I0720681

PRINT EDITION

THE TIME TRAVELLER'S RESORT AND MUSEUM © 2016 by Mirror World Publishing
Written by David McLain
Illustrated by Felix Eddy
Edited by: Robert Dowsett and Justine Dowsett
Published by Mirror World Publishing November, 2016
All Rights Reserved.

*This book is a work of fiction. All of the characters, organizations and events portrayed in this novel are either products of the authors' imagination or are used fictitiously. Any resemblance to actual locales, events or persons is entirely coincidental.

Mirror World Publishing
Windsor, Ontario
www.mirrorworldpublishing.com
info@mirrorworldpublishing.com

ISBN: 978-1-987976-24-3

To F.M., A.M., and R.E.M.

THE TIME TRAVELLER'S RESORT AND MUSEUM

By David McLain

Illustrated by Felix Eddy

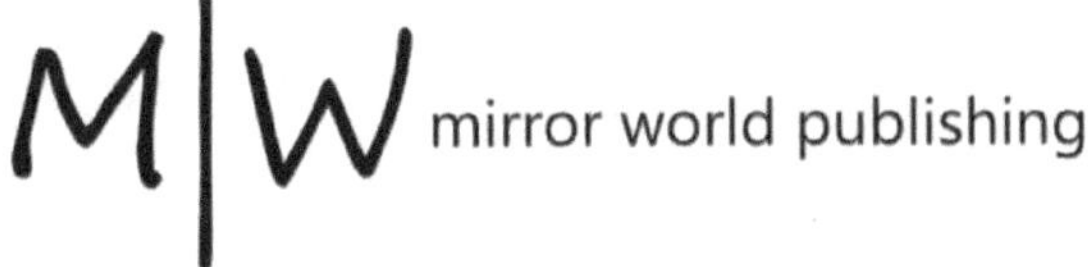

The Five Basic Laws of Time, as used in this book:

Everything written is real.
You cannot break the laws of physics.
The past has passed.
The present always rolls forward.
The future is unwritten.

The rest you can figure out yourself.

-D.E.M.

PART ONE
THE AMAZING MISTER QUICK

Gypsies Travelling

The prophetical tribe, that ardent eyed people,
Set out last night, carrying their children
On their backs, or yielding to those fierce appetites
The ever ready treasure of pendulous breasts.

The men travel on foot with their gleaming weapons
Alongside the wagons where their kin are huddled,
Surveying the heavens with eyes rendered heavy
By a mournful regret for vanished illusions.

The cricket from the depths of his sandy retreat
Watches them as they pass, and louder grows his song;
Cybele, who loves them, increases her verdure,

Makes the desert blossom, water spurt from the rock
Before these travellers for whom is opened wide
The familiar domain of the future's darkness.

- Charles Baudelaire

Chapter 1
Riothamus

When the young man finally came to, an arm was laying at his feet. Not an arm attached to a man, *an arm*. He wondered whom it belonged to. He shuddered instinctively. He tilted his head back and a sharp pain struck the back of his head, like a hammer coming down on an anvil. It took him another thirty minutes to stand up. There wasn't any hurry. The battle was over and the Gauls had retreated. The sound of clashing metal had faded; the dead and the dying were left to suffer in peace.

The smell of carrion in the young man's nostrils was overwhelming. He tried to imagine telling his mother about what had happened here. There were the things he would never be able to tell her about – the arm, for one, and the smell. How could you explain *that* to a woman who fed you, clothed you, and cared for you in sickness and health? How could he explain the arm, and the smell, and the pieces of good men that lay all around him? His mother had lost two children already. She never needed to know. No one ever needed to know.

Slowly, painfully, he stood up and surveyed the field. He seemed to be on the far end of the battlefield, though most of the conflict had taken place in the area just east of where he stood. Through the mist he could make out a few women tending to the injured, and a few young boys running back and forth. There had been twelve thousand men on the field that day. The young man had never seen so many men at once – in fact, no one had; it was the largest assembly of men for any purpose since the Romans had left Britain. How many were left now on his side? On any side?

Before the young man had lost consciousness, the numbers appeared to have thinned out to eight or nine hundred. He surveyed the field again. It was difficult to tell how many were still standing.

Slowly, he lurched forward toward the centre of the field. There was a sharp pain in his ankle and he limped on his left leg. *'The battle is over,'* he reminded himself. *'The battle is over, and the Gauls have retreated. The King will be King of everything south of Hadrian's Wall, at least for now, and I will be able to go home. I'll go home and all of this will be over. I'll go hunting, and fishing, and riding. Mother will cook for me. I'll dance with pretty girls underneath a silver moon. I'll go home, and all of this will be behind me. It's all over now.'*

He lifted his legs over the fields of trampled grass, doing his best to find a path around the piles of flesh that littered the field. A dying horse looked up at him. Its belly was slit open and a bone fragment was sticking out of its left foreleg. The eyes of the horse turned grey as its neck twitched. The young man turned away and shuddered. He kept walking forward, through the fog toward the east. There had been some kind of a town over there; a fishing village or something. If he could get there, everything would be all right. He just had to get there.

He almost ran into the young boy before he saw him. He had seen him somewhere before, in the fields, or maybe at a banquet, he wasn't really sure. They were only three or four years apart in age – under other circumstances they might have gone fishing together, or gone out with some girls and gotten drunk late at night on a beach. The boy didn't seem to be injured. He looked frantic, as if they had been looking for each other for a long time. The young man wondered if he looked as desperate as the boy before him did.

"*Glædne heahfrea*," the boy said.

'*How can he call me that?*' the young man wondered. '*Isn't there anyone else?*' But of course, the look in the boy's eyes answered his question before he had time to even ask it. '*No, there isn't anyone else. That's why he looks so happy to see me. He's been looking for hours and I'm the first he's found. Everybody else is dead. That's why he's here. He's looking for you, expecting you to know what to do. The Kin–*' the young man's train of thought suddenly derailed. He looked at the boy's eyes, and almost instantly understood.

"*Rioðamus*?" he asked.

The boy ran a hand through his short, brown hair, and scratched the back of his neck. The young man nodded and closed his eyes. The back of his head was killing him. When he opened his eyes, he saw that the boy had turned around again and was walking back toward the opposite end of the field. "*Cwom mit mē*," the boy said, and he turned around and trudged back across the field.

Rioðamus – The River King. Greatest King. If ever anyone had deserved the title it would be him. It was his love of his men that had been his greatest strength, and they had returned the favour with the title. To him, all men great and small were like long-lost brothers. He could talk to the poorest beggar and the highest Lord with equal aplomb; everyone felt like he was their friend, like their problems were his. Even though he was King, he remembered the name of every man he'd ever shaken hands with. He would remember their names, and the names of their family. He wasn't what you expected a king to be. He had a wicked sense of humour, and was known to tell the dirtiest jokes of anyone in the country. He was noble, too, and brave, and kind. It was hard to accept that now – all that was over. Now, everything was over. The young man tried to push that thought out of his mind. *'Resignation,'* the young man thought. *'That's understandable. You have to do what needs to be done, and after that we'll see.'*

The young man and the boy trudged forward in silence. Slowly, but surely they made their way over the field and into the small town that they had just finished defending. The young man wondered what the name of it was. It wasn't much of a town, really, just a few ramshackle stone cottages thrown together on a small strip of land between water and rock. As they walked past, frightened women quickly shut doors and shutters on the small stone cottages. Playing in the mud, a group of small, dirty faces stared up at them. The young man could hear the sound of the ocean roaring far away. In the distance, the young man saw an abbey, right on top of a small hill. They would have brought him there. Somehow the young man knew that at this point there was nothing else that could be done for him.

They found their way almost effortlessly. The young man and the boy climbed the hill to the abbey, where a young woman met them at the stones steps of the church. She stood there, mute, a serene expression on her face, neither moving nor speaking as they approached. She was lovely, but her feet were bare and there was a wild, feral look about her, like a child raised by wolves. Her hair was pitch black, and cascaded down her shoulders in ringlets. The boy looked at her, and nodded before turning around and heading back toward the field of battle. She stared at him passively. Her eyes revealed neither pride nor shame.   *'She's beautiful,'* the young man thought, shocked at the random, scattered thoughts that popped in and out of his mind. *'She's beautiful. The King is dead. We fought a war today. The Gauls retreated. I will get to go home again. I can never go home again. She's beautiful. I need to hold on.'*

"Þā cyning?" the young man asked. (*The King?*)

"Þā cyning is nēah," she said as calmly as if he had asked her about the weather. "Cwom."

They turned around, and walked through the chapel. The young man thought about saying a prayer, but he couldn't think of what to say. The chapel was small and hard and grey. The young woman faced a statue of the Virgin Mary and bowed her head. The young man took a moment and stared at the floor before walking out into the back room of the church.

It didn't seem like a place for a king to die. He lay there on a simple stretcher, with no more ceremony than a common soldier might have. His beard was bloody, and his arms looked disjointed, but he didn't look like he was dying. Maybe it would be all right. It was difficult to tell. The young man knelt down beside him. The smell was overwhelming. *'The smell of death,'* he thought. *'I have to pretend. I have to pretend I don't smell it. Just look at him. He looks fine. Just look at him.'* The young man looked at the King's face and tried to smile. The King opened his eyes and stared at him.

"Hwæt!" he said. He spoke with a small laugh, as if all of this were a practical joke on him. "Adam," he said. The young man nodded. He had never been sure why it was that the King called him that. It wasn't his name. Normally he would object, but of course things like that didn't matter just now. With great effort, the King raised his hand to his chest. It was only then that the young man noticed the sword.

The King's beautiful sword was still clutched in his left hand; or rather, the hilt of his sword was still in his hand. The blade had shattered, leaving only a small stub where the deadliest weapon in Britain had once been. The cold flat steel of the hilt was still perfect, but its power was gone now, gone forever. It had shattered like a chicken bone, or an old piece of wood.

"Wē wunne," the King said.

"Wē wunne," the young man repeated.

"Ond min deað," the King gasped.

"No," the young man said firmly, as if his insistence would be enough. The King laughed again.

"Nū morgen," the King said. "Nū cyning. Ic Fæder fæþmum, ond Ic spræce mit mitig."

And with that, he died.

They buried the King at the abbey. He was laid in the hollow of an oak tree, near the men who had died so willingly protecting his kingdom and his throne. The hilt of his sword was laid on his chest. The young man had a local blacksmith lay down the engraving on the hilt, so that the world would know him for all time. It was nothing extravagant, just a simple dedication in Latin. The plot was marked with a stone pyramid and nothing more. The funeral was attended by the men who had survived, and those who were there were convinced that he would have been honoured. He was now the past, and the future.

A new morning. A new king. I embrace the Father and I speak with might.

Those were his last words, and they haunted the young man until he became an old man, long after the old king had become a myth and a shadow. When the young man was asked about the old king, and he was asked more times than he could remember, he would usually talk about his love of the people, of all people, and the way he could make men laugh. But sometimes, just sometimes, when it was late at night, he would tell people about the last words of the King, and the engraving the blacksmith had put on the sword:

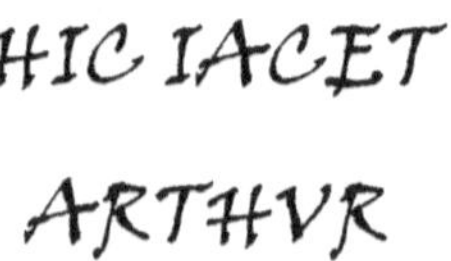

Chapter 2
1500 Years Later

With *The Times* spread out across her lap, Alice pushed her left ear into the tiny pillow the stewardess had given her and did her best to pretend she was asleep. It was one of those funny little tricks; whenever you took the flight from New York to London you had to spend the night on the plane regardless of whether you took off at eight o'clock at night or nine in the morning. The Flight Attendants on British Airways compensated for this by giving you a blanket that appeared to be made out of a blend of fiberglass insulation and horsehair and a pillow that would have been comfortable if you had a head the size of a squirrel. Alice loved going back to England, and was excited to be a part of the conference, but the flight – oh, the flight. Alice would have been much, *much* happier taking the QEII, even if it did take an extra week to come into port. Of course, she would probably just throw up over the side on a boat like that. She supposed there was no winning either way.

"Hello, this is your captain speaking," a voice said. "We'll be landing at Heathrow in just over thirty minutes."

Travel was the both the bane and the saving grace of Alice Anderson's existence. She had long since learned to hate the smell of airports, the feel of the drab polyester seats, and the uncomfortable pounding in her head that came with a night where the sun only went down for three hours. On the other hand, there was the feel of the cobblestoned London streets underneath her feet – *that* was worth something. In cobblestone-street-free America, there was a saying: In Britain two hundred miles is a long way and in America two hundred years is a long time. For Alice Anderson, either one could go by in the blink of an eye.

"Please put your tray tables in their full and upright positions," the voice said.

Alice rubbed her eyes and stretched. The key to successful travel, in her opinion, was a rigid adherence to a schedule. In thirty-seven minutes her flight would be landing on the tarmac. In two hours she would be arriving at the hotel. In three hours and forty-five minutes she would be having a quick drink with her sister before heading back to the hotel room, and mercifully, a good night's sleep. In a little over twenty-four hours she and Malcolm Oliver would be standing in a lecture hall in Cambridge University, talking to a group of the world's oldest astrophysicists about the importance of new technology when educating the next generation. After that there would be three days of conferences, meetings, presentations, and general hobnobbing with her brother and sister wizards, before getting back on another flight to New York. Alice was like a pocket watch, wound and polished, a precision instrument moving exactly according to schedule.

"Thank you for your business," a voice said. "We will be exiting the plane shortly. On behalf of British Airways, we hope you will enjoy your trip."

'It's a brave new world,' Alice thought to herself as she found her way to the plane door.

Heathrow Airport, being first and foremost an airport, and secondly, a product of the military industrial transportation complex, had clearly been designed by an architect who worshiped at the altar of some unknown god of confusion and banality. In a haze of forgetfulness, Alice muddled through the maze of escalators and coffee-coloured hallways, finally finding her way to baggage claim. She had been there for exactly nine-and-a-half seconds when her mobile rang.

"Hello?" she asked, sleepily.

"Either you have taken a job at NORAD and you're on twenty-four-hour missile watch or you've just gotten off the flight from Heathrow," Malcolm said.

"I should have gone to graduate school in Tokyo," Alice mumbled. "I could have taken the Orient Express whenever I came back home."

"I can't imagine that the stars would be much to look at under the Tokyo lights."

"I just spent the night sleeping between two strangers, in a chair the size of a dishrag. Changing majors seems like a small price to pay."

He considered this. "Strictly speaking, there's really a very small pool of Astrophysicists who have spectacular breasts. It would be a shame to lose you to French Literature."

"Why would I be studying French Literature in Tokyo?"

"You know, I hear that Baudelaire isn't the same until you've read it in the original Japanese."

Alice groaned. In the world of Astrophysicists, there are claims to fame, and there are claims to fame. Albert Einstein, Edwin Hubble, and Isaac Newton had the former. Alice on the other hand, had the latter. Alice was known far and wide as the world's sexiest astrophysicist. Her hold on the title of sexiest astrophysicist had nothing to do with appearance; anybody walking through the airport would see an attractive but ordinary woman, in possession of soft curves, pale blue eyes, and a head of curly red hair that seemed to prove the laws of electromagnetism fairly distinctly. For the past two years, Alice had been the sultry, deep-throated voice of Astropod, a weekly podcast about astronomy, physics, and the known universe. Alice had over twenty thousand regular listeners. It was a project that she had begun at the invitation of Malcolm Oliver, who had invited her to be his co-host after hearing her give a presentation on galaxy superstructures as an undergraduate student. Although starting the podcast had been Malcolm's idea, she hadn't actually heard his voice in a while. She didn't want to admit it, but his deep intonation and dry delivery were comforting. "Is that what you're working on, these days?" she asked him. "Baudelaire?"

"I'm exploring the theoretical parameters of multidimensional space time with regard to fictional realism," Malcolm said. "Baudelaire wrote poetry, so unless you're planning on visiting a universe where everyone speaks naturally in blank verse, I think that probably his work and mine aren't going to intersect. How was the flight?"

"I'm exhausted, my back hurts, and I need to take a shower with roughly the same level of urgency as a monkey at a rock concert," Alice admitted. Then, without thinking about it, she admitted something else. "I've missed you," she said.

Malcolm, who was apparently doing his best to be both warm and distant, decided to ignore both her embarrassing admission about needing a shower and her desperate confession about their relationship, and asked about her life instead. "How's America?" he asked.

"Terrible," she admitted.

"It can't be all bad," Malcolm offered. "You're in New York, after all."

"I'm in *upstate* New York," Alice pointed out. "It's about as close to the Great White Way as Cheapside is to the Outer Hebrides."

"Ah, they never put fifty inch telescopes in prime real estate, do they?"

"I suppose not," Alice sighed. "Anyway, I'm home now."

"I'm glad," Malcolm said, and Alice could tell that he really was glad. She silently hoped that he was glad to have her back in his life for some grand, sweeping romantic reason. It was a hope blown in on the winds of desperation, and was dashed upon the rocks of despair a moment later. "I have something to show you."

"What's that?" Alice asked.

If Malcolm had been there in person, he probably would have shrugged. "Just something to do with my research," he said, not shrugging.

"You could have sent me a picture," Alice suggested.

"Some things are worth seeing in person," he said. "Come by my flat before the presentation tomorrow?"

Alice said that she would, she and Malcolm made their pleasantries, and then Alice hung up. She picked up her bag and headed toward the nearest exit. It was exactly four-and-a-half minutes before the phone rang again.

"Hello," Alice said, with a certain degree of reluctant enthusiasm.

"You sound American," an annoyed voice on the other end of the line said.

Alice dropped her bag. "I've been in New York for three years," Alice said. "You're lucky I don't sound like I'm from the Bronx."

It was Alice's sister, Wendy, giving what by her standards was a remarkably warm and friendly greeting. "You're lucky I don't steal your passport while you're here and force you to teach Electrical Engineering at the University of the Orkneys. Electrical Engineering, that's what you do, isn't it?"

"You do realize that I just spent an entire evening in a metal tube, sitting on a very small seat that appeared to have been made from rocks confiscated from terrorists at security?"

"Terrorists use rocks these days?"

"Well, they're harder to spot going through metal detectors, aren't they?"

Ending a sentence with a question apparently sounded appropriately British and Wendy seemed to ease up a little.

"How was the flight, then?" she asked.

"I believe I aged three years," Alice answered, looking for the way to the exit. "Do you want to have a drink?"

"Is that a rhetorical question?"

"In America, it's considered polite to ask."

"I believe that the University of the Orkneys has early tenure."

Wendy took pride in her absolute loathing of all things American. She saw Alice's decampment to New York as nothing less than a complete betrayal.

"Would you mind if we met in at my hotel?" Alice asked, trying to sound as if this were a polite request and not a desperate plea.

"I don't know," Wendy said. "There aren't going to be a lot of randy outer-space types there, are there?"

"It's an astronomy conference," Alice insisted. "Not a Sci-Fi convention."

There was the unmistakable sound of pursing lips on the other end of the phone. "What hotel are you staying at?" Wendy asked.

"The Kensington."

Wendy thought about it. "I'll meet you, but let's meet somewhere else. There's a pub down that way that I've had my eye on."

"Wendy–"

"I have to drive in all the way from Brixton. You can walk a hundred metres out of the hotel lobby."

Alice sighed. She decided not to point out that in fact she had come quite a bit farther than hundred meters. "What's the name of the place?" she asked.

"The Gristle and Thorn," Wendy said.

Alice spotted the word "EXIT" on the far side of the hall. "Couldn't find any place with a ghastlier name? Was the 'Skull and Crossbones' already booked?"

"Just meet me," Wendy insisted, and for a moment, she did her best to sound kind. "I've missed you."

It has been said that all journeys begin with a single step, and while it might seem that Alice's journey began all the way back at JFK, in actuality the first step of Alice's journey began with a decision. It was not a big decision, not the kind of thing that would strike a historian as a significant chapter in the decline and fall of the Western Empire, but for Alice Anderson, it was the equivalent of crossing the Rubicon. It was the simplest thing really – a choice of restaurants.

"The Gristle and Thorn it is," Alice said, picking up her bag again and shuffling through the crowd.

If Baedeker had ever written about the Gristle and Thorn, it would have delighted in pointing out that it was exceptionally sleazy. (Rick Steves, on the other hand, would have called it an excellent place to meet full of "local colour," but this is neither here nor there.) The decor was garish, the atmosphere suffocating, and the food was an impressive combination of expensive and unappetizing. The building it was housed in appeared to have just barely survived the London Blitz, and the street it was on was one that Sweeney Todd would have gone whistling past rather quickly. Oddly enough, in a millennium of travelling writing, no researcher had stepped into the Gristle and Thorn, not even once. If the proprietors had ever noticed this, they wouldn't have cared. The G and T catered to a fairly exclusive clientele.

Why exactly Wendy had decided to have a drink there is one of those mysteries lost to history. Older, wealthier, and less intellectually driven than her sister, Wendy had made a career out of finding obscure places to get drunk. In that respect, the G and T would have been quite a feather in her cap, although in almost all other respects, it was rather dreary. That Alice arrived before her sister was hardly surprising. Wendy regarded punctuality slightly above American Culture and popular music in terms of importance. Alice was used to this, and took a seat at a table in the corner that looked like it was the least likely to be infested with cockroaches.

This being the twenty-first century, Alice sat down, took out her cell phone, and quickly became engrossed in the world of email. Her father had sent her a message which she didn't read, and her colleagues from New York were asking questions that might have had relevance if she wasn't on another continent. Alice became so distracted that she didn't notice that everyone in the pub was trying not to stare at her.

The bartender came over and handed Alice a drink. "Mango liquor, Kina Lillet and Cranberry Juice, with a thin layer of pomegranate seeds and a large slice of lime," he said cheerfully.

"I didn't order this," Alice said, staring at him blankly.

"I'm sorry, miss?" he asked.

"The drink," she said "I haven't ordered anything."

The bartender smiled. He was a bald little man with large eyes like ping pong balls and the pleasant smile of an insurance salesman. His accent was Cornish, and his manner was a little stiff. "I'm sorry, miss," he said, still smiling.

"That's all right," Alice said. She didn't know what to order and the drink looked lovely. "I'll keep it anyway, if that's okay."

The bartender continued to smile. "If there's anything else, miss, I'll be behind the bar."

Alice took a sip of her drink and looked around the room. It was an odd sort of bar, that was for sure. Everybody seemed to be dressed as if they were going to some sort of costume party. The couple sitting at the table by the window were wearing pith helmets and tan shorts. An elderly gentleman in the corner was sporting a Nehru jacket and a cigarette holder. A man at the table behind her – Alice couldn't see his face, but he seemed to be wearing a top hat and an opera cape, and nobody was paying him the slightest bit of attention. Instead, everyone seemed to be stealing sideways glances at *her*. Why wasn't clear. She was wearing nothing more spectacular than a black t-shirt and pair of jeans – it was hard to compete with the woman at the bar wearing spats. It was odd; being the world's sexiest astrophysicist wasn't the kind of claim to fame that got you a lot of attention in bars.

"Hi stranger," a familiar voice said.

Wendy Mittlestadt was, without question, the best and the worst of sisters. She was equal parts Emma Woodhouse, Joan Collins, and Florence Nightingale. A bitch for all seasons, as it were. Alice was happy to see her sister, but was rather painfully aware that this particular meeting was going to involve a certain amount of griping about Wendy's least favourite subject – her sister's occupational move to America.

"You look like you've been over ten miles of bad road," Wendy said, sitting down.

"I spent the night on an airplane," Alice replied. "It isn't exactly the Holiday Inn."

"You were the one who decided to leave the country," Wendy countered.

"I left the country for a reason," Alice said curtly.

Wendy bristled. Bristling was something that Wendy was very good at, and she tended to play to her strengths. Wendy's resume largely consisted of graduating University, marrying a wealthy man who was two decades older than herself, and consuming large quantities of alcohol. In general, she could be counted on to while away the hours from Monday through Saturday shopping, drinking, and then complaining about how absolutely exhausting it was to shop and drink, usually to her husband, who had not actually heard his wife's voice for the better part of three years. It was an existence that Alice wanted no part of, and this angered Wendy, in part because she simply couldn't understand how one could go through life believing that there was more to this world than money. The truth was, Wendy loved and cherished her sister, but was very, very worried most of the time about the large number of things that she had absolutely no control over, Alice's wanderlust being not least among these.

"How is New York, anyway?"

"Oh well, you know," Alice said. Alice knew that the cool waters of Lake Cayuga, the rushing sounds of giant waterfalls, the green forests of the state parks, and the rolling hills of Ithaca would sound absolutely dreadful, but the truth was, it wasn't that bad.

"And how are American men?" Wendy asked.

"Starting in with twenty questions pretty quickly, aren't we?" Alice asked.

"Well, I need to know the basics," Wendy said. "Your emails read like Japanese Haiku."

Alice took another sip of her drink. "If you must know, American men are basically the same as English men, except that when they talk about football, they mean something completely different."

Then Wendy said the thing that Alice had been silently dreading since she had gotten on the plane. "I noticed that you're giving your talk with Malcolm," she said, hopefully.

"I am," Alice admitted. "It's on using new technology to get kids interested in scientific exploration. Do you want to come?"

Wendy's eyebrows made a distinct downward turn, and her lips pouted just slightly. "You are my sister," she said, in a tone that was genuinely warm and kind, "and I love you, but you are frustrating."

"You're frustrated that I moved to New York," Alice surmised.

"I'm frustrated that you have moved to the ends of the Earth to teach little kids about the wonders of the planet Jupiter and are not meeting any men," Wendy snapped.

"That isn't what I'm teaching–" Alice protested, ignoring the comment about men.

Wendy rolled her eyes. "It might as well be. Please tell me that you're at least doing some sort of final frontier thing that I can be proud of."

"I was looking at the Large Magellan cloud last night," Alice said. "There was a supernova there last week. It was one hundred and fifty thousand light years away, but it was one of the most brilliant stars in the sky. The light had been travelling here for 1500 centuries. It was a million times brighter than the sun, and then it blew out, like a candle."

Wendy stared at her. "What is that that you've been drinking?" she asked.

Alice took a sip of her drink. "I don't know," she admitted, "but it's lovely."

"Perhaps I'll have one too," Wendy said. She waved at the barman, but he seemed distracted. "Bloody man," she cursed.

"It's on me," Alice said, getting up and walking up to the bar. The bartender came over and gave another pleasantly inoffensive smile.

"Could I have another one of those drinks?" she asked.

The bartender nodded, turned around, and reached for the Kina Lillet. That was when Alice turned to the right, and saw him.

In any other bar, the man sitting next to her would have been considered decidedly odd, but at this place, he seemed to blend in like sugar in water. He was dressed like a World War One flying ace, wearing a leather jacket, white scarf, and leather cap, with a pair of antique motorcycle goggles perched on top of his head. (The latter was especially odd, since he was also wearing glasses.) Alice found herself staring at him.

"I know," he said, without looking at her. "I shouldn't be drinking before I go out to fly, but the Red Baron drinks like a fish."

Alice laughed. The man put down his drink to look at her, and then suddenly everything on his face seemed to stop. "Have we met?" the flying ace asked. He looked like he was about thirty, and spoke with the sort of flat, American accent that Alice tended to associate with places like Iowa. His eyebrows had gone so far up on his head that they were hidden underneath his leather hat.

"I don't think so," Alice said, furrowing her brow. Certainly she would have remembered someone who dressed so oddly. Granted, it was possible that he didn't always dress like that, but it seemed to follow that if you were willing to don an early twentieth century flying helmet for a casual drink at the pub, then you probably weren't a t-shirt and jeans guy.

There was a long pause before he spoke again. "My mistake," he said awkwardly. He suddenly seemed to be trying very hard to look at absolutely everything in the world but her. Alice couldn't help noticing that he was drinking the same odd drink that the bartender had given her.

"You're here for the astronomy conference?" he asked.

This was, to say the very least, surprising. Especially since, although the man had *phrased* the sentence as a question, it *sounded* as though he already knew the answer.

Alice answered his question with one of her own. "How did you know that?"

The flying ace looked embarrassingly smug, an expression that American men seemed to deal in almost exclusively. "Well, the world's sexiest astrophysicist can hardly be expected to walk into this place and not be noticed," he said.

Alice blushed slightly. "Michio Kaku owes me a sash," she mumbled irritably.

"Michio Kaku has unfortunately never stepped into this bar," the flying ace said. "Pity, I would buy him a drink."

"That drink?" Alice asked, pointing to the pink concoction that they'd both been drinking. "The bartender poured me one."

"He must think you're special."

"It had Kina Lillet in it. Probably going to cost me a fortune."

"Probably, but everything good involves a little sacrifice."

Alice stared at the man. She had the odd sort of feeling that she seen him before. "Are you going to the Astronomy Conference? It would be nice to see a few young faces."

He smiled. "It's been my experience that the attendees of the Royal Astronomy Conference tend to think that life begins when you're at least as old as a quasar. I'm surprised that you're going, actually."

"The current holder of the Isaac Newton chair is embarrassed that I have more Twitter followers than him," Alice admitted.

"The current holder of the Isaac Newton chair looks like he should be playing a game of riddles with Bilbo Baggins and talking about his favourite Golden Ring," the flying ace said. "You, on the other hand—"

Alice, who sensed that now might be an appropriate time to get offended, raised her eyebrows haughtily. "My audience is comprised of students who are interested in Astronomy," she insisted.

"Let's just agree that your audience is interested in heavenly bodies at rest and in motion, and leave it at that," he suggested.

There was a silence. There is nothing quite as ugly as a long journey followed by an unbearable truth.

"It's a shame," the flying ace said then, "because you could knock down Einstein. Right hook, third round, you'd take him down."

Alice probably should have found a politer way to ask what she said next. "Who are you?" she asked.

The man stretched out a gloved hand. "My name," he said. "Is–"

"Alice?" a voice called. "Alice? My drink isn't going to consume itself, dear."

Alice grabbed Wendy's drink and stood up. "My sister without alcohol," she said. "It isn't a pretty sight."

The flying ace raised his glass, and Alice walked back to her table. She spent the next twenty-two minutes and thirty-four seconds listening to her sister talking about the joys of being wealthy and English. She would not remember this later on. She would not remember the flight from that morning, or how exactly she made it from the airport to the hotel. These were fairly unimportant details that would be washed away in the ocean of time.

She *would* remember the phone call from Malcolm, as it was the last time that she would ever talk to him, and she would be forced to recount the details later on. She would also remember the drink, the first of many she would have at the Gristle and Thorn (the bartender, as it turned out, had been quite right to bring it to her), as well as the odd dress of the other customers. More than anything else she would remember the phrase "Have we met?" because over the next few years she would hear it many times in many different places. You see, Alice didn't know it, but there was a reason that everybody in the pub was dressed so strangely, why the bartender knew her drink better than she did, and why the flying ace had known so much about her. The Gristle and Thorn, as it turns out, is a time traveller's bar.

Unfortunately, Alice was still "living in the moment," as they say, so absolutely none of these things seemed significant in the short term. What did seem significant was that after talking to her sister for another twenty-two minutes and thirty-four seconds, Alice Anderson went back to her hotel and fell asleep. She was exhausted.

It was several hours later and Alice was having the most wonderful dream, wonderful and strange. She seemed to be lying on her back in a small field, in what she could only imagine was some sort of national park. It was a beautiful spring day. A man was lying next to her. He was holding a small leather-bound book, and was looking at her intently.

"That time of year thou mayst in me behold," he said.

"Shakespeare," Alice mumbled absentmindedly.

"Of course," the man agreed. He had the sort of faceless quality that people in dreams sometimes have, but as near as Alice could figure, he seemed to be a good-looking man with thick, black hair and long sideburns. Alice didn't recognize him, but he seemed very familiar. He was dressed in the sort of ridiculously formal outfit that

Alice tended to associate with historical productions on the BBC. Indeed, judging by his breeches, white waistcoat, long jacket, and riding boots, Alice could probably expect a new production of *Northanger Abbey* sometime soon. All of this might have been odd, if Alice herself hadn't been wearing a billowing blue skirt with an empire waist and what appeared to be a flowery blue bonnet.

"You know it then?" the man said, looking at the book.

"I think even Grendel followed that one," Alice said playfully. Grendel, she could only assume, was the smallish-looking triceratops that was stretched out in the field next to the carriage. (*'Carriage?'* Alice wondered. Well, it was just as well. She certainly couldn't drive a car with the bonnet on.)

"Grendel," she called out playfully, "how's your Shakespeare?" Grendel turned up his horns, but didn't say anything.

"If you know the poem," the man said with an approving but slightly disingenuous smirk on his face, "then you can recite it to me."

Alice sat up, holding her hands together like a proper English schoolgirl. She said:

> *"That time of year thou mayst in me behold*
> *When yellow leaves, or none, or few, do hang*
> *Upon those boughs which shake against the cold,*
> *Bare ruin'd choirs, where late the sweet birds sang.*
> *In me thou see'st the twilight of such day*
> *As after sunset fadeth in the west,*
> *Which by and by black night doth take away.*
> *Death's second self, that seals up all in rest.*
> *In me thou see'st the glowing of such fire*
> *That on the ashes of his youth doth lie,*
> *As the death-bed whereon it must expire*
> *Consumed with that which it was nourish'd by.*
> *This thou perceivest, which makes thy love more strong,*
> *To love that well which thou must leave ere long."*

She studied his face – what she could see it, of anyway. He was obviously impressed, almost as much as she was. Alice had absolutely no idea where the words had come from.

"Only you would try to woo a woman with a poem about death," she said, and stretched back out into the grass again.

"Woo?" the young man played with the word like a boy with a new toy at Christmas. "Woo? Well. I suppose that isn't inappropriate. I think that the idea though is that *I* should be impressing *you* with poetry, not the other way around. How did you do that?"

"I think you will find that wearing a dress inhibits neither my ability to comprehend literature or to remember its content, Mister Cassidy," Alice said curtly.

"That isn't what I meant," the man said. He tossed the book aside, leaned over, and kissed her. As his lips touched hers, an odd feeling came over her. There was pleasure, of course, and warmth, and joy, but there was something else. It was understanding.

Alice woke up. Something was happening, something important enough to pull her out of the pleasant dream of summer fields and handsome men and William Shakespeare. What was it that was happening? Couldn't she just ignore it?

The phone was ringing.

Alice looked over at the clock. Much to her surprise and horror, it said 2:00 AM. She listened to the sound of the ringing phone and came to what must be the only logical conclusion – that someone back in New York had simply forgotten that she was in London and was trying to call her, thinking that she was still on Eastern Standard Time. She picked up the phone.

"Hello," she said sleepily.

"Miss Anderson?" a clipped-sounding female voice said. "My name is Detective Enid Williams. I'm with the Metropolitan Police Service."

If you've ever gone into a meeting at a great job that ended with you been sacked, you will recognize that moment of immediate dread, when you both know something awful and don't know it at the same time. That was what Alice was feeling now. She knew that whatever reason Scotland Yard had for calling her in the middle of the night, it wasn't that they had an abundance of good news. What she didn't know was what that reason actually was. In a desperate attempt to grasp onto the least dramatic reason that she could be talking to someone with the rank of detective, Alice came up with the idea that Wendy had been driving home drunk and had gotten arrested. Had Alice had been wide awake, she would have realized that this was dead wrong, but she was not wide awake, and when you are talking to a police detective at two o'clock in the morning, you are desperate to grab onto something.

"Yes," she said, doing her best to sound as though they were having this conversation at another time of day. "Yes, I understand."

"We're contacting you about Mister Malcolm Oliver," the detective said.

Malcolm. Of all the strange things that the police detective could have said, there was nothing that could have been as strange as the mention of Malcolm Oliver.

"Malcolm?" Alice asked. The sound of Malcolm's name was much, much, better than good strong cup of coffee and a good, clean kick to the head. "I know Malcolm, yes."

"I'm afraid I'll need you to come down to New Scotland Yard, Miss Anderson," the Detective said. "I can send around a car for you, if you like."

If the phone call at two a.m. wasn't bad enough, then the promise of a police escort was certainly a sure sign that something was terribly wrong. "Please," Alice said. She didn't know what else to say. There probably wasn't anything worth pleading for, but she needed to say it just the same. She needed to say it, and then she needed to ask the question that probably absolutely everyone would have asked in the same situation.

"Is he all right?"

"I'm afraid that I can't discuss that over the phone," Detective Williams said. "I'll have a car pick you up immediately."

That did it. If they weren't willing to tell Alice on the phone, then it had to be the worst. Malcolm Niles Oliver. Of all the people in the world to turn up dead, didn't it just have to be poor Malcolm? Alice told the detective that she would be ready in ten minutes and in the Hotel lobby.

Once, in the distant memory of his youth, Malcolm Oliver had had an argument with his high school physics teacher. Teaching Malcolm physics was one of those lucky draws in the same way that being Muhammad Ali's sparring partner was an incredible opportunity, so the argument was probably more or less inevitable. The argument concerned the universe, and how many dimensions of time and space we live in. The teacher (who apparently thought that Einstein was some kind of upstart whose theories were akin to pop music and movies starring teenagers who aren't wearing underpants) was telling the class how even though it seemed as though we live in three dimensions, we actually lived in four, the first three being the dimensions of space, and the fourth being time. The instructor went on to point out, rather smugly, that although all objects move forward through time, it was only the creatures on this planet who really experience it, which was one of the things that made the Earth special. Malcolm, who knew perfectly well that the universe consisted of more dimensions than men could ever count, tried to at least bring the teacher into the twentieth century by pointing out that we don't live in four dimensions, but six.

"How do you mean?" the teacher asked.

"Consider, a road," Malcolm suggested. "You're travelling down a highway and you come to a fork. As it happens, one path leads to fame and fortune and the other path leads to certain destruction."

"All right," the teacher said.

"Well, as it happens, you happen to take the right path, the one that leads to all the good things in life. Good for you, but that doesn't mean that the other path isn't there. It just means that you don't perceive it, and the consequences that it entails."

"So?" the teacher said.

"The fifth dimension," Malcolm said, "is choice."

There was tension in the air that was broken by one of the students shouting out. "What do you think the sixth dimension is, then?"

"Now consider all of the roads," Malcolm suggested. "All of the roads that you won't turn down. All of the roads you will never see. All of the roads that have never been made, but someday will be. They all exist. They're all out there. The consequences of you going down them would be the same, whether you go down them or not."

"The sixth dimension," Malcolm explained, "is imagination."

The teacher responded to this by moving on to a lecture about the laws of electromagnetism and giving Malcolm a D minus, which he judged as proof that Malcolm would never make it through Oxford. Malcolm, in turn, would eventually react to this by tearing through Newtonian physics with a wrecking ball.

Now he was gone.

Sitting in a police station is a lot like sitting at the emergency ward in hospital. Everything has an odd antiseptic quality, except for the people, who appear to have been dragged out of the less than savoury corners of a Dickensian novel. Having been met by a young-looking police officer, Alice had been taken to New Scotland Yard, where she had been led down a maze of confusing-looking hallways, past a number of men who should probably be kept away from children, and into a room that looked like precisely the sort of place where they should be attending to you after a long night of hard drinking. For roughly ten minutes, Alice sat there alone, with nothing but two chairs and table to occupy her mind. The minutes seemed to creep by like days. With nothing to occupy her thoughts (pulling out her phone and checking her messages seemed incorrigible somehow), Alice's mind went to the first place that almost anyone's would in the same situation – was she a suspect in Malcolm's death?

Alice told herself that this wasn't likely, although this was extremely difficult to do. While it was true that Alice hadn't seen Malcolm in a year, and that they'd parted on good terms, it was also true that she and Malcolm had a history, and that she had been alone for most of the day. These were details that were hard to ignore when you were sitting in the detective unit at New Scotland Yard. She wondered if she should call Wendy. Wendy, of course, would rush here in a heartbeat with the best solicitor in London on retainer, but she would also be hungover, brash, and a general embarrassment. Still, in moments like this, you wanted to call someone you loved. This led Alice to a second thought. Was it possible that she was still Malcolm's emergency contact? This thought made her almost as embarrassed as the notion that the police might think she would try to murder him.

With thoughts like this, it was easy to understand that Alice was rather frightened and confused when the detective finally came into the room.

Detective Williams was a short woman with square shoulders who looked a little bit like she had been trying to prove herself to people for much, much longer than she had hoped. Alice wasn't sure that this was a good sign. She sat, waiting to be told news that she already knew.

"Miss Anderson," she began, "I've brought you here to talk about Malcolm Oliver. As I'm sure you've surmised by this point–"

"He's dead, isn't he?" Alice mumbled. She was surprised by the tone in her voice, so dull and flat and hollow. She would have thought she would have cried buckets at the death of Malcolm Oliver. She supposed there would be time for that. Right now nothing seemed like it was real.

"I'm afraid so, Mrs. Anderson," the detective confirmed. "999 received a call from his neighbours about two hours ago. Police arrived on the scene approximately ten minutes later and found the door to Mister Oliver's flat open. A body that was later identified as

Malcolm Oliver was found on the floor. I'm afraid that he had been shot in the neck."

There were so many questions to ask that beginning seemed to be an exercise in futility. Alice started with what seemed like the most obvious. "Am I a suspect?"

The detective shook her head. "No, ma'am. We don't have any suspects at this time. I contacted you because Mister Oliver's mobile indicated you were the last person he talked to."

"Oh," Alice said, her voice giving in to just the slightest hint of sorrow.

"Can you tell me the nature of your relationship with Mister Oliver?"

"We used to work together," Alice said numbly. "We did a podcast," she clarified. "We used to date, too," she added. "We used to do a lot of things, but then we – sort of stopped."

The detective nodded. She had taken out notepad and was writing something down. "And he contacted you today?"

Alice nodded.

"May I ask why?"

"We're to give a talk at the Royal Astronomy Conference tomorrow, on using new media to get kids interested in Science. I flew in from New York today. He called to make sure that I'd arrived safely."

Sorrow burst out of Alice in a moment when she wasn't expecting it. Something about the idea of arriving safely was a little too much. "I'm sorry," Alice said, wiping her eyes.

The detective nodded. She said nothing. Alice felt the need to fill the silence, and she found herself talking.

"Malcolm and I met at University," she said. "We were both at Cambridge, in the Astrophysics Department. It was his idea to do the podcast. I'd like to think it's been fairly successful, only Malcolm stopped doing it last year."

"Why is that?"

Alice shook her head. "He wanted to focus more directly on his research," she said. It seemed like an appropriate thing to say. This had, officially, been Malcolm's answer at the time. The truth, of course, was more complicated, as truths always are. It was actually Alice who had left, for America anyway. Although they certainly could have continued with the show, Malcolm had decided that he needed to step back from the podcast. He had insisted that the two things weren't related, but that was like insisting that there was no causality between a bomb and an explosion simply because you couldn't see the bomb afterward.

"What was his research on?" the detective asked.

"He was working on Fictional Realism," Alice said. It occurred to her that the phrase 'fictional realism' made it sound like Malcolm was a professor of modern literature, but that didn't seem to matter now.

The detective nodded and wrote something on her notepad. "This is always an awkward question to ask, but is there anyone you know of who might have wanted to hurt Malcolm? A jilted lover, an old rival, someone who might have held a grudge?"

Alice shook her head. "I'm sure you have heard this time and time again, Detective, but there is absolutely no one on the face of the Earth who I would believe less likely to be murdered. I would have put even money on my own mother before Malcolm."

The detective said that she understood, and then added that although it was merely a formality, she would have to take down Alice's whereabouts for the day, along with some information about where she was staying and how to get in touch with her. Alice was asked to notify Scotland Yard in the event that she planned on leaving the country. Alice thanked her, and then asked if she could use the loo.

Alice didn't have to go to the bathroom, she just needed to, well, she didn't *know* what she needed to do exactly – run her fingers through her hair, splash some water on her face, throw up; she didn't know, just something. She needed to be alone, she supposed. Alone and secure.

Alice looked at herself in the mirror. It can be said that young women are never truly happy with their reflections, and indeed, staring into a pool of water, Helen of Troy could have found flaws. However, it was understandable if looking into the mirror at this ungodly hour, Alice found the woman staring back at her a shell of who she normally was. She had dark circles under her eyes, and her bright curly hair looked both matted and tangled. She would have dreaded the thought of going to the Astronomy conference now, but of course, she couldn't give her presentation anymore, anyway. She would need to send an email to the event coordinator, as soon as she got back to the hotel.

Alice stepped out of New Scotland Yard and onto the street. It had gotten cold during the night, and she wished she had a coat with her. She looked up. The stars were, technically, out, but in the middle of downtown London it was difficult to see them. It occurred to her that this was the first starlight that she would never share with Malcolm.

"Are you all right?" a voice asked.

Alice spun around. It was the man from the bar. He was still dressed in his World War One flying ace costume, although there was a look of obvious concern on his face. Alice, who liked surprises about as much as diarrhea and taxes, asked what seemed like the most logical question.

"What are you doing here?"

"You aren't the only person Malcolm Oliver talked to yesterday," the man said.

Alice, feeling less unsure of herself than she did a moment ago, asked the question she hoped would provide her with at least the smallest degree of orientation.

"Who are you?"

The man stretched out a gloved hand. "My name," he said, "is Keith Quick."

Well, I won't have any trouble remembering that one, Alice thought. She looked at the man. He was smiling warmly, but there was a distinct level of concern in his face. He had a small nose and long eyelashes. This was only her second time meeting him, but he seemed very familiar somehow, as if he were an old friend who she had been very close to once, but whose face seemed somehow distant and forgotten.

"Are you all right?" he asked again. She didn't answer. He could probably tell that she was feeling a little uncomfortable talking with this strange man who kept popping out of nowhere, so he began again. "I was brought down here because I was one of the last people to talk to Malcolm

I had a feeling that the next person they would want to talk to would be you, so I waited. I thought you might be upset. I was standing right over there when they brought you in, only you had your head down and you didn't notice me."

Alice nodded. Her brain was still catching up with the events of the night. "I didn't know that you knew Malcolm," she said.

"I didn't," Keith Quick admitted. "At least not in person. He had contacted me recently about his research, which, let me tell you, isn't easy to do."

He pulled the receiver of what looked like an early twentieth century telephone out of his bag and then put it back again.

There was an awkward silence. It seemed very much as though he wanted to say something, but was having a time working up to it, as if he were a doctor and was trying to tell her that she had cancer. (After hearing about Malcolm's murder, it probably wouldn't have surprised her if he told her that she needed an emergency sex change operation, but that was neither here nor there).

"Can I buy you a cup of coffee?" he asked.

She could tell from the tone of his voice that he meant no harm. Even so, Alice sighed with the exhaustion of heavyweight boxer who had just gone twelve rounds. "I'm sorry," she said. "I'm exhausted, jet-lagged, and probably in the middle of one of the five stages of grief. I need to get some rest. I need to get back to the hotel, cancel my presentation at the Royal Astronomy Conference, and get some rest. You'll have to forgive me."

Keith Quick shook his head. "No, you see that's what I was afraid of. I'm afraid without a doubt that you're going to have to give your speech at the conference."

Alice rubbed her temples. It seemed that in the two minutes that they'd been talking the sky had brightened significantly. "Why is that?" she asked, thinking that perhaps it would be best if she simply walked back into the police station and asked if there was some sort of petty crime she could commit that would force them to lock her in a room by herself with a bed. "Why on Earth would I want to give my presentation without Malcolm, especially after the day I've had?"

"Because," Keith said, "the police think you're a murderer."

Alice's eyebrows moved all the way to the top of her head and stayed there. "Really?"

Keith nodded. "C'mon, I need to tell you what I know. I know a place not far from here that's always open. We can catch a bite to eat and get caught up."

Chapter 3
At Glastonbury

It is widely accepted by scholars everywhere that the twelfth century was not a whole lot of fun. Why exactly it wasn't fun is a matter of debate. Perhaps it was the climate, which, it must be admitted, was a lot cooler than it is now. It may have also been the instability brought down by the fall of the Roman Empire, which undoubtedly caused a certain degree of political turmoil. Mostly though, it seems to have been the poverty, disease, famine, repression, and general misery that contributed to the general inability to find anything cool to do on the weekends.

The monk digging the grave would have been aware of this, but only vaguely. He was, after all, knee deep in the twelfth century, and as with most things, it is difficult to see what is going on when you are in the middle of it, not unlike the hole he was digging. He looked up at the sky and shouted. "I have, god woot, a large hole to ere. Why did the old man have to die?"

From somewhere up above him a voice, much older than his, said, "Right so, there livede never man, in all this world, that som tyme he ne dyed."

The grave digging monk leaned against his shovel and wiped the sweat from his brow. "Of course, but for some drope of pitee, he might hae picked anothere tyme to do it. Hell hath nothinge on the morninge sun."

A bald, greyish head popped over the mountain of earth and looked down at him. "Ne," he said dismissively.

The young monk groaned. "By myn troth, do you want to kill won man burying anothere?" he asked.

The head had apparently gone back to where it had been a moment ago. "Ye shovel like myn suster," he said.

The young monk sighed and went back to work, thinking that he would go down another foot or so and then declare the job done whether the old monk thought so or not. He pushed his shovel further into the dirt and hit something that felt like stone.

"Oy," the young monk said. He picked up his shovel and dug again. It struck rock a second time.

"What?" the old monk asked.

"I thought you sayd noon was buryd here," the young monk said.

The old monk stood up with a groan that seemed to imply that the real work in grave digging lay in showing patience to young men. "Noon is buryd there," he insisted. "It's a rock. Put ye back into it,"

The young monk grunted back at his superior and tried another spot. This worked for a while, but eventually he hit rock again. "It's huge," the young man complained. "Like a mountain under the earte."

"God doesn't burye mountains," the old man said irritably.

"How do ye know?" the young monk asked. "Goode Lord tell ye everythynge, then?"

"Juste a bigge rock," the older monk insisted. He crawled down into the grave. "We'll find the bottome."

Three hours later, they did.

The secretary ran down the hallway, a lamp shaking in his hand in spite of the dwindling daylight. It was the secretary's job to disturb the abbot in his bedchamber, a chore that had all the career satisfaction of driving a cab in New York City. About the only really spectacular perk about being an abbot in the twelfth century was looking down your nose at a wonderfully large group of people. (If you don't believe this, feel free to take a moment to Google the word "hairshirt." Be advised you may want to take a shower afterward.) As such, the abbot tended to be about as soft and cuddly as a thorn bush covered in double-edged steel. This meant that the secretary didn't usually like to disturb him, even if the news he had to deliver was really astonishingly good. (Indeed, on the whole, the secretary wasn't sure that he would wake the abbot in the event of the resurrection, especially if it happened in the middle of his daily nap.) Today he would have to chance the lashing, and knocked on the abbot's door. The second coming was one thing. This was important.

The secretary's loud knock on the oak door was met with an even louder grunt. "Father?" he asked, and from the other side of the door the abbot's secretary heard the words "Shite hool!"

The secretary cleared his throat rather loudly. "News from the yarde, father," he said nervously.

The secretary of the abbot heard the unmistakable sound of a bodily function. "Thy burye bruther Michael?"

"The bruthers have dug up the earte," the secretary said, clearing his throat a second time.

"Thy burye hym?"

"Thy cane not," the secretary insisted.

The door opened. The abbot was a bald man with a round face and a curious lack of eyebrows. This made him look a little bit like an enormous round baby who had just come into this world and found it tremendously unsatisfying. He appeared to have been in a state of deep meditation. The secretary could see the lines the pillow had left on his face.

"Hae ye not understoot what the words 'Doe ne disturbe' mean?" he asked.

"I am sorrye," the secretary began.

"Sorrye?" the abbot said angrily. "I hath been at the accounts all daye. Do ye knew what it tekes to kepe this place running? Ye knew I hath the chance a snowball hath with the devil of keping the counting house at bay! The walls in the kitchens are crumbling, the pews in the chapel hath termites, and the casks from last summer hath turned into Vinegar! The abbey does ne hae tuppence to rub together, and everyone is turning to me for answers! All I ask is fore a moment's peace afore I go at it agayn."

They had been having variations on this same conversation for months now. Glastonbury Abbey had built a new hall last year. The cost of construction, and the poor harvest that had followed, had left the abbey on the verge of bankruptcy. Indeed, there had been lengthy discussions between the abbot and the archbishop about consolidating this abbey with the one in Sussex. These were discussions that frequently became quite heated, and usually involved both the abbot and the archbishop going to confession, a situation that was made awkward by the fact that the abbot usually confessed to the archbishop and the archbishop confessed to the abbot. Until now, the secretary had been trying his best to keep the abbey moving, hoping against hope that his superior would take his head out of the sand.

The secretary took a deep breath, and tried again. "The bruthers," he said "They–"

"What?" the abbot said irritably. He had turned around and began to pace back and forth in the room. The abbot's room was decorated in a manner that in almost any other century would be described as sparse, although for the age it was considered more than adequate. The secretary did notice that the ledger was sitting open on small table, next to a narrow bed. The pages were scribbled with impossibly tiny script, detailing the accounts. The secretary wondered if, in fact, any progress had been made.

"They were burying bruther Michael," the secretary said, a tad more courageously.

The abbot groaned. "Pious olde farte," he grumbled. "Ye would have thought he pooped angel's wings. I suppose thy neede a prayer sayd o'er the bodye?"

"Ne," the secretary insisted. "They were shovelling the earte when they founde," he didn't even know how to put it, "a grayve. Centuries olde."

The abbot sat down on the tiny bed and rubbed his temples. The news that the issue was not financial in nature seemed to calm him, but only momentarily. "I tolde them to bury him in the west field. The olde yard is full."

"They did bury him in the west field," the secretary insisted.

The abbot placed his forehead in his palms in a manner that suggested his cerebellum was made out of marble. "There has ne been a buryel o'er there in–"

"Centuries?" the secretary surmised. In the verbal chess match between these two men, the secretary frequently felt something akin to Boris Spassky, if he were pitted in a tournament match against a rhinoceros with irritable bowel syndrome. However, for just a moment, the tables turned and the abbot, looking at the younger man's face, saw the power in his strength and humility.

"What'd they find?" the abbot asked grumpily. "A Centurion? A Pictish invayder? What is it?"

"The answer to our prayers," the secretary said. "You must come quicke."

It bears repeating that there isn't really a lot to do in a twelfth century abbey, even less then there might have been in the world at large. Indeed, the four daily hours of prayer at Glastonbury were initiated, not so much as a symbol of piety, but rather as a tool to keep the men busy during the day. Still, there were always a few idle hours, and occasionally, on hot summer nights, the men would trade stories about a king buried centuries before at Glastonbury Abbey.

The secretary had never believed this story. Indeed, he would have been wise not to. You see, nearly every town within a hundred miles of the Severn had a similar story about this same king. Either their town was the home of his castle, or his birthplace, or the local mountain had been the sight of his greatest battle, or the town inn had been the spot where he'd gotten spectacularly drunk. The secretary would nod politely when monks mentioned the King's grave, and say nothing, privately thinking that in all probability, he had never existed.

Oh, how wrong he had been.

It was well past midnight as the abbot wandered through the library with the secretary following close behind him, nervously carrying a torch in one hand. The stacks were high and narrow, and the secretary knew that if he as much as wavered with the flame, the whole place would go up in cinders. They were in the most ancient section of the library, where the books were centuries old and had pages and spines that could do little more than act as kindling. If the room burned, a treasury of history would be lost, to say nothing of their lives. The secretary couldn't help but think that this might have waited until morning, though he appreciated the abbot's sense of urgency.

"Hae ye written to the Kyng?" the abbot asked, stopping in front of a bookshelf.

"E'en now the messengers are off," the secretary confirmed. He did his best to make sure that his voice sounded crisp and alert. He doubted that the abbot would see sheer exhaustion as an excuse for dereliction of duty.

The abbot reached for a book on the top shelf. "Did ye tell him about—"

"Ne," the secretary interrupted nervously. "If the messenger were stopped by highwaymen, it could be dangerous for the abbey. I only told hem that the grayve had been founde."

The abbot nodded. "Good," he said confidently.

"Do ye think he will come?" the secretary asked.

"If he does ne leaf within the houre, I should be surprised," the abbot replied, putting the book back on the shelf and taking down another.

In the distance, there was the sound of oak creaking unpleasantly.

"I thought he was buryed on an islande," the secretary said, turning around nervously.

"This was an islande," the abbot confirmed. "In the tyme of olde. Avalon was its nayme. Look at the landscape, ye can tell. The eastern pasture, the swamps, and the craig down by the river, it was all under water in the tyme of my grandfather's grandfather's grandfather. Aethelbert drained it all to make room for more farmland. Looke at the groundes, ye can tell."

He opened the second book and studied it closely. "Here," he said. He opened the volume, and it cracked like a rotted tree branch blowing in the wind.

"What is it?" the secretary asked.

"Notes from my predecessors," the abbot said. He flipped through the pages slowly. The secretary brought the torch down slightly to shed more light. The writing was old. The secretary could barely make out the lettering.

"I founde this, yers ago," the abbot said. It looked like some kind of a diary, written presumably by some other abbot, in days long forgotten. "I was looking for the papers of Joseph of Aramathea. I knew ne what to mayke of it. Until today."

He turned the book around and held it up for the secretary to read. The words were in a tiny Latin script, which the secretary translated in his head.

March 29th, the year of our lord, 485

The King was buried today, even as the forces of chaos pour in around us.

They brought him to us after the battle, hoping against hope that we could provide a miracle that not even God himself could perform. We were able to provide comfort and safety only, and even these would not last long. Although in pain every second, the King seemed to be in good spirits, asking after his attendants, hoping he might have some information about their health and safety, of which we had very little, or at least, very little that was promising. About his son he did not ask, and although this might not be surprising, it made me wonder – did he know the young prince was killed, or did he simply not want to know? If he was dead, he would not come for the King, and if he was alive, he might. Neither outcome was promising. I have not known the King personally, but it does not take a seer to know that he had been haunted by the ghosts of his past for a long time.

When at last some lieutenant of his could be found, the King breathed his last almost immediately. I had offered to take his confession, but he refused, saying with a smile that he would meet Saint Peter at the gates of Heaven and work out the matter for himself. Then he spoke with his man and gave his last breath. So help me, I've never seen a man who took to death as though it were a mother's kiss, or something black, and rare. Even in death, the King surprises me.

His Highness had been insistent that he be buried in the ways of the old gods, but on this point I refused.

This is an abbey. We will not paint our faces and dance like pagan men. We buried him in the enormous hollow of a tree, placing his mark on top of it. In keeping with his desires, I told him that his queen would one day be buried with him, although I was unsure if the wretched woman could even be found. The monks laid a fine stone pyramid atop the grave, a testament to who he was.

Of his death, there is little more to tell. As for his honour, I buried it with him, it wouldn't serve anyway.
Geoffrey of Avalon,
Abbot

"That's it, then?" the secretary asked.

"A little more toward the end of the volume," the abbot insisted.

Quickly flipping through the volume, the secretary found his way to a page at the end that had been marked.

April 7th, the year of our lord, 493
It is as I feared.
The pyramid that was meant to last for an age has started to sink. Heavy rains these last two weeks have left the fields muddy, and the stone, already more than the earth could bear, has fallen at least a foot. I fear that although his name will never be forgotten, the world may marvel that there is no grave for Arthur.

"How long afore we can expect Kyng Edward?" the secretary asked.

"He's in France," the abbot said. "Could be a fortnight before he gets the news."

"He will surely want the object the bruthers tooke frome the grayve," the secretary observed.

"Whether the story be true or ne, it will sit in the hande of every kyng to take the throne for a thousande year," the abbot said.

A thought rolled through the secretary's mind as he put the book back on the shelf. It was the kind of thought out of which political careers were made, which is to say it was brilliant, but also self-serving, underhanded, devious, and might change the face of a country besides.

"The Kyng will think it is his birthright," the secretary said very, very quietly.

"The right of kynges is devyne," the abbot agreed.

"And as such, he should reward us handsomely?" the secretary asked.

"We can only hoope," the abbot said.

The secretary held his breath for just a moment before speaking again. "There are others who might pay moore."

"Who?" the abbot asked, although of course he knew.

"The right of kynges is devyne," the secretary said "but even the devyne hae competitors."

The abbot looked at the secretary, sizing him up. In the dark shadows of the library, the secretary appeared to be less nervous. He looked older and more powerful. The abbot wondered if he could trust him with his life. If they were not careful, it could come to that.

"A pretender to the throne," the abbot said. He swallowed hard. "You thinke he would paye–"

"Moore?" the secretary suggested. "Almost certainly. A man with power hae everything an ordinary man hae ne, sayve one, the need for that power. And power is what we found in that grayve."

"You're thinking of William the Rough," the abbot said.

"Or Phillip of Arris, or Llewylyn of Caer Leon. Father, we must send word. We can sell it to the highest bidder."

"We hae already sent word to the Kynge," the abbot said, looking around the darkness nervously. "He will make for Glastonbury as soone as he has heard."

"But I hae ne tolde him anything othere than the grayve hae been found," the secretary pointed out. "He does ne know–"

"Without it, it is nothing moore than an old grayve," the abbot said. "A noble man of an ancient house that hae long since passed into mythe and shadow."

"We could make somethyng," the secretary suggested. "A cross, with his nayme on it."

"We must be discreet," the abbot said.

There's something dark and wonderful about being a part of a conspiracy. The secretary rode out of the abbey before the sun rose and made his way hastily to Caer Leon. From there, if necessary, he would head on to Edinburgh, riding as if the hounds of hell were at his heels. In Wales he met with resistance, but in Edinburgh, ahh…the Scots were more than happy to pay off the abbey's debts and then some – a pittance for the privileges that the opportunity of possession would provide. For years, the King of the English had been insisting that he was the rightful heir to the Scottish throne. Well, now, oh how the tables would turn. A river of gold would flow into the abbey, the King of Scotland would lay claim to the English throne, the secretary would be made the successor to the abbot, and the abbot could take the counting house receipts and set them ablaze. Everybody wins, or rather, everybody would have won, if the United Postal Service Company had been founded sometime during the twelfth century.

Unfortunately, it had not.

"God woot, I hoope the Inn hath a fine ale," the young monk said. He turned his head towards the sun, and bathing his face in the sunlight, he smiled with the satisfaction of a lazy man who for once in his life had done the easy thing. "Perhaps a pretty maid to turn my eye. Lord, by my troth we hath had a longe ryde."

The old monk grunted. "We'll be sleeping in the forest," he grumbled.

"Aaghh," the young monk spat back. He got off his mount, a small mule, and stretched his back muscles. Truth be told, he hadn't expected to sleep anywhere other than the cold hard ground. Still, a man could always hope. It was a long trip to Scotland, and although the young monk was grateful for the opportunity, it would have been nice to spend a little time in a wayside inn, if only money allowed "The abbot is as flint a man as ever was born," he grumbled.

"Ne an abbot borne whose shite hoole did ne pucker when he was passing out gold," the old monk said. He had been irritable all day, and had largely confined his conversation to a series of grunts and bodily functions. "Surprised he let us hae the mules. There isn't an inn for miles, anyway. Still, better than digging grayves, God be praysed."

They stopped on the edge of a clearing and built a fire, letting their mules graze and take water from a nearby stream. Dinner that night consisted of a sliver of mutton and a jug of wine, a meal the monks considered a movable feast. In another century their location would have seemed almost embarrassingly close to where they started, but for two men who had expected to live the rest of their lives inside the walls of the abbey, they might as well have been on the far side of the Moon. The trip north would take weeks, a prospect that almost anyone would look at as an adventure.

"I hae ne'er seen the north," the young monk said, pushing a wedge of kindling into a newly made fire. "Will we hae to cross Hadrian's Wall?"

"We shall," the old monk said.

"I hae always wante to see the wall," the young monk said. "My father saw it once, afore I was borne. Always said it was beautiful. Like a great big line drawn all the way down the country side. Hae ye seen it?"

The old monk sighed. The young man got the impression that this was a subject that the old man hadn't wanted to discuss, although how the old monk thought they were getting to Scotland without the subject of the wall coming up wasn't clear.

"I was there, loong ago," the old man said, "when I was a knight."

The young monk did something that fell somewhere between a sneeze and a spit. "You were a knight, were you? I suppose you fought with our faire Kynge then?"

The old man stirred the fire. "Twas the olde Kynge I fought fore."

This wasn't surprising, or at any rate it shouldn't have been given the old monk's age, but the young monk raised his eyebrows just the same. "You fought with the olde Kynge?" he asked.

"Even he," the old monk agreed.

"Did ye meet him?"

The old monk stirred the fire. "I strode with him against Llewellyn," the old monk said. "Shoke his hande after a tough battle. He was in the middle of his life. Fierce as a lion."

"Guess it's fitting that the abbot sent you on this mission, then?" the young monk said. He was lying down on his back so he could look at the stars. "We need a man of your bravery on a mission like this. Carrying the–"

"The Kynge," the old monk interrupted, "would have us hanged for what we're doing right now."

"Hanged?" the young man asked. "Hae ye been at the ale, man?"

The old monk shook his head grumpily. "Do ye na understand what we founde ye daft–"

The young monk looked up. It was clear from the expression on his face that he had absolutely *no* idea what the old man was talking about. He also felt it was better to feign disinterest, rather than admit ignorance. "Rusty ol' bit o' metal?" the young monk sniffed. "Scots are welcome to it."

The old man stood up. He seemed angry. "That thing?" he shouted. "That thing we've got sitting in the saddlebag? That is na an olde bit of iron. It's the seed which gave life to this country. It is the touch of the hande of god, the miracle of this nation, the thinge that says that this place, and these people, they are a country that will see the sun rise and set, till the heavens fall."

In another century, this would have been considered a truly remarkable speech, worthy of applause, quotations, and re-blogging on various social networking websites. This being the twelfth century, it earned the old monk little more than a raised eyebrow. This was a shame, really, since it would be the last time the old monk would ever get a chance to finish a sentence.

"If you think so much of it," the young monk asked dryly, "why are you taking it to the Scots?"

The old monk sat back down again. "I do what I'm tol'," he grumbled, "an' I'll tell you another thing–"

Just then there was a strange sound in the distance. If the young monk were to have described it, he would have said that it sounded a little like the howl of a wolf and a little bit like thunder. It was curious, reminding both men of things that never were and couldn't be. They both stood still and stared in the direction of the sound. At first there was nothing, then there was a silence, and then there was nothing again. Then, just as the two men were about to sit down again, a hooded figure stepped out of the forest.

"I beg your pardon," the hooded figure asked, "but could I join you?"

It was an odd voice that spoke, both smooth and angular, like cold steel. Unfortunately, the young monk was too stupid to notice this. "Why na? We've a little mutton left, if you finde yourself hungry. The two of us haf eaten already."

'So,' the hooded figure thought, *'there isn't anybody else with you.'*

"We should hae stopped at an inn," the young man offered, "but the abbot is a chepe bastard. Na an inn near here, anyhow."

'So,' the hooded figure thought, *'no one else is around.'*

"Come, sit!" the young monk said. "Tell us your tales of the road. We are on our way to Edinburgh, to see no less a personage that the Kynge of Scotland."

'So,' the hooded figure thought, *'no one will come to your aide.'*

From under the hooded cloak emerged a long, thin piece of steel. "This doesn't have to end badly," the figure said. "I only want the package."

The old monk, a survivor of battle, tensed up. He might not understand exactly what the thing in the figure's hand was, but he understood the stance of a warrior. It was difficult to describe, but there was something in the shoulders of the hooded figure that let the old monk know that he was in danger.

The old monk stood up and balled his fists. "Now see here—" he said, not finishing his sentence for a second time.

"What is that, anyway?" the young monk asked, leaning in closer to look at the strange piece of metal.

"A Winchester," the stranger said.

The hooded figure raised the rifle and pointed it at the monk's chest. In a split second the old monk leaped forward, which was a mistake. There was a scream, and then a noise, and then a scream again. The hooded figure took what it wanted from the saddlebag before retreating back into the night.

Gristle
&
Thorn
Est.
10072 B.C.

Chapter 4
The Royal Astronomy Conference

In spite of the lateness of the hour, the Gristle and Thorn was open, and was doing a fair trade of business. Again, the pub was catering almost exclusively to people whom Alice would have described as oddballs. At a table next to her a man in a black judicial robes and a powdered wig was talking with a woman in a short black leather skirt, a cape, and a bustier, and at the bar a man in a cowboy hat and chaps seemed to be chatting up a woman dressed like Queen Victoria. Alice found her eye drawn in particular to a wide-eyed man in his thirties who was slipping martinis from underneath a black fedora. He seemed familiar, although in a very different way than Keith did. Alice was so tired that she scarcely noticed that in spite of Keith's suggestion of a cup of coffee, the bartender had given her the same drink that she had that afternoon, again without asking. The thought occurred to her that she had never paid for the drink the first time.

Keith had been quiet on the way over, hailing a cab for the two of them and directing it to the bar's address. Now that Alice had been given a chance to look at him, he seemed a little off somehow. There were his eyes, for starters. He didn't seem to know where to look, and he kept thumping his chest nervously with his right thumb. Under normal circumstances, she probably would have found the thought of sitting across a table from him a little frightening, but right now she was much, much more frightened of everything else. Keith had ordered a strong cup of coffee for himself, along with something that appeared to resemble breakfast. Having spent some time in America, Alice was aware that Americans would eat breakfast at any time of day. At another time, she might have questioned the wisdom of that decision, but right now there were bigger fish to fry. She decided that she should start by asking the single most obvious question:

"Why do the police think I killed Malcolm?"

Keith didn't answer, but leaned forward and stared deeply into her eyes. "You haven't been sleeping well," he said.

"It's four o'clock in the morning," Alice reminded him, not a little tartly. "I doubt that anyone in this room has been sleeping well. You said that Malcolm had contacted you."

"I'm not easy to get a hold of, but yes, he left me a message. He said he had something I would like to see."

Alice recalled that Malcolm had said the exact same thing to her the last time that she had spoken to him – he had something he wanted to show her. She hadn't thought much of it at the time. For all she knew he could have bought a new car, but in light of his death she started to wonder. Was a new car the kind of thing you could get killed over? She supposed it probably was. It didn't seem likely that it was the case here, though. Malcolm was killed in his flat, and had contacted Keith, both of which seemed to rule out that idea. If someone killed him for a car, he would have been found in a parking lot or something, and a new car wasn't the sort of thing that you contacted a total stranger about, unless he was a mechanic.

"What did he want to show you?" Alice asked. "Was it important?"

Keith shrugged and sighed and shook his head. (He was still wearing his World War One pilot's helmet, which made this a fairly dramatic gesture. Indeed, a woman at the next table had to duck rather quickly.) "I'm sorry," he said, sincerely. "There are so many, many things to tell you, that it's difficult to know where to begin."

"You could begin," Alice told him, "by answering my questions. Why do the police think that I killed Malcolm? And how do you know about it?"

Keith bent over and pulled a small package out of the leather satchel that he'd been carrying. "The police think that you killed Malcolm because you used to date him, you've just come back from the states, you don't have an alibi for the last few hours, and Malcolm has just been shot twice in the neck. But that's the least of our worries. We need to start with the broader strokes first and work out the nitty-gritty details later on. For starters, I should probably explain why the waiter keeps giving you free drinks."

Alice raised her eyebrows. "You think *that's* the most important thing to discuss right now?"

Keith nodded. "How much" he asked, "did you know about Malcolm Oliver's work?"

On the Richter scale of non-sequiturs, this lay somewhere between 9.6 and 9.8, making it roughly the verbal equivalent of the 1906 Earthquake in San Francisco, but Alice decided that she'd play along. "Malcolm's work?" she asked, surprised. "He was working on something called fictional realism."

Fictional realism is the bi-product of taking the more irrational ends of quantum mechanics to their absolute most ridiculous conclusion. To understand what fictional realism is, you need to start with the basic idea that every choice we make, and every choice we could make, is real. All of our choices all exist out there somewhere, in a multitude of universes, each one existing like a drop in an ocean of time. These choices could lead you to some strange places. In one universe you might be a billionaire, in another a pauper, or a murderer, or a saint. You can be, and probably are, almost anything, given the right choices.

Now, for just a minute, imagine that in one universe, just one, things go astoundingly, amazingly well. Let's say that in this particular universe, your parents, whose names just happen to be Andrew and Monique Bond, happen to have settled in Scotland, named you James, raised you with a desire to serve on Her Majesty's Secret Service, and driven home a thorough respect for a good martini. So there you are, wearing a tuxedo and a packing a Walther PPK, and insisting to Miss Moneypenny that there would never be another girl other than her. *Is this possible?* Yes, it is. This is the idea of fictional realism. It turns out that you live considerably more than twice.

Malcolm Oliver had a fairly concise way of stating this theory. In his words: "Everything written is real." It was Malcolm's fascination with the ideas brought forth by fictional realism that had caused him to quit doing the podcast with Alice, and had led Alice to eventually take the PHD fellowship offered by Cornell University. Before she left, Alice, along with everybody else, had said repeatedly that as theories go, fictional realism was an idea that was unrealistic, illogical, and downright absurd. What she didn't know was that it also happened to be correct.

"Fictional realism," Keith repeated. "You must have hated that one."

"It wasn't exactly a career building decision," Alice admitted.

"There's probably better funding for pulsars, or dry Martian river beds," Keith said. "It's always easier to get money for questions that people already know the answers to."

"It probably would have been easier to get money for almost anything," Alice complained. "Trying to prove that the Moon is made out of green cheese or making a space station out of Popsicle sticks. Diving into the realms of the unreal just made him seem crazy."

"It apparently wasn't completely crazy," Keith pointed out. "It might have gotten him killed."

Alice swallowed. "Are you saying that Malcolm might have been killed because of his research?"

Keith leaned in closer. "I am not trying to explain Malcolm's death," he said. "I'm trying to explain why the bartender is giving you free drinks."

Startled, Alice looked down at the drink in her hand. It was lovely. She didn't even know what it was called. Kina Lillet must be pricey, but the bartender had handed it to her like it was nothing.

"It's called a Venutian Sunrise," Keith said, answering her unspoken question. "Doesn't it seem odd that the bartender knew your favourite drink before you did?"

Alice put the drink down.

Keith pushed the package a little closer to her. "Open it," he insisted.

She started opening the package. It was wrapped in several layers of ragged brown paper. "The first time I met you, I asked you 'have we met'?" Keith said. "Do you remember? The reason I asked that was that I honestly wasn't sure if we had."

Alice nodded, but made no other reply. She just kept pulling layers off of the package.

"In my line of work, things sometimes happen in the wrong order. It gets confusing. It's usually best to ask if you need to introduce yourself, just to make sure. It was because of my line of work that Malcolm Oliver got in touch with me."

"What are you saying?" Alice asked. In fact, she knew precisely what Keith was trying to say, but for reasons that were obscure even to her, she decided to keep opening the package. Whatever it was, it was hard, and curved.

"I am a collector," Keith said, "for the Time Traveller's Resort and Museum."

Alice finished opening the package. It was a large ceramic and ebony pipe that smelled so awful Alice wondered if it had been used in some sort of carbon-14 dating.

"What's this?"

"That," Keith said, "is the pipe of Sherlock Holmes."

Apart from a semester where she lived with a sculpting major, Alice didn't have a lot of experience dealing with truly crazy people. Given the evening that she'd had, calling the police seemed like a bad idea. It would be a shame to end up at Scotland Yard twice in the same night. Instead, as she had already done at least once that evening, Alice decided that for the moment she would play along. She had absolutely no reason to trust him, but it seemed like a truly dangerous man wouldn't seem so ridiculous.

"This pipe belonged to Sherlock Holmes?"

"Yes."

"The *actual* Sherlock Holmes?"

"Yes."

"The *real* Sherlock Holmes?"

"You can add as many adjectives as you like, but it will still mean the same thing. Somewhere out there, there's a universe where Sherlock Holmes exists, and, by a curious coincidence, he doesn't bother locking his front door." Keith picked up the pipe and looked at it. "I'm sure that he was mad as hell when he noticed it was gone," he added. "He notices everything."

Alice seemed to have entered into some sort of contest where her companion was determined to make sure that each thing he said was more outrageous than the last. She took a deep breath. She supposed that there was no point in using words like 'impossible' or 'crazy.' Perhaps it might be better to point out the holes in his story. "You're saying that you stole this," she pointed to the pipe, "from the world's greatest detective?"

"That's right," Keith insisted.

"And the reason you were able to do this," Alice made an unnecessary swirling motion in the air, "is because you're a time traveller?"

Keith poked a finger at her, putting on what Alice suspected was as close as he could muster to a serious expression. "What I'm saying, is that *everyone in this pub is a time traveller. Including you.*"

"Of all the gin joints in all the towns in all the world," Alice muttered.

"I've actually been to the Cafe American," Keith said brightly. "Delightful place. Funny thing though, in real life, everything is in colour. Except for Rick's tuxedo, of course. That's the same. Nice guy, Rick, little touchy on the subject of women, but…"

That was it. Alice was willing to entertain his fantasy for the purpose of avoiding a scene, but when the discussion came round to the quality of the cocktails served by Humphrey Bogart, things had taken an awkward turn. "Thank you for the drink," she said curtly, "but I think it's time for me to leave now. I need to cancel my lecture and get some sleep." She nodded to him briefly and stood. She was just about to step away when she heard his voice again.

"You noticed the man in the fedora, didn't you?"

Alice glanced over at the man in the large black fedora, who quickly began to look in the other direction. The truth was, she *had* noticed the man in black fedora, but how did Keith know that?"

"He looks familiar," Alice admitted, turning back around.

"Indeed," Keith said. He stood up, presumably so he could look her squarely in the eye. Alice noticed that there was an earnestness in his deep blue eyes. It seemed odd, especially since Keith had treated her impending indictment on a murder charge fairly dismissively. She looked at him. He had obscenely long eyelashes and a nose that would have fit in the coin pocket of a pair of jeans. He wasn't unhandsome-looking, in spite of the leather hat and goggles. He reminded her of one of those little owls with big blinky eyes and a little tiny beak.

"So you're saying that the pipe belonged to Sherlock Holmes?"

"Yes."

"The *actual* Sherlock Holmes."

"We've been here before. Maybe we should stop and ask for directions."

"And so the man over there in the fedora–"

"Is Orson Welles, yes."

Alice sat down and sighed. The whole point of learning Astrophysics was to discover order within the chaos of the universe. It was a beautiful, enchanting thing to study, revealing the very fabric of the universe. Now, this man sitting across from her, who was dressed like he was flying a Sopwith Camel, seemed to be cutting through that fabric with a weed whacker.

"He's working on rewriting the script to *The Third Man*," Keith commented, filling in the pause in the conversation.

"Did you suggest he go out and rent the movie, or did he not want to spoil the surprise?" Alice asked.

"Actually, I did better than that. I introduced him to Harry Lime. The conversation was awkward. Would you like to meet him?"

"No," Alice snapped. "I would not like to meet him. Orson Welles is dead, or at any rate he was until a minute ago. I do *not* want to meet Orson Welles. What I want to do is go back to my hotel room, get a good night's sleep, cancel my presentation, take a flight back to upstate New York, and go rearrange the furniture in my flat. It has a view of the lake and I've got a little tree with oranges on it standing by the door. I like that view and I like that tree. Instead, I get you. I thought that you would at least tell me why the police think that I killed Malcolm, and instead you're sitting there, dressed like you're in the RAF, and insisting that the reason all this is happening, that man, and that *pipe,* Malcolm's murder, all of it, is because you're a time traveller!"

"Actually, I'm saying that the reason that all this is happening is because *you* are a time traveller," Keith corrected. "Or at the very least, you will be. A very special time traveller. It's why I know that you didn't kill Malcolm Oliver, even though on the surface, at least, you look extremely guilty. It's also the reason why the bartender keeps giving you free drinks."

The sudden hint that she might actually appear to be guilty snapped Alice back into the present. "I want Malcolm to be alive again," she admitted, wanting to cry. She paused, and neither for the first nor the last time, a wave of sorrow rushed over her. She was not proud of it, but a tear ran down her cheek.

Keith reached out and squeezed her hand. "I'm sorry," he said. "Malcolm had left me a message saying that he knew who I was and that he had something I would want to see, but the truth is I never met him. At least, I don't think I had. Not yet, anyway."

Alice gave him a dirty look. "You," she said, "are a very strange man."

Keith smiled and then smirked and then smiled again. "I am strange and getting stranger," he admitted, "but that *is* still Orson Welles sitting at the table behind you."

Alice didn't have a response to this, so she decided to switch tactics. She frowned and put her head in her hands. "Can I go to bed now? I don't mean to put you off, it's just that I'm exhausted."

Keith's eyebrows did something which suggested a great deal of control over the endocrine system. "I'm very sorry," he said. "I'm sure that you must be exhausted, but daylight is coming up, and you'll need to get to your presentation."

Alice's eyeballs did their best imitation of dinner plates. "You're off it. There is *no* way I can give a presentation now. I've been up all night, I'm under a cloud of suspicion, and half of the talk was supposed to be delivered by Malcolm, anyway. I'm sorry, but I'm obviously in no state to give a presentation tomorrow. After all, *I'm talking to a man who thinks he's a time traveller."*

Keith laughed. He had a laugh that sounded like someone had crossbred a dog bark with a thunderclap and had gotten the worst genes from both. "I'm sorry," he said, still laughing, "but no matter how crazy I sound, you're going to have to realize that you absolutely have to go to the Royal Astronomy Conference today."

Steam seemed to come out of several different parts of Alice's head. "And why is that?" she asked.

"Because I think that the killer will be there too," he said, and for the first time since she'd met him, Keith was making sense. "Let's get you that cup of coffee," he suggested, "and you can tell me about your dreams."

"It's called drifting," Keith explained, his long white scarf trailing after him as he walked rather briskly through King's College. He looked delightfully out of place, like a small dog running through the House of Lords while it was in session. He strode purposefully past bewildered undergraduates, who seemed to be eying him as if he was some sort of hurricane. "It's happens when you get close to your first trip."

"Drifting?" Alice repeated. In the intervening hours she had taken a shower, downed several aspirin, gotten a fresh change of clothes, and had several cups of coffee. Even so, her head and her back were stiff, and her eyes were dry. She would have liked to have been charitable and said that she wasn't sure if her companion was a time traveller or not, but that wasn't the case. Truth be told, Alice didn't have even the slightest doubt that he was simply crazy. How exactly he'd managed to get an Orson Wells lookalike to show up in that bar, or what purpose that served, Alice wasn't sure.

Luckily, he wasn't much bother to her, and he did seem to have at least one key point – showing up at the talk Alice was supposed to have given with Malcolm did seem like the sort of creepy thing that a crazed murderer might do. (Were they looking for a *crazed* murder? Alice wasn't sure. She supposed it was fair game to refer to whoever had killed Malcolm as crazed. Malcolm had once lost an arm wrestling contest to a twelve-year-old girl. It wasn't like you had to kill him in self-defense.)

"Drifting," Keith said again, unaware that Alice's mind itself had drifted off to another part of the country. "You see, when you're close to your first time trip, your Cerebral cortex tends to forget which things it's seen and which it hasn't. Usually you'll have a few dreams about people you've never met or things that you've never done. You can see it in people's eyes, if you know what you're looking for. They have an exhausted, hungry look."

Alice decided not to point out that she was actually both hungry and exhausted, and chose to play along. "So you're saying I'm going to have a picnic in the countryside with a small dinosaur?"

Keith turned and raised his eyebrows and turned again. "What I'm saying is that anything is possible," he said, a sad look in his eyes. "Anything short of dragons, that is."

"And why not dragons?" Alice asked wearily.

Keith looked at her. "Because fire breathing reptiles violate the laws of physics, of course," he said. "Surely *you* know that. Pity. I always liked dragons."

There was a part of her that wanted to tell him to shove off, but she kept restraining herself. He seemed like such an equal measure of kindness and absurdity. *'At least I have an ally,'* she thought as they reached the lecture hall, silently wishing that her sister was more willing to attend her lectures.

The faculty of both the Astronomy department of Cambridge University and the Royal Astronomy Conference weren't technically old enough to remember the publication of the Principia Mathematica, but you wouldn't have known it to look at them. Indeed, during Alice's time as an undergraduate at Cambridge it had been a point of pride among the faculty to tell the story of how they remembered hearing about the discovery of galaxies for the first time. Conferences were largely an excuse for the aged wizards of the Astronomical Profession to bond with their brethren, and none of them were ever going to get any better at talking to young women than they'd been in their youth, and they probably hadn't been very good even back then.

It was only because Alice was a primary speaker of the day that she was given even the curtest nod by the organizers of the conference, who otherwise would have looked at her as if she had been given a pass as a present for her sweet sixteen. Mercifully, the talk that she was giving was part of the opening session of the conference, which meant that regardless of how things went, she could skip the proceeding events, a chore which Alice would have normally thought of as painfully dull, but now seemed to have all the pleasantness of a Chinese Water Torture. After a good deal of time getting everyone settled, the announcer, an elderly woman who looked a little like Albert Einstein, announced that they were, naturally, "Proud and delighted," to have the opportunity to host the Royal Astronomy Conference. Judging by the look on her face, by "proud and delighted" she clearly seemed to mean "bitter and annoyed."

Although Alice had gone to school here, she saw very few familiar faces in the crowd. It seemed that in the years since taking her undergraduate degree, the faculty had merged into one elderly grey-haired blur; a curmudgeon for all seasons. After she had introduced herself to the event's organizer, she quickly took a seat in the front row of the conference hall. Looking around, it was hard to believe that these people would really enjoy listening to a young woman renowned for being the world's sexiest astrophysicist talk about the joys of new media. They looked more like their idea of new media was a gramophone.

"I have no idea what I'm doing here," she whispered to Keith.

"You've been planning this. You were supposed to be prepared," Keith whispered back.

"I was prepared to do this with Malcolm," Alice pointed out. "Malcolm was supposed to open and he never shuts up. What are we looking for, anyway?"

"Anyone weird," Keith said.

"That's it?" Alice asked. "We're on a weirdo hunt?"

"Anyone who looks like the sort of people we saw in the bar," Keith said.

"You mean *time travellers?*" Alice asked, rolling her eyes.

"Time travellers, that's right," Keith insisted. "They're not known for their understated style."

"Is that why everyone at the Gristle and Thorn was dressed so garishly?"

"Time travellers tend not to stay in one place for very long, and usually don't do a whole lot of background research," Keith clarified. "Frequently they're spending one week in the twenty-first century and one week in the eighteen nineties, and they try to compensate by doing both. You end up with a woman wearing a petticoat and a corset with tattoos on her right arm. It's a little mixed up."

Alice would have liked to have given a reply to this, but just then she heard the speaker say the words, "I'd like to welcome Miss Alice Anderson to the stage, She's a graduate of this University and the host of Astropod, a weekly fact-based show on physics, astronomy, and the universe in general…"

What the photon Alice said that day was anybody's guess. She seemed to forget the words even as they were coming out of her mouth. She was reasonably sure that she hit upon her major topics: interactive social media as an education tool, the importance of getting young women involved in science, the changing nature of Astronomy in the classroom, the future and, well, just the future. She tried to stick to her notes, but there were times when she got off page and the words came out like spiraling free form jazz, spinning out of control into dark and difficult areas. She could only hope that it went well. If there was anyone in the crowd who was strange in any way, then Alice didn't see them. Except for one – a strange-looking woman seated almost all the way in the back. She wasn't odd in an out of this world sort of manner, she was just severe. Tall and angular, with dark sunglasses and a sharp chin, she looked about as happy to hear Alice talk about the joys of teaching children science as the Duchess of York would have been at a Megadeth concert. Alice had given this same talk many times and was used to a few glassy stares, but this was different somehow. Under normal circumstances, the woman would probably have seemed like a haughty graduate student, but today Alice wasn't sure. Perhaps it was just that the members of the Royal Astronomy Conference were so very, very white and old. Alice supposed that there probably wasn't anything significant about the woman, but she thought she might mention it to Keith, as it would give him something to obsess over.

Alice finally made it to the end of her talk when she heard, much to her shock and horror, her own voice say the words, "Any questions?"

A grey-haired man in a cardigan sweater, who looked like he probably had fond memories of the reign of Oliver Cromwell, stepped forward to the microphone that had been set up in the audience by the organizers of the conference. "Yes, Miss Anderson?" he asked, his voice just above a whisper.

'Here we go,' Alice thought.

The old man looked at the microphone as though it were some sort of new fad that hadn't quite caught on. "Miss Anderson? Paul Hopper here, holder of the Edward Gibbon chair in History. Pardon me, but what I understand, Miss Anderson, is that you were supposed to give this talk with a Mister Malcolm Oliver?"

Alice swallowed. "That's correct," she said.

The old man adjusted his glasses several times before speaking again. "And forgive me, news here trickles down slowly, I believe Mister Oliver died last night?"

"That's correct," Alice said again.

"Have you talked to the police?" a voice asked.

There was a general murmur throughout the crowd, and a look of absolute panic appeared on the face of the old man. Alice's voice gave the answer that her eyes had undoubtedly already given.

"Yes."

This time the murmur was almost twice as loud. The old man tried unsuccessfully to turn his mustache at a ninety-degree angle. "Excuse me then, but–" he paused dramatically, hoping perhaps that someone else might finish this question. "Why are you here?" he asked, when else nobody did.

Alice swallowed hard. "I'm here," she admitted, her voice quaking, "because I thought that one of you might have killed Malcolm."

The outburst that this statement caused was the closest thing that the University had seen to absolute pandemonium since the reign of Richard the Third. Immediately everyone was on their feet. There were shouts of "my god!" and "incredulous!" and Alice took a moment to give thanks that that the University didn't have an agricultural department, because at this point someone probably would have brought out rotten tomatoes and pitchforks. Keith ran forward immediately and grabbed Alice by the hand.

"You looked at the audience," he said. "Did you see anything? Anything at all?"

Alice looked up. The woman in sunglasses had stood up. She glanced up at Alice expressionlessly, before putting on a floppy black hat and turning around and striding rather purposefully toward the exit on the far side of the room. Standing up, the woman was tall and imposing. For a moment, she looked over her sunglasses and their eyes met, and when they did Alice felt a little chill go up her spine. "At the back," she said, and she tried to express urgency with her eyes. "There was a woman wearing sunglasses, all in black."

Keith scoured the crowd. "I see her," he shouted, and he started purposefully cutting through the crowded room. Keith was making headway, but the tall, dark figure had turned and was making her way purposefully towards the door. Alice, feeling that her question and answer session had come abruptly to an end, did her best to find her way to the exit. By the time she had found her way out of the hall again, the crowd of astrophysicists had dispersed in a thousand different directions. Keith was standing in the square in front of the building, shading his eyes and trying to find the woman in black.

"Did you see her?" Alice asked.

"I caught a glimpse of her as she was headed out the door. Seemed like she was in a hurry."

"Do you think that she was the one we were looking for? Do you think she killed Malcolm?"

"Whether or not she killed Malcolm I couldn't say, but a six-foot-tall Asian woman does have a tendency to attract the eye. I'd like to know who she is, at least."

"We could ask around, perhaps someone will know who she is," Alice suggested.

"We could," Keith agreed, "but you seem to have brought the conference to a rather abrupt conclusion. Besides, I have a feeling that she was an outsider."

Alice walked over to the edge of the fountain and sat down. "I suppose it was a long shot," she said.

"She was looking at you like you were liquid death," Keith observed. "She knew something, I'm sure of it."

Alice leaned over and put her head in her hands. "What do we do, then?"

This question wasn't posed at Keith as much as it was directed at the universe in general. She desperately wanted to know what it was that she was supposed to do next. She had a bad feeling that going back to the hotel and going to sleep wasn't the answer.

Keith sat down next to her and put a hand on her shoulder. "Let me take you somewhere," he suggested. "Somewhere warm and wonderful, where all of this seems no more relevant than a darkened dream."

Alice had already given this strange man enough of her time, but his tone was so warm and so comforting that she couldn't help but feel sorry for him. "What did you have in mind?"

He patted her on her leg. "Home," he said simply.

"I've been living in America for two years," Alice said. "It's nice, but it never really felt like home. Before that, I went to school here. I've been back for the better part of an hour and I almost caused a riot. I'm not really sure that I know where home is anymore."

"That's because you've never been there, not yet, anyway," Keith insisted. "Come on, let me take you back to the hotel. You can get some sleep, and then pack your bags."

"Get some sleep?" Alice repeated.

"As much as you like," Keith said. "Get some rest, take a shower, and get ready. After that we've got a flight to catch."

Chapter 5
On the Run

Alice thought about her hotel room like it was a long-lost love. A nice, long nap would make her right as rain. She could sleep until the evening, and perhaps even go to bed early. Children on the night after Christmas wouldn't sleep as well as Alice would sleep tonight.

For a crazy person, Keith was surprisingly chivalrous. First, he arranged to have a car drive them all the way to her hotel in London, so that they wouldn't have to take the train. Then he insisted on walking her to room, although she had made it very clear that he would be leaving her at the door. Why exactly he was following her around, Alice couldn't guess. Surely he must have something else to do. *'Two largely dateless years in New York and I come home and meet a crazy American in less than eight hours. It wasn't like there was a lack of them over there.'*

"You seem to be handling this pretty well," Keith said. They had just gotten into the hotel elevator and were headed up to Alice's room. He was still wearing his aviator's hat, scarf, and bomber jacket. Alice wondered if it made him hot.

"I suppose that later on it will set in," said Alice. She didn't mention Keith's suggestion that they go away together. Indeed, she didn't mention anything that had happened at all. She just wanted to put her problems aside for a moment and focus on getting her head on straight before she worried about contacting a barrister and figuring out what she needed to next. She would like to know who the strange Asian woman was, but that would have to wait, at least for now. She supposed it was possible that the woman was simply a teaching assistant with an odd demeanor, but it was difficult to either forget or ignore the hatred apparent on woman's face.

"Don't try to take it all in at once," Keith suggested. "Let it come in waves. I know it doesn't sound right. It sounds like the worst thing you could go through. You need to take a little of it in and let it go. You need to do that, over and over and over again, until it's gone past you."

"What makes you say that? Have you lost someone?"

"We've all lost someone."

Alice didn't know it, but the very last thought she would have as an astrophysicist would happen between the fifth and sixth floors of the hotel, when she would make a note to see the sun set from the millennial bridge while she was in town. She had walked across it with Malcolm once when he was alive, and they'd made a point of watching the stars come out. It was nice. She smiled as the elevator came to a stop on the sixth floor. As the doors opened, she saw the police detective standing at the end of the hallway.

For a moment, Alice and DI Enid Williams looked at each other, neither one moving nor speaking. The detective was holding a walkie-talkie and there were three large uniformed officers with her. They all looked tense. In another context, Alice would have supposed that they were there for some sort of follow up, or with information about what had happened to Malcolm. It didn't ring true, though. You could see it in their eyes. *'This is it,'* Alice thought. *'They're here to arrest me.'*

Keith pushed the 'close door' button and then the one for the top floor.

"What are you doing?" she asked.

"We need to head in another direction," Keith said.

"How do you know they'll have people waiting for us in the lobby? And what good is going to the top floor, anyway? What are you going to do up there?"

"The walkie-talkie," answered Keith. "She was talking to someone downstairs. As for what we're going to do on the top floor, obviously I haven't the foggiest idea. I'll improvise."

'I hope he doesn't think he can fly,' Alice thought. *'Maybe he thinks flying is a part of time travel.'*

The elevator opened on a floor that looked exactly like the one that they'd just been on, only with an absence of police officers. Alice and Keith got out and the door closed behind them. "You do realize that they can see where we've gone, don't you?" Alice said, looking at the elevator behind them.

Keith looked around frantically. "This way," he said, projecting a confidence that he almost certainly didn't feel. He strode off down the hallway, taking fierce strides so that Alice had to run to keep up.

"Stop," she shouted. "This is crazy. Surely the police will catch the killer eventually."

"The funny thing is, I don't think that they will," Keith insisted. He got to the end of the hallway, looked out of the window, and promptly turned left down another hall. "But–" he added, running to the end of another corridor, "I'm hoping that we can."

Keith reached the end of the second hallway and grabbed a door handle. "Damn hotel room doors," he muttered.

Alice tried the door on the other side of the hallway. "What are you looking for, a place to hide?" she asked.

"Not at all," Keith said, trying another door. "We've got to look on this side."

"Look for what?" Alice asked frantically.

"Your hotel is old," he pointed out. "Really old."

"So?" she asked.

"So old hotels that were built before fire codes tend to have fire escapes on the outside of the building," Keith said as he stared at the locked door to a room.

"How do you plan on getting it open?" Alice asked.

"Easy." He bent over and pulled something out of his bag. It was a round metal object that looked a little bit like a pocket watch, if perhaps a pocket watch could be made out of liquid mercury. He placed it over the lock. The object whirred and then clicked, and then whirred again. Keith opened the door.

"That's a handy gadget," Alice commented.

"It'll also make you a cup of tea," Keith said.

"How did you pick that lock so fast?" Alice asked.

"The owners of imaginary objects tend to want to keep them for themselves," he said.

"I suppose the wedding rings of Romeo and Juliet are kept under lock and key?" Alice asked snarkily.

Keith looked at her, and smiled. "I bought the wedding rings of Romeo and Juliet in a pawn shop," he said. "Getting the skull of Yorick, now *that* was hard."

The room they were in was only marginally different from the one that Alice had rented for the weekend, except that Alice's had a slightly smaller bed and a slightly older television set. Keith strode over to the window and stared out. Alice realized that he was staring at the iron fire escape.

"You're barking mad," Alice said, her eyes widening. "There's no way I'm climbing down that thing."

"Of course not," Keith insisted, sliding a lock and opening up a window. "We're not going down." With some difficulty, he stepped out onto the metal fire escape and looked upward.

Alice, silently weighing the merits of going to prison over hanging off the edge of a building, tentatively looked out of the window. "This is crazy," she shouted.

"If you were looking to attract the attention of the police, by all means, keep shouting," Keith said.

"I–" she said, and then stopped. As much as she didn't like the idea of running, the thought of attracting attention suddenly seemed even worse.

"I believe the expression is 'in for a penny, in for a pound'," Keith said, turning and looking at her. "You should know, it's your country."

With a great, exasperated sigh, Alice climbed out of the window. "What's it like being you?" she asked. "Is it like driving a car toward a cliff, or is it more like being one of those little dogs that barks all of the time?"

Keith smiled. "It's like being anyone else, only much faster," he said, and without another word he climbed up the metal ladder at the end of the fire escape, his aviator hat and white scarf flapping in the wind.

There wasn't anything for Alice to do but follow him. She ran to the far end of the fire escape and stepped onto the ladder, silently thinking it would be a much, much better idea to go back inside and throw up. Keith was reaching the top of the ladder, looking upward at the rooftop above.

"Yes," he shouted, climbing upon the top of the roof. "Yes, this is better."

'Don't look down,' Alice thought to herself, and she climbed the ladder to the roof.

It's difficult to imagine the abject terror that ran through Alice's mind at the thought of climbing six metal rungs on the edge of a hotel. Facing fear had never been Alice's strong suit, and she would have been better for it if she could have simply gone back to her room, but this was out of the question. There are moments from which you can never return and Alice had passed one. She stepped up and climbed the ladder onto the rooftops of the world.

Looking at the city from a rooftop is a completely different experience from looking from the ground; you are instantly confronted with a third dimension that you don't otherwise feel when you are walking down the street. The view was spectacular, although the rooftop itself had an odd, unused quality, like an attic, or a basement. Keith seemed to be surveying the landscape. "Excellent," he said. "This way."

He ran toward the far side of the roof. Alice didn't have the foggiest idea what he thought he was doing. He seemed to be acting as though being on the rooftop was some sort of new and exciting opportunity to violate the laws of physics. Alice looked down. There seemed to be a small group of uniformed police officers assembling on the street below. *'Right,'* she thought, and she ran after Keith.

In spite of anything you might have seen in a comic book, it's actually a surprisingly challenging thing to cross from the top of one building to the next. Nonetheless, Keith was trying to figure out how to do just that. He was staring in front of a large stone wall about six feet high, and appeared to be making designs on the best way to get the two of them up it and onto the rooftop of the next building. "Give me your foot," he said. "There, now grab onto the edge of the building. That's it. Ignore how undignified it is.

With great difficulty, Alice found herself being vaulted upward and grasping at the top of the wall. With a large push from Keith, she was on top of the next building.

"What about you?" Alice asked, but Keith was already working on launching himself up the wall. Backing up several paces, he made a run at the wall, leaping against it and vaulting himself upward. Alice grabbed him and managed to pull him up onto the ledge.

"Does this sort of thing come up often in whatever it is that you do?" Alice asked.

"You'd be surprised," Keith said. "Now let's make our way back down."

Thankfully, there was a way down off the rooftop – a large metal door erupted out of the middle of the building, presumably for rescuing stranded fugitives in times just like this. Keith opened the door with his gadget, and in just a few moments Alice found herself wandering through the upper floors of what appeared to be some kind of empty office. It was easy to imagine people selling bonds or writing computer software on a weekday. Thank goodness it was Saturday. Keith was searching around frantically for the elevator. "Over there," he said, pointing.

They got into the elevator. Keith pushed the button for the main floor. There was a silence, and then a pause, and then a silence again. Alice realized that she'd been running very quickly and was out of breath. "How does this work?" she asked.

Keith looked at her. "How does what work?"

Alice swallowed hard. "Running," she said.

Keith swallowed hard back. "It's easy. Every time they turn one corner, we turn two."

"We can't run forever," Alice said.

"Any object can achieve orbital status if it's going fast enough. If you get moving fast enough, you can travel forever, all you have to do is fall."

Alice frowned. "Orbital velocity at ground level is 707 miles per second," she pointed out. "We may have to run a few red lights."

Keith reached out and squeezed her hand. "Just trust me," he said. There was another pause, and another silence, and another pause again. The elevator opened out onto the main floor. Alice stepped out.

"When you get out onto the street, your instincts are going to tell you to run," Keith suggested. "Don't. It will only attract attention. Walk slowly. Stare at your shoes."

"Where are we headed?" Alice asked.

"The bar," Keith said.

"The Gristle and Thorn?"

"It's about a block and a half from here, but it's going to feel like it's on the far side of the Moon," Keith said. "Here," he said, handing her his aviator hat.

"Your hat?" Alice asked, surprised to see that underneath it he had a head of longish, wavy brown hair.

"A bit of camouflage," Keith suggested. "Just remember, all you have to do is put one foot in front of the other. If we get caught, avoiding arrest isn't going to seem like much on top of a murder charge. Let's go."

They were still holding hands when they walked through the building lobby, although Alice was much too nervous to notice. There was a lump in her throat as she walked to the door. She took a deep breath as they walked out into the world, looking up into the sky, and wondering if this would be the last time she saw it without looking through a set of steel bars.

Keith had said the walk to the pub was going to seem like it was on the other side of the Moon, but he hadn't mentioned why. The street was filling up with policemen, as if there had been a threat on the prime minister. They were going to have to go right through the growing crowd of police officers that were gathering around the hotel.

"We could go around the block," Alice suggested as Keith steered them down the street.

Keith put his arm around her, holding her firmly. "By the time we made it back around, the whole street would be blocked off," he said. "Besides, if we turn around now, it would only attract attention."

Alice looked up. She noticed that DI Williams had found her way to the top of the hotel. It wouldn't be long before they spotted the open door on the adjacent building. Looking up, Alice didn't see the police officer in front of her, and she bumped into him, shoulder to shoulder.

"Sorry," she said. The policeman grunted in reply and Alice kept walking. She remained cool as they crossed the street. Only half a block to go. They were halfway to the pub when Alice heard someone shout "Hey!"

The funny thing about being in the middle of a chase scene is that you never get to look back and find out just what it is that the people chasing you are actually doing, because real life has no actual cut scenes. As such, Alice never got to see who it was who shouted 'Hey!' or if, in fact, they were shouting at her. However, it probably didn't matter much, since Keith took off like a buck at the sound of a gunshot.

Alice ran after him. "There's no use trying to run, they've spotted us. We won't be able to hide in the Gristle and Thorn."

Keith turned the corner. "Leave that to me," he said.

They crossed the street and ran into the bar. The Gristle and Thorn, as usual, seemed to be doing a brisk trade today. Alice gave the man who looked like Orson Welles a nod. She looked at Keith. She was still wearing his hat. Without it, he looked a little like he'd been made out of rubber. "Look!" he said and pointed out the window. Alice looked. Several police officers were meandering about in the street, but their attention seemed to be focused further down the road.

"Obstruction field," Keith said. "It's meant to keep out the riff-raff, but right now it's working in our favour. For the moment, we're safe."

Alice rolled her eyes. "If it keeps out the riff-raff, how exactly did Wendy and I get in?"

"You're a time traveller. Time travellers will always find this place."

"And what about Wendy?"

"Well, Wendy's a drunk, she was bound to drink everywhere sooner or later. Listen, I would really love to discuss the ins and outs of post-temporal physics, but there isn't a lot of time. The obstruction field isn't a brick wall, if you follow me. Sooner or later someone out there is going to spot the pub which they're currently overlooking, and if we haven't moved on by then our goose is cooked. Every time they turn one corner we have to turn two, remember?"

"Is there a back way out of here?" Alice asked.

Keith smiled and then grinned and then smiled again. "There's an alley. It's where I'm parked."

"If you have a car, why didn't we take it to the conference?"

Keith shook his head. "So many, many things wrong with that sentence," he said, and then, without explanation, he patted her on the shoulder and strode purposefully toward the back of the bar.

There are moments that change your life forever. By and large they do not happen in a bad-smelling alley behind a bar, but when Keith Quick opened the door, there it was.

Alice reflected later on that Keith had technically said that he was parked; he didn't actually say that he either had, or didn't have, a car. Still, Alice felt that *parking* usually implied that there would be four wheels involved, so she was certainly surprised to discover the small black motorcycle parked in the alleyway. She would have found the motorcycle surprising even if it didn't have a bullet shaped sidecar, which it did, but perhaps not shockingly so if it hadn't had a small blue triceratops sitting in the sidecar, which it *also* did.

The strange thing about seeing a dinosaur for the first time, is that even though you know precisely what it is, you still feel the need to express a certain disbelief that you're looking at it, if only for convention's sake, which is why Alice found herself saying, "What the hell is that?" even though it was painfully clear what it actually was. Azure blue and about the size of a medium-sized dog, the three-horned member of the ceratopsian family stared back at her happily. Alice didn't know what to think.

"This?" Keith said, patting the gas tank of the motorbike. "This is a 1947 Triumph Motorcycle. I bought it new—"

"Not the motorcycle," Alice objected. *"That thing."*

Keith climbed on the bike. "Oh, that's a miniature triceratops. Bred for size, or lack thereof."

"Nark!" the triceratops said, happily wagging its tail.

"You own a dinosaur!" Alice said in disbelief.

"Of course not," Keith insisted. "You do." He gave the motorcycle a kick and the engine roared to life. "I don't mean to be rude," he added, "but this is really going to work best if you get on."

Alice got on. She was still wearing Keith's hat and put his goggles on over her face. They pulled out of the alleyway and into the street.

One of the lesser known disadvantages of living in a fifteen-hundred-year old city is that there is almost no way to lay out a well-designed road block. Keith was able to pull out into traffic quickly. He took an immediate left turn at the next intersection, but before he was around the corner, Alice heard sirens.

"They're after us," she said.

"How many?"

Alice turned around. There were two police cars following them, along with a number of officers running up the street. "Two police cars," she shouted, over the roar of the motorcycle.

"Not a problem," Keith shouted back, although it seemed to Alice to be very much of a problem. Traffic was busy that day and it looked like they were going nowhere fast. Keith gunned the engine, zipping around a taxi, and took the motorcycle up onto the sidewalk.

People jumped to get out of the way. "You're crazy!" Alice shouted.

"Doing your greatest hits?" Keith asked, and he zipped around an old woman before crossing onto another street.

The triceratops seemed to think that this was a tremendously exciting ride and was leaning his gigantic head over the edge of the side car. Alice might have worried that this was attracting a good deal of attention, but as they had the police after them and had just been driving on the sidewalk, it hardly seemed to matter just now.

"We're going to have to get off of the street," Alice shouted. "We stick out like sore thumbs out here."

Keith, who apparently took this as a cue that he was going to have to ditch the motorcycle, didn't seem to approve of this plan.

"Do you have any idea what a bike like this is worth?" he asked, bitterly.

"If you wanted to keep it, then bringing along a dinosaur was probably a bad idea. Makes us pop out rather prominently."

"I couldn't help it, he was too excited," Keith said. "He's never seen you this young. Besides, do you have any idea how much a kennel costs? It's absurd."

Keith quickly turned another corner and then another. He pulled up onto another sidewalk and then skidded to a halt. They were in front of a tube station.

"Come on," Keith shouted, jumping off the motorcycle. "Let's get out of the light."

London underground stations generally seemed to be built out of deep bedrock, presumably to avoid the possibility of accidentally excavating the remains of a Saxon military latrine or something, and this one proved to be no exception. Alice found herself going down an impossibly long narrow spiral staircase that appeared to have built by gnomes during the Victorian era. This might have been for the best, though, as it seemed to minimize the number of people who were traumatized by the small dinosaur trotting happily behind them.

"Hang on," Alice said, stopping up short. "Take off your coat."

"What on Earth would I do that for?"

"Well, we could put it over the dinosaur," Alice suggested.

"Why would I do that?" Keith asked.

"So everyone will think that you have a dog under your coat," Alice said simply.

"Why would I have a dog under my coat?" Keith queried.

"Yes, that's precisely what I'm hoping everyone else will ask, and since that's much, much better than asking 'why does that man have a dinosaur under his coat?' I figure it's a step in the right direction."

"Nark!" the triceratops said cheerfully.

Keith nodded. "Good point," he said, and he took off his coat and threw it over the triceratops. It didn't cover him very well, and it was only going to fool people if they thought there was a breed of cocker spaniel that had hairless blue hindquarters, but at least it would keep other passengers from staring at the horns.

They paid their fare and found their way down to the platform. The station was mostly empty, with only a few weekend stragglers here and there. Alice led the triceratops over to a bench in the corner, where he curled up happily at her feet, acting as though this was a wonderful game. He tried to take off the coat, but one of his horns had gotten stuck in the sleeve.

"Where are we going?" Alice asked Keith.

"There's an airfield in West Ham," Keith said.

"There's an airfield in Heathrow," Alice countered.

"There is, but we're not going to Heathrow. My plane is in West Ham. How often do the trains come, exactly?"

Alice didn't answer, but instead mouthed the words *'my plane?'*

Keith appeared to be staring hard at the far end of the platform. "Policemen," he whispered.

Alice looked up. Sure enough, a policeman was standing on the platform, about fifty feet away. There was nothing about him to suggest that he had been chasing her, he simply seemed to be a transit officer monitoring the platform. Still, Alice didn't relish the thought of marching Grendel past him.

'Grendel,' she thought to herself. That was his name in the dream – the one that she had the other night before Malcolm was killed. She remembered what Keith had called it – drifting. Alice had a huge number of questions that she wanted to ask Keith, but just then the train rolled in. Alice stood up. Looking at the police officer, she stepped forward. She wondered if it was illegal to bring a dog on the underground. If so, it might not make any difference that they'd covered Grendel with a coat. They walked within twenty feet of him, and when they passed, Keith gave the officer a perfunctory nod. The officer nodded back, but just as they got onto the nearest train, Alice heard the sound of a walkie-talkie squawking on the policeman's hip.

Alice didn't look at him. She sat down on the seat with her back to him, directing Grendel to her feet. Keith stood facing her, his expression taught but not panicked. Just as the doors closed, Alice heard the policeman answer the call on his walkie-talkie. She tried to turn around casually to look at him, and just as she did, their eyes met. He looked at her and said something Alice didn't catch.

"I think we've been spotted," Alice said. The cop was walking at a brisk pace, following the train and talking into his walkie-talkie.

"Right," Keith said. "We'll get off at the next stop, then."

"What if they're waiting for us at the next stop?"

There was darkness, then a creaking, and then darkness again. As the neon light of the next station came into view, Keith grinned broadly. "I told you the dinosaur was useful," he said. He pulled his coat off of Grendel. "Are you up to this, boy?" he asked.

"What?" Alice asked. Looking out the window, she watched as the train pulled onto the next platform. This time there were three police officers, and they seemed to be staring at the train rather intently.

"The train only opens on one side," Keith clarified, a tad unnecessarily. This was true. Although there were doors on both sides of the train, they would presumably only open on one side, since the other side would have let them out onto an empty track. The police were clearly counting on this, since they'd all lined up on the side where Alice and Keith would have to get out.

"I'm not clear how that's a relevant detail," Alice said.

"Wait," Keith said. "Don't step off of the train."

The doors to the train opened. Alice stood up. Various passengers stepped off, and two police officers got on. A third quickly followed, and they all began walking down towards Alice.

"That's it, then," Alice said, but Keith shook his head. He had the firm look of a man who wasn't beaten, not yet, but knew that even the slightest mistake would mean his downfall. One of the police officers looked at the little dinosaur. Alice wondered if they thought he was real. Perhaps, out of context, he might just seem like an expensive toy. Judging by the wide look in the policeman's eyes though, he seemed to understand exactly what he was seeing.

"Alice Anderson," a gruff-looking police officer said. "You're under arres–"

"Henry," the wide-eyed police officer said, pointing at Grendel. "Look at the–" He didn't finish his sentence, but simply stood there, open-mouthed. The other two police officers looked down at the little triceratops. The eyes of all three policemen grew very wide. Alice could tell that for just a moment, they realized what they were looking at.

"Keith," Alice said, grabbing him by the arm.

"Wait," Keith said again.

The policemen were clearly trying to judge whether or not Grendel was dangerous. "Do you want me to call Animal Control?" one of them asked.

"Now!" Keith shouted, and on command, Grendel rammed clean through the door on the opposite side of the train. His horns tore through the metal like it was wet paper and the dinosaur bounded down onto the train tracks below.

"Jump!" Keith shouted, and before anyone knew what was happening, the three of them had jumped off of the train and onto the opposite side. The police stepped forward as if to follow, but just then the train took off, and it seemed that however ambitious the police officers were feeling about capturing Alice, that ambition didn't include jumping off of moving trains. They were carried away to the next stop. Keith picked up Grendel and hoisted him onto the platform. In another minute, all three of them had gotten to the opposite side of the station.

"Just out of curiosity, couldn't you have just used your fancy door opener to do that?" Alice asked, dusting herself off.

"Lacks the drama," Keith said, running towards the exit. "Come on, I figure that I've got about ten minutes to steal a car."

They stepped out onto the street, doing their best to look like calm, ordinary people who hadn't spent the better part of the morning running for their lives. Keith placed his coat back on top of Grendel and then followed his own advice, turning down one street and then another, before ducking into an alcove. Alice stood next to him, silently breathing hard. Once or twice she heard a police car go by, but they didn't seem to be coming down the street.

"I thought you might need to catch your breath," Keith said.

"Thank you," Alice said. She hadn't realized how hard she'd been running. Her lungs felt like she'd been shot square in the chest. It was a relief to stand still, if only for a moment.

"I wish I had a cigarette," Keith said.

"I didn't know that you smoked," Alice asked, surprised.

"I don't," he said, "but it would look like we have an excuse to stand here. Nobody asks questions if a smoker is loitering outside a building."

"So kiss me," Alice said.

Alice was so surprised by the words that she wondered if she were channeling her sister somehow. Keith, who raised his ears, and then his eyebrows, and then his ears again, seemed equally surprised. "What makes you think I want to kiss you?"

"Your ears, and then your eyebrows, and then your ears again," Alice said. And she pressed her lips against his.

For thirty minutes, or thirty seconds, she wasn't sure which, Alice pressed her lips against Keith's, letting the excitement of feeling his face and his body against hers wash away the agony and the terror of the last twenty-four hours. For just a few moments, there wasn't anything. Malcolm wasn't dead, she wasn't on the run, and her speech at the Royal Astronomy Conference wasn't a disaster. There was just an odd man with soft lips, and she was kissing him. She wondered if she was being selfish.

"I'm sorry I said you were crazy," she said.

"It's all right," Keith said.

"But I said it an awful lot," she admitted.

"When you have lived a life where causality has broken down, you get accused of being a little strange from time to time," he acknowledged. "Now, let's give the police a few minutes to spread out and then we'll steal a car."

"I wish we didn't have to break the law," Alice said fretfully, not liking the idea of putting someone out.

"If you like, I can eventually double back and place the car back in the same spot the moment after we pull out," Keith suggested, "but that's a lot of quantum energy to spend on returning a used Fiat. We're currently on the street with a miniature dinosaur. We may need to focus on our priorities. Make sure Grendel stays put. He squeezed her hand gently and spun around, turning his attention to a smallish red sedan that was parked on the street. Alice knelt down and patted the triceratops under the chin.

Things had been happening so quickly that Alice hadn't had time to look at the happy little dinosaur that had been trotting around at her feet. It was almost impossible to believe that he was real, but nonetheless he stood there, wagging his tail happily, apparently unaware of the contradictions his existence seemed to inspire. The closest thing Alice had ever seen to a trike was maybe something like an alligator, which was a little like comparing a bottle rocket to a NASA space flight. His skin was smoother, and less scaly than she would have expected, and his body was soft and warm against the palm of her hand. Alice wondered if any paleontologists knew that there was a triceratops wandering around twenty-first century London. It certainly made digging for bones seem quaint.

"Nark!" the little dinosaur said, staring up at her with wide eyes.

"I don't think we're looking to attract attention," Alice whispered back. From behind her, she heard someone shout "Hey!" and she knew that Keith had broken into a car.

It appeared that Keith had used the same clockwork mechanism that he had employed earlier. At any rate, the device was attached to the drive shaft where the key would usually be. Alice let Grendel into the back seat and slipped into the passenger's side door.

"What is that thing?" Alice asked, looking at the device attached to the steering column.

"It's called a Houdinometer. It's dead useful. Opens any lock. This one's the old model. It has a little trouble with Yale locks occasionally, but it still works."

"Is it," Alice struggled to get the right words out of her mouth, "you know, from the future?"

Keith pulled the car out slowly into the street. "Strictly speaking, past, present and future are terms used by people living linear existences. I prefer to think of my door opener as coming from someplace else."

"Someplace else?" Alice repeated.

"Another dimension, another time. Call it what you like. A place precisely like this one, except that it's been nudged just slightly into a different light. Once you stop living one moment to the next, all kinds of wonderful things can happen."

A million questions burst forth from Alice's mind. "How do you break down causality, exactly? And what about General Relativity? How is anything you're suggesting even possible?"

Keith made a right turn and stuck a hand into his pocket. "With this," he said, and he promptly dropped something into Alice's lap.

Alice picked it up. It was a large crystal ball about the size of a grapefruit, with what looked like the infinity symbol etched on the top. It looked a little bit like a clock, but instead of having two hands, it had three, all of which were currently at right angles from each other, which of course no regular clock could do. The hands were all suspended from a tiny golden ball at the centre of the crystal, in a manner that suggested that the laws of physics were more like guidelines than hard and fast rules.

"It's a dimensional browser," Keith explained. "For travelling from one part of the multiverse to the next. I could technically use it to get us out of this mess, but I prefer to be above cloud cover when I punch a hole in the space time continuum. It attracts attention."

"So this is a time machine?" Alice asked. "It's so small."

"I know. It seems like it should be built into a refrigerator or something."

"How does it work?"

"It's psychically activated, but if you're asking me how the damn thing does what it does, I've no idea. That was always your strong suit, not mine."

"My strong suit?" she repeated.

"Well, you are the world's sexiest astrophysicist," Keith said. "Of course, that was before you were on the run with the law. Speaking of–"

Alice turned around. Behind them, a police car was flashing its lights.

"Must have put an all points out on the dinosaur," Keith said. "I can only imagine what that sounded like. Hang on."

Keith sped up and took the next left, going against the light and speeding into oncoming traffic. Alice closed her eyes and screamed but didn't hear any crashing noises. When she looked up again, they were heading down a different road.

"That was good," Alice said, by which she meant that they were still alive.

"They're still on our tail, though," Keith said. This was true. The police car had turned around and was still on their tail, lights blazing.

Alice was starting to wonder if they were going to be on the run for the rest of their lives. "What will we do?"

"I've got an idea," Keith said. Then he did something that Alice didn't expect. He turned left onto a larger street and slowed down. The police car caught up with them almost instantly. Alice looked out her window. She saw a young-looking policeman staring at her sternly. The policeman rolled his window down and shouted "Stop your vehicle!" in the sort of voice usually used by members of law enforcement to ensure that you never invited them to parties. Keith didn't stop, but instead rolled down the back window behind Alice, allowing Grendel to stick his head out of the window in a manner much like a Golden Retriever.

The police officer's eyes grew to the size of dinner plates. It was clear that his brain was processing what he was seeing on several different levels. Alice could tell he was feeling shock, disbelief, joy, and possibly something in the anxiety family, as he stared at the dinosaur in the back seat of the car. Grendel barked at him happily. The policeman was so impressed by this, in fact, that when his car crashed into an oncoming vehicle moments later, he hardly seemed to notice.

"He's all right, isn't he?" Keith asked, not looking back. "I didn't mean to hurt him."

"I hate to think about the deductible on your insurance policy," Alice said, looking out the back window and staring at the wreck behind them.

Chapter 6
Down the Rabbit Hole

I f the last hour had been one of the longest of Alice's life, it was followed by another that was only slightly less harrowing. For the moment though, they were safe, although safety in this case was a relative term. Keith had made his way onto a highway and was barreling westward at a relatively unassuming speed. Alice wasn't sure if she should ask more questions or take a moment to reflect on everything that had happened in the last few minutes. She compromised by doing neither. Instead she turned around and looked at Grendel, who seemed to be celebrating their escape from the police by curling up in the back seat and taking a nap.

There was no doubt about it, he was real. Although Alice had been willing to momentarily go along with his existence, there was a part of her that had wondered if he was some kind of a trick – a toy, or a hallucination, something. No, he was a dinosaur. As far as Alice knew, Grendel was the only triceratops to walk the Earth for, say, sixty-five million years, and Keith said he was hers, but where did he come from?

She was still holding the crystal that Keith had given her. Was it really a time machine? It looked much, much more like an elegant paperweight than anything else.

And then there was the way Keith had been talking to her ever since they first met. She had seen it in his eyes the first time he looked at her. He had said that she was a time traveller; a very special time traveller, that was how he had put it. What did he mean by that, exactly? Alice wasn't sure that she wanted to ask. For all she knew the answer might be crazier than everything else he'd said.

Somehow all of this had *something* to do with Malcolm's death, of which she was now the chief suspect, and his work on fictional realism. She sighed. *'Maybe I should turn myself in,'* she thought. *'At least the police would let me get some sleep.'*

They had slipped off the highway and into a relatively quiet looking suburb, where Keith found his way to a large, empty field. It was odd. Alice had certainly been to West Ham before, but she didn't remember ever seeing the field, and it was certainly big enough that you would have noticed it if you been in the area. It was at least half a mile long, with heavy trees on either side. It was dominated by a large, rusty metal warehouse out front, which looked like it had been left incomplete by construction workers during the reign of Edward the Eighth. Alice recalled Keith saying something as they dashed through the Gristle and Thorn about the pub being protected by an "obstruction field," whatever that was. Alice wondered if maybe this was the same kind of place. Keith parked the car and opened the front door to the building with the kind of casualness usually reserved for someone walking into their own home. Alice got Grendel out of the back seat and followed nervously.

On an old rusty sign on the front of the building Alice read the words: "Herbert George Wells Memorial Airport."

The building's size was incredible, but then again, it had to be. Alice immediately realized its significance, as well as that of the giant field that lay behind it. It was an airplane hangar, or rather it would have been, if it had exclusively airplanes in it. When Alice walked through the door she found herself staring at an enormous airbag, one which was not, surprisingly, a Member of Parliament.

"A blimp?" she asked, eyebrows raised. That's what it appeared to be, anyway, specifically a bright blue one with a pattern of golden stars on it. Alice wondered how someone picked out the pattern for something like that.

Keith stopped and momentarily looked upward. "Strictly speaking, I think it's a dirigible, not a blimp."

Alice raised an eyebrow. "You feel like this is a significant detail at this point in time?"

"As long as you don't feel like lighting a candle, then no, I suppose not. Don't worry though, we're not going up in that one. It attracts an awful lot of attention. Fergus!"

Alice, who had become accustomed to Keith's non-sequiturs, decided that this last was probably not a sign that he was having a stroke. In a few moments, her patience was rewarded with the sound of a loud crash from the far side of the hangar, at which point the bartender from the Gristle and Thorn came running forward.

Except that it couldn't be the bartender. They had just run through the Gristle and Thorn only a few minutes ago, and Alice had seen him there serving drinks. He couldn't have possibly have beaten them here, much less have changed into the odd outfit he was wearing now. A pith helmet covered his bald head, and he was wearing a waistcoat with gears on it, along with a set of Wellington boots and a pair of enormous black gloves that looked greasy. Oddly enough, he didn't seem even remotely surprised to either see them, or to discover that they had a blue dinosaur in tow,

which, upon reflection, hadn't caused much of a commotion in the pub either. Alice recalled what Keith had said about time travellers looking odd because they skimped on research. Perhaps they tended to be less shocked when they ran into something that was completely out of sync with the world around them.

"Have we met?" Alice asked. (She remembered Keith saying this to her and it seemed like an appropriate way to begin. Of course, she had met him before, at the pub, but they hadn't really talked, and he'd been dressed differently.)

Fergus looked at Keith. His ping pong ball eyes seemed to grow even larger, if that was possible, and his mouth seemed to twitch just slightly. Keith rolled his eyes and pinched his nose before saying, "Go ahead."

The bartender exhaled as though he were holding his breath. "Miss Anderson, may I just say, it is an honour." He spoke with a Scottish accent that Alice didn't remember him having in the bar.

"An honour?" Alice repeated. She didn't know what else to say. If it really *was* an honour meeting her, she didn't have the foggiest idea why.

"Of course," Fergus insisted, "I–" but at this point Keith coughed rather loudly. Fergus looked at him, and then at Alice, and then he looked at Keith again. Then he did something stranger – he studied Alice from head to toe. It looked to her like he was staring at her clothing. (At any rate, he spent a lot of time looking at her shoes.) How this was significant, Alice couldn't tell. She was still wearing the same black jumper and blue skirt that she had put on for the conference, several hours before. (It felt like several days.) Somehow though, the man came to some sort of conclusion that made him change his tone fairly significantly.

"I – take it this is your first trip, then?" Alice was about to say that she had just gotten off a plane from New York when Keith said under his breath, "She's linear." Judging by the size of the man's eyes, this was apparently a very controversial thing to say.

"My plane?" Keith asked Fergus, in a tone which seemed to indicate that this was almost certainly the task at hand. "Is it ready to fly?"

Fergus gave Alice just the slightest second glance before speaking again. "Right as I can make 'er. Changed the oil, put a new air filter in 'er. She could probably use a new carburetor, but it'll be a bit of a wait, I'm afraid."

"I'm afraid we don't have the time," Keith said, doing his best to keep the man focused. "As long as I can get it up in the air, we'll be fine."

"Are you sure? Only I wouldn't want you up in that thing if I didn't think it was safe."

"It's all right," Keith insisted. "We may be in a bit of a hurry."

Fergus gave a look of disapproval. "What 'ave you been up to?" He turned and looked at Alice. "He didn't try to get you to nick something, did 'e?

"No," Alice said, although of course they had stolen the car. "He was actually helping me." There was a part of her that wanted to defend Keith and admit that she'd been accused of murder, but it didn't seem like a good idea just now. She was pretty sure that Fergus wouldn't call the police. In fact, she had the sense that whoever these people were, they had about as much to do with everyday society as a Jackson Pollock painting had to do with a portrait by Da Vinci. (Alice, who never studied art, would have been surprised to know that while Pollock was a big fan of both Da Vinci and Renoir, Da Vinci, through the magic of interdimensional time travel, would eventually be quoted as saying he thought Jackson Pollack was "full goose gonzo.")

"Keep 'im honest, Miss Anderson," Fergus said. "The plane is ready to fly, Mister Quick, far end of the hangar." He handed Keith a set of keys.

"Was that the bartender?" Alice asked.

Keith paused for a second before answering. "No," he admitted.

"It looked like him," Alice pointed out.

"It did," Keith agreed.

"But there's no way he could have gotten here before us."

"Probably not, no."

"Do you want to explain why he's here, then?"

He shook his head. "You've had a long day. Dinosaurs, accusations of murder, breaking up a science convention. Androids may be a little much for one day."

"Fergus is an android? There are androids, now?"

"We'll have a Q and A session later. Right now we've got to get up in the air."

Keith led them past the dirigible, a B-12 Bomber, and something that resembled an enormous paper airplane. He stopped in front of a large red and white biplane with the mathematical symbol π painted on the side. Suddenly, the aviator's hat and goggles made a little too much sense.

"You're barking," Alice said. "There's no way I'm going up in that thing."

"It's a two-seater," Keith said with an air that was remarkably devoid of any trace of defensiveness. "You're going to want to put my hat back on. It's a warm day, but it can get cold up there."

"This is your plan?" Alice asked incredulously. "Fly us out of the country in a *biplane*?"

He walked over to the plane and gave it a loving pat. "Look at it this way, I'm almost positive that the Metropolitan Police don't have a Sopwith Camel."

"What about Grendel?" Alice asked, wondering if there was a luggage compartment with a large dog carrier in it.

"Well, strictly speaking, I have to fly the plane, so–"

"Oh good Lord," Alice groaned. "You want him to sit in my lap, don't you?"

"Well, I don't think he'll fit in the luggage compartment," Keith said.

The biplane had two seats, a front and a rear, each with its own set of controls and a stick. Alice graciously agreed to get in the rear, since regardless of where she was sitting, there was no way she was going to look out the front of a plane. *That* was crazy. At any rate, it was clear that Grendel had ridden in the biplane before. He hopped into Alice's lap quite willingly and she had to hold onto his collar to keep him from sticking his head out the top of the plane. With the two of them in the cockpit it was going to be quite snug, but perhaps that was for the best. Unlike the Trike, Alice had never ridden in anything so ridiculous, and was quite sure that she was going to die. She had logged more frequent flier miles than anyone she knew, and while it was true she had no love for cabin pressure, she understood the proper way to fly – in a comfortable cabin where a stewardess brought you a cup of tea and a hot towel. Sir Edmund Hillary, fresh off his conquest of Mount Everest, might have gladly told you that while the thrill of being the first man on top of the world is truly exhilarating, there's nothing like flying in a biplane, with the wind blowing in your face as you fly through the air with the whole world spread out in front of you. Alice Anderson, on the other hand, would have gladly told you that Ed Hillary was an idiot who was lucky that he hadn't been killed crossing the street and should be thankful that his mother didn't have a heart attack every time he went out the door. Biplanes were not for her.

"How's the cloud cover?" Keith shouted to Fergus.

Fergus was busy opening the enormous metal hangar doors, a process which seemed to involve pulling on a long, heavy rope in a manner that suggested Quasimodo. "It doesn't look like much from down here," he said, "but once you're up above a thousand metres, no one will see you."

"All right," Keith said. He turned around and looked at Alice. "Have you still got my dimension browser there, beautiful?"

Alice, who had been clutching the glass ball rather tightly since Keith had given it to her, said "Yes" and made no other reply.

Keith pulled a second aviator hat and pair of goggles from seemingly out of nowhere and put them on. "Keep it handy, and don't let Grendel jump out of the cockpit."

"Should we go through the checklist?" Fergus asked, walking up to the front of the plane.

"There isn't time. By the way, there's a red sedan parked out front. You may want to dispose of it later."

"What happened to the motorcycle?" Fergus asked. "Or don't I want to know?"

"Let's just say I'll be happy to be home," Keith said, and then he asked, "Contact?"

"Contact!" Fergus shouted, and then he reached up and gave the propeller a twirl. The motor of the plane sputtered, then swirled, and then roared to life. Fergus quickly pulled away the blocks holding the plane in place, and slowly they began to inch forward.

By the time the plane had rolled forward a good fifteen feet, Alice had silently reiterated her opinion of what an absolutely brilliant thing an interior cabin was. The biplane's motor had the subtlety and rhythm of a Jackhammer. Indeed, between the plane and the motorcycle, Alice was giving serious thought to buying a sailboat, if simply to travel in peace and quiet. Slowly, it picked up speed. Alice had trouble reading the instruments, but it seemed like they were going about thirty, maybe forty, but certainly not more. The wings were shaking like leaves in the wind. They were going sixty. How fast did they have to go to take off? The propellers were roaring and the plane bounced, but they didn't get airborne. Alice was sure that they were going to crash into the trees on the far side of the field. They were going seventy. The plane bounced and took off. They cleared the trees and soared into the skies.

There were a couple of things about flying in a biplane that Alice noticed right away. The second one was that flying the plane clearly took a lot of strength. Keith was raising the plane up into the air using little more than his forearms and Alice watched the stick shake as the plane banked upward. She gripped Grendel tightly and tried to keep from focusing on how high they were getting, but this was tough. Staring at the ground meant looking at how high they'd gotten, looking up at the sky meant feeling how high they'd gotten, and looking down into the cockpit meant glancing at the dials on the dashboard, which meant *knowing* how high they'd gotten. Alice did her best to stare at Grendel's leathery skin, trying not to glance over at the altimeter as it moved from 100, to 500, to 1000.

By the time the altimeter had reached 1500, the air was as cold as it would have been on a winter's night, and the ground below was difficult to see. When they were on the ground, the sky hadn't seemed like it was covered by anything more than a light haze, but once they were up there it was thick enough that Alice had no sense of where they were – they might have been over the Atlantic Ocean or Piccadilly Circus for all she knew. Alice had assumed that they'd been heading toward France, but she now had the vague impression that they were going in the wrong direction.

"How long is this journey going to take?" Alice asked, thinking that at the very least it would be fair to point out that she and Grendel were pretty cramped.

"We should land within the hour," Keith shouted back from the front of the plane.

The altimeter crawled up to 2000.

"This is it!" Keith shouted. "Grab the orb!"

Alice couldn't have let go of it if she wanted to. "What do you want me to do with it?" she asked.

"You need to open a hole in the fabric of time and space!" Keith shouted.

"Are you out of your mind? I can't!"

"You can!" Keith insisted.

"Do you mind telling me how?"

"We're going to the Island of San Tiempo," Keith said. "It's the most beautiful place on Earth. Just picture an island paradise – a wonderful spot full of sunshine and ocean spray – then tell the orb to take you where you want to go. It will do the rest."

"Are you sure?" Alice asked.

"Just trust me!" Keith shouted.

Alice had been to the Virgin Islands once, several years ago. She had gone snorkeling in a blue bay and had gotten a suntan on a golden beach. She pictured the beach and said quietly to herself, "I want to go to San Tiempo, please." Then, trying to sound like she thought this would really work, she added. "Now."

The orb whirred, and then hummed, and then it glowed bright green. All three hands on the inside started spinning wildly. Then it opened up a hole in existence.

The odd thing about a hole in the fabric of the universe is that you know one the moment you see it, even if you've never seen one before. It was big, and black, and empty, and it hung huge and black in the sky in the same way that the sun never could. It was a giant ball of nothing, and they were headed right for it. The dials on the plane started spinning. Alice grabbed onto Grendel and held him tightly.

"You've done this before, right?"

"Hang on," Keith shouted. "Here we go!"

There was nothing, and then there was darkness, and then there was nothing again.

Alice Anderson travelled through time.

The sky was flickering like a television set with a bad transistor. This was strange for two reasons. The second one was that it made the sky seem dark, which a moment ago it wasn't. Up above the cloud cover, the air had been sunny – but now, well, something seemed darker somehow. Darker and flickering.

"Why is the sky doing that?" Alice shouted up to Keith.

"Doing what?" Keith asked.

"*That!*" Alice shouted, as if adding extra emphasis would make it clear. "That *thing* the sky is doing!"

"Oh," Keith shouted back. "You'll see once we slow down."

He took the biplane into a descent, slowing the engine and bringing down the wing flaps. As they began to descend, Alice realized what the flicker was. It was night, and then day, and then night again. Someone was flickering the daylight on and off, like a child playing with the light switch. She could see it now: daylight, evening, daylight, evening, daylight, evening. Look, there was the Moon. No, that was the sun. It was all changing so fast. How was that possible? And then, suddenly, Alice understood. It wasn't that the sky was flickering. It was *them*. The little biplane was circling the Earth at a speed that would make the Apollo 12 mission look like the Wright brothers. In spite of herself, Alice looked down at the ground below. The world was spinning like a top.

"Hang on," Keith said. "Just a few more minutes."

Slowly, the days and nights got longer, going from mere moments, to seconds, and finally minutes. It occurred to Alice that she'd just orbited the Earth more times than any astronaut in the history of the NASA space program.

"We're coming in!" Keith shouted, although from Alice's point of view she couldn't see how this was true. They passed by something that looked a little like Panama rather quickly.

Finally, the daylight came up one last time and didn't leave. Alice looked at the controls. The dials had stopped spinning wildly. The altimeter read 1000, and then 500.

They descended over the ocean, coming into what appeared to be an enormous bay. In front of them was a luxurious-looking green island, capped by a majestic-looking mountain, which Alice hoped wasn't Krakatoa. Just beyond a beautiful-looking lagoon, a thin stretch of an airfield turned up. It was just the place for a landing. The biplane touched down and Alice was on terra firma. She was so happy she thought she might kiss the ground. Grendel, eager to get out, got up on his hind legs and began barking "Nark! Nark! Nark!" as the plane came to a stop.

Alice took off the hat Keith had given her. The air was warm, like an August afternoon, although the last time she had checked, it was March the twenty-ninth. Keith stood up and smiled. "Looks like there are a few others coming in," he said, glancing skyward. Alice looked up. Directly above them, something that looked like a model A Ford but with wings attached, and something else that almost certainly was a Nasa Space Shuttle, were landing on the Tarmac behind them. In the lagoon just beyond, a large wooden pirate ship was laying anchor. Ahead of them, what was unmistakably a B-52 bomber was readying for takeoff. Alice noticed that the maintenance man loading cargo in the cabin appeared to be the bartender from the Gristle and Thorn.

"Okay," Alice said. "This is weird."

From a tinny loudspeaker sitting on top of a little metal building came a voice that said, "Welcome to the Island of San Tiempo, home of the Time Traveller's Resort and Museum. The time is fifteen minutes to infinity o'clock. Please adjust your dimensional browsers accordingly. We hope you will enjoy your stay."

Chapter 7
Curiouser and Curiouser

C aptain Martin Taylor of the United States Army Air Force was a man destined to have a major impact on the culture, politics, and history of an entire decade. He would do it by dropping a pencil on the floor of his office on a Thursday afternoon.

The pencil had been sitting in a coffee cup on his desk. He had picked it up to make some notes on a map of the French Alps, and it slipped from his fingers. He had two other pencils in the same cup, so he grabbed another, intending to pick up the one that he had dropped in a minute or two. When Captain Taylor stood up he stepped on it, and when the pencil rolled, his foot rolled with it. He landed wrong and twisted his left ankle, breaking the bones in his foot and putting him on reserve duty for the next week and a half.

Because he was out, his plane, a B-52 that went by the name of Beautiful Betty, was taken off the mission list for a bombing run into Western Germany – the first invasion of Nazi airspace by the allied forces. Colonel Fitzwilliam, the man in charge of planning the mission, was forced to ask for volunteers to fly Captain Taylor's run. One man in particular, a young pilot by the name of Joseph P. Kennedy Junior, stood out head and shoulders above the rest.

Kennedy was arguably the most promising young pilot in the Army Air Force Corp. Young, popular, and a graduate of Harvard University, Kennedy was the eldest son of the US ambassador to Britain, and was widely believed to be planning on running for Congress upon return home. The next morning Joseph Kennedy got to his plane, and he and his crew prepared for the long flight to Germany. Due to a lack of cloud cover, always considered a bonus on missions like this, the flight was delayed until later in the evening. This presented other hazards, but the Captain and crew felt confident.

Just five minutes into the flight, Captain Kennedy got into trouble. Under circumstances no one was able to explain, the Beautiful Betty went down. Whether the darkness had been a factor was difficult to say, but it certainly didn't help matters any. There were no survivors, and the body of Captain Kennedy was never found.

Kennedy's father, Joseph P. Kennedy Senior, was devastated by the loss of his oldest son. He had planned for Joe Junior to carry on his legacy in politics. Instead, Joe passed this mantle onto his second son, John Fitzgerald Kennedy. Admittedly, John Kennedy didn't strike the impressive figure that his older brother did. Skinny and weak, with a bad back, John had nearly been branded four F before he joined the navy, although during his time there he served with distinction. Upon returning home the war, John Fitzgerald Kennedy did what was expected of him and ran for Congress in 1946. Although he was initially seen as little more than an example of nepotism acting through democracy, he eventually rose to the challenge, and in 1952 he ran for the US Senate Seat in Massachusetts. He had very little chance of winning. His opponent, Henry Cabot Lodge, was a long-term incumbent who was very well funded. Normally a junior congressman wouldn't have stood much chance against a man like Lodge, and Lodge didn't take the campaign very seriously. Instead he focused on aiding General Eisenhower in that year's presidential election. Unfortunately for him, the young congressman's charm proved to be more formidable than anyone could have imagined, and Henry Cabot Lodge lost.

Senator Kennedy would be re-elected in 1958. In 1960, much to the surprise of many Democratic strategists, he would run for the presidency. Again, he was largely expected to lose. His opponent, Vice President Richard Nixon, was an excellent debater, and was much better known. Still, Kennedy was charming, and the race would be close. As 1960 pushed toward November, the two candidates would be running neck and neck. In the weeks before the Election Day, they would meet in what would become a famous debate.

In any year before 1960, the debate would have been awarded to Richard Nixon. He was obviously much more knowledgeable and better prepared than his opponent. However, in 1960, for the first time in history, a majority of Americans owned a television set. For the debate Senator Kennedy wore a nice black suit, which looked good on TV, and appeared to be young and good-looking. Vice President Nixon wore a suit that blended in with the background and looked like a potato. So, by the narrowest of margins, John Fitzgerald Kennedy would become the 36th president of the United States. Nixon, who was actually a friend of Kennedy's, was heartbroken.

No relation would define Kennedy's presidency more than the one he had with Russian President Nikita Krushchev. After the invasion of the Bay of Pigs, a public relations disaster, Kennedy was determined to beat the Russians in any competition that he could find, and the most obvious playing field was space. However, the Russians were clearly far ahead of the American space program, so Kennedy asked the head of NASA for the recommendation of a goal that was far enough away that they might be able to beat the Russians to achieving it. The head of NASA made the laughable suggestion of landing a man on the Moon and returning him to the Earth by the end of the decade. It was an absolutely ridiculous idea, potentially costing the taxpayers billions of dollars. Still, it sounded good, so the president announced it as a goal on a campaign stop in 1963. It was likely to be one of those promises that normally came and went over the course of presidential politics, and if it weren't for the events of the 22nd of November, then it would have remained that way.

By all conventional accounts of history, the three bullets that killed JFK were one chance in a million. Lee Harvey Oswald was, by all accounts, a poor shot, and the chances of his ever being anywhere near the President of the United States were extraordinarily slim. Somehow, perhaps because of fate, or luck, or coincidence, in spite of everything, he pulled the trigger, and in 5.6 seconds the world changed. And so, because of the tragic manner of the President's death, the next President, Lyndon Baines Johnson, and his successor, Kennedy's friend and former competitor Richard Nixon, would to do everything they could to meet Kennedy's goal of landing on the Moon, in spite of the costs and the dangers involved. So in August of 1969, at a cost of roughly one billion dollars for every minute they were there, two men named Buzz Aldrin and Neil Armstrong walked on the Moon. And they did it, at least in part, because of a series of events that began with a man knocking a pencil off of his desk. Because of Martin Taylor's pencil, and all the events that followed, mankind crossed from one world to the next.

Perhaps the Moon landing would have happened anyway, but imagine for one minute what it might be like on all of the worlds where all of those things didn't line up in quite the same way. How many of those incidents did you have to nudge for the Russians to land on the Moon first, or to make Joe Kennedy the President instead of his brother? You have to ask yourself: what would happen then? These are world-altering changes – if you doubt that, just ask Marilyn Monroe.

Temporal scientists like to tell this story because it demonstrates the delicacy of the fabric of time and space. Keith Quick liked to tell this story because once, in the nineteen-sixties, he had stolen the Lunar Excursion Module and taken in for a joy ride. He claimed the controls pulled a little to the left.

Although the airport on San Tiempo was tiny, it was bustling with people. Strange people they were, too. Everyone Alice looked at seemed to possess a fashion sense that had been borrowed from the nineteenth century by way of the psychedelic era. There were bright blue bowler hats and handlebar mustaches dyed pink. A man with no hair and eyeballs that looked like pinwheel galaxies was wearing a leather kilt and a Sex Pistols t-shirt, and he was talking with a woman in a rose-coloured bustier with a matching top hat and thigh-high boots. Each one seemed stranger then the last, and everyone seemed to be staring at Alice, who wasn't wearing anything more spectacular than a black sweater and a blue skirt.

"We'll need to check in at the desk over there," Keith said as he led her across the room toward an airport check-in. His voice was calm and reassuring, as if he somehow thought that this was going to be a traumatic experience for her. This made absolutely no sense. Most of the traumatic experiences in Alice's life had come and gone in the past few hours, and Keith had acted as though they were nothing more than mildly amusing anecdotes. Why exactly he would think that walking through an airport was a big deal, Alice couldn't say. Suddenly, she heard someone call her name from across the room. "Alice!" a distant voice shouted out, and then someone else said, "Alice Anderson!"

Alice turned around and looked to see where the cry was coming from, only to discover that entire airport was looking at her. Every single person in the room had stopped what they were doing so that they could stare. Slowly, but building to a tumultuous roar, the entire assembled crowd started to applaud. Alice raised her eyebrows. She had no idea what to do. Was she supposed to beam and wave, like a politician? She lifted up a hand and smiled weakly. This only caused the assembled crowd to applaud louder. Alice wondered if there was something that she could do that would make them go about their business.

"Have we met?" Alice asked. This was apparently a marvelous thing to say, because the entire room burst out laughing. This was followed by another round of applause, which caused several queasy flip-flops in Alice's stomach.

"Come on," Keith said, and he spun her around quickly. They stepped on up to the airport check-in desk behind them. In principle, it didn't look that different from any other airport terminal, except that the frenzied hostess standing behind the desk appeared to be typing on a large black and white typewriter, and was talking into the business end of an Edwardian candlestick telephone.

"May I help you?" the hostess asked, putting the phone down. She looked very nervous, and appeared to be breathing heavily, although this might have been caused by the corset she was wearing. (It did look a little uncomfortable, but without it, Alice supposed that the petticoat she was wearing would just look silly.)

"Alice Anderson and Keith Quick checking in," Keith answered.

The hostess looked at them, wide-eyed. "Please," she stammered. "May I have your orbs for synchronization?"

"Here's mine," Keith said, handing over the crystal dimensional browser. "Alice is on her first trip."

The hostess' eyebrows did three things at once. "This is your first trip?" she said.

"It's all right," Keith insisted, although it didn't sound as though it was all right. He looked a little nervous. Alice watched as he began picking imaginary pieces of lint off of himself. Yes, Keith was nervous.

"All right," the hostess said. "You'll want to purchase an orb of your own at some point, I expect. I trust that you'll be staying here on San Tiempo?"

Alice looked at Keith, who nodded. "Very good," the hostess said. "I – yes, well, very well. Welcome to the island." She smiled, and then grinned, and then smiled again. She placed Keith's orb in a little brass holder, which caused the three little hands inside it to spin wildly before pointing at the infinity symbol again.

"Thank you," Keith said. He took the orb back, and stuck it into his bag. "I'll be staying at the Hotel Kronos."

This made the hostess' eyes pop out just slightly. "Very good," she said again, coughing heavily this time. "We hope you will enjoy your stay."

Keith turned around and strode purposefully for the exit. Alice followed him with Grendel at her heels. No one seemed surprised by the sight of a dinosaur at all. She wondered if there was a leash law for little dinosaurs.

Keith and Alice strode out of the airport and walked down a little path toward a small town that seemed to be made primarily out of little white huts and its own sense of self-esteem. It was a beautiful day. Wherever it was that they had landed, it had a very different feel then downtown London. In England it might have been a warm day in early spring, pleasant enough if you didn't mind wearing a sweater. It was nice, but it was nothing like this. The air was warm and fresh and exciting. It felt like the kind of day when you would go to the beach, which Alice supposed was appropriate, since they were so close to the ocean that she could hear the surf in the distance. There was just a touch of humidity in the air, and puffy white clouds were scattered overhead. For another thing, there didn't seem to be any cars, or at least, any normal ones. A man on a unicycle went by, and a woman on a Vespa road past, as well as a morbidly obese gentlemen pulling a rickshaw with a group of puppies in the back, but there didn't seem to be anything along the lines of a Volvo anywhere. The whole thing put the motorcycle with a sidecar in a certain perspective.

"We could get a cab," Keith said, eying the rickshaw, "but I thought you might like to stretch your legs. The walk isn't far."

Wherever they were, the city wasn't large. There wasn't a building in sight of them that looked like it was more than two stories high. Keith walked at a brisk pace down the small dirt road, which was lined with palm trees and daffodils.

"Are we going to visit this museum of yours?" Alice asked, showing a little bit of genuine curiosity.

"Not today," Keith said. He stopped momentarily to allow a small family of dodo birds to walk in front of them. (Grendel growled at these, but Alice warned him to stay put.)

"So this place is…" Alice said. She wasn't sure what to ask first, so she decided she might start out with the obvious. "Is this the past, then, or the future?"

"This is the Island of San Tiempo," Keith said.

"Saint Time," Alice translated.

"Very good," Keith said encouragingly. "And to answer your question, it's not exactly the future, or the past, it's more three blocks over and two to the left, if you get me."

"Just how many laws of physics are you planning on violating?" Alice asked. "There isn't a perpetual motion machine lying around here somewhere, is there?"

"No perpetual motion machine," Keith insisted. "I always play by the rules. You see, up until now, you've been what we would call linear, which is to say you've never travelled in time or known of time travel's existence. When you're learning about time travel, San Tiempo is a good place to start. The island is a kind of temporal way station. It's quantum locked, so that you don't have to worry about running into yourself while you're here. Everyone here is a time traveller. By design, it's a place where we can all get together and trade stories and information about the complex world that we live in."

Keith took a right at a palm tree that stood almost one hundred feet tall, and began walking up a path that led up the mountainside. Alice struggled to keep up. "So what exactly is the situation with this museum you work for?"

"The economics of time travel are slightly different," Keith said.

"How so?"

"Well, for starters, if you deposited one pound in a savings account on the day that Brutus killed Julius Caesar, by the time that you and I were born you would have earned enough money in interest to buy a ball of gold approximately the size and weight of the Earth."

"No one had invented either the pound or the bank account in Cesar's time," Alice pointed out.

"In your timeline, that's true, but you see my point," Keith said. "I can buy Coca-Cola stock the day after the stock market crashes, and sell it the twenty-first century an hour later at a five thousand percent profit. It rigs the game. So the economy here is based on something a little more sophisticated than, well, money."

"What do you use then?" Alice asked.

"Nostalgia," Keith said, with a smile. "We search for the greatest objects in the universe, the things that are too good to be true, things that never were, but should have been, and we bring them all here, to the Island of San Tiempo, home of the Time Traveller's Resort and Museum. I'm one of the museum collectors, and today, woo boy, I brought in a big one."

"Sherlock Holmes' pipe is rather impressive," Alice said.

Keith looked at her "That too," he said, raising his eyebrows.

As they walked up the mountainside, Alice noticed that people continued to stare at her, although it was easier to avoid their gaze if she walked past quickly.

"Keith," she asked, trying to sound casual, "why exactly is everybody looking at me like I was on Top of the Pops, last week?"

Keith stopped walking.

"We'll get to that," he said.

"We won't," Alice said. She stopped in her tracks and gave him a dirty look. "A group of total strangers applauded because I walked into the room, for goodness' sake. I think that there's something going on here, something that you know about. You stuck your neck out for me today, even though you barely knew who I was." Alice paused. "I think you know something. Something about me."

Smiles are not, generally speaking, subject to volume control, but nonetheless Keith smiled quietly. "I said the island was quantum locked, so that you don't have to worry about meeting yourself. However, that doesn't mean that you always show up in the right order, or that you haven't met someone outside of this place unexpectedly. So, yes, I know a few things about you. Quite a bit, as a matter of fact. The question is, how much do *you* want to know?"

Alice considered this. "What is it that you know? Do I die, or something?"

"Nothing so dramatic," Keith insisted. "Although if you're asking what *will* happen, or what *is going* to happen, I have to tell you that it doesn't really work that way."

"Well, how does it work?"

"Well, I've never been particularly adept at explaining temporal physics where causality has been removed," Keith said. "Strictly speaking, I can only tell you what *I* remember. Whether it *will* happen to you, I couldn't say."

"So, you may assure me that I yet may change these shadows you have shown me, by an altered life?" Alice said, quoting Charles Dickens.

"Ebenezer Scrooge couldn't have put it any better," Keith said. "The things that I know about you might be thought of as what might be, or what never was."

"If it's all the same to you, I'd like to know what everyone else seems to know."

"Are you sure?" Keith insisted.

"It would at least explain why Fergus keeps giving me free drinks," Alice said.

Keith started walking again, then he jumped, then he spun around on his toes, and then he stood still. "The funny thing about time travel," he said, "is that no one is sure who invented it."

This didn't make any sense to Alice, but at this point that was just like saying that the sun rose in the east. "How's that?"

"Well, you have to remember, by the time that the first trip had taken place, we'd already gone back in time and visited almost every era before that, going back thousands of years, so figuring out exactly who was the first person to actually jump across the space time continuum can be a little difficult. As soon as one person claims to have done it first, another person travels back to the same spot and does the same thing five minutes earlier. It makes things tricky."

Alice shooed Grendel away from a bush that looked like an enormous Venus Fly Trap. "Your life seems chaotic," she observed.

"Life without chaos is like dessert without chocolate. Technically possible but statistically unlikely, and ultimately unsatisfying," Keith explained. "But this is beside the point. The point is that the discoverer of time travel has been completely shrouded in myth and legend, spoken of rarely and seen by no one, well, almost no one."

"You have an odd habit of taking the longest possible route to a point," Alice said.

"The point," Keith said, a slightly disparaging look on his face, "is that the legend has always been that time travel was first discovered by Alice Anderson, in the year 1815."

"Alice Anderson?" Alice Anderson said.

"Yes," Keith said. He stopped walking and gave her a little bow.

"That's me," Alice said.

"I agree," Keith agreed.

"You're telling me I invented the time machine?"

"Well, in the same way that some people learn that George Washington chopped down a cherry tree, or that Saint Patrick drove all the snakes out of Ireland, or that Richard the Lionhearted was a glorious English King who fought a grand crusade, young time travellers are taught that time travel was invented by Alice

Anderson." Keith stopped and looked at the sky. When he spoke again, it was in a sing song voice:

> *"If you need to know men's secrets*
> *Or if there's something you need to find*
> *If you want to see the dinosaurs*
> *Or the insides of your mind.*
> *If you want to watch the Earth begin,*
> *Or see what the apocalypse will leave behind,*
> *You need to thank Alice Anderson,*
> *For Alice is the Mother of Time."*

"Are there going to be a lot of instances where you're going to be speaking in rhymed couplets?" Alice asked.

Keith shrugged. "That's the story," he said.

"And I'm going to be doing this in the year 1815?" Alice asked.

"Well, it would be silly to do it now," Keith pointed out, "although I suppose you could if you wanted to."

"But I was born in the twentieth century," Alice said.

"Now you see why that strikes me as really strange," Keith replied.

"Excuse me, but are you telling me that I'm going to end up living in 1815?" Alice surmised. Suddenly she remembered the dream she'd had from the night before, good Lord, had it only been a night? She remembered that she had been wearing a bonnet in the dream, and that Grendel was there. Keith had called it 'drifting.'

"The legend of Alice Anderson is the reason that everyone here keeps acting like the Queen just walked in," Keith surmised. "It's also the reason I know that you didn't kill Malcolm Oliver. When I saw you in the Gristle and Thorn, well, it was a little like seeing Winston Churchill in the crowd at Woodstock. I knew that something was up. Then, when you were accused of murder – well, it was like I saw my whole world crashing down in front of me, quite literally. So I grabbed you, and I ran, and here we are."

Alice stopped and stared at him. "You would do well to stop making claims that border on the ridiculous," she said, furrowing her brow.

"I suppose I could have hired some sort of lawyer who specializes in cross-temporal physics," Keith replied. "They might be able to secure an acquittal for you. I'm sure the law offices of Einstein and Schultz would have somebody. Maybe, if I wasn't hard pressed for time, I could have found a more diplomatic solution to your problem. In the moment it seemed best to move you somewhere safe, so here we are."

They were heading up the mountainside. Alice definitely had the feeling that they were a fair way up now, and she found herself turning and looking at the ocean behind them. (What Ocean was it? Alice didn't know.) The water was a lovely cerulean blue of the sort that she tended to associate with places like Hawaii. She supposed it could *be* Hawaii. The air was warm enough.

"Where is this museum of yours anyway?" she asked.

Keith grinned like a proud parent. "The far side of the island," he said. "It's a wonderful place. We've got Elizabeth Bennett's dress, Robin Hood's black arrow, Moll Flanders' bustier, Sam Spade's Gun, and Oliver Twist's bowl of gruel. We've got the canoe of Hiawatha, the riding crop of the Man from Snowy River, the tassels of Gypsy Rose Lee. They're all here. This," he patted his bag, presumably giving Sherlock Holmes' pipe a comforting feel, "will be an incredible addition to the collection."

"So are you going to give me a tour?" Alice asked.

"I will," Keith said. "But first we have someplace more important to go."

He had stopped in front of a smallish villa. It was slightly larger, but in principal more or less the same, as the little white huts further down the hill. If there was any particular reason that they had stopped here, Alice couldn't see it, but Grendel was wagging his tail vigorously. They walked up to the door and Keith entered without knocking. It seemed as if it was an ordinary twenty-first century home, distinguished by nothing more than a handsome oak bookshelf and a white leather couch. Alice noticed what looked suspiciously like the copy of Principia Mathematica from her flat in upstate New York sitting on the coffee table.

Keith put a hand on Alice's shoulder and gently directed her to a hallway on her left. "The bedroom is down there," he said.

Alice didn't have to be told twice. In another five seconds she was at the end of the hall, staring at a large master bedroom with a beautiful king-sized bed. "That's a bed," Alice said. She was so happy that the words sounded like a song.

Keith didn't answer, but walked over to the window and touched it. The view outside instantly changed from day to night. It wasn't just tinted; it was night – you could see the moonlight reflected on the bay. Grendel hopped up on the bed and curled up into a ball.

"I can sleep," Alice said.

"I hope so, the house is yours," Keith explained.

The thought that she actually owned a house she'd never heard of didn't faze her even remotely. "I can sleep," she said again.

"For days, if you want to," Keith agreed.

Alice turned around. Slowly, but firmly, she began to push Keith out the door.

"I'll need to stop by the museum and drop off my–" Keith began, but Alice interrupted him.

"That's good," she said. "I need to sleep."

"I'll check in later," Keith said.

"Sleep," Alice repeated, pushing him out the door.

Keith nodded, and then he shrugged, and then he nodded again. "I'll be by in a couple of days. When I come back, we'll talk about the Laws of Time."

Chapter 8
1457

f all the things that *you could do* to annoy your wife, Sir Thomas Malory had found spending several years in prison to be truly the most satisfying. It had given him time to himself, embarrassed her in front of her friends, gotten him out of going to parliament, and nearly caused his mother-in-law to have a stroke. It was this last bit of which Malory was the proudest. The old bat had been telling her daughter what a mistake she had made in marrying him for most of a decade now, and Malory had laughed himself silly when he heard that the decrepit hag had taken to her bed when he'd been placed under arrest. Thomas Malory was familiar with the idea of being a nice person, and he wanted nothing to do with it.

However, as much as he enjoyed gloating over his wife's misery, he was really too busy to deal with it right now. It wouldn't seem like a person who had been locked away would have so much work to do, but the little desk in the prison cell was covered with stacks of papers three feet high. These were written in a tiny, obtuse script, filled with cross outs, strange markings, and footnotes that generally made it look as though the author had been given some sort of vague description of the Latin alphabet and had decided to give it a go.

To Thomas Malory, it was *the* story. He was going to tell it, all of it, from beginning to end. Saint Peter had written the Bible, Thomas Malory had this, and it was proving to be almost as long. He was determined to tell all of it, every twist, and every turn, every thread of it that had ever been told. He was going to write his name across the legend of his country, even if he had to lock himself away in prison for the rest of his life to do it.

To the guards walking past his cell, the contents within looked like a tremendous fire hazard, but since they never really liked the prisoner, they didn't seem to mind. Indeed, in the Warwickshire dungeon Sir Thomas was widely regarded as an unpleasant mix of self-serving intellect and devious opportunism. As the captain of the guard walked over to his cell, he was filled with an overwhelming feeling of joy that he would be able to walk away again in a few minutes. He tried to focus on that feeling as he walked up to prisoner and cleared his throat.

"Russell Baker hath accused you of raping his wife," he said.

Thomas Malory didn't even look up from his papers. "I suppose you hath some testimony that the good woman stopped by my cell? Otherwise I think that the Good Lord will pardon me."

The Captain of the Guard snorted derisively. He had worked hard to achieve the station he had found in life. His father had spent his days cleaning out pig slop, and he believed that hard work was its own reward. He always tried to use those feelings to bolster his pride when talking to Malory, who seemed to view hard work as some sort of pyramid scheme. "You were on a furlough on night the woman claims you attacked her. 'Twas a fortnight past, I remember it clearly," he charged.

This time Thomas Malory looked up. "Hereafter you may refer to my weekend as an 'escape', my good sir."

"So you admit thy guilt?" the Guard said. "The Right Honourable Baker hath–"

"I admit that the Right Honourable Baker hath a wife with a bottom lighter than air. I suppose I was raping his sister that night as well?"

At this the Captain of the Guard developed an embarrassed look on his face. "There were some stories," he mumbled.

"Both women hath fine singing voices. No doubt that there were many who heard their chorus that night. You may tell the fine ladies of the town that if any of them feel like singing, I will be breaking out again three nights hence."

The Captain of the Guard bristled at this notion. "I think that highly unlikely, sir," he insisted, squaring his shoulders and giving the prisoner a haughty stare.

"I have met your guards, sir, and I think it slightly less likely than the rising of the morning sun, but I'll leave it your good offices to sort that out."

"You are a villain, sir," the Guard said, indignantly.

"And for that you hath placed me in this cell. I hope it has given you a certain satisfaction. I'm sure that being a guard is good work for a man of your station. By the way, my chamber pot needs changing."

The Captain of the Guard groaned. "I'll see to it, sir."

"Very good. Now, did you come simply to accuse me, or do you have my letters?"

"No letters," the Guard said, "but someone is here to see you."

"Who is it?" Malory said. "Perhaps the butcher come to claim that I stole his wife or his cow? To be frank, it's a miracle the man can tell one from the other."

"Not the butcher," the Captain of the Guard replied. "It's – well, you'll see."

"Show them in, chop-chop. Oh, and I will be wanting my dinner in another hour. See to it, my good man." The Guard turned around and walked away again, quite pleased that he wouldn't have to talk to the prisoner again for the remainder of the evening.

From the far end of the hallway, a shadowy figure stepped forward. It was a bright day toward the end of March, but the figure seemed to bring darkness with it. Perhaps it was the enormous black cloak, an anomaly even in the fifteenth century, or perhaps it was something more intangible. Saying the dungeon was a fairly depressing place is one of those fairly obvious statements along the lines of pointing out that teenagers tend to make poor life decisions when left to their own devices, but it was depressing, undeniably. Even so, the hooded figure seemed to cast a dark shadow over the room. So much so that Malory could have sworn that the pages on his desk were a little harder to read.

"Sir Thomas Malory?" an icy voice asked.

"I think it's safe to say that's my name," Malory said. "What would yours be?"

The hooded figure lifted its cloak just slightly. Malory glanced casually at the person underneath. It was a mark of his bravado that he didn't flinch. Even so, he couldn't help but give the eyes staring down at him just the slightest second glance. *'My god,'* he thought.

"My name," the figure said, "is unimportant. I am a–"

"I know what you are," Malory replied. He dipped his quill in the inkwell and started a new page. "You're not the first." *'Although you're the first with eyes like that,'* he thought. *'They're beautiful. Terrifying, but beautiful.'*

"I didn't think I would be," the figure said.

"My jailers do not understand this endless pile of paper that I insist on having," Malory commented. "I might tell them it's a book, a book of such importance that I would lock myself away toward seeing it finished. The Captain of the Guard told me I would do better to write a book about hymns."

"Your book is a hymn," the stranger pointed out. "He doesn't understand that."

"The guard doesn't understand that when you add two and two you get four," Malory commented dryly. "Most men don't. I would not expect them to understand what I am doing here." He stood up and walked over to the little prison window. "So, imagine my surprise when people started coming to ask me questions about a book that I haven't even finished writing yet."

"You haven't finished," the stranger said, "but you will."

"Are you asking me for an advanced copy?" Malory asked.

"I am asking you to tell me what isn't in the book," the stranger admitted.

Malory shrugged. "Why?"

"Because knowledge is power," the figure said.

"Knowledge known only to you is power," Malory said. "Knowledge known to everyone is for scholars. Why should I tell you what I have told other men already?"

"Because," the hooded figure said, "I have something that you want."

Malory turned around. "Beggars can't be choosers, I suppose. Come on in, then. The bed is narrow and hath slightly more give than a stone floor, but I assure you, 'twill serve."

The hooded figure appeared to roll her eyes. "Not that," the figure said, and a gloved hand held out a package wrapped in brown paper.

Malory took the package and opened it. His eyes grew wide. "I've never seen this before," he said, obviously impressed.

"Nor are you likely to again," the figure said.

Malory placed the package on the desk. "Very well," he said grumpily. "If you're looking for the Grail, I don't know where it is."

"I *already* know where the Holy Grail is," the stranger said. "It doesn't interest me."

Malory narrowed his eyes. "What is it that you want?"

"Centuries ago, the monks at Glastonbury Abbey found the tomb of an ancient King. A king who wasn't supposed to exist," the figure said.

Although the icy voice had been very calm, it clearly wasn't an easy subject for the prisoner. Thomas Malory shook his head and walked back to the far end of his cell. "The story I'm compiling is a myth," he dismissed. "It is the tale of a forgotten age. It stands for a race of men who are all but lost, but in whose deeds lay the foundations of the Earth. I want document to the myth so I can document the men who made it. You are talking about ghost stories."

"What's wrong with ghost stories?"

"They obscure the memories of the truth," Malory said. "And the truth is already obscure enough already. Is it the bones of the king you want, or his deeds? I assure you that the man himself would think that it was his deeds that speak for him, and not the earth that made up his body."

"The devil is in the details," the figure said.

"The devil is in ignorance," Malory spat. "He exists in the details, and in the process and in every other thing that men cannot be bothered to learn. Why is this detail so important?"

"The course of history is not turned by waves, or currents, but by raindrops in an ocean of time," the hooded figure said.

"A metaphor that means much the same thing as your last," Malory pointed out.

"You know the story," the figure said. "Tell it to me, or it will be lost forever."

Malory shrugged and returned to his desk. "There are thousands of pages here," he said, gesturing to the stacks in front of him. "Much of it I wrote myself, but I have other works here too. I have the writings of Nennius, and Saint Gildas, and the book of Taliesin. I have others too, by poets whose names are forgotten but whose words have been passed down. There are dozens of stories about King Arthur, hundreds may-haps, many are pious, a few are bawdy, one involves a knight wearing a girdle for reasons that aren't clear."

"I think that's supposed to be interpreted as a belt," the icy voice said.

"It's a belt he borrows from a beautiful woman, you be the judge," Malory said. "They're all here, every one, and they all have one thing in common – they are all full of lies. They were designed to make this miserable cold lump of rock we call a country seem bigger than it really is, and while I find glimpses of the truth in all of them, none are historical documents. Except for two."

Malory shuffled the papers on his desk until he managed to pull out a thin leather journal. "One of them is a one-page history of Wales," he said. "This one is the other."

"What is it?" the hooded figure asked.

"It is the confession of an abbot who bore witness to the excavation of the tomb of an ancient Celtic King. It details the particulars of an item taken from the grave site."

"What item?" the stranger asked.

Malory swallowed. He wasn't sure why the subject made him nervous, but it did. "A cross," he said. "Although you might say that it wasn't one item, but two."

The hooded figure's breathing seemed to change. Malory could sense the excitement that was coming from the other side of the bars. "Two?" The icy voice spoke quietly, but Malory sensed danger.

"The abbot knew that the King of England would want the piece for himself, would expect it, even, as his divine right. However, it seems that the abbot got greedy. He sold what he had found to William the Bruce, the King of the Scots. This was in the days of King Edward the first, when tensions ran high. The abbot knew that it would have given the Bruce a claim to the English throne, and he would pay handsomely for it. In order to hoodwink King Edward, some sort of a copy was made."

"What happened to it?"

"According to the confession, the fake was taken to the court of King Edward, " Malory said, "who was probably as dim a flame as the guards out there. I have seen a drawing of it. It was as obvious a piece of costume jewelry as I have ever seen. Still, it made the King happy, but then again, so did Queen Elinor. Takes all kinds I suppose."

"And do you know what happened to the original?"

Thomas Malory shrugged. "Disappeared," he said. "Never seems to have made it to Scotland, as far as I can tell. Now that it comes to it, I don't know where the fake one is either. It seems to have disappeared sometime during the reign of Edward the Second. I would imagine that the man had an eye for spotting fake antiques. I don't judge."

Malory squinted at the figure through the bars. A thought occurred to him. One which he scarcely dared to speak out loud. "You know this," he said quietly.

"I know it," the icy voice agreed, "because I stole the item in question from a pair of monks who were trying to smuggle it into Scotland."

Thomas Malory looked like he didn't know whether to be frightened or impressed. "You have the holy Cross of King Arthur? The original one, buried with the King himself?" The figure removed its hood. Malory found himself staring again. *'Those eyes'* he thought. *'What is this creature?'*

"The reason no one ever found the cross," the figure said, "is that it has been skipping through time."

Malory ignored the fact that he didn't understand the last sentence. "If you have it, then what do you want of me? What are you here for?"

"I'm here," the figure said, "to find out who is trying to steal it from me." Two sets of bony fingers grasped the iron bars. "I know you told this story to someone else. I want to know who."

A better man might have wondered if admitting this last piece of information was really the wisest course of action, but Thomas Malory was not a better man. "As a matter of fact, someone was here just the other day, asking all the same questions."

The dark eyebrows on the other side of the bars did several things at once. "Who?" the icy voice asked. "Who was here?"

"It was a funny chap," Malory admitted. "Wore a monk's hat, with something funny on it I can't describe. Odd nose, Toothy Grin."

"What," the stranger asked, "was his name?"

"His name," Malory said, "was Keith Quick."

Chapter 9
PARADISE FOUND

ALICE ANDERSON WAS STANDING ON THE BACK DECK of what she could only assume was her house. At any rate, the clothes in the wardrobe seemed to fit her. Tonight she was wearing a simple white dress and a pair of sandals, which, given the warm air, had struck her as both elegant and practical. Between the clothes, and the presence of an entire bookshelf of astronomy textbooks, there seemed little doubt that the place was hers. Certainly, in the three days she'd been lounging around there, no one else had come by to claim it. It would seem that Alice had come home for the very first time. *'I wonder if I have bills to pay,'* she thought, staring up at the stars.

Alice had spent most of the last seventy-two hours asleep in one fashion or another. She had been that tired. Now she was enjoying the night air, standing on the deck and drinking a glass of white wine, and waiting for the inevitable knock on the door that she knew would come.

Grendel heard it before she did. "Nark!" he shouted, wagging his tail and running for the door. Alice turned, but before she could take more than two steps toward the door, Keith was letting himself in.

"How are you?" he asked. After being at her side almost constantly during that absolutely most frenetic episode of her life, Keith had made himself scarce for a few days. Perhaps he had known how tired she was. Alice couldn't help but wonder if he was suddenly feeling a little skittish. He seemed to have lost his aviator hat and goggles. He was wearing a tweed jacket and a button-down shirt that made him look like he should be giving lectures on *Paradise Lost*.

"I'm fine," Alice said. She was surprised at how happy she was to see him. Not talking for three days can get a little lonely, although lord knows that she had needed the rest.

Grendel ran back and forth between the two of them as Keith stepped out onto the deck. The little dinosaur seemed to feel that this was a moment of truly epic importance, which he commemorated with an odd butt wiggle and several excited wags of his tail. Alice made a mental note to find some kind of round ball to put on the end of his horns. If she wasn't careful, he was going to put a horn through someone's thigh.

"Enjoying the stars?" Keith asked, looking up at the night sky. Alice had remembered that Keith seemed to know about her podcast. She wondered how much he knew about Astrophysics. She suspected that the answer was something approaching zero, but she had a few things she wanted to talk about just the same.

As an astrophysicist, Alice was always on the hunt for 'dark sky' areas, that is, areas in the middle of nowhere where the stars are easy to see. It was the reason she had gone to school in the frigid wasteland of upstate New York. The Finger Lakes were nothing, though, compared to the view off the back deck here. Stars twinkled brilliantly all the way to the horizon. "That's the constellation Leo," she said, pointing up at a bright patch of sky. "It took me awhile to recognize it, because Regulus has drifted all the way over to the far side of the sky. And in the front of the house you can see Orion, only it's way in the North, and Betelgeuse is missing. It's just gone, like someone rubbed out a piece of the sky."

"It's called the Betelgeuse Nebula now," Keith explained. "It's a little hard to see with the naked eye, but it's there."

"We're in the future," Alice said. She wasn't quite sure if that was the correct way to put it, but she had no doubt about the statement's accuracy. "We've jumped ahead by tens of thousands of years, maybe more. We're a long way south from where we started, although I don't know where." There was a pause, and a silence, and a pause again. "I've been trying for two days to figure out a way to prove everything you've told me. All those years of studying physics and that was all I could come up with – two misplaced stars."

Keith nodded. "There's more in Heaven and Earth, Horatio, then is dreamt of in your philosophy."

"I suppose you're here to tell me why exactly I can't go back and prevent Malcolm's murder," Alice said quietly. "Because if we really can travel through time, that's the first thing that I would want to do. Only I can't figure out for the life of me why I haven't gone back to save him."

"Actually," Keith said. "I'm here to talk to you about the Laws of Time. I suspect you've already figured out a few of them."

"I don't know," Alice said. "In the time I've known you, you seem to have violated various laws written by Isaac Newton, Charles Darwin, and both houses of Parliament. It's hard to believe that there are any rules that you live by."

"Believe it or not, nothing we've done violates the rules of physics. Newton, Einstein, and Heisenberg are all in play. I can take you to oblivion and back, but I can't walk on water or float through walls, and breathing fire is out of the question. I can take you to meet Julius Caesar, or Michelangelo, or even Robin Hood if you like, but I can't ever introduce you to Merlin, or a fairy, or a dragon. Especially a dragon. Everything you've learned in school still applies."

"So we can go anywhere?" Alice asked.

Keith smiled. "Just about. If you can imagine it, and it could be real, then we can go and see it, if you like. The past, the future, and the present – the real and the unreal – it's all yours, if you want it."

"Why can't we go back and rescue Malcolm, then?" Alice asked.

Keith smiled again, although a little sadly this time. One of the great proofs that time travel *couldn't* exist was the life of Adolf Hitler. Surely, it was argued, if time travel could exist, then you'd *have* to go back and kill Hitler. That went without saying. Keith understood that the question Alice was asking him now was a variant on that same idea. He knew that in fact, that you *could* go back and kill Adolf Hitler. The three day 'Go and Kill Hitler' package was actually one of the most popular mini-breaks offered by the Time Traveller's Resort and Museum, so much so that many hipster time travellers considered the 'killing Hitler' mini-break to be passé. The trouble was that even if you *did* kill Hitler, that didn't stop Hitler from *existing*. It just created a different world that Hitler had no part in. Likewise, saving Malcolm wasn't going to stop Malcolm from *being* murdered, it would just create a world where Malcolm's life played out in a different way. This in and of itself wasn't a bad thing, but Keith knew that it wasn't going to be the answer that Alice was looking for.

"The truth is, we *could* go back and save Malcolm," Keith admitted. "Although it might not make you as happy as you'd like, and it wouldn't come out quite the way that you would hope."

"Why is that?" Alice asked.

"For one thing, whenever we travel through time, we can only go to the same day of the year that we're already living in. If you want to go back ten years, we can, but it has to be *exactly* ten years, dead on the nose. As useful as it would be to jump forward six months, or go back a week and half, it actually can't be done."

"It can't be done? Why is that?"

"You're the astrophysicist," Keith pointed out "You tell me."

Alice thought about this. She could think of at least a dozen reasons why you couldn't jump forward six months in advance. In particular, 'common sense' seemed to strike her as jumping out and leading the pack. As an astrophysicist, though, there seemed to be one thing in particular that struck her as particularly problematic. "The orbit of the Earth," she guessed.

Keith nodded. "Right as rain," he said. "Six months from now, the Earth–"

"The Earth will be one hundred and eighty-two million miles away, on the other side of the sun," Alice finished for him. "Yes, I can see how that would be a problem. How do you compensate for galactic rotation and expansion of the universe?"

"By hiring a bunch of temporal scientists and giving them a lot of computers," Keith said. "My understanding is the entire solar system is temporally locked, but I don't really know the specifics. You're the scientific one. I'm just a collector."

Alice sat down on a metal deck chair and called Grendel over to her. "So if today is April 7th, 10 million and whatever, and I want to go back to March 29th in the year that we just left–"

"You would have to wait for the better part of a year to get there," Keith confirmed, with an apologetic expressing covering his face.

Alice gingerly scratched around the base of Grendel's middle horn. "I would wait most of a year to save Malcolm, but I suppose that there's some reason I can't do that either."

Keith bent over to pet Grendel's hindquarters. "Well, the past is always the past," he said. "If you want to save Malcolm, you can, but you have to understand, it won't be *your* Malcolm. At best, it would be a *different* Malcolm, who would go off with *his* Alice Anderson, who would be someone else entirely. Like it or not, death is always final. The past has passed, they say. I guess that's one of the Laws of Time as well."

"This seems unpleasantly like metaphysics," Alice observed. "Can you tell me what year it is, at least?"

"In as much as these things matter, the year is forty thousand, seven hundred and eighty in the magenta range, but at this point, what a 'year' is has become a little hazy. You're right about the location, though, we are a lot further south. You wouldn't know it to look at it, but Edmund Hillary set up base camp right over there." and he pointed to a spot where some lights flickered on the far side of the island.

"Ed Hillary?" Alice asked. "That would make this–"

"Mount Everest, that's right," Keith insisted.

Alice decided that she was simply going to have to accept a few of Keith's more ridiculous statements on faith. "Then I suppose that the rest of the world is underwater?" she asked.

"Most of it," Keith admitted. "You can still see K2 from the far side of the island. The Andes are still there too, although Machu Pichu has worn away."

"I can't believe I'm here at the end of existence," Alice reflected. She stopped scratching Grendel's horn, which he responded to by pushing his head underneath her hand in order to convince her to scratch her again.

"I'm sure that for a twenty-first century woman, this must seem like the end of time," Keith said, "but San Tiempo is a wonderful place. What's more, we've got the whole of unrecorded and reimagined history to poke around in. You can see the ice age, or the second war, or watch the *Argo* come into port. We can meet Elizabeth Bennett, or Prospero, or Captain Nemo. Most of those things are just stories where you come from, but for me they're real things. They're real people and real places, and you and I could go and visit any one of them."

Alice could tell from the slightly deranged look in Keith's eyes that he had hoped this speech would be inspiring, but it only made her feel a little tired again. "If I can't go back and save Malcolm, then what can I do?"

"We," Keith emphasized, "can clear your name."

Alice didn't want to admit it, but the thought of heading home sounded blissful. Although the island was nice, the thought of never going home again was absolutely terrifying. "Okay," she said. "How do we do that?"

"No idea," Keith admitted, shaking his head. He sat down in the chair facing Alice, and stared up at the stars. He had been such a fountain of aid up until now that Alice was quite surprised to see that he seemed to have run dry. *'Well,'* she thought, *'at least I have all of the time in the world to figure it out.'* "Can I get you a drink?" she asked.

"Just a cup of tea," Keith said.

Alice nodded. "I honestly don't know if I have any," she admitted.

"Come on," Keith said. "I'll show you where it is."

The kitchen was on the far side of the house, adjoining another balcony. Alice had eaten breakfast out there that morning before taking an early nap, and she had enjoyed staring out at the thin blue of what she now knew to be the Indian Ocean, just visible out in the distance. Somehow she had never gotten around to making tea. Keith found the kettle and a tin of Earl Grey, and set to work immediately.

"You have a strange taste in drinks," Alice said, "for an American." In her experience, Americans drank very little but soda and watered down beer.

"I left the States a long time ago," Keith said. "I never much cared for it over there. America is a giant country for tiny men. Too big in one way, and too small in another."

"Were you always a time traveller?" Alice asked. "I mean, I know you didn't invent it, or whatever, but how did you get started? Were your parents time travellers or something?"

"Hardly," Keith said. "I was born in Omaha in 1908. My father is a District Attorney, and my mother bakes the best pies in town."

"Is that right?" Alice asked. "What kind?"

Keith grinned and then he smiled and then he grinned again. "She bakes apple, cherry pie and lemon meringue. She won a blue ribbon at the Omaha State Fair for the lemon meringue, but I always liked the cherry best."

"Do they know?" Alice asked. "Your parents? Do they know that you're a time traveller?"

Keith shook his head. "My mother thinks that I moved to Great Britain during the depression and that I'm flying puddle jumpers across the channel. I send her a postcard every week."

"That's nice of you," Alice complimented.

"In her world it's 1938, and the biggest issue is whether or not my father should get the new Model A. She thinks that I'm successful and happy, enjoying French wine and English Cheddar. I don't know what I'll do when she gets up to World War Two."

Alice poured herself a little more tea. "It's strange to think that I'm talking to someone older than my Grandfather."

"On San Tiempo, the father is often younger than the son," Keith said, in a manner that suggested that this was the sort of slogan you might find on postcards down at the local tourist shop. "It takes a little getting used to."

There was a pause, and a silence, and then a pause again. Alice found the quiet awkward. After the most manic episode of her life, the three days of silence that followed had been an incredible relief, but now it felt so good to talk again, especially about nothing in particular. "So do I seem incredibly futuristic to you?" she asked, her eyes wide. "Do mobile phones and computers and satellites and all of *that* seem like something out of another world, or have you travelled all over by now, and it all seems like old news?"

"For the life of me, I don't understand mobile phones," Keith admitted. "It seems like you took the Saint Louis Post Dispatch and shrunk it down to size of warning labels on medicine bottles for the sake of being able to stick it in your pocket."

"Well, there really is a lot more to it than that," Alice countered.

"In my time, the Dispatch cost a nickel, *and it still fit in your pocket,*" Keith insisted. "To answer your question though, yes, some of the things in the future seem odd, but people always seem the same no matter where you go, in any era. I'm always surprised by it. They all want the same things. They struggle with the same feelings, and they have the same hopes. All of them, except people from Massachusetts. Those guys are nuts."

"Is that right?" Alice asked.

"One of the amazing things about this place is that it brings people of all ages of history together, breaking barriers in ways I've never seen."

Suddenly Alice thought of something. "Keith, do all time travellers come to San Tiempo?" she asked.

"Most," Keith said. "Why?"

"Well," she said. "You said that Malcolm had left you a message, that he had something that you wanted to see."

"That's right," Keith agreed. "I don't know what it was though."

"You also said that you weren't easy to get in touch with," Alice pointed out.

"I am hard to get in touch with," Keith agreed. "Leave me a message, and I may not get it for a few minutes, or for another decade."

Alice had been expecting this and had her next question all prepared. "So if you are so difficult to get touch with, how did Malcolm manage to do it?"

Keith seemed to realize what she was thinking. "Most likely he was referred to me by another time traveller, although he might not have known it at the time."

"So Malcolm must have met at *least* one other time traveller," Alice surmised. "Someone other than you or me?"

"I suppose that he must have," Keith agreed.

"And if another time traveller were looking to get out of London, because, say, they were afraid they were going to be implicated in the murder of a promising astrophysicist–"

"Most likely they'd come here."

Alice considered this. "And is there some sort of place on the island where we might run into a large number of people, the better to question them and see exactly who's here and what they know? Some sort of restaurant, or function, something like–"

"Something like the Time Travellers Museum Gala tomorrow night?" Keith asked.

"Something like the Time Travellers Museum Gala tomorrow night," Alice said. "I love a good party."

Truth be told, parties made Alice nervous. As such, she ended up spending most of the day getting ready. This was not so much a matter of primping, bathing, and beautifying, as much as it was a problem of organization and inquiry. It seemed that at some point Alice ended up using time travel to buy a wardrobe that would have rivalled the costume department at MGM. There were dresses and shoes from nearly every century. There were bodices and corsets. There were spats, spangles, and jewelry pieces of every conceivable style and price range. There were hats of every kind – bowlers, top hats, cowboy hats, fedoras, and something which very clearly seemed to resemble Nefertiti's headdress. It was all strange. (There wasn't a pair of jeans in sight.) If Alice ever ran into herself, she was going to have to have a serious conversation about the knee-high copper-heeled boots that she found under the bed. If the future Alice was a clothes horse, then she was a Clydesdale.

In the end, she decided to wear a little black dress. It was the sort of thing that twenty-first century women wore to museum galas, and this particular Alice was still a twenty-first century woman. *'A closet full of historical outfits, and I wear the one thing that seems timeless,'* she thought.

Keith came to pick her up around eight-thirty. He was wearing a tuxedo with tails and was carrying a cane. He'd slicked his hair back in a manner that suggested he was going to a party being held by Fred Astaire.

"You look nice," he said, squinting. (Keith was, clearly, blind as a bat – a characterization that bats everywhere would have found unfair.)

"You're not wearing your glasses," Alice said, laughing.

"I was trying to look nice," Keith said, and he tripped over a coffee table.

"You know, in my time we have these things called 'contact lenses'," Alice said, laughing.

"Oh, god no," Keith said after she explained what they were. "In your eyes? Why in god's name would you – no, never mind, I don't want to know. Come on, let's go."

It still seemed that cars were some sort of social faux pas on the island. (Although old time nineteen-century bicycles never seemed to go out of style. In the past few days Alice gotten quite used to a parade of men determined to bike up to the top of what she now knew to be Mount Everest, usually while wearing jodhpurs and top hats.) Alice thought that perhaps that she and Keith might have walked to wherever the Time Travellers Museum was, but there was a carriage waiting out front. Alice would have found this very charming, even if it weren't being pulled by a set of four large ostriches.

"Horses take up a lot of space on the island," Keith explained, somewhat apologetically.

"It's all right," Alice said with a smile.

The coach was being driven by Fergus, previously the bartender at the Gristle and Thorn, who was dressed in an elegant riding coat and seemed to have a French accent this time. "Mademoiselle," he said, happily hopping down and opening the door for her. "Your carriage awaits."

"Thank you," Alice said, stepping inside, silently thinking that it was lucky that she had worn the black dress and not a ball gown. The carriage, while charming, was slightly roomier on the inside than the Fiat that they'd stolen the other day.

"To the museum, Fergus," Keith snapped, hopping into the seat across from her. Fergus picked up the reins, and the ostriches hopped along.

It took about half an hour to get to the museum. The road was winding and beautiful, but Alice still couldn't shake the feeling that she was a stranger in a strange land. For a while she stared in silence at the Ocean. It was a warm night, probably all nights here were warm, and the air was pleasant and relaxing. She was reminded of something her father used to say to her a long time ago – that no matter how bad things were, it was always nice to look at the sea. She supposed that her father had been dead for a long time now. It made her feel a little bit empty inside to think about it.

"It's still a little sad to think that we're here at the end of the world," Alice commented, "even if it is beautiful."

"It's not the end of the world, exactly," Keith explained. "Just a convenient point where we are more or less left to ourselves. There are other timelines where the world isn't a giant fish tank, but giant holes in the sky do seem to attract a lot of attention, so the city was built here. Think of it as an island not in water, but in time."

"I take it that there aren't many time travellers?" Alice asked.

"Oh, there are a few thousand," Keith said. "Enough certainly that you would never see them all, but spread out over the whole of human existence, it doesn't seem like much. For the most part, this island, the Gristle and Thorn, and *L'ostello Illegale* in Rome are the only places where you will ever meet another time traveller. Time travellers tend to be misfits. Never quite at home anywhere, except for here, maybe."

"How far is it to the museum, anyway?" Alice wondered, but Keith didn't have to answer because they were already there.

Alice would eventually discover that the museum of the time traveller was a sprawling complex, with buildings of every conceivable kind. Indeed, it would serve quite well as an excellent display of western architectural styles, if nothing else. However, on first glance, as happened with all incoming tourists, Alice's eyes would be completely overwhelmed by the sweeping glass tower stretching up over the cliff face. It leaned out forward over the ocean, so that it looked like an enormous wave breaking against the rocks. It was topped by a brilliant light, so bright that it looked like a star.

"What is *that?*" Alice asked. "Some sort of lighthouse?"

"That," Keith Quick said with pride, "is the Tower of Imaginary Objects, or as I like to call it, the office."

Chapter 10
Conspiracy

Locrinus stirred the fire and stared out of the mouth of the cave at the large metal beacon winking in the storm outside. He knew that the beacon's signal would cut through the clouds and snow, but he couldn't help but wish that the light on the end was brighter. Locrinus was a man of old Earth. He knew what the beacon did, but did not understand its power, and it seemed like Black Magic to him. Not that the fact that it was Black Magic bothered him. If anything, it gave him a warm feeling to think that his employer's power was so vast. He took great delight in the thought that the misfortune of so many, many people across the folds of space and time would be his gain, and if he used some dirty tricks to get there, so much the better. Locrinus had fairly rigid ideas about what constituted good and evil, and he had very little doubt which side he was on.

'They will come,' he thought to himself as he stirred the fire. *'They will be drawn to his will like moths to a flame.'* Although, in truth, the master would in fact be elsewhere tonight, and for that matter there wasn't a moth within a thousand leagues of here. Indeed, with the amount of snow that had fallen in the last two days, it seemed like a miracle that there was any life out there at all. Still, none of that mattered. They would come.

Slowly, in the distance, a dark figure stumbled through the snow.

Locrinus peered out of the cave at the figure stumbling towards him. Whoever it was appeared to be unaccustomed to this weather, not that this was surprising. The location had been chosen specifically because it wouldn't be settled for several centuries. Judging by the sheer volume of clothing that the figure out in the snow had chosen to wear, it might seem a wonder that it was ever settled at all. The person in question (if it actually was a person, Locrinus could not swear at this point that it wasn't a Neanderthal) was wrapped up so tightly that it looked as though an enormous mitten was waddling this way. The figure stopped in front of the beacon. Locrinus saw a gloved hand pull out a pocket watch. Then the figure turned and headed toward the cave.

"Good Lord!" a high pitched, but unmistakably male, voice said. "It's cold out there!"

"It is the age of ice," Locrinus said simply. In almost any age he was a severe-looking man – his bald head and pointed beard had all of the subtlety of a broadsword laid next to a dessert fork at a fancy dinner party. His voice was low and scratchy, and simple statements suited him.

The overly-dressed figure began removing layer after layer of clothing. Underneath, he was revealed to have a slender figure with a surprisingly long nose, and rather impressively large ears. On his face he wore a bristly red mustache, as well as a futuristic piece of technology Locrinus had come to know as "spectacles." In spite of the cold weather, underneath his outer layers he wore a black topcoat with long tails, a pair of elegant pressed trousers, and a dashing bow tie. His presence in a cave made about as much sense as an astronaut riding into the middle of the battle of Agincourt. Locrinus didn't trust him and wasn't interested in hiding that fact.

"I knew it would be bad, but good Lord!" the well-dressed man said. "I believe I saw a wooly mammoth. An actual mammoth!"

Locrinus grunted. "'Twas a rhino," he said, picking up a wooden goblet and taking a swig of ale.

The bespectacled man dusted frost and snow off of his remaining clothes. He looked both oddly enthralled and disappointed at the same time. "A rhino?" he asked, his eyebrows raised.

Locrinus found a jug of ale and refilled his goblet. "The mammoths have moved north. I know, I've hunted them."

"Really?" the bespectacled man asked, a little too keen to make conversation. "I've been thinking of hunting elephants on the African Serengeti. What kind of gun did you use?"

"No gun. A spear," Locrinus said, taking another swig.

The bespectacled man clearly didn't know what to say to this and eventually pretended that he hadn't heard it. "Chesterfield," he said, stretching out a hand that had, without a doubt, never hunted a mammoth, but had done other things, possibly knitting. "Milton Chesterfield."

Locrinus didn't shake the hand, but poured a second cup of ale and offered it to the stranger. "Welcome to London," he said.

It was the year 11945 BC.

Milton Chesterfield's decision to become a time travelling criminal was one of those bizarre life choices that could probably be compared to Arnold Schwarzenegger deciding to take up acting classes, or Adolf Hitler thinking he would be better off dropping out of art school. In another reality, he would have been an upscale gentleman, who attended meetings and private clubs, drinking port and giving his opinions on the important matters of the day. Chesterfield was meant for politics and port, but unfortunately he'd had a run in with a very, very bad crowd. So there they were.

One of the advantages to being a time traveller was that if you committed a crime, you could hang out a very long way away from where they were looking for you. It was very difficult to catch you for stealing the Mona Lisa if you were hiding out in the Roman Empire. This irony was not lost on the *United Bureau of Chronological Affairs,* the agency that governed these things. Unfortunately, resources were fairly slim, and it was widely known that if you went a little way out of the time stream, say a century or two in either direction, then you were probably in the free and clear. Of course, if you had done something incredibly awful, with serious implications to the world at large, then you were probably better off moving to another millennium all together. In this case, they had gone back roughly ten thousand years, and they hadn't actually broken any laws yet. Even then, Chesterfield was concerned that they hadn't gone far enough. He was wondering if they should have moved to a different part of the continuum altogether, perhaps one where the Roman Empire never fell, or where Panda Bears ruled the Earth. Chesterfield had recently read a book on the Far East, and had heard of Pandas. Surely Pandas must rule the Earth somewhere, at some point. They sounded like such fearsome creatures.

"How many are coming?" Locrinus asked.

"Including you and I? Six," Chesterfield said. "I take it I'm the first to arrive?"

"Six?" Locrinus asked. "So few?"

"The Professor is too close to the object and won't be able to extract himself until after the job has been done, and we lost one, a few days ago," Chesterfield admitted.

Judging by the look on the faces of both men, there was no question that this wasn't good news. Locrinus picked up a stick and stirred the fire.

Time travel is a science of precision, a quality human beings are not known for, and even with the beacon in place it took a good ninety minutes for everyone to arrive. During that time Locrinus sat contemplating the fire, while Chesterfield tried a number of different tactics to hide how badly his nerves were fraying. This included making some of the most awkward small talk ever known to man, during which he appeared to have an out-of-body experience and may have heard himself talking about cucumber sandwiches and ladies' ball gowns. (Chesterfield was a nineteenth century man, born and bred, but even in his own era, a man talking about ball gowns was a little odd.) He also retied his boots (several times), cleaned his glasses, combed his mustache, and inspected the inside of his pocket watch for grime. Eventually, Locrinus, perhaps trying to keep the man from wetting himself before the others arrived, offered him a bowl of something. It was a hot warm liquid that smelled like soup, provided that the soup in question had been made by baboons.

"Hungry?" he asked, handing over the bowl.

"What is it?" Chesterfield said.

"Gristle and thorns," Locrinus mumbled.

'So that's where the name comes from,' Chesterfield thought.

Luckily for Chesterfield, the others began to arrive before he was forced to eat it. Esther Wilcox showed up first. She was a cross-temporal clairvoyant, and had an almost preternatural sense of other timelines. They'd picked her up in the seventeenth century, shouting omens of doom at passersby. Her predictions were remarkably specific and accurate, and they'd had to rescue her from getting burned at the stake. The nice thing about hiring people about to be torched during the Salem Witch Trials was that they work super cheap.

The Glycerin brothers came next. They were hired as muscle out of the army of Genghis Khan, and their knowledge of horses and weapon making had proved quite useful, especially in periods of antiquity. Chesterfield tended to look the other way when they spoke, which, thankfully, wasn't much.

Federico Faya showed up as the sun was going down. He was either from the past or the future, Chesterfield wasn't sure which. He was dressed in the manner that Americans did in the west, provided that westerners wore cowboy hats with goggles on them and brandished brass ray guns. He wore a brown leather cape, embroidered with an octopus and gears. Chesterfield did his best to make sure that he was standing on the opposite side of the cave from him.

With Federico, that made six. Including the Professor, who wouldn't be there that night, there would be seven. Yes, they had lost one, but they still had seven, and seven, Chesterfield couldn't help but think, was *a proper number of people for a conspiracy.'*

"Well, well," Chesterfield spoke in the sort of bright chipper tones normally reserved for garden parties, "I'm so excited to have you all here." He adjusted his topcoat and looked brightly around the cave. The faces that stared back at him looked like they had come here to take part of some sort of advanced rage study, but that couldn't be helped. "I'm sorry the Professor is not here, but he's asked me to speak to you on his behalf. For those of you who have not had any news in a while, I'm happy to report that our progress is moving forward as planned. Our attempts to get a virtual timeline up and running are going smoothly, and the quality improvement and larceny teams have been coming up with some really excellent ideas. Also, the move to get everyone onto the new healthcare plan is going exceedingly well–"

"There is news," Locrinus growled, as if Chesterfield had never spoken.

"There is news, yes. It seems that–"

"What is it?" one of the Glycerin brothers asked.

"News, yes," Chesterfield said. "It seems that–"

"What is it?" the other one of the Glycerin brothers asked. "Is the Professor backing out?"

Chesterfield's mustache bristled. "Not at all," he said. "It seems—"

"The Mother of Time has been found," Locrinus interrupted.

Inside the cavern there was a murmur that would have disturbed Martin Luther.

"The past has passed," Esther Wilcox said. She was an older woman of about fifty, who looked like she'd seen too many winters and too few meals. Chesterfield had noticed that she had been eying the gruel hungrily while the others had been coming in. "What has happened will always happen."

"The past can be avoided," Locrinus countered, and on this point there was some murmuring. "What has happened before may not happen again."

"Where is she?" one of the Glycerin brothers asked, giving his brother a knowing look.

"She turned up in San Tiempo," Locrinus said. "I saw her. I was there."

This time there wasn't a murmur, but instead a silence — one that the Dalai Lama would have found a little awkward. Even Federico Faya, who had been polishing his ray gun, looked up. "I sought zat ze Mother of Time, she was a myth," he said, speaking in a thick Spanish accent, but still obviously surprised.

"Everything written is real," Esther said, folding her arms and holding her chin up proudly.

"You should have killed her," one of the Glycerin brothers suggested.

"I would have done so at the expense of my own life," Locrinus dismissed. "It was too crowded."

Esther rocked herself back and forth in front of the fire. "Too soon," she squawked. "Too soon. Too soon. Too Soon. The Mother of Time has a role to play yet."

"Did she recognize you?" one of the Glycerin brothers asked.

It was a fair question, and it occurred to Chesterfield that he would like to know the answer as well. If they had been spotted, it might mean an end to everything.

"She was in a room full of people," Locrinus said. "They applauded when she came in. She was young, so young. I'm sure that it was all new to her."

Federico Faya took off his cowboy hat and ran his fingers through his hair. "Who has 'er?" he asked.

"She was with Quick," Locrinus said, his voice barely above a whisper, but dangerous nonetheless.

There was another murmur. One that Jesus probably would have found a tad unsettling.

"Quick will use her to his advantage," one of the Glycerin brothers pointed out.

"No," Federico Faya insisted. "He weel want to keep 'er safe."

"He will do neither of those things," Locrinus said, his voice quiet again, but unmistakably dangerous. "He wants the prize as badly as we do."

"The greed of men will always be their undoing," Esther Wilcox said, and at this there was a more pleasant-sounding murmur.

Chesterfield cleared his throat rather loudly. "This moment was always coming," he said, mustache bristling. "We knew it would come, and we have prepared for it. We all need to trust the Professor and stick to the plan."

"Trust the Professor," Locrinus agreed.

"What," asked Federico Faya "ees the Professor's plan?"

"The plan is to use Quick's strength against him," Chesterfield said. "The Professor has planned for this and knows precisely what to do."

"He knows what to do," Esther said "because it has happened already."

"It has already happened," one of the Glycerin brothers said, "but it may be avoided."

"Quick will not want to avoid his destiny," Locrinus argued. "He will put her at risk, in order to create himself."

"His beginnings and ends are one," Esther added. "To destroy one, we must destroy the other."

There was a silence, and then a murmur, and then a silence again. This was broken by Federico Faya. "So what do we do?" he asked.

"We stick to the plan." Chesterfield said. "We trust the Professor."

"Trust the Professor," the conspirators chanted.

Chapter 11
THE BALL

ALICE STEPPED OUT OF THE CARRIAGE. They had pulled out in front of a grand museum entrance, with stone pillars and beautiful wide marble steps flanked on each side by statues of large octopi. Alice was reasonably sure that the time traveller's museum gala was going to be a fairly odd affair, and her expectations were met almost immediately, when at the museum's front entrance they were met by an entire line of Generic Ferguses, all dressed in matching powdered wigs and livery.

"How many of the jobs on the island are done by Ferguses?" Alice asked Keith as they got out of the carriage.

"Only the ones that nobody else wants to do," Keith admitted. "Food service and auto mechanics, primarily, although how they get that woman to work at the airport check-in desk is beyond me. They do good work, though, plus you don't have to tip them."

There was something about this last statement that seemed ugly and unfair, but Alice was momentarily distracted and didn't dwell on it, instead focusing on doing her best to smile and be impressed. "Good evening, miss," each of the Ferguses said one after another in a variety of accents, each giving an elegant bow as she walked past. "Good evening," Alice responded to each one in turn as she walked past, and each one seemed to stand a little taller and prouder when she did.

"Are we going to see your work?" Alice asked as she reached the end of the processional. The glass tower was just behind them and Alice imagined that the view from the top must be quite beautiful.

"We'll get there eventually," Keith reassured her. "The gala tonight is being held in the twentieth century historical hall, which is quite popular with the locals but might seem less significant to you. I'm afraid that you're going to have to make an awful lot of small talk in a room filled with total strangers, most of whom will be much more interested in telling you the petty details of their personal lives."

"So it will basically be like any other party the world has ever known?" Alice asked.

"Yes, except that if we're very, very lucky, there will be someone there who knows why you've been accused of murder," Keith clarified.

"And how exactly are we going to know if anyone here knows anything significant? Should I just mingle throughout the crowd, shake everybody's hand, say 'Hello, I'm Alice Anderson, I may invent time travel one day, and by the by, did you happen to murder my ex-boyfriend and frame me for it? You see, I've been accused of murder back in what in my primitive state of existence I would call the present, and I would really much, much rather not spend time in prison, thank you so very much.' Is that what you're thinking?"

"Well, I'd like to tell you that I can spot guilty people just by looking at them," Keith said. "However, I'm afraid that statement is only really useful if you're trying to get out of jury duty. Remember, this was your idea. Now, I'm sorry to do this to you, but I'm afraid we're going to have to split up."

Alice liked to think of herself as a strong-willed and independent person, but having been through so much change in the past few days, the plain and simple truth was that the thought of being alone in public terrified her. Keith seemed to have all of the predictability of an off-centre roulette wheel, but still, he had met Alice Anderson, graduate student in Astrophysics, a person who was already starting to seem like a stranger after less than a week's time. Keith seemed to sense this and placed a friendly hand on her shoulder.

"I'm hoping that maybe someone who is smart enough not to talk to you will be dumb enough to talk to me," he said. "Just maybe I can find out something that you can't. In the meantime, just mingle a little bit and see if you can find out something interesting. Remember, in cases like this, the shortest distance between two points isn't always a straight line. Just see what you can find out. We'll see where it leads us."

"It seems to me that the problem with this place is an overabundance of interesting things," Alice said. "You don't have some sort of driver and vehicle licensing agency, do you?"

"It's going to be fine," Keith said, and without any further ado, they stepped into the museum.

The foyer of the museum was in many ways not all that different from the sort that you might see in any art museum in a major city – the MET in New York came to mind. The interior was a giant marble dome similar to the Pantheon in Rome, a little smaller and less ornate, perhaps, but nonetheless impressive. Like many museums, the foyer was largely empty; the curator had focused instead on the majesty of open space, with a single piece standing free in the centre of the room. There was a large crowd, and Alice couldn't clearly see what it was at the room's centre. *'If you have a museum devoted to time and space,'* she wondered to herself, *'what do you stick in front of the ticket booth to get the punters to go have a look inside?'* Certainly Keith had demonstrated that time travellers had abundant resources, so what would they put in such a prime spot? The true cross, maybe? The crown of Richard the Lionhearted? They could probably set up a nice display case with the unpublished manuscript of something by William Shakespeare. Personally, Alice would have put Galileo's telescope dead centre in the middle of the room, probably on a nice marble pedestal with velvet ropes all around. Of course, that was just her. An art historian would have probably had other ideas, undoubtedly involving Christopher Wren, or Da Vinci, or maybe a statue of Einstein done by Michelangelo, and rendered in six dimensions. (Alice wasn't really sure about this; at this point anything seemed possible.) She moved in for a closer look.

There, in the centre of the room, was the unmistakable sight of the orange tree that sat by the door in Alice's flat in upstate New York. It was much, much bigger, and appeared to be dying on one side, but there was no mistaking it, it was the same tree. Alice didn't know what to think. She walked up to the tree and stared at it blankly. As she stood there, admiring the fruit tree that she had bought on sale at a garden centre for fifteen American dollars, she became dimly aware of two things. The first thing was that Keith was no longer with her. The second thing was there were camera flashes popping off all around her in every direction. Almost everyone in the room was taking pictures, using cameras of almost every conceivable kind. (Brownie Instamatics and cell phones seemed to have appeared in equal numbers.)

'Maybe if I just stay here, they'll get bored and talk amongst themselves,' Alice thought.

"Do you like it?" a voice behind her asked.

Alice turned around. A small, voluptuous woman in a Greek toga was standing behind her, smiling pleasantly. She was middle-aged, perhaps fifty, with salt and pepper hair that was almost as curly as Alice's was. She had friendly indescribable eyes and a warm inescapable smile. Alice liked the look of her. She was the only one

in the room besides Keith who wasn't acting like they should be hanging her somewhere on the museum's wall.

"I always did like it," Alice said. "I bought it on sale."

"It was a gift from the museum's founder. Artifacts from the Mother of Time are quite rare," the woman said with a smile.

"The Mother of Time appears to have pruned it rather badly," Alice said, noting how the tree seemed to be leaning to one side.

"It has almost died a number of times," the woman said, brightly. "They've always managed to revive it." The woman in the toga offered a hand. "I would ask if we have ever met, but I can tell by that glassy-eyed look on your face that everything's new right now. I am Phaedra, daughter of Minos. I am curator of this museum, and your host for the evening."

"Phaedra?" Alice repeated, flashing back to a rather unpleasant memory of her A level in French.

"Oh, you've heard the stories, haven't you?" Phaedra asked with a coy smile. "The downside of fame, but I imagine you've been finding out about that already. Well, I suppose it can't be helped. They're all written by men, love, did you know that? You know how men are, they're always prone to exaggeration when a woman bats her eyes at someone."

"I only read the French," Alice admitted.

"Oh, that one's the *worst*," she said, rolling her eyes.

"I only read it because they made me in school," Alice said, hoping she wasn't going to be pinned down on the details.

"I hope you cheated on the exam, and focused on something important, love, like mathematics, or engineering, or watching the football team run around in tiny pants," Phaedra suggested, her eyes sparkling devilishly.

"Astrophysics," Alice insisted, "although the football team did come up a couple of times."

"Well of course, love. Now I hate to be a bit on the pushy side, but I have roughly two hundred people here who are hoping to shake your hand. Tell me, love, have you ever been the bride at a wedding?"

MUSEUM

"No," Alice admitted.

"Good, love. Try and keep it that way. You can trust me on this. Tonight, though, you're going to find out what being a bride is like. Being famous is a similar experience. Everywhere you go there's always a large group of people, and they all want to talk to you."

"Okay," she said. "How long will it last?"

"Till you're dead, love. I'm sorry, I thought you would have understood that bit. They do have television and things where you're from, don't they? Or has that become passé? Honestly, I can never keep up. Anyway, get ready to meet more or less everyone."

"I meant how long would the party last?" Alice clarified, wondering if the time would ever come when she didn't need to ask so many questions.

"Two hours, love. Three, tops. At the most, four. We'll get you home by dawn, love, I promise. Now come on, let me introduce you to your best and brightest."

Alice had never been to a museum gala before. It seemed more like the sort of thing that existed in movies and on television, and the idea conjured up images of rich people with too much money passing out giant cheques while listening to string quartets and drinking champagne. Certainly some of that was true. In many ways the Time Traveller's Museum didn't appear to be all that different from any other museum. It had elegant halls, delightful open spaces, and a sense of majesty to it that made you believe that the things inside *must* be important. True to form, they had set up a bar where you could undoubtedly get an overpriced but elegant drink, and there was a string quartet, but any resemblance to a fundraiser at the Smithsonian or the Louvre seemed to stop there. Here the barman (another Fergus, naturally) seemed to be favouring Venutian Sunrises over Dom Perignon. The string quartet seemed to be dressed in liveries and looked like they had been brought in from the court of the Holy Roman Emperor. (In fact, all four had played with Mozart, but there was no way that Alice could have known that.) In the halls themselves, the Time Traveller's Museum was littered with objects that probably meant a lot in the year eleven thousand and whatever, but in the twentieth century would have been things that Alice would have thought of as brick-a-brac, at best. In the first hall that Alice stepped into there was a collection of half-chewed pencils, an old movie poster, a weather-beaten guitar, an old wheelbarrow, a blue gingham dress, a fairly nice group of Russian nesting dolls, and a hundred more objects that Alice would have thought nothing of overlooking at a yard sale, much less here. The artifacts were hung on the walls in a proud, stately manner, suggesting that each had a kind of sympathetic magic to it, as if it held the power of some bygone hero or heroine that could be passed on just by being touched. *'I suppose even the Holy Grail was once just someone's china,'* Alice thought.

Alice spent the next five hours making small talk with strange people. *Very strange* people they were, too. She saw men in ruffled collars and suits of armour; Ladies in bustles and hats, and in some cases opera gloves and bustiers. It seemed to Alice that everyone had come in their own culture's version of their Sunday best, from whatever century and area they had come in from, and they must have come in from everywhere. She did her best to smile politely, nod, and listen to people as they talked to her, and everyone in the room had a story. Alice heard stories about their first time travel experience, stories about how they had travelled through history and beyond, stories about places that never were, or shouldn't have been. A few seemed to have grown up here on the island, and related tales of how they had grown up, hearing about Alice, and how she had made all of this possible. At this, Alice couldn't help but think, *'That's nice, but I haven't actually done anything yet, and I don't know if I ever will. All of this just seems like a dream.'*

With names she was hopeless, although with so many people to remember she could hardly be blamed. Even with characters with colourful monikers like Robin Finn-Fellows and Heather Silvernail, names seemed to pass through her like a west wind through a screen door. She apologized several times, most notably while talking to a lovely couple in some kind of traditional African dress, whose names she could barely pronounce, let alone remember. *'These are nice people,'* she thought to herself. *'I know they mean well. It's just that I don't really know if I'm one of them.'*

What she did not see was someone who looked or acted as though they were unapologetically guilty. If Alice shook hands with the person who shot Malcolm she never knew it, and she shook hands with almost everybody. If anyone knew of the personal turmoil she'd been through, they didn't mention it or offer any details about Malcom's death. She realized that coming here had been a long shot, but still, it was disappointing. She had hoped, perhaps foolishly, that she might come across the severe-looking Asian woman who had been at her lecture at the Royal Astronomy Conference. It was a ridiculous idea, but Alice couldn't help but think that it would have made a weird kind of sense to see her here. Sense, though, seemed to have been left behind in the United Kingdom, or worse yet, back in America. *'America, the land of sense,'* Alice thought. *'That seems wrong for so many, many reasons.'*

Keith seemed to disappear for the most part, although Alice caught a glimpse of him a couple of times. He seemed to be hanging around the makeshift bar they had set up in the foyer, talking to people as they came up to get drinks. He looked like he was in good spirits, and Alice was glad to see that he was enjoying himself, even though she couldn't help but feel that he was ignoring her. *'Maybe he'll find something out,'* she thought hopefully.

Phaedra remained at her side throughout the evening, alternately introducing her to people and then making catty gossip about them as they walked away. This wasn't terribly useful, but it was entertaining, as time travel gossip had its own unique spin to it that Alice hadn't anticipated. "Lovely to see you Hilda, that's Hildegarde Albrecht, usually ends up living in a house in the Black Forest made of candy, trying to convince little children to stop by for a visit. Doesn't end well. Hello, Robin! Robin Goodfellow, lives in a time traveller's commune near Athens, gender questionable, as is his taste in clothing. Over there, that's Hiram Bingham, discoverer of Machu Pichu, only he didn't discover what his wife was doing while he was there." And so it went, on and on and on. Somewhere in the second hour, Alice needed a breather.

"I'm sorry," she said, turning to Phaedra, "do you know where the loo is?"

"Of course, love. Come on, you can use the one in my office, that will give you a bit of privacy," Phaedra said. "I'm sure you could use a few moments to yourself. It's right down this way."

Phaedra led her down a flight of stairs off the main hall and into a long hallway that appeared to be closed to guests for the evening. Like the items in the other parts of the building, everything had the look of a well-organized collection of Knick Knacks. Alice had been so busy introducing herself to everyone that she hadn't had a chance to look at the exhibits, and found herself taking a moment to focus on a collection of bird skulls handsomely mounted on the left side of the hall. She peered at one as she walked past, thinking that it might be a specimen of scientific significance. Underneath it was a bronze sign, which read:

Raven, found on the bust of Pallas, upon the chamber door of Edgar Allen Poe

Nevermore

'Morbid,' Alice thought, wondering what the skull next to it had belonged to. (It actually belonged to Long John Silver's Parrot, but Alice never got a chance to read the sign.)

Suddenly she thought of something. "Phaedra, you said you run the museum?"

"Yes, love. Not a difficult job, really. There's a lot of chatting people up at functions like this. Why do you ask?"

"Well," Alice asked. "Keith Quick works for you, then, right?"

"Not directly. The museum is a big place, with many different departments. I am familiar with his work, though. Brought in quite a prize the other day, I understand."

"The pipe," Alice said, remembering the parcel that Keith had handed her back at the Gristle and Thorn.

"That too, love," Phaedra said, beaming.

"I was just wondering, what do you make of him?" Alice asked.

Phaedra sighed in such a melodramatic manner that Alice wondered if the older woman had been expecting this question all night long. "The real question, I think, is what do *you* make of him?"

"I couldn't say," Alice admitted, and as soon as she had said the words she realized how true they were. "He's been tremendously helpful over the last few days, but I honestly don't know him all that well. I guess that's why I asked you."

"He knows more than he's letting on," Phaedra admitted.

Alice didn't know what to make of this. "What do you mean?"

"Well, we all do, love, don't we?" Phaedra suggested. "It's part of being a time traveller. If you had been to someone's wedding, or their funeral, or the birth of their son, and it hadn't happened to *them* yet, would you tell them? Nevermind that just the act of telling them might alter their lives so much that whatever you had seen might never happen at all. Imagine someone coming up to you, patting you on the shoulder, and saying, 'Hello, I just went to your wedding, Steve seems like a great guy, beautiful ceremony, although I think those flower arrangements might look a little dated in ten years. I know, because that's the decade I grew up in.' Only you've only just met Steve at a party, and he seemed a little on the dull side, and you didn't talk to him much, and of course you hadn't given a thought to flowers yet at all. No, you're better off not saying anything."

Alice could see how this would be an awkward situation, but didn't really feel like conceding the point just now. "Nobody seems to mind telling me what's in my future," Alice muttered, thinking of all the people who had praised her for inventing time travel.

"Well that's different, love. You're an institution, aren't you? Besides, everyone assumes that you've invented the damn thing already, don't they? No one thinks that you would have started time travelling beforehand."

They stopped in front of a brown office door. "My office. Door on the other side of the room is the toilet, love. You're lucky," she said, adjusting her toga. "You've got no idea how hard it is to pee in this thing. Of course, if I left the house without a toga, my father would be ashamed of me. He's already ashamed of me, come to think of it, but there you are."

Eventually the night seemed to wear down. The crowd began to thin out, and Alice's appearance seemed less significant to the people who remained. She thanked Phaedra profusely for everything and promised to visit the museum on a less auspicious occasion. When she finally found Keith, he was sitting on a wooden bench in a corner, nursing a Venutian Sunrise and watching a Fergus in a jumpsuit push around a broom. The bow tie on his tuxedo was undone and his hair was a little disheveled, although he still looked handsome, if a little down in the dumps. "Hi beautiful," he mumbled, carelessly.

"What did you find out?" Alice asked.

"Less than nothing," Keith said. He shook his head and rubbed his neck, and then he ran his fingers through his hair "There seems to be a code of silence in place, at least as far as you're concerned. Plenty of gossip about absolutely any other subject though. Did you hear about Hiram Bingham's wife? I was shocked, I don't know about you."

Alice sighed and sat down next to him on a bench. "I suppose it was a long shot," she admitted. "Now what do I do?"

"Well, I could sneak back down to your timeline and see if the police know anything," Keith suggested. His tone sounded hopeful, but there was a certain futility in his eyes.

"I don't suppose we could just go into the future and see if anybody was ever convicted of the crime?" replied Alice.

Keith shook his head. "It doesn't really work that way. The future is unwritten. We might find that someone *had* been convicted of the crime, but the events heading up into shooting might be different. Maybe Malcolm would even still be alive, in which case there might be a completely different Alice wandering around London. There's no guarantee that anything we found out would have anything to do with the details of your life."

"Surely there can't have been *that* many people who would have wanted to kill him," Alice protested. "Even if it is a different situation or whatever, it would still give us a clue."

"I'd agree with you, if I had any idea why he was killed in the first place," Keith said. "But I don't. You have to remember that someone thought killing Malcolm was a completely logical and rational thing to do and we don't know who or why. There might be other people who would have the same motivation. Or they might not. It's tough to say."

"I suppose it's a little like assuming someone's guilty just because they've been arrested," Alice said, imagining what everyone back home must think of her.

"A little bit," Keith said. "It's a messy business, mucking about in your own future. There's a reason most time travellers don't go there."

"I would have thought it was because people don't want to end up killing their future selves," Alice mused.

Keith made a sour face. "Everybody says that, but honestly, how hard is it not to kill yourself? If you see yourself, and you've got a gun in your hand, you just don't *shoot* it. No, the problem is more complicated than that. Imagine seeing yourself going through a painful divorce, or finding out that your father has cancer. Then throw in the added uncertainty of the fact that there is absolutely no guarantee that what you've seen will ever actually happen to you. What you've seen might be nothing more than the shadows of what might be."

'He's afraid they'll never catch anyone,' Alice thought, *'and he's right. If the person who killed Malcolm can time travel, there isn't really any way of explaining that to the police. Of course, maybe it was just a burglar, and I'm overthinking this whole thing.'* She buried her face in her hands. "I suppose being able to go home again was a little too much to ask," she said, trying hard not to cry.

"Beggin' your pardon, miss," a voice said, "only it seems to me that what you'll be needin' to do is go back and speak to that professor fellow."

Alice looked up. This had come from the Fergus pushing the broom around the hallway. Alice had been talking like he wasn't even there. She stared at him now. He was leaning on the end of his broom and beaming at her. Alice wasn't really sure what to say. "I'm sorry," she stammered. "I haven't the foggiest idea what you're talking about."

"Well, miss–" this Fergus spoke with a cockney accent, "I knows that you've been looking into the murder that you've been accused of. I was just tryin' to suggest that you might want to check in with that professor that come to that speech you gave. Seems to me that 'e must know somethin'."

This made slightly more sense than the last thing he said, but Alice was still feeling confused. "I'm sorry, but I – my talk? How do you know about that?"

Fergus gave her a knowing look. "People might not be wantin' to talk to *you* about your problems, miss, that's human nature, but you're sure they'll be wanting to talk about you behind your back, once your companion is out of earshot, that is," he added, giving Keith a nod. "They like it especially when they thinks you're out of earshot, like when they're in the loo," the Fergus paused for dramatic effect, "and I cleans the loo," he finished.

Keith stood up excitedly. "You heard something?" he asked.

"Well, nothin' that you probably hadn't heard already, miss, 'ceptin' maybe a few choice comments about that dress that you're wearin'. I understand that you turned up at the Gristle and Thorn and you caused a bit of a stir. Well, I got to wonderin'. You see, miss, the other Ferguses and I, we have a method of communicatin' across the time stream."

"You never told me that," Alice said, looking at Keith.

"They use it to relay messages and information, and apparently to spread idle gossip," Keith said, raising his eyebrows.

Fergus ignored this. "So I asked the barman, over at the Gristle and Thorn, exactly what had happened on the night that you showed up. He said that he had heard most of the story of your comings and goings, in particular how you had brought the Royal Astronomy Conference to a rather abrupt halt, as it were."

"How did he get the story? Were there other time travellers there?" Keith asked.

"Oh there were other time travellers there, and also a reporter from The Times," Fergus said. "By the by, I didn't read the article, but I understand that it didn't do you justice. Anyway, the point is, I heard things, and one of the things I heard was that you took questions at the conference, although only from one gentleman. A professor–"

Alice stood up. "It was a chaired professor," she said. "He held the Edward Gibbon Chair."

Keith didn't get the significance. "So what?"

Alice's face brightened, and she grabbed Keith by the shoulders. "Don't you see? That's it! We have to go back! The professor who asked the question, what was his name? Ooh, I can't remember, but he was asking about Malcom's death."

"Hopper," Keith said. "I remember. He was an old fellow, not that that distinguished him in *that* crowd. Looked old enough to have been a classmate of Edward Gibbon's. Probably had been at the University since the early Renaissance, at least. Now that you mention it, he did say that he was the Edward Gibbon chair, whatever that means. So what?"

"So," Alice was doing her best to mentally prod Keith and not physically poke him, "Edward Gibbon–"

"Edward Gibbon wrote *The Decline and Fall of the Roman Empire,*" Keith said. "I am aware, although I'd be lying if I said that I'd read the whole thing. So what?"

Fergus beamed at him like a grammar school teacher who had just taught an especially slow student how to read. "So, that would make him a history teacher, wouldn't it?"

"What was a history professor doing at the Royal Astronomy Conference?" Keith asked.

"I don't know," Alice said. "It's something, though, isn't it?"

Keith laughed, and then he grinned, and then laughed again. "First rule of a fancy dress party. If you want to know what's really going on, ask the help. How stupid of me."

Alice turned around and kissed Fergus on the cheek. Fergus blushed and dropped his broom.

"Get that biplane of yours ready to go," she said excitedly. "We need to go back to London."

Chapter 12
Returning Home Again

It was only going to be her second trip, but Alice was pretty sure that she was never going to enjoy the physical experience of time travel quite as much as she loved an early night and a hot bath. She could see its value, but the thought of the empty nothingness between one period and the next, and the Earth spinning beneath them, was a little more than she could bear comfortably. Also, and Alice was a little ashamed to admit this, she was disappointed to be heading back to the present, and not to someplace more interesting – like the Ming dynasty, or Sherwood Forest, or Ancient Rome. She promised herself that the next trip would be more impressive. *'Maybe Edwardian London,'* she thought to herself. *'I'm pretty sure I saw a dress in that closet that would look perfect.'*

Keith had spent quite some time trying to convince her not to go, insisting that he could go and interview the Professor on his own. After all, Alice was still wanted for murder, and they wouldn't want to attract any undue attention. Alice pointed out that Keith had also been questioned in Malcolm's death, that he had been seen fleeing the hotel with her, that he'd parked a motorcycle with a sidecar on the sidewalk in front of the tube station, and had given London its first glimpse of a miniature triceratops. "Chances are neither one of us is going to be able to walk into a police station," she pointed out.

"Yes–" Keith said, "but–"

"I know the University and you don't," she interrupted. "You'll need my help to find the Professor. For that matter, I know the century, too."

"All right," Keith said, "but we should leave the trike behind this time."

This undoubtedly Alice *should* have agreed to, but she had become so attached to Grendel that she didn't want to leave him behind. Besides, Alice was new to San Tiempo, and had no idea what sort of shots a triceratops would require to board at a local pet hotel. "All right," Keith said, "but he's staying in the car."

"What car?" Alice asked.

Keith adjusted his aviator's goggles. "There are a lot of details to work out with you, aren't there?"

"I'm the Mother of Time," Alice said. "I think my life may be a little more complicated than most people's."

Alice was still a fugitive from justice, so they took some pains to disguise her. She wanted very much to blend in, maybe find some sort of twenty-first century headgear, but it didn't seem like her future self had a great love of conservative clothes. Instead, she settled on a brown leather blazer that looked like it belonged to Keith and a dark suede bowler with some nineteenth century magnifying equipment on it. To this she added a pair of round blue sunglasses and pair of brown velvet gloves. She supposed she should have dyed her hair, but she was anxious to clear her name and she didn't fancy herself a blonde anyway. Instead, she pinned her hair up and put on a large red scarf. This seemed to go well with a long charcoal grey dress that she found, and black t-shirt with a scooped out neck. The effect was dramatic – certainly anyone who looked at her would be drawn to stare at the hat and glasses, which of course could be easily discarded. If they were lucky, they might not even realize that she was a ginger.

The trip to the present seemed to take about thirty minutes, although its real length was impossible to judge. They were changing time zones and millennia, and the sun spun round like a top again. Alice made a mental note to buy herself a pocket watch, just so she could keep track of how long she had been awake. Keith had given Alice the job of hanging onto the time orb during the flight, and she opened up a giant hole in the sky simply by holding it in her palm and saying to herself *I want to go home again.* The orb had responded to this with a bright green glow, and the three dials spun in all directions before coming to a halt just before they landed. The plane came down on the same airfield that they had taken off at, where the same Fergus flagged their plane into the hangar. "Do you want this back?" she asked Keith, offering him the orb as she climbed out of the biplane's back seat.

"No, I want you to hang on to it," he insisted. "Without it, you could get lost in time and I'd never find you. It's very easy to get lost in the fabric of the continuum, never to be seen again. I should have gotten you one of your own before we left the island, but I knew what a hurry you were in."

Somehow Keith had acquired a bright green Jaguar and had left it parked out front. "I suppose it would have been too much to ask that you get a four door," Alice sighed as Grendel hopped over her.

"It has a back seat," Keith said, and he started up the car.

"Eyes on the road," Alice warned him. "You know the way to Cambridge, right?"

"Yes. Do you know the where we will find this old geezer?"

'American colloquialisms,' Alice thought. "I actually don't know, not exactly. I assume he'll be somewhere over in Claire College. That's where most of the history types were when I was there, anyway. It's not like these things change over at breakneck speed."

"They may not move at breakneck speed, but we may have to," Keith pointed out.

"Half a moment, and I'll check the Internet and figure out where we're headed," she insisted. She remembered that Keith came from another era, and might not be familiar with how technology really worked. "Just trust me," she added.

The drive to Cambridge was the most dangerous part of the endeavor, and if Keith could have teleported them to the university, he probably would have, but it seemed to violate the laws of physics, so unfortunately it couldn't be helped.

Out on the highway, Alice reached into her purse and pulled out her mobile. (Not having checked her email for most of a week, she was unsurprised to see that she had 1,538 messages. She put these aside with much the same feeling an alcoholic has on their first night of sobriety.) She pulled up the Internet and consulted the website of the University's History Department. It was a little tough to read, owing to the fact that the head of the department viewed the Internet as some form of witchcraft, but Alice managed eventually.

"I was wrong, he's in Christ College," Alice said, swallowing hard. She supposed that it was too much to ask that Paul Hopper be tucked away in some obscure, overly wooded section of campus. No, he had to have an office dead centre in the middle of everything. *'This is going to involve more running,'* she thought to herself.

And then, it happened. The phone rang. It was her sister, Wendy.

The funny thing about getting a phone call from someone you talk to all the time is that you can develop the disobliging habit of answering the call, even when you should very, very obviously let it go to voice mail. (Grown men, in the midst of the most profound bowel movements of their lives, have been known to pick up their mobiles, even though this is unquestionably a bad idea.) Alice couldn't help herself. She picked up the phone. "Hello?" she stammered, grateful that polite society had dictated what she should say first in circumstances like this.

"I don't want to bother you," Wendy said, "but you said I could call."

There were three things about this statement that struck Alice in rapid succession. The first, and probably least significant, was that Wendy (for once) appeared to be both sober and contrite, making this a particularly special occasion. The second, and most overwhelming thing, was the wave after wave of pure unadulterated joy that Alice felt in hearing her sister's voice. This was so incredible that she almost didn't notice the third thing, which is that she had no idea why she would *need* to tell her own sister that it was all right for her to call. Wendy had once picked up her mobile during the middle of the funeral. She could hardly be expected to need prodding now.

"I – I'm in the car," Alice sputtered. This seemed like a fairly pointless observation. Keith was actually doing the driving, not her, but Alice simply didn't know what else to say. The sound of her sister's voice seemed like a distant artifact from her youth, like the song that played on her first date or the smell of her mother's cooking.

"I know your life is complicated right now," Wendy said.

"Yes," Alice agreed. (Thank goodness *that* one was easy.)

"I don't know when you're coming back this way, but when you find him, and I know you will, I want to see him."

"See him," Alice repeated. She didn't have the foggiest idea what her sister was talking about. It sounded like Wendy was giving a prepared speech, but Alice had no idea what the subject was.

"I think it's important," Wendy said. Her tone betrayed absolutely nothing. She might be talking about the end of the world or about wedding plans. Who was it that she wanted to meet?

The only answer that Alice could think of was Keith, but why on Earth would Wendy even know who he was? "I think you're right," Alice said. She wondered if she had just agreed to some sort of time travelling family dinner.

"Just call me when things have calmed down a bit," Wendy sighed.

"Of course," Alice insisted. "Wendy – I"

"That thing that you asked me to say last time I spoke to you, I won't say it," Wendy insisted, her voice taking on a waspish tone.

"Okay," Alice said. "Okay."

"Well, I know that you're off," Wendy said. "When you're safe, call."

"I love you," Alice said, but Wendy had already hung up.

Keith was negotiating a busy roundabout. It wasn't agreeing with him. "Did you just talk to your sister?" he asked, turning the wheel.

"I did," Alice admitted.

"No way can *that* end badly," he grumbled. "What exactly did Wendy want?"

"Wendy–" Alice didn't know what to say. Should she tell the truth? That would be easier to do when she knew what the truth actually was. "She wanted to get me legal representation," she lied.

"And you took the call?" Keith asked. "Very brave."

"She was trying to help, I'm sure," Alice said.

"And I'm sure there's very little chance that she called from the police station. Almost none, really. Do you know where exactly I'm going? The college is just up ahead."

As a life form, University campuses rate somewhere in between Giant Sequoias and Antarctic Lichens in terms of speed of change. These were, after all, institutions that still acted, at least on formal occasions, as if the Roman Emperor was going to show up sooner or later. Change did not come easily for them. Even so, after only a week on San Tiempo, the school seemed like another world. As they got out of the car, Alice couldn't help but notice how young students coming across the campus in groups of two or three seemed like children, and the doddering old professors seemed like quaint throwbacks to another era. (To be fair, they *were* quaint throwbacks to another era, but it was *definitely* an era that Alice was not a part of.) Alice felt like she was watching videos from her childhood. Even the smell made her sigh deeply.

"So where is the office of the Edward Gibbon Chair?" Keith asked, oblivious to the nostalgia trip that Alice was on.

"This way," Alice said with more confidence than she felt. "Is anyone looking at us?"

"Yes, but not because they recognize you. They're only staring because we look odd. Come on, let's get this done quickly."

Paul Hopper had almost reached that long sought after level of professorial nirvana – he almost never had to speak to students. He only met with students in his office by appointment, which were presumably made via carrier pigeon or telegram, whichever was the most inconvenient. The few young men and women who wandered into his office often wondered how they had gotten there, or in fact, what subject the Professor actually taught. At times it seemed to be some sort of linguistic history, at other times it was anthropology, and some occasions it seemed to be medieval statistics. Paul Hopper was essentially a man paid to live inside books, an idea reinforced by his office, which was full to bursting with books of every kind. The University had tucked him away in a quiet hall at an obscure end of Christ College, and the dusty historical tomes that filled his shelves spoke to the very ideals of the University system – that change is always bad, and the more you can resist it the better. Indeed, there was very little in the room that would have been out of place in 1945, and a good deal of that would have been antiquated even then. Unfortunately for Paul, today was the day the future was going to come crashing in on him.

Alice Anderson probably could have found a politer way to enter the sacred hall of a learned professor (knocking might have been a start) but desperate times called for desperate measures and politeness didn't really strike her as the most useful tool right now. Having located the Professor's office at the end of a lengthy hallway, Alice grabbed the handle, and strode in through the door as if it were her own.

Professor Hopper, knee deep in a book on the art of Roman cement making, looked up. "Hello?" he said, placing the handsome volume down on his roll top desk.

"Professor Hopper?" Alice asked, stepping into the room. She was followed by Keith, who took off his aviator's hat and humbly held it in his hands.

It might be imagined that having achieved a certain level of acknowledged brilliance, the holder of the Edward Gibbon Chair would instantly recognize who Alice was, and have deduced why she might be there. This, unfortunately, is a position that can only be described as "winningly naive." In fact, Paul Hopper obviously didn't have the foggiest twinkling who Alice was and looked up at her rather bewilderingly. "May I help you?" he asked, struggling with the words.

Alice could see that the Professor was perplexed, so she took off her hat. "My name," she said, "is Alice Anderson."

The Professor didn't answer right away, but seemed to look around the room. Alice saw him glance at the telephone. "Yes," he said quietly. "Yes, you are."

Alice did her best to speak warmly. She didn't want to frighten the Professor, but she needed him to know that she meant business. She pulled up a straight-backed chair and sat directly in front of him.

"I gave a talk last week at the Royal Astronomy Conference," Alice said. "A talk I'm sure that neither one of us will forget."

Professor Hopper nodded. "Indeed not."

This time it was Alice's turn to glance at the Professor's phone. "I know you want to ring for the police, and in a moment, I'm going to let you, but before I do, I need to ask you something, if I may."

"Certainly," the Professor said.

"What was a history professor doing at the Royal Astronomy Conference?" Alice asked.

Paul Hopper looked at her. Alice very much got the impression that the phrase 'stiff upper lip' was floating through his mind. "I usually tell students who burst in to make an appointment. I don't suppose that you would like to come back another time?"

"I'm afraid not," Alice said. She leaned into him. "Someone killed Malcolm Oliver, and I need to know why. Now I'm not saying that you know who did it, but I think that you know something. Something you might not have told the police."

"I came to your conference because I was invited by Malcolm Oliver, shortly before his death," Paul Hopper admitted.

Alice nodded. "How did you know Malcolm?"

"He came to me, about a week before he died," Professor Hopper said. "He was looking for information."

"Professor," Keith said, "do you mind picking this up a little? We've got a triceratops waiting in the car."

Paul Hopper stood up. He looked around the room, peering at the bookshelves with a keen eye. "Do you know how many versions of the story of King Arthur there are?"

Alice certainly didn't know the answer to this question, if in fact there was one. "Hundreds?" she suggested.

"The better answer would be thousands," Paul Hopper said. He stared at a shelf behind him. It was filled with several paperback books that looked like they had been through the Boer Wars. "The story has been done in every conceivable manner. Malory, White, Walt Disney, to name a few. A heavy metal guitar player did a version on ice in the seventies. There are cartoons. There are musicals. I've always been partial to the Monty Python film myself. I was interviewed last year about King Arthur for an American television program. It was one of those programs where they talk about what the 'real' King Arthur would have been like. Do you know how many references to King Arthur are reported to be based on historical fact?"

Alice shook her head. "I have no idea," she admitted.

The Professor took a book down from the shelf that he had been staring at. "There are two," he said. He flipped through the pages until he came to a spot that was well marked. Alice had a feeling that if they'd closed the book and dropped it on the ground, it would have fallen open to that same spot.

"This is the first," he said, handing over the book. "It's about halfway down the page, on the right."

On the page was some sort of timeline. The text was printed in two columns. The first column was in Latin, and the second in English. On the English side of the page, she read:

516. The battle of Badon, in which Arthur carried the cross of Our Lord Jesus Christ for three days and three nights on his shoulders, and the Britons were victorious.

531. Arthur and Medraut fell, and there was a plague in Britain and Ireland.

Alice looked up. "That's it?" she asked.

Professor Hopper nodded. "That's it." he said.

"Not very long, is it?" Alice said.

"It's called the Annales Cambrae," Professor Hopper explained. "Every student who comes in and asks me about the *real* King Arthur, that's what I show them. Two lines in a one-page timeline, written six hundred years after the events in question. As you say, it's not very long."

"Did you show this to Malcolm?" Alice asked.

"I did," Professor Hopper said. "It did not spark his imagination."

"You said that there were two historical documents," Alice said. "What is the other one?"

"The other one is lost," Professor Hopper said. He took the book back and started flipping through the pages. "It disappeared in the nineteenth century. Probably destroyed, although nobody knows for sure."

"Destroyed?" Alice repeated. "What was it, a letter, or a book or something?"

Professor Hopper shook his head. "Neither," he insisted. "It was a cross, reported to have been recovered from the grave of King Arthur in the twelfth century. There isn't a photo of it, but at one point somebody drew a picture." He turned the book around again and handed it to her. Alice looked at the sketch:

"What do you think?" the Professor asked.

Alice didn't know what to say. Fortunately, Keith did. "It's a fake," he insisted, looking over her shoulder.

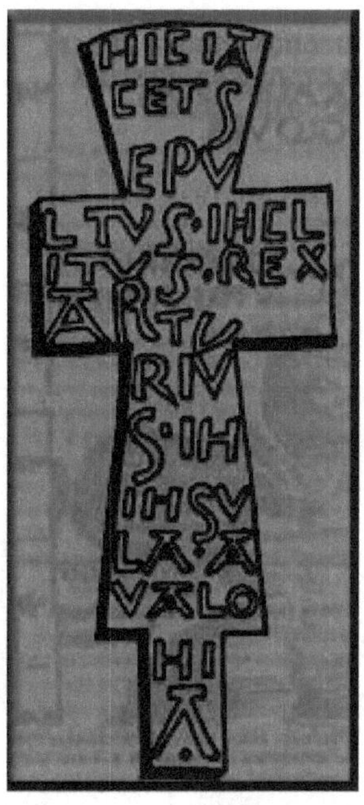

"Right," the Professor agreed, "and not even a very good one. No sixth century King would have been buried with a cross and the writing is obviously from the wrong era. The abbey was in financial trouble at the time and the moment that King Edward found out that the Once and Future King had been found, he thundered across the kingdom, purse in hand. Even monks have to pay the bills."

"Did you tell this to Malcolm?" Alice asked.

"I did," Professor Hopper admitted.

"And did it *spark his imagination?"* Alice asked.

"Like a match over petrol."

"What did he want to know?" Alice asked.

"Everything I knew, which wasn't much. As I said, it's been missing for two hundred years. Supposedly it was about ten inches long and made of lead. Although the drawing is quite detailed, written accounts suggest that there might have been a different wording. Models based on the picture have been reproduced endlessly. You can buy them in gift shops in little towns all over Wales and Cornwall for about twenty pounds or so. None of this struck Mister Oliver as important, nor did I think it would. Indeed, he seemed to have found out as much from a casual glance from the Internet before he came to me. Then he told me something that sparked my curiosity."

"What was that?"

"He told me a story of a medieval manuscript, the journal of a monk who had been at the abbey at the time. Apparently it said that the monks *had*, actually, in fact, found the grave of King Arthur, and they did recover something from the tomb, but it wasn't a cross. The cross was forged by the monks as a cover."

"A cover?" Alice asked. "What for?"

"So that they could sneak the real item out of the country," Professor Hopper said. "Presumably to tell sell it to the highest bidder. Remember, this is the age of kings. Edward the First is trying to claim the thrones of both Scotland and Wales. If you had an opposing claim, well, the idea that you were connected to someone like King Arthur would be quite a way to turn the tables and make a claim on the English crown."

"Had you heard this story before?" Alice asked.

"No," Professor Hopper admitted, "which is what I told your friend at the time. If there had been an eleventh century manuscript like that out there, certainly I would have been the one to know. I suspected that it was some kind of online rumour, one that I simply wasn't familiar with. I told him that it probably wasn't true, and then he told me that he was giving a lecture at the Royal Astronomy Conference, thought I might enjoy it, and gave me a pass. After that, of course, he died. I suppose that you know the rest."

"You didn't tell this to the police?" Alice asked.

The Professor shook his head. "They haven't asked and I haven't volunteered. I didn't think it relevant. It's hard to view it as evidence, really. It's more of a fun story. I mean, medieval manuscripts, King Arthur, and political intrigue, who doesn't think that's fun?" he added, a slight smile spreading across his lips. He seemed to have forgotten Alice was a fugitive and that her presence frightened him. Perhaps they might get through this.

"The item," Keith said. "The item that the monks took from the grave of King Arthur. What was it?"

"The *real* item, if you will?" the Professor asked.

"For lack of a better term," Keith said impatiently.

"The hilt of a sword, of course," the Professor said. "What else?"

"Thank you, Professor," Alice said, standing up and putting her hat on. "I think that we have all of the information that we need." She turned around to leave. They were almost out the door when the Professor called her back.

"They say that King Arthur will return in Britain's darkest hour," he said, looking up at her through thick spectacles, "that he will return to vanquish our enemies with the fury of God's own thunder."

Alice smiled faintly. "I'm not sure how that's relevant, professor."

The Professor sighed. "I suppose it isn't," he admitted, "but I've always wanted to say it."

Alice smiled, and closed the door.

Keith jumped, and then he skipped, and then he strode purposefully down the hallway. "Do you want to say it or do you want me to?" he asked when they had gotten out of earshot.

"Malcolm was killed because he had found Excalibur," Alice sighed, "and when we find it, we'll find out who killed him. Come on, I'm pretty sure that Grendel is going to need a walk."

Chapter 13
China 1538

he old man sat on the porch watching the sun set behind the hills on the far edge of the valley. The hills were covered in rice fields, and had been shaped and flattened over the centuries so that they looked like an enormous curved staircase leading up to the sun. It was a little tricky to see things through the haze, but at this distance the old man could just make out peasants weeding fields on the far side of the valley. It was still spring, and the old man knew that he would be able to smell the flowers in just a few weeks' time. *'It's a beautiful day, but once the sun goes down it will be cold,'* he thought to himself. *'I should get inside and build a fire.'* The old man grabbed his cane, and started to stand up.

The most beautiful woman he had ever known came walking down the path to his house. He smiled and waved at her. She held up a gloved hand and waved back, although with a little less enthusiasm. The old man hobbled down the stone steps to greet her. As she got closer the woman tried to smile, but this was difficult to see. She was incongruously dressed all in black, including a pair of black sunglasses, and with her back to the sun she seemed to be little more than a silhouette, but the old man grinned at her nonetheless. Looking close, the old man thought he saw a forced quality in her smile, but he didn't let it bother him. With great effort, he came down the walk and threw his arms around her.

"Do you have to cover up your face?" he asked, standing on his toes so that when he embraced her he looked almost as tall as he did. "Your eyes are so beautiful."

"The sun was bright," she said, removing her glasses.

"So it is. My neighbours, on the other hand are not. You have your mother's eyes. Take off your glasses so that I can see them."

His daughter stuffed her sunglasses into the pocket of her overcoat. She tried to smile, but it didn't take, and there was no hiding the truth now. The old man could see the sadness that only a moment ago she had been able to hide. He wondered if it would be better to draw out the sadness like poison from a wound, or simply treat the issue symptomatically, like a fever or a cough. "There. Now I can see your mother," he said, ignoring both impulses and choosing to make himself happy instead.

"You could try a photograph," his daughter suggested. "I have several."

"Then I would have no reason to smile so broadly when you come to visit. Besides, photos would make the neighbours suspicious. They would think that I was a witch, and stories of how I had captured a beautiful princess and held her inside a magic painting would spread across the kingdom."

"Mother wasn't a princess," the woman insisted.

"No," the old man said, "but the story of the pediatrician from California who was trapped in a painting would be a tougher sell.

Come on in, we'll have a cup of tea. You can help your old man make a fire."

While the exterior of the house had a very traditional ornate Chinese roof that implied a certain level of wealth and power, the interior would have been sparse even by prison standards. A tiny cot and a little cupboard lay across the room from a little hearth, and a handful of cooking utensils hung on the wall. Beyond that, there was almost nothing. His daughter, dutiful as always, found a hook by the door and removed all her accoutrements – hat, topcoat, boots, and sword. She sat down on the wool rug, which was the only thing to sit on.

"Comfy?" her father asked, sitting down beside her.

"I'm surprised you indulged yourself so luxuriously," the daughter commented dryly.

"We all atone for our sins in different ways," the old man said. "I don't need much, and I like it here. The past is suited to old men."

"My house would suit you better," his daughter insisted. "The guest room has a beautiful view of the bay. There's a lovely garden, and you could go and see a doctor."

"The bay is never more beautiful than it is in my mind. I have a lovely garden here, and the doctor will only tell me that I'm dying and I should quit smoking. I've given the same advice many times during my career. Doctors make poor patients."

"If treatment would spare you pain–"

"Nothing will spare me pain, not entirely anyway. You didn't come all this way to hear an old man complain about his problems. Something is bothering you, I can tell."

His daughter pressed her hands against her head in the same way that she did when she was nine. "There's so much to tell you, I don't know where to begin."

"Then don't."

The young woman raised her eyebrows.

"Have dinner with your father. Then take a walk with me. Look at the stars and tell me how your cousins are doing. Let your troubles go into remission, at least momentarily."

This was not a bad suggestion, but it was not one his daughter could take him up on. "I must overlook the murder of an angel in order to save a demon," she blurted out, "and I don't have the stomach for either."

The old man stood up. He grabbed the flint and steel, and began to spark the fire. "I spent my life treating the sick, so I would have to say 'saving the demon' is the better part of the bargain, but I imagine that if things were that simple than you wouldn't be here."

"If I were doing an internship at Saint Francis, I would agree with you, but this isn't a residency. It's a war."

"Is it?" the old man asked.

"It could be," his daughter insisted.

The old man struck at the flint and steel. "They say that the Mother of Time has been found," he said.

His daughter nodded. "I saw her with my own eyes," she admitted.

"And which was she, the angel or the demon?" the old man asked.

His daughter didn't answer, but looked down at the floor. She seemed to collapse into herself. Her father sighed. "When we became time travellers, we did it for the adventure, and the excitement, and the opportunity," he said. "I don't think we did it to make the world a better place for our children."

"A comforting admission, but not one that helps me out of my current situation," his daughter replied.

"If you are looking for advice, I would suggest doing whatever involves giving me grandchildren, but I am old, and this is a self-serving argument."

His daughter's smile was unmistakably bittersweet. "I'm afraid that grandchildren may be a little way off," she said.

"A pity. What happened to that nice young man that I met awhile back?" he asked.

"The less said the better," his daughter admitted.

"I'm sorry. What is it that you really want to know?"

"I suppose I want to know how you set your moral compass when causality has broken down? I could kill someone one night and then have dinner with her the next."

"I take it that you're leaning towards murdering the angel," the old man said. He struck the flint once more and the fire sparked. He blew on it vigorously.

"It seems the lesser of two evils," she admitted.

The lesser of two evils is still an evil that you have to live with," the old man said. "Perhaps you'll do your penitence in a little house like mine."

"WHAT WOULD YOU HAVE ME DO?" his daughter screamed. She was obviously agitated. She had come to him looking for answers, just as she had when she was a girl. Back then, ice cream usually solved the problem. It was a little more complicated these days.

Her father replied, "When I did my residency in Oncology, we used to have an expression: *'Make sure that you know everything.'* If you don't know everything, you're just making a lucky guess."

His daughter seemed satisfied with this. "Okay," she said. Her tone was reluctant, but firm. "Trust in the Laws of Time?" she asked, repeating an oft-used phrase of his.

The old man laughed. "Trust in the Laws of Time," he repeated. "Whatever you do, I will be proud of you."

A light breeze blew in and the fire started to spread. There would be no stopping it now.

Chapter 14
An Unexpected Turn

"Excalibur," Alice said blankly.

They had retreated back to the car, where Grendel had greeted them lovingly with great sweeps of his tail. They had pulled out of the university parking lot just a few steps ahead of security, who were responding to the report of a group of students who insisted that they had just seen a happy-looking triceratops staring out of the window of a silver Jaguar. Keith had brushed past two puzzled-looking security guards, shouted 'Weird, isn't it?' and hopped into the car without any further explanation. They found their way quickly to a wooded grove, where Grendel was noting with some disdain how few other dinosaurs had marked their territory in the area.

"Excalibur," Keith repeated. "Well, I must admit – wow. It would be the lord of the knick-knacks."

Keith was obviously excited, but Alice's mind was more of a blur, as much as because of what her *sister* had said as the thought that Malcolm had been killed over a medieval sword that positively *couldn't* exist. After everything she had seen, the thought of meeting Lancelot and Guinevere didn't seem that out of the ordinary, but her sister behaving like a rational adult, *that* was something. She tried to remember her sister's words exactly.

"I don't know when you're coming back this way, but when you find him, and I know you will, I want to see him. I think it's important."

That was what her sister had said. What did that mean, exactly? Who was the person that Wendy had wanted to meet? And why would she need to ask so politely? At the time the obvious answer seemed to be Keith, but now she wasn't so sure. For one thing, Keith didn't need finding. For another Keith had rescued her from a life behind bars at least half a dozen times. Certainly if she had told Wendy about him, Wendy wouldn't have to ask for special permission to meet him, as if it were some kind of favour. And that was another thing – Keith had said that because of the rotation of the Earth, the present was always rolling forward. (Alice remembered it clearly, as it was one of the few things he had said that made sense.) It definitely seemed as though Alice had talked to Wendy in the past couple of days, but Alice had spent the last week in San Tiempo. She hadn't been back to the present until today, and she didn't have any way of talking to her sister when she was on the island. How was it that she had talked to Wendy? And why? For that matter, why had she lied to Keith about what Wendy had said? Although the impulse to want to explain things to herself first was perhaps understandable, certainly she *could* have told him, but why did it make her so nervous?

She supposed that the underlying concern behind all of these questions was the thought that Wendy hadn't been talking about Keith at all, she had been talking about the killer, the shadowy figure in the background of Alice's life, whoever it was. Again, this fit what Wendy had said. *"I don't know when you're coming back this way, but when you find him, and I know you will, I want to see him."* She had followed that up by adding, *"I think it's important."* However, this also had its problems. For one thing, if Malcolm's killer was found, it wouldn't be up to Alice whether or not Wendy got to see him. Certainly there would be a trial, and if there was, Wendy could attend, but that wouldn't be up to the two of them to sort out. Perhaps Wendy was trying to make a show of support, stating that she *would* attend the trial when the time came for that, but that still didn't explain how Alice had gotten in touch with her sister in the first place, if in fact she had. Perhaps someone had been impersonating Alice and had given Wendy a call? No, that didn't seem likely either. Even at her most inebriated, Wendy would have recognized her own sister.

Then there was the troubling idea that Malcolm had been killed for *Excalibur*. Alice knew very little about King Arthur, but high on the list of things she did know was that the Knights of the Round Table weren't real, or at any rate they weren't *supposed* to be. Even Keith seemed to agree with that. After all, hadn't he specifically told her that he *couldn't introduce her to Merlin?* It seemed to Alice that if someone had found out that Malcolm had the sword (or at any rate, *knew* about it) they would have reacted in the same way Professor Hopper did – thinking of it as an interesting story, but nothing more. Surely an ordinary person wouldn't kill for it, if for no other reason than a simple lack of conviction. Of course, if you had been roaming through time on a regular basis, that might be a different matter.

Alice sighed. She supposed that no matter how you looked at it, time travellers had been mucking about in her life for a while now. Well, at least now she was aware of it. That was something.

"I can't figure out for the life of me why King Arthur's sidepiece ended up in the hands of your boyfriend," Keith observed.

"He wasn't my boyfriend," Alice said. "At least, not when he died."

"Clarifying your relationship doesn't explain how he got the sword," Keith said.

"It must have had something to do with his work," Alice said. "Fictional realism, the idea that a real King Arthur could actually be out there was exactly the kind of thing he was trying to prove."

"Prove it yes, but how did he *get* it?"

"I don't know," Alice admitted, then she asked the question that she had been trying to avoid asking. "Have you been to Camelot?"

Keith shrugged. "I've gone looking for it, of course. Most time travellers have, but no one has ever found it. Wherever it is, it's buried somewhere in the time stream, clouded in a layer of myth and shadow."

"Buried in a layer of myth and shadow, but out there somewhere?" Alice asked. "It's real, then? I thought you said that you could never take me to meet Merlin."

"I can't," Keith said. "Not the way that that TH White wrote him, anyway. King Arthur, Guinevere, and Lancelot don't break the laws of physics, though. Which means that they're out there, somewhere, making each other miserable in a golden age. Lost, but real. That's not really the problem, though." Keith Quick turned, and then he spun around, and then he turned again. "The problem," he said, still spinning, "isn't *where* the sword came from, it's *where* it ended up. If you had a sword like that, where would you take it to?"

Alice considered this. "Professor Hopper said that King Arthur would return in England's darkest hour."

"Then that's where we have to go," Keith said.

"England's darkest hour?" Alice said. "That would be–"

"The war," Keith shook his head. "My mother is going to kill me."

By the end of the day, they were in the middle of the Blitz.

They had arrived in 1941 under cover of darkness. This suited Alice better than the daytime time trips that she'd made before. She still saw the sunlight flicker overhead, but the empty black void of nothingness was less disturbing against the night sky. Keith complained that it was difficult to fly through, but did it just the same. He had given her the time orb to handle, saying he preferred to keep both hands free to fly. Technically, Alice had told the orb to take her to 1941, and not 'England's darkest hour,' but make no mistake, they were one and the same. It was close to eight o'clock Greenwich Mean Time when they landed. Alice had spent a few of the intervening hours finding a jewelry shop, where she had bought a nice-looking but relatively inexpensive pocket watch, the better to keep track of how long she'd been awake on days when they circumnavigated the globe at breakneck speed. As it had before, the orb glowed red and the three hands inside spun around wildly, before coming to a halt in a position that made it look like there was a tiny ballerina inside doing a pirouette.

Previously, HG Wells airport had seemed like little more than an empty hangar, but in this time period it was bustling with people, most of them dressed in olive green fatigues of one kind or another. Everybody looked like they were in a hurry, and for once nobody seemed interested in staring at Alice, which she found a relief.

"I'm surprised it's so busy," Alice remarked. "Are people trying to leave before the Blitz?"

"Trying to leave, trying to get here, trying to help out in any way that they can," Keith said.

"It must be strange fighting a war when you already know the winner," Alice remarked.

"This is the past to you, but it's the future to me," Keith said. "For many time travellers, it's the present. This is their time."

Alice looked around the room. "For many?" she asked, wondering how many people in the room had come from her own time, or from somewhere else for that matter, to this unpleasant moment in history

Keith grinned wickedly. "Well, time travellers like to be where the action is. If they didn't, they'd spend their days in Bermuda."

When they left the airport, Keith's motorcycle was waiting for them in front of the building again. "I'm sorry, but has this bike actually been built yet?" Alice asked.

"We're travelling with a dinosaur and *that's* the continuity flaw that concerns you?" Keith asked.

Alice looked up at the night sky. She noticed that the sign over the airport was obviously newer and shinier than the first time she'd seen it. She could just make out the constellation Andromeda over the airfield. It was beautiful, but there were other bright lights that were more foreboding. "I'm more worried about the bombings," she admitted.

Keith climbed onto the motorcycle. "Don't be," he insisted. "I checked the history books. There isn't another attack until after midnight."

"After Midnight?" Alice repeated. Instinctively, she took out the pocket watch and looked at it. "That's cutting it a little close, wouldn't you say?"

"Normally I would agree with you," Keith said. "If I could jump ahead a week, or a month, or a year, I would, but it doesn't work that way. We do this now, or not at all. Besides, the Professor said that King Arthur would return in England's darkest hour. This is the night before the last major bombing. If England has a darkest hour, this is pretty much it."

"I just wish that we weren't cutting it quite so close," Alice said, securing Grendel in the sidecar and climbing on the motorcycle behind Keith.

"Remember, we're not going anywhere that isn't still standing in your time. If the bombs start going off, we just stay put."

"And what if we're travelling when the bombs go off?" Alice asked.

Keith stepped on the engine's kickstarter. "Then we hang on tight and ride like the wind," he said, and the engine sprang to life. "Let's go."

Alice had made a great deal of small talk at the museum the other night, and one of the stories she had heard the most was the tale of people's first trip through time. These stories always seemed to contain the phrase "And when I got there, the first thing I noticed" in them somewhere. "And when I got there, the first thing I noticed was that the Golden Gate Bridge had fallen into the bay" or "And when I got there the first thing I noticed was the giant sloths, grazing on the hillside" and so forth and so on. This wasn't Alice's first trip through time and space, but it was her first trip to the past, and the first thing she noticed was the cars. Even though they were really nothing more than glowing headlights rushing in the other direction, you could see it. The smooth contoured lines of twenty-first century automobiles had been replaced by sharp little circles that looked narrow and strange. They lumbered by at a slow, odd pace, revealing little of the world in front of them. Even though there wasn't anything particularly dramatic about it, Alice couldn't help but marvel. *'This is it,'* she found herself thinking. *'I've really taken a step into the past. I've gone someplace other astrophysicists can only dream of.'*

As they moved into the city centre, the street lamps started to fill in the details of the era. In many ways, things were the same as they always were, or at the very least, the way Alice had remembered them when she was younger. London was old, and a lot the differences in the landscape were subtle, especially at night. Still, you could see them if you looked close. In front of them, two women in hoop skirts hurried across the street. They were being eyed by two men in uniform who were smoking cigarettes and staring at their legs hungrily. A newsboy wearing a cap and short pants stood in front of a shop selling papers out of his bag. (Alice half expected him to shout out 'Extra! Extra! But this was probably something they only did in the movies.) As they rounded a corner, Alice caught a glimpse of a movie theater marquee. The words *"The Maltese Falcon"* were displayed in big black letters.

"I can't believe we're really here," Alice shouted as she clutched onto Keith. "We've actually gone back into the past."

"The past for you, the future for me," Keith said. "I like this era, although I try not to come here often. My mother would worry."

As they rolled past the Gristle and Thorn, Alice noticed immediately that it was exactly the same, although her perspective on it had changed completely. Before it had seemed like a dark and unfriendly place, filled with strange characters in ridiculous dress. Now, it seemed friendly, welcoming, and comforting. She knew it was there in her time, which made it feel safe, and it was a connection to world that she had left behind. It was still filled with the odd mish-mash of people, but Alice was one of them now. The jacket and the bowler hat she had put on earlier in the day seemed like a strange caricature of early twentieth century outfits now. She hadn't planning on coming to this era, it was true, but even so, the Gristle and Thorn was the kind of place where fitting in made you feel self-conscious. Alice remembered something that Keith had said the first time he met he met her. "Time travellers tend to skimp a little on their research." *'I should have dressed like a proper female astrophysicist,"* Alice lamented to herself, before she realized that in this era, there were none.

They sat down at the table that Orson Welles had been sitting at the first night that Alice had arrived. The Fergus on duty came over immediately.

"Two Venutian Sunrises," Keith said, without asking Alice what she wanted.

"Very good," Fergus said. (Alice wondered if it was the same Fergus as in her time. She suspected not, though he looked and sounded the same. For all she knew the Ferguses could be immortal or something.) "Can I get you anything else?" he asked.

"I'm looking for a man by the name of Chesterfield," Keith said. "Stuffy Guy. Glasses. Usually looks like Benjamin Disraeli shoved a stick where the sun doesn't shine. Have you seen him?"

"Milton Chesterfield is over there," Fergus said brightly. "Shall I let him know you're here?"

Milton Chesterfield arrived over at their table about the same time their drinks did. He seemed to be a nineteenth century fellow.

He was dressed in a black top hat and tails, with bright white spats, and the sort of spectacles that had no earpieces but you had to pinch onto the edge of your nose. *'Good thing Keith doesn't have to wear those,'* Alice found herself thinking. *'They would slide right off the end of his tiny little nose,'* and she giggled at the idea.

"Herb—" Keith said, patting the other man on the shoulder and taking a large swig of his drink.

"Milton," Milton Chesterfield corrected.

"All right, *Milton,*" Keith said. "Do you know Alice?"

"Yes. Have we met?" Milton asked.

"I don't think so," Alice said. "I meet a lot of people these days, though, so if I've forgotten you, you'll have to forgive me."

Chesterfield shifted in his seat nervously. Alice could tell from the look on Chesterfield's face that whether he had met her before or not, Milton Chesterfield definitely *knew* who she was. He probably had some sort of Mother of Time related story that he was tempted to tell, though for politeness' sake he kept it to himself. Keith, presumably unaware of these subtle interactions, plowed ahead as though nothing was going on.

"Milton," Keith said. "Alice and I are looking for someone who might have been hoping to sell something on the black market.

Milton Chesterfield shifted his hair uncomfortably. "The black market?" he repeated. "What was it they were selling, exactly?"

"Well, I doubt that anyone would have been stupid enough to shout it out in the middle of the bar, but it was a medieval item, probably stolen, and whoever had it would have been looking to fence it for a lot of money. The item in question was last seen during the nineteenth century. Now, that's your era."

Milton swallowed. His throat looked dry. "And you think that they would have brought it here, to this era?"

"It's a reasonable bet that they would," Keith said.

Milton nodded. "Well, I did—" he began, but then stopped. "I'm sorry, would you mind if I got a drink?"

Alice thought that this might be an opportunity to ingratiate herself to an unwilling witness. "I'll get it," she offered. "What are you having?"

"Just a glass of water for right now, if you'd be so kind," Milton said. "My throat is dry."

"Sure thing," Alice answered, and she got up from the table and walked over to the bar.

"Could I get a glass of water, please?" Alice asked.

"Absolutely," Fergus said. He turned around momentarily and handed her a tall glass. She picked it up and started to walk away before a thought from the last time that she was here brought her back. "The last time I was here," she said. "I got a drink, but I don't think I ever paid for it. They never brought me a cheque, anyway. Is there any way I could settle that? I bought it in the future, so technically I haven't even drunk it yet."

"A drink?" Fergus asked. "Well, I expect that they will have put it on your tab, won't they?"

"My tab," Alice swallowed hard. She imagined the bill for a night of drinks quietly collecting interest for a century. "Just out of curiosity, when did I open up that tab?"

Fergus looked confused. "You didn't open it, miss," he said.

Alice frowned. "But you said it was *mine.*"

Fergus nodded. "That's right. Mister Quick opened it up."

And suddenly everything that happened to Alice in the past few weeks made a terrible kind of sense.

Chapter 15
Nazis

It occurred to Alice that one of the few good things that had happened to her lately was that she had developed a good sense of bravado. This was good, because what she had to do next absolutely terrified her. She took a sip of water and walked back to the table. By the time she had gotten there, Milton Chesterfield had walked away. "Where did he go?" Alice asked.

"He went to the bathroom, said he wasn't feeling well. It's just as well. He didn't know anything. He said he had heard a story about someone who had found Don Quixote's lance or something, but obviously that's not what we're looking for."

Alice technically heard this and she knew that she had to respond, but at the moment she was completely distracted. Keith had left his leather satchel on the floor. It was lying open. She couldn't see the keys to the motorcycle, but…yes! The Houdinometer! Keith's weird lock-picking gadget. That would work, but could she reach it? She stuck her foot out, and slowly started to drag the bag over to her side of the table. "The Lance of Don Quixote," she mumbled without inflection. "Pretty exciting."

"What?" Keith asked. "Oh, yeah, I guess. If you're into that sort of thing."

Alice kept dragging the satchel towards her side of the table. "It's not really in the same league as Excalibur, is it?"

"No," Keith said. He took a swig from his drink. He didn't seem to notice that she was slowly pickpocketing him. "*Excalibur,* now that is something."

Alice had to be very careful here. The bag was almost all the way to her side of the table. She moved ahead with the next part of her plan. She reached across the table and grabbed Keith's hand. She turned it over, pretending to be studying his palm. There! On his ring finger, a dark red line as straight as an arrow, with a smooth patch just underneath it. "Excalibur would make an excellent addition to the museum," Alice said.

"Excalibur is everything I got into collecting objects for in the first place," Keith admitted.

"Would you *kill* for it?" Alice asked, looking down at his hand.

Keith looked surprised. "*Kill for it?*" he repeated. "No, of course not."

Alice looked directly into his eyes. "What if the man who had it was in love with your wife?"

Keith stared at her. His eyes betrayed nothing, which in Alice's mind was as good as an admission of guilt. There wasn't the slightest trace of shock, or anger, or bewilderment, or for that matter, shame. Alice could only imagine that his heart was pure ice.

Alice gripped his hand tightly, staring down at the red mark on his ring finger. "You take your wedding ring off while you're around me, but the band still leaves a mark."

Keith pulled his hand away. He stuck it in his pocket and pulled out a silver ring with little golden gears on it. "What gave it away?" he asked.

"The night I first came into the bar, I never paid for my drinks. I inadvertently put them on my tab, which, as the bartender just informed me, is actually *your* tab. But there were other things too. When I almost got caught by the police you knew all about my sister, even though I never told you about her. Then, at the airport, you told the girl at check-in that you'd be staying at a hotel, and she looked at you bug-eyed. Normally, of course, you'd stay with me."

"Actually, normally *you* stay with *me*," Keith insisted, but Alice pretended he hadn't said anything.

"You said that Malcolm had contacted you, but you were vague on the details. He must have wanted you to tell him whether or not the sword was real. Was that it?"

Again, Keith didn't say anything. Somewhere in the back of Alice's mind, she became grimly aware that the bar had become very quiet.

"Did he tell you that he and I used to date, or did you know that already? Maybe he mentioned something about hoping that we'd get back together. So you went over to see him. How am I doing so far?"

Keith didn't respond to this. He wasn't even looking at her now. His breathing had become laboured and there was a wet look in his eyes.

"He must have invited you into his flat, because that was where he died," Alice concluded, "and you got angry and shot him, except that he didn't have the sword with him, so you're still looking for it. What did you do, shoot him with James Bond's gun? That seems like your style. Probably nicked it from the museum!"

Keith swallowed. He looked like he was working hard to think of something to say to diffuse the situation. "We've been married for three years," he said. "I didn't want to mention it before, because you weren't ready yet."

Alice's temper erupted like Mount Vesuvius. "We were *never* married. Maybe *you* were. I never was. Whatever alternate universe version of me you married apparently wasn't bright enough to figure you out. That's not me. I know what you are, and Malcolm did too."

Keith gave her an angry look. "Malcolm isn't–"

But Alice didn't get the chance to find out what qualities Keith thought Malcolm lacked, since at that moment she flipped the table up and over into Keith's face, causing a tumult and knocking Keith off balance. This was a decidedly calculated gesture. While Keith was distracted, Alice bent over and grabbed the Houdinometer. As quick as lightning, Alice was out the door of the bar and headed around back to the alley, to where Keith had parked the motorcycle.

"Nark!" Grendel called out happily as Alice ran around the corner, but Alice didn't pay him any mind. She was in much too big of a hurry. She knew absolutely nothing about how the Houdinometer worked and knew only marginally more than that about motorcycles. She sensed intuitively that if she was very, very lucky, she might have upwards of ten seconds to figure out how to use both. She hopped on the motorcycle and put the Houdinometer down over the ignition. Fortunately, the first part was easy. The little silver beetle-like mechanism affixed itself over the ignition, whirring and clicking until it was firmly in place. Alice turned the Houdinometer like a car key, which caused the motorcycle to make a groaning noise. *'Clutch,'* Alice thought to herself. She grabbed the left handle of the motorcycle and gave it a squeeze. Nothing happened. *'Kickstarter,'* she realized. She kicked downward in the manner that she had seen Keith do earlier and the engine sputtered.

Just then Keith appeared out the back of the bar. "Alice!" he shouted. "Wait!"

But Alice wasn't interested in listening. "Too late!" she shouted back. She gave the motorcycle a second kick and the engine sprung to life. She rounded one corner and then another. *'Every time you turn one corner, I turn two,'* she thought. Only Grendel looked back, giving the air behind them a disappointed sniff as they pulled away. The motorcycle went so slowly that if Keith had possessed even as much as a skateboard he could have caught up with her. Alice knew that the bike had gears, but wasn't really sure how to operate them, so she gunned the engine in first, topping out a speed just beyond that of a bicycle. She pulled around toward the main entrance to the building, convinced that Keith would be running after her, probably screaming her name. She didn't want to hear him. It had taken every fibre of courage she had had just to make it this far, and now all she wanted to do was run, run to the far ends of the Earth. She wanted to run back to New York, to Ithaca, and to her fellowship. She wanted to go back to where everything made sense. She missed her world, where everything was predictable and governed by the laws of the Universe as Alice understood them. She wanted out of this strange world where everything seemed touched by magic and chaos.

The severe-looking Asian woman turned the corner in front of her.

Alice was so shocked that she let the motorcycle come to a halt. The woman was coming down the far side of the block. She was roughly forty metres from Alice, but there was no denying that it was her, even in the dark. She had removed the dark glasses, but she still had on the same large black hat and overcoat that she had had on the first time that Alice had seen her. The Asian woman stopped dead in her tracks and raised her eyebrows. It was clear that she was just as surprised to see Alice as Alice was to see her.

Alice was so angry that she wouldn't have thought twice about running the woman over just out of spite, but then she was distracted by two events that happened almost simultaneously. The first, and least significant, of the two events was that Keith came bolting around the corner, shouting out Alice's name and running down the street towards her. The second thing was that the air raid siren went off.

Keith had said that he had checked the history books, and that the next bombing was some three hours off, but apparently no one had told the Nazis. Grendel tucked himself down in the sidecar, apparently scared by the noise. Alice gunned the engine, and took off into the night.

'At least the police aren't chasing me this time,' she thought as she turned one corner and then another. Somehow, she found her way to the gearshift underneath her left foot. She ground the gears, but somehow figured out how to shift into a higher gear and sped away at a faster pace. Alice had no real idea where she was going, left was as good as right. She just needed to run, run and get back home.

"The time orb," she remembered suddenly. "It's still in my pocket." Keith had made her hang on to it again during their last trip and Alice had stuck it in the pocket of her coat. "If I use it, I can get back home," she thought. She wondered what would happen if she used it right here on the street. Given the amount of Earth spinning that seemed to go on when they did it in the air, this probably wasn't a good idea. "I need to get up in the air," she thought, wrenching the motorcycle in the direction of the H.G. Wells memorial airport.

It was amazing how fast the bombs came in and how little time Alice had between the moment the sirens went off and the moment that the world came crashing down around her. The first wave came in behind her. These sounded like fireworks. Alice couldn't see them, but she could make out the flashes reflected against the night sky. It was scary, but Alice was pretty sure that she could handle it. She ground a few more gears and sped off to the east.

The second wave of bombs landed to the left of her, perhaps a mile or so off in the direction of the Thames. These sounded closer, and the explosions had the unpleasant cacophony of gunshots at close range. By now, Alice had gotten the bike up to a fair speed. She was barreling through the streets, moving out of the city proper and heading into the quieter neighbourhoods. She felt certain that she could make it to the airport, if she could just hang on.

The third wave of bombs came right down on top of her. An explosion that felt like the eruption of Krakatoa took off the top floor on the right hand side of the street, leaving a hole in the facade the size of a football goal and showering the street with a pile of rubble. Alice had just barely dodged this when another blast came down directly behind her, knocking her bowler hat into the street and shaking the bike violently. A third landed directly in the road right in front of her, blowing a hole in the street and throwing up chunks of brick and asphalt. Alice gripped the handlebars and swerved up onto the sidewalk to avoid hitting the newly made crater. This shook the sidecar considerably, causing a frightened yelp from Grendel, who was still huddled in the bottom of the sidecar, and was trembling considerably. Still, they were moving forward, and after going around a lorry, they were back on the road again.

'I've seen this motorcycle in the future,' Alice thought. *'I don't suppose that means that I'll be safe.'* Unfortunately, Alice knew that it did *not* mean that. Right now World War Two was the present and even an Allied victory wasn't even assured. Still, it meant that surviving was possible, and that was something. At times the bombs drifted away, and at times they seemed to be almost on top of her, but Alice pressed forward. As frightening as the Nazis were, Alice knew that Keith would be behind her, and she knew that she had to stay ahead of him.

H.G. Wells Airport was completely empty by the time she arrived. (Apparently even time travellers had the good sense not to fly away in the middle of an air raid.) Alice helped Grendel out of the sidecar and ran into the building.

The hangar was empty. The only sign of life was a Fergus, who came running up in a grey jumpsuit and stared at her with his large, ping pong eyes. "Please, miss," he shouted in an American Midwestern dialect. "Please, miss, how can I help you?"

"I need a ship," Alice said.

The Fergus's already big eyes bulged outward. "Miss Anderson, you can't, the Nazis–"

"Are honestly the least of my problems, please. I need a ship."

It is a curious fact about human beings that they will run full tilt at a brick wall if they are being chased by an angry rhinoceros. It might be argued that as a lifestyle, running at a brick wall has a surprisingly low quality of life, with an astonishingly short life expectancy, but that doesn't matter. Humans will do what it takes to survive, and if running at the wall allows you to live right up until you hit it, so be it. At that moment, standing in the hangar, Alice hit the proverbial brick wall. She had been running towards it the whole time, but she had been too busy worrying about the rhino to see it.

There were a number of different flying machines there. At first glance, Alice saw a B52 bomber, a Wright Brothers plane, and something futuristic that looked like a flying car. They were all wonderful to look at, but they all had one basic problem – Alice didn't know how to fly any of them. She looked at the Fergus, and tried to express with her eyes how terrified she was. "I don't know how to fly a plane, but I need to get out of here," she said. "Is there anything you can do? Please."

The Fergus shook his head and sighed. "Well, there's something out in the field, ma'am. I suppose you could take it, but it's on your head."

Alice and the Fergus ran through the hangar to the door on the far side, leading out to the landing strip. There, out on the tarmac, was a bright blue dirigible with golden stars on it. It was the same one that Alice had seen back in the present, on her first trip as a time traveller.

"It's full of hydrogen, ma'am," Fergus pointed out. "If the Nazis shoot it, it'll go up like a roman candle."

This was a fair point, but Alice didn't have time to argue just now. "It's dark, and it's painted with a pattern of the Moon and stars. The Nazi's won't even see it," she insisted.

The Fergus nodded. "If you insist," he said. Alice scooped up Grendel and climbed into the dirigible. A thought occurred to her. She turned to face the Fergus. "You knew I would be coming for this, didn't you?" she asked.

The Fergus nodded. "Yes, ma'am," he said, solemnly bowing his head, and untying the rope that kept the ship held to ground.

Alice decided that she probably didn't want to know any more about that. She turned around to face the dirigible, working out how to take it into the sky. Strictly speaking, she was not overly familiar with the concept of dirigibles. She knew a little about blimps, and she had taken a ride in a hot air balloon once a few years ago, but she certainly wasn't an expert on either. She remembered the hot air balloon having a small, sturdy gondola, and she knew that blimps were larger and seemed to have some sort of interior cabin. The dirigible seemed to be a hybrid of these two. It had a large open deck that looked a like the bridge of a wooden ship, with a number of sandbags all around the edge and a large iron contraption on one side. It seemed to be a steam engine, probably one from the nineteenth century, maybe earlier. Alice was certain that there was no way she could get the engine moving, but the sandbags were easy enough. One by one, she grabbed the bags and began heaving them over the side. It was slow work; the bags weighed at least fifteen kilos each, but slowly, an inch at a time, the dirigible started to rise into the air. It was up a foot, and then two feet. Little by little, Alice was getting away.

The dirigible was six feet in the air when the inevitable happened. How he had done it was a mystery, but Keith came running out of the back of the hangar. "What are you doing?" he shouted.

'I suppose I should have expected him to show up,' Alice thought. "You're too late!" she shouted.

"Are you actually flying that thing into the middle of the Blitz?" he shouted back. Alice didn't answer, but dumped another sandbag. Keith ran out and grabbed a rope dangling from the dirigible's platform. He held tight with both hands, and dug his heels into the ground.

"Let go!" Alice shouted.

"You're still my wife!" Keith shouted back. "I'm not going to let you get yourself killed!"

Alice picked up another sandbag and dropped it right on Keith's face.

"Ow!" he shouted. "That hurt!" He let go of the rope, just for a moment, and wiped his eyes. Alice didn't respond to this. The dirigible was seven feet into the air now and was starting to pick up speed. "You're too late!" she shouted back.

"You're still my wife!" Keith repeated, grabbing onto the rope again. His weight slowed the dirigible, but it wasn't enough to stop it. It rose up into the air, taking Keith with it. The dirigible rose above the rooftops.

Alice kept dropping sandbags and the balloon's ascent began to accelerate. She wasn't sure how high she would need to go in order to open up a hole in space and time. Keith had always taken the biplane up to stratospheric heights when they travelled through time, presumably to avoid hitting a mountain as it zoomed past. Alice certainly didn't want to crash, but if she went too high–

Nazis.

The first plane came at the dirigible so fast that it looked like a grey streak against the night sky, its engine's cracking like a chainsaw. Alice could tell that it was a lot more sophisticated than Keith's biplane; it seemed to have the silver airfoil and cigar-shaped body type common to World War Two planes, although as it went by in slightly more than an instant, it was difficult to tell. She could only imagine what the dirigible looked like, with its moon and stars pattern it would be all but invisible, and the platform behind it only slightly less so. Only Keith's legs swinging from the bottom of the platform were likely to attract any attention at all. He must look like a mountaineer, climbing up an invisible cliff side.

"Alice," Keith shouted out *"This is crazy!"*

Alice couldn't help but agree, but it seemed too late to turn back now. "You invited yourself along on this trip!" she yelled back without looking at him.

A second plane whizzed by, closer than the first. This was followed by a third that went by on the opposite side, guns blazing.

Gunfire seemed to come from the opposite direction. Presumably an Allied plane was engaging them and returning fire, although it didn't seem to improve the situation, as far as Alice was concerned. She grabbed Grendel and bent over, holding the little dinosaur close to his chest. (Grendel, for his part, urinated on her foot, but under the circumstances he could hardly be blamed.) In the distance, Alice saw a plane explode and go down. The sky rang out with more gunfire. An Allied plane seemed to be determined to take the Nazis down, engaging them head-to-head in a dogfight. (Alice wasn't to know this, but this was the Black Betty, whose Captain, Joseph P. Kennedy Junior, was engaging the Nazi planes, and was sadly on his way to doing his part in history.) A Nazi plane exploded, and the platform gave a sharp jolt to the left. From the sway and the sound, Alice was willing to bet that the airbag of the dirigible had just been perforated.

"Alice!" Keith shouted. "They're coming around for another pass! The dirigible is leaking hydrogen! You need to get us out of here!"

"I – I don't know that I can!" Alice admitted.

"Use the orb!" Keith said. "Get us out of this era!"

"If I do that, you'll be killed!" Alice said, thinking of the horrible void in between space and time. Surely you couldn't survive going through *that* hanging on to only a rope.

"It's all right," Keith said. In spite of all of the excitement, his voice sounded quietly resigned. "Save yourself."

Alice stood up and looked over the side. Keith was hanging on about two feet from the bottom of the platform, gripping the ropes so tightly that blood was running down his right hand. He looked absolutely terrified. The flaps on his aviator hat were flapping in the wind and his left ankle was twisted in a manner that looked unhealthy. Alice grabbed the rope. It took tremendous effort, but she hauled him up onto the platform. Keith smiled warmly. "Thank you," he said.

Alice didn't answer this, but put her hands in her pockets and glared at him.

"Alice," Keith started. "I–"

But as soon as he started speaking, Alice turned her back. "I don't want to hear it," she said. "I wish that I could go somewhere where time travel never existed."

A hole in space and time opened up just in front of them.

Alice hadn't been expecting this and wasn't braced for it. She was knocked over as air went rushing into the emptiness on the other side of the void. Keith was thrown to the other side of the platform. "Alice!" he shouted. "The orb!"

"I don't understand!" Alice shouted back. "I didn't open up a time window!"

"You put your hand in your pocket!" Keith bellowed. "You must have made contact with the orb!"

Alice pulled the orb out of her pocket. Keith was right. Without realizing it, she had pressed her palm against the orb while it was sitting in her pocket. It was glowing bright purple and the hands were twirling. "You need to close it!" Keith shouted. "Close the hole!"

Alice wrinkled her brow. "I thought that you wanted to get out of this era?"

"Yes!" Keith agreed. "But don't you see? You said that you wished that you could go somewhere where–"

Boom.

The Nazis had come around for a second pass, and this time the dirigible's air bag exploded. It lit up the night sky in a ball of fire. Alice was thrown completely off kilter, striking her head against Grendel's ridge plate. The platform was sucked into the empty black void just as the Nazi plane clipped the fireball with its wing, undoubtedly sending the pilot to an untimely death. The back end of the platform broke off and Keith was thrown into the air. The last thing Alice saw before she passed out was Keith, reaching out into the open air as he plummeted into the empty black void.

PART TWO
INNOCENTS LOST IN TIME

Introduction
THE ODDS

KEITH QUICK HAD DONE HIS BEST to make sure that Alice learned the ins and outs of time travel, but there was one thing that he hadn't quite gotten around to mentioning, and that was the very large amount of coincidence that seemed to creep into your life once you started mucking around in time. This isn't that surprising. When you have the opportunity to visit your own past, the temptation to leave yourself or someone you know little clues as to what to do in the present can be overwhelming. Alice hadn't considered this, so she wasn't aware of the significance of a small lead cross made in the Middle Ages for the purpose of swindling the King of England out of a whole lot of money.

The cross found its way to the court of King Henry the Second, who, barring any real expert he could bring the cross to, showed it to his friend Thomas Beckett, the Archbishop of Canterbury. The Archbishop took the cross and spent about five minutes looking it over before he declared it a fake. Things did not go well from there on out, with King Henry and the Archbishop going on to discover that they had quite a lot that they wanted to argue about. Beckett eventually went on to become an advocate for draining all of the fun out of life, while King Henry went on to send a group of well-armed men to engage the Archbishop in some philosophical debates. (For future reference, if the King of England asks you if he is in possession of something that once belonged to King Arthur, the correct answer is 'yes.')

King Henry the Second ignored the opinions of others and hung onto the trophy, eventually passing it on to his son, Richard the Lionhearted. Richard did not share his father's belief that the cross was genuine, and being a Frenchman at heart, did not much care if it was. He sold it to his brother, who perhaps understandably gave it to his son, Arthur of Brittany. The twelfth century Arthur made the cross a family heirloom and it was passed through his family for several generations, until long after the Plantagenet holdings in France had passed into other hands and the English crown had been passed onto other men.

The men who took possession were primarily French, ironically enough, although the cross made it back to Britain on at least one occasion. This was during the reign of King James the First, and at that point it was owned by a poor but proud country squire, who held on to it as proof of his family's proud ancestry. He had shown it to a British historian, before bringing it back to his home in Normandy, where he eventually bequeathed it to his son, a young man with a gambling problem. The young man would eventually lose the cross in a card game to a gambler from Paris, who would sell it in a pawn shop for one hundred francs.

From there the cross would end up in some strange places. It was on the mantelpiece of the mayor of Paris at one point, and at another point it ended up in a brothel. It hung behind a bar in Le Mans for most of a century. Then, during the middle of the Napoleonic Wars, someone believing they understood what it was, and feeling that it would be important, bought it. Then in a gesture of goodwill, rarely seen since perhaps the fall of classical Greece, they brought it to the Emperor in the hopes that it might aide in the reconciliation between the French and the British and bring an end to a long and bloody war. For once in his life, Napoleon did the sensible thing – he agreed to present the cross to Britain as an olive branch. It was promptly shipped across the channel, where unfortunately it was lost to a band of English pirates, who had mistaken the envoy for a French military vessel.

Alice would not have appreciated the long, strange route that the Cross of King Arthur had taken to get to back to the England, but it would have struck her as an absolutely amazing coincidence that roughly twenty-four hours after hearing about it, she was heading straight for the cross on a raft made of the bits and pieces left from the airship she had been flying in when the time vortex opened up and sucked her in. Coincidences are a part of life when you are a time traveller. Just how big a part was something that Alice hadn't discovered just yet.

Chapter 1
At Sea

he first thing Alice became aware of was the ocean stretching out in every direction.

When Alice was little, her father had gotten in the habit of taking her and her sister to the ocean when he needed to relax. This was after their mother had died but before Wendy had started secondary school. Alice must have been about ten the first time and she was knee deep in that golden period of her youth before adolescent awkwardness has set in. Her father, convinced that any crowd had the potential to be an angry mob, tended to take them on days when swimming would have resulted in hypothermia, but you could always stare at sea, which was what Alice liked best. No matter how ugly the day was, or how sad you were, the sea was always beautiful. It was beautiful now. Alice wondered which ocean she was floating on. Wherever she was, it was a spectacular day. There wasn't a cloud in the sky and the sun was shining high overhead. That meant that either she had been out for a long time, or they had travelled a long way. Either one was certainly possible. (Or both, for that matter.)

She had no idea how she managed to stay with the dirigible's platform. Any traces of its blue airbag with stars on it were gone. The black steam engine had broken off and floated away. Most of the sandbags were gone.

Keith was gone.

Alice wondered if he was dead. She imagined he probably was. She wondered how she should feel about that. On the one hand, he had done so many things to help her, on the other hand – no, there really wasn't any debating it. Malcolm wasn't coming back, and there was no bringing back her opinion of Keith, either. Still, she wondered if he had survived. If it were any other human being the answer would undoubtedly be no, but Keith seemed to live one of those lives where things come up all sevens. *'I wouldn't wish him dead, but I shouldn't feel sorry for him either,'* Alice thought to herself.

"Nark!" a voice called from behind her.

Alice sat up and turned around. The little dinosaur was at her feet, wagging his tail happily. "Nark!" he called out, apparently relieved that Alice was finally awake. She cheerfully scratched him on his front horn, for which he was very grateful. "Glad to see you, sir!" she said, beaming. "We've been through a rough patch, haven't we?"

"Nark!" the little dinosaur said, crawling into her lap.

"The one man in my life who hasn't let me down," she said sadly. She grabbed Grendel by the frill and rubbed him all over, giving his hindquarters an extra bit of attention.

Relieved to be alive, regardless of the circumstances, Alice took a moment to list her assets. These were remarkably slim. In addition to the sandbags, there were a few ropes left on the platform. Alice didn't know if she had any use for these, but made note of them just the same. Mercifully, her clothes seemed relatively dry. She had lost her hat, but her leather jacket was in good shape, and would keep her warm. She checked the contents of her purse. She had her wallet, makeup, keys, several ballpoint pens, roughly enough change for a diet soda, the sunglasses that she'd been wearing earlier, a pack of gum she had bought before the flight to New York, her cell phone with its charger and earbuds, a tissue packet, and a butane lighter which she occasionally used in demonstrations for students to explain why extrasolar planets are so difficult to spot.

"Well, that's something, anyway," Alice thought.

She checked her pockets. The pocket watch she had purchased was still there, as was Keith's Houdinometer. Other than the gum, she didn't have any food or water. Also, the time orb was gone.

It took a minute for the significance of this to set in. The dimensional browser was gone. That meant that wherever Alice was, she was stuck there. Well, she would have to hope for the best.

The platform crested over a particularly large wave. Alice's stomach made a point of letting her know how much it disapproved. The dirigible's platform was big enough that she didn't really have to worry about balance, like she might on a raft or a surfboard, but it was still small enough to risk being flipped over if Alice ran into a storm. *'I suppose we'll cross that bridge when we come to it,'* Alice thought, and then she sat down, waiting to die.

'Water, water everywhere, and not a drop to drink.'

Everyone who has ever been marooned at sea has found themselves thinking this phrase at one point or another. Alice thought it now. She wasn't overly thirsty, but still, how long could you last without water? Four days? Five? She didn't want to think about it. Still, there was always the possibility that she would be rescued, but of course, to be rescued, you had to be *seen*. She knew that visibility at sea level amounted to roughly 5 kilometres in every direction. That meant that any ship that might rescue her would need to come within a circle approximately 10 kilometres in diameter. This was big when compared with something like London, but when compared with the *Pacific*, well, that was another matter entirely. *'Perhaps I'm near a shipping channel,'* she hoped. It occurred to her that even if she did get near a ship, there was no guarantee that they would ever actually notice her. *'It's a shame I don't have Wendy's purse,'* she thought, imagining that her sister would at least have a small quantity of alcohol.

'At least I have fire,' she thought, checking the butane lighter and making sure that it worked. She knew that she would have to do something to get someone's attention, so she got to work constructing a signal. She started by gathering all the driest bits of material that she had. One of the remaining sand bags was tucked in a corner behind her. She dumped the sand out of it, cleaning it out as best she could. (It was still dry, which was lucky.) Once it was empty, she made a small hole in the bottom, stuffed the tissues through it, and then attached it to the longest bit of rope she could find. A quick test proved that she could swing it over her head easily. Lit on fire, it might be visible for quite a distance, provided of course that anybody was looking in that direction.

'Nothing to do but wait,' she thought, and that was exactly what she did.

There are very, very few people who can testify about how scary and uncomfortable being stranded at sea really is. All of them would be happy to tell you how lucky Alice was. Acts of genuine desperation are not uncommon. As it turned out, Alice was in the Atlantic, not far from the Strait of Gibraltar. She would have to wait for about six hours before spotting a ship on the horizon. This would be long enough that she would need to work out going to the bathroom over the side of the platform, but not long enough that she would consider doing something completely crazy. Still, for Alice, it was a very unpleasant few hours, easily as intimidating as the motorcycle chase or the dirigible ride had been. There was really nothing to do but wait, and wait, and wonder.

Alice found herself thinking about her father. She hadn't called him on her last trip because her stay was so short, and she had been feeling guilty about the decision ever since she had landed in San Tiempo. An awkwardly distant man, he tended to look at his daughters as pale reflections of his wife, and his attitudes towards both of them tended to swing wildly, if that was possible, between formally cold and unpleasantly aloof. Nonetheless, he would be worried. As far as he knew, his daughter had been accused of murder and then vanished without a trace. Alice could only imagine what *that* looked like. Although, come to think of it, she wasn't really sure *what* her father would say, exactly. She had been sure that she would know what her *sister* would say, but Wendy's behavior hadn't reflected what Alice would have considered an ordinary level of concern. Her sister's tone had sounded worried, it was true, but the words she had chosen had an odd, off-kilter quality. The phrase "Are you all right?" was noticeably absent from the entire conversation. This was not really a big deal; it was just *odd.* It seemed like such an obvious thing to say. It had been the first thing out of Keith's mouth when he'd seen her. Alice tried to put Keith out of her mind.

She thought about her mother, but this was also a touchy subject. Alice and Wendy's mother had been killed in a car accident when she was very young, and the photographs her father kept seemed much more vivid than any actual memories of her mother in person, although a few Christmases and Birthdays stood out. Like Wendy, she had straight dark hair; Alice's curly red hair had come from her father. She hoped her mother would have been proud of her. She knew her mother had never been a fan of science, but had travelled extensively during her youth. Alice had a feeling that she would have been proud of her daughter for travelling through time. It occurred to her that in just a few years she would be older than her mother was when she died; Wendy was almost older than her now. It would be a strange moment, to be sure, but this was assuming, of course, that she somehow survived her current predicament.

Just to steer her thoughts away from death, she tried to focus on her work back in New York. The Astronomy Department had been trying to find money for an x-ray telescope, and there had been a bit of a row with the physics department, who wanted the money spent on a low-level particle accelerator instead. She remembered hearing the Head of Department in Physics give an impassioned speech on behalf of the particle accelerator. He had proudly proclaimed that the accelerator would be used to *'Teach a new generation how to unlock the secrets of the universe.'* This seemed positively ridiculous now. Alice could imagine Keith going to a department Christmas party and taking the mickey out of anyone who used the phrase "quantum particles." She still didn't want to think about Keith right now, which was a pity, as up until last night, she had really liked him.

It was around sunset when she saw it. It wasn't much more than a black speck on the horizon. Alice stared at it for a while, unsure if it was anything more than a piece of driftwood, or a seaweed patch that had floated out to sea. Whatever it was, it didn't move very much. She ruled out a bird almost immediately. She had almost decided that it was nothing when the fading light caught a glimmer of white and Alice realized she was staring at a sail.

"HHHEEEELLPP!" she shouted. "HEEELLP!" She knew that this was pointless; the boat was obviously out of shouting distance, but it was human nature to give it a try. She stood up and grabbed her signal, fishing the lighter out of her purse.

Every fibre of her being wanted to light it right away, but she knew it would last for only a few minutes, and it certainly would be easier to spot the flame if the sun had gone down below the horizon. She waited for a few minutes, and then a few more. *'Now,'* she thought, as the sun finally disappeared, *'now, in that moment after the sun has gone, but before the stars come out. Now I'll do it,'* and she lit the tissues sticking out of the sandbag on fire. The fire came to life, first catching on the tissues, and then spreading to the sandbag. Alice swung it back and forth gingerly. With any luck, you could see it from a distance.

There is a long and largely undocumented tradition of brilliant people making astonishingly bad decisions. Alice, in her moment of peril, was about to follow in that tradition, and while this particular misstep wasn't going to rival Julius Cesar's feeling that the fifteenth of March would be an auspicious day for a speech, it was still remarkably bad. (Alice, being a scientist, would have preferred to go with the example of Marie Curie deciding to play with the glowing green material that was lying around the lab, but regardless of the metaphor, this is a case of stupid is what brilliant does.) Alice's stupid decision was to try and elevate her signal as much as she could. She did this by standing on what was left of the platform's sidewalls, and swinging the rope over her head. This seemed like a good idea, it got the fire up where it was easier to spot, and for a brief moment it worked, until the platform crested a wave, and Alice slipped. The rope slipped from her hand and then dropped straight into the water.

The air was filled with the sound of a young woman cursing at the top of her lungs.

"Nark!" Grendel said, happily trotting over to her.

"I'm sorry," Alice said, scratching his horn. "I'm afraid I've done us in. My survival skills are limited to ringing for the police if someone tries to break in."

And then it came to her. *'Ringing for the police,'* she thought. *'Of course.'*

Digging into her purse, Alice pulled out her cell phone. The light from the phone was a little on the pale side, but the flash – yes! That was perfect! Alice took a picture. For a moment the sky turned blue. She turned another, and then a third. She paused. She took three pictures in rapid succession, followed by three pictures timed a little farther apart, and then three fast ones again. There! An SOS signal! But would they see? She did it again, and again. It worked, but did they see it? She tried again, and again.

'*It has to work,*' she thought. '*Please, it has to work.*'

The last thing Alice saw before the sky went completely dark was a white sail twisting in the wind.

Chapter 2
THE OFFICE OF THE CURATOR

ALTHOUGH THE OFFICE OF THE CURATOR had its own bathroom, it seemed surprisingly small, mostly because it was so cluttered. Phaedra, daughter of Minos, had been born in an age when the concept of writing was a fairly new idea, and as such had never really taken to the concept of paperwork. She did her best, but try as she might she could never keep up with it, and at least once a month she would have a Fergus shovel the stacks of memos and invoices into a box, which she then moved to a desk of the head of some department or other, who more often than not used it as kindling for his backyard barbecue. The last Princess of Crete was not a fan of organization.

Phaedra was in the middle of a particularly long and dull day. It had started with a meeting of the island's Board of Scientific Anomalies. This was followed by a conference with the Unminister of Paradoxical Timelines. (Irritable man, was constantly reminding you of the oppression of those who couldn't possibly exist.) Then Phaedra had lunch with the Holy Roman Emperor Charles V, which was followed up by a quick telephone call with the Chairperson for the Committee on Wasted Time. (Wasted time became an epidemic shortly after the great apathy wars of the twelfth millennium.) All in all, it had been a very tedious day, and Phaedra was looking forward to capping the night with an elegant cocktail and a very hot bath.

There was a knock on the office door. *'Please be a group of handsome young men in tiny pants,'* Phaedra thought, allowing exasperation to flow over her for just a moment before saying, "Come in."

A tall, handsome young man with thick black hair and heavy black spectacles walked into the room. He wasn't wearing tiny pants, but was dressed in an elegant three-piece suit with a red necktie. Phaedra looked up at him and smiled with a little more brightness than she actually felt. The young man returned this look with a professional nod.

"Do you know, I was looking at a lovely volume on twentieth century civil servants," Phaedra said. "The firemen had these delightful hats. They were sort of oblong. I'm thinking we should get you one."

The young man looked at his watch. "I'm not sure that it would go with my suit," he said dryly.

"Oh, you would look charming," Phaedra insisted. "You're far too uptight, love. You need to relax – have a little fun. Have you ever been to the nineteen-sixties? They have this thing called the 'Summer of Love?' It's absolutely wonderful."

"A little before my time," the young man said. "I was seven that year."

Phaedra had been batting her eyes at Assistant Director Smith for nearly a month now, and was very frustrated by how little he seemed to notice. She had tried jokes, heartfelt confessions, bawdy stories, several low-cut togas, and an embarrassing luncheon involving a watermelon that she would rather not remember. Nothing had worked. So far he had reacted to her attentions as though she was a Greek statue, which to be fair, she had actually been the subject of on several occasions. For a woman who had once turned the head of Theseus himself this was truly a letdown and she had resolved to celebrate his inevitable pledge of undying love by taking the underside of his scrotum and shoving it up his nose.

'It isn't his fault,' she thought to herself. *'He's twenty-eight, maybe twenty-nine, and I'm forty – too old for him. Time catches up with us all, no matter how much we try to cut through it.'*

"You've had a busy morning," Smith observed. "I came by your office looking for you, twice."

"I've been talking to every self-important windbag who ever managed to escape his own era," Phaedra admitted.

"What did they want?" Smith asked. Judging by the tone in his voice, this was a rhetorical question. Assistant Director Smith very rarely asked a question that he did not already know the answer to. Phaedra knew this tactic well and resented it, especially when it worked.

"They all wanted the same bloody thing," Phaedra said tartly. "My head on a platter."

"Sure they weren't all *that* graphic," Smith replied dryly.

"The Holy Roman Emperor went into great detail about a new device called the 'guillotine.' Ghastly man."

"He's frightened," Smith observed. "They all are."

Phaedra shook her head. "I had her here. She was here, *right here,* in this office."

"I know," Smith said. "You introduced me to her briefly. Nice woman, seemed to be a little overwhelmed. Didn't have the foggiest idea who I was, or any of us, for that matter."

"Well, of course not, love. You saw how young she was. She couldn't have been older than twenty-five. She hasn't become the person we all know, not yet anyway. That's why I let her go. Not that I could have stopped her anyway."

"It was a curious decision," Smith observed, "letting her run off with Keith Quick."

"Well, who she was with wasn't really something I had a choice about. He found her and brought her in, or hadn't you heard?"

"I assume that she doesn't know who he really is," Smith remarked.

"*He* doesn't know who he really is," she snapped. "What good would it do to tell her?"

"Our enemies will try and use this against us," Smith said.

"Our enemies," Phaedra repeated derisively.

"Everybody has them," Smith said as casually as if he were talking about the weather.

Phaedra sighed. "I'm not the oldest time traveller there is, but I'm close. Did you know that? There are almost no time travellers born in the era before mine. There I was, standing in the museum foyer, trying to give advice to this woman, born three thousand years after me, upon whom my entire life depends."

"I understand," Smith said.

"Do you, love? I wonder. Did you know I met her once? Not that night at the museum, I mean. I met her years ago, in Greece. I was one of the few. She was older, older than me, and married. She seemed happy. She was patient, and kind, and explained everything, all of the strange things that were happening to me. Now, in this era, she comes to me, and I had absolutely no idea what to say. I introduced her to everyone like it was a garden party."

"Keith Quick does work for the museum," Smith pointed out. "You could have told him to leave her alone."

"If he had a lead on the belt of Orion, I could tell him to leave well enough alone. Telling him not to fall in love is a little outside the employer/employee relationship."

"Does he love her?" Smith asked.

"I don't know," Phaedra admitted. "They were young and looked happy. I suppose that they have as good a chance as any."

"Maybe. Maybe not. Other people's relationships don't have lives hanging in the balance," Smith said.

Phaedra glared at him.

"Present company excluded, of course," he added, sticking his hands in his pockets and giving a rare smile. "Even so, the present is always dependent on the past. So it always has been, so shall it ever be."

Phaedra nodded and stood up. Greeks understood the importance of looking down on an inferior and she knew that standing up showed off her figure to its greatest advantage. She was quite an attractive woman, in spite of her greying hair and middle age. "I suppose that you have some sort of news of her whereabouts," Phaedra suggested. "Otherwise you wouldn't be here."

Smith looked at his watch. "Apparently she showed up in the twentieth century. Near the time and place Keith picked her up. After that, they were seen in London, during 1943." Smith's face looked grave. Phaedra could tell that there was something that he wasn't telling her.

"What is it?" she asked.

"The Fergus working at HG Wells says that he saw Alice and Keith take a dirigible up during a Nazi bombing raid on the city. They did not return."

Phaedra asked the question even though the answered had already been implied. "So nobody knows where they are?"

"They've since disappeared," he acknowledged, looking down at the floor.

Phaedra gasped, but recovered herself quickly. "She must have survived," she concluded. "Otherwise–"

"I concur," Smith said, cutting her off before she could speak the worst out loud. "Still, it does not bode well."

Phaedra walked around her desk. She stepped as close to him as she dared. "I should never have left Greece," she admitted. "I should have been a dutiful daughter, and a dutiful wife, and stayed married to Theseus, and ignored my feelings, and done all the things that I was supposed to have done."

"If Alice Anderson doesn't become the Mother of Time, you may get your wish," Smith pointed out. "Consider yourself lucky."

Phaedra shook her head. "That isn't what I want. You know that."

Smith raised an eyebrow. "What is it that you want?"

Phaedra gave him an exasperated look. "What I want is to roll back time, and I can't. I can jump over it, change its course, move it around. We can do anything but make it roll backward, which I suppose is why I let Alice go. She has to achieve her own destiny, and I can't interfere. You said so yourself – so it always has been, so shall it ever be. Now come on, I have a meeting with the Undersecretary for Island Affairs, who is probably going to want to do a whole lot of shouting. You can come with me, and help me calm him down."

Chapter 3
The Ship

For a *long, long, time* Alice sat in the darkness, taking pictures of the night sky. If the boat was still there, she couldn't tell. She could only hope. Around the time that the Moon found the middle of the sky, she started to think that maybe this was a lost cause. Although she had seen the ship briefly, she also knew that she would have been very difficult to spot, even if someone was looking for her, which, of course, they weren't. Finally, after one last flash, the phone gave up and charged down. Alice had done everything that she could. Either they would rescue her, or they wouldn't.

Exhausted, she put the phone back in her pocket, lay down on her back, and started staring up at the stars. Grendel walked around in a series of concentric circles before laying down at her feet. She swallowed. Her throat was still dry. "Look, Grendel. There's the belt of Orion. I can see Betelgeuse, so we must be somewhere close to the present. We're in the Northern Hemisphere, too. You can see Polaris off in the north."

Grendel snorted and breathed deeply.

"It's funny," Alice mumbled. "For an astronomer, I haven't spent a lot of time looking at the stars. Just looking, I mean, as opposed to talking about relative luminosity data, or looking at pictures from the Hubble Telescope. I always meant to, but somehow I got distracted. Doing the podcast and finding new ways to get kids excited about science seemed more important somehow." She nudged Grendel with her leg. "Did you know that last semester I built a replica of the Voyager 1 space probe using a 3d printer and showed it off to a bunch of Girl Scouts? It was lovely. Of course, now I'm here."

Grendel sighed heavily, and indicated with a nudge of his horn that he thought that Alice's energies would be better focused on rubbing his head crest.

"I should have spent more time at the observatory," she said. "I suppose as far as regrets are concerned, though, that one is pretty small." She closed her eyes. "Maybe if I just sleep for a while–"

Suddenly, from out of the darkness, Alice heard a voice in the distance call out, "Ahoy?"

Alice sat upright with a bolt. "Hello?" she said, surprised.

"Ahoy?" the voice said again.

Alice's voice croaked when she spoke. "Help!" she called out, doing her best to project, although her voice wasn't much above a whisper. She took out the phone again, forgetting for a moment that it had run out of batteries.

"Ahoy!" a second voice shouted. It might have been a little louder, closer, maybe two hundred yards away.

"Yes!" Alice shouted. "Yes! I'm here! Yes!"

"Man overboard!" a third voice shouted. It occurred to Alice that it was an English voice – judging by the accent the speaker was from Blackpool, maybe, or Leeds. She must be near home, or at any rate, she could get there. "Yes!" she shouted, a little more confidently this time. "Yes! Yes! I'm here! Yes! Help!"

From out of the darkness, an enormous form started to take shape, appearing as if out of nowhere. A gigantic black on black silhouette. A shadow of a shadow that was consumed by midnight. Still, it was there. Someone on the ship held out a light, which gave off the warm flicker of burning oil.

"Someone throw down a rope!" yet another voice shouted.

There was a splash in the water nearby. Someone had thrown down a rope.

It would take some experimentation to find. Alice would end up fishing around in the water with both an arm and a leg, and would end up almost completely drenched in the process, but eventually she would find it and grasp the rope firmly, pulling on it with both hands. *There's something odd about that,* Alice thought to herself as she picked the rope up out of the water, but she couldn't think of what it was. She was tired, and thirsty, and wasn't thinking clearly. If she had been, it would have occurred to her that usually in the water a rope would have had a buoy or a life preserver attached to it, and the fact that it didn't might be seen as a clue, but things being what they were, the thought didn't occur to her. Instead, she wrapped the rope around her waist, grabbed Grendel, and shouted, "All right, I'm ready."

The rope dug into her flesh as someone hauled her up, rubbing her skin raw. This was also distracting, and as such it didn't occur to her that the unvarnished wood of the ship's hull was strange, although she did marvel that it stood so high out of the water. However, when she reached over the side of the ship, and saw the enormous white sails stretching up into the sky, there was no doubt where she was.

Alice was on a pirate ship. There was no other phrase to describe it. It might have been a clipper, or whaling ship, or something, but Alice, being a thoroughly modern woman, couldn't see it as anything else. She stared upward at the crow's nest, trying to see if the Jolly Roger was flying overhead. A man in a white ruffled shirt and three-cornered hat was helping her onto the deck. He was surprisingly short and square-shouldered, and had the lean look of a man who had never had much to eat and had needed to work hard all of his life for everything that he had. He had a cutlass belted to his side and his clothes were spectacularly dirty. He was being assisted by another smallish man with a large scraggly mane of grey hair. The grey-haired man was missing the three-cornered hat and the cutlass, but did have an impressive jagged knife tucked into his waistband.

Now that she was safely on deck, Alice dropped Grendel and removed the rope from her waist. She found herself completely out of breath, and bent over on her knees and started gasping for air. She was happy to be alive, but it was a little tough to fathom just where exactly she was at the moment. Getting her breath, she looked up, trying to get a sense of her bearings. The strange thing about being on a pirate ship is that it looks exactly as you would have expected it to look like, even though you've never actually seen one before. Everything that Alice looked at was exactly the way you'd have thought, as if Alice had walked onto some sort of movie set. In other circumstances, she would have exclaimed how impressive it was, but she expected outing herself as being from another time would have been a bad idea.

"What," asked the man in the three-cornered hat "the bloody hell is that?"

"That," a younger-sounding voice said "is a woman."

Alice looked up. Standing over her and leaning on the ship's wheel was a tall young man with a smirk on his face. He was wearing a long black coat with tails, and was marginally less dirty than the others. He had a thick Scottish accent and a thin pointed chin. A three-cornered hat sat on the back of his head, but it didn't stop his thick black hair from falling into his face. "I know that we been at sea for a long while, but surely you haven't forgotten what a woman looks like," he said.

234

"Not 'er," the pirate standing next to Alice said. *"That,"* he clarified, pointing to Grendel.

The young man raised his eyebrows. "You know, I have no idea what that is," he said. "But it looks like the only one who ever was."

"Nark!" Grendel said, sniffing the smellier of the two pirates and wagging his tail.

"It's a dog," the grey-haired pirate exclaimed. (A deep sniff from Grendel confirmed that this pirate was in fact the stinkiest, a state of being that the little dinosaur clearly approved of.)

Pirates were quickly coming out of the woodwork. They were all were staring at the new arrivals with very wide eyes, and a few smiled at Alice with grins containing very few teeth. All of them looked very dirty, and more than a little lost, in Alice's opinion. *'Maybe I haven't been rescued by pirates,'* she thought. *'I've been saved by lost boys.'*

"It's not a dog," the pirate with the three-cornered hat insisted. "Might be a rhinoceros."

"A rhinoceros has two horns and is six feet tall," the young man observed. He climbed down off the poop deck to have a better look at Grendel. "That," he added, "is something very strange." He looked at Alice, and studied her as well. "Stranger still is what you're doing here. Was your vessel attacked?"

"As a matter of fact, it was," Alice said, smiling faintly. She knew that she would need to tell a wide variety of lies in the next few minutes, and it was relaxing to tell the truth, at least at first. "My name is Alice Anderson. I have made an incredible journey, and I'm grateful to be alive." She looked at the young man, and addressed him directly. "Tell me," she asked, "is this a pirate ship?"

This earned a round of laughter from the crew. "We should be so lucky," someone shouted.

The young pirate smiled. "We're not pirates," he said. "We're privateers."

"Oh," Alice said. She tried to sound bright and chipper about this, but the phrase *'a rose by any other name,'* floated in and out of her mind.

"Are you the Captain?" Alice asked. The young man and most of the crew laughed at this as well, and as soon as she had said it, Alice realized that it was a silly thing to say. The young man looked like he belonged in the front of the Introduction to Astronomy class Alice was supposed to have taught next semester.

"Begging your pardon, Madam, I'm only the Captain's Valet," the young man said, making a polite bow. "The Captain and his First Mate are indisposed."

"They were indisposed over the side of the ship after that last battle that we had," a voice coming from somewhere on the masts above said.

The young man looked up. "Very true, but it's impolite to say so in front of a lady. As your coxswain, I must insist that you refrain from telling this woman the details of our current predicament."

He turned to face Alice, and bowed formally. "My name is Jack Cassidy," he said darkly. "Welcome to the Black Spot."

One of the difficult things about getting lost in time, and Alice was pretty sure that she was only marginally less lost than when she had been adrift, is how very, very difficult it can be to find out what blasted year you're stuck in. It is, of course, the first thing you would actually want to *know*, but simply asking someone to tell you what year it is a really spectacular way to convince people that you're *crazy*. On her first night aboard the Black Spot, Alice found out the names of most of the crew, their location in the Atlantic, the weather that they'd been having, and the amount of time before they would come to port. What she did not know was what year it was. She wracked her brain trying to think of a way to make somebody let on, and when it became clear nobody was going to make some kind of identifiable pop culture reference, she did her best to sneak a glance at something – a calendar, a coin, the inside of a book cover – anything, but this also proved fruitless. Wherever she was, it was clear that the twentieth century seemed a long way off. Alice was pretty sure that she wasn't going to find a tube station or a telephone when she got back to the mainland. The question was: what would she find? Alice didn't know.

One thing that was sure, if Alice thought that the pirates were strange, this was nothing compared to how the pirates seemed to feel about her. After all, she had seen pirates; they were part of her cultural consciousness, which gave her a certain frame of reference, one that, while apocryphal in many respects, gave her a jumping off point that explained who these people were and what they were doing. Grendel, on the other hand, was a completely unknown entity to them, and Alice only slightly less so. It was clear that wherever they were, a woman travelling alone was something of a novelty, although this could be explained by the circumstances in which they had found her. (In one respect she had been lucky – the dirigible's platform had looked like a piece of a ship's deck, so the idea that she'd been shipwrecked was plausible.) Other details of her presence were a little harder to explain. Fortunately for Alice, Grendel was such a simultaneously outrageous and endearing figure that he seemed to distract most of the pirates from other anomalies about her that might have caused them to ask difficult questions. The little dinosaur lapped up their attention like warm milk,and the pirates gathered around him like little children on their first trip to the zoo. "He's amazing," a skinny pirate with a large nose and a shaggy mane of hair exclaimed, his eyes as bright as a schoolboy's. "I've ne'er seen his like, and I've been to Florida. Twice."

"Florida," Alice said with a slight smile. "Very impressive."

"They had alligators there that was twelve feet long," the pirate added, eyebrows raised. "They was like dragons."

"I've heard stories," Alice replied, doing her best to sound impressed.

"I can't say that I've heard stories about this creature," Jack Cassidy remarked, looking at Grendel. He was standing at a fair distance from the others and seemed to be watching the action with a certain detachment. This struck Alice as odd. She'd never met a kid who didn't love dinosaurs.

"Where did you find it?" he asked.

It was a fair, and fairly obvious question, but even so, Alice wasn't quite prepared for it, and she found herself swallowing hard before she spoke. *'I need to learn to lie, and I need to do it quickly,'* she thought to herself.

"Yeah," the pirate with the large nose and shaggy mane said. "Where'd you get 'im?" (Alice was pretty sure that he was hoping to get one himself. She imagined an era where pet dinosaurs replaced parrots among the pirating community.)

"I found him in Tasmania," Alice said. She didn't know what made her think of that, it just seemed like a spot a very long distance from where they were, hopefully one that no one had ever visited. "He's from the forest there, very rare. I don't know if I will look upon another like him."

"That light," Jack asked, "the one that you used to signal us, how did you do that, exactly?"

Several curse words went through Alice's head. "Well, a lady never reveals her secrets," she said, curtsying. Jack seemed to appreciate this and bowed politely in her direction.

"What you're wearing," he said, "it's – very unusual."

Alice had long since lost the bowler hat she'd been wearing yesterday, and the round blue sunglasses were in her purse, but she was still wearing the leather blazer and the charcoal grey dress that she had put on earlier. The dress was perhaps anachronistic, albeit in a manner that was forgivable, but the blazer clearly belonged in another era. (It also occurred to her that her hair, normally a little wild, even on its curliest days, must be an absolute disaster.) "My coat," she said. "When we were attacked, I wasn't properly dressed. The coat belonged to a sailor – in the cabin adjacent," she added quickly, thinking that it would probably best to avoid ruining her reputation in an era when such things were important. "I grabbed it because I was in my nightgown." She looked down at the charcoal dress. Could it pass as a nightgown? She supposed it might. "The man who owned this coat, I suppose he's dead now," she added, and she tried to look sad.

For a woman who could barely get through Christmas without admitting what was hiding in all the wrapped packages, this was really quite an achievement. Unfortunately, Alice's clever answer only lead to more questions. "I've never seen a woman dressed so somberly," Jack Cassidy observed, "unless she was in mourning. Have you lost someone so special that you must mourn him when you sleep?"

"I suppose that I have," Alice said. It was the second time she'd been able to tell the truth, although this time she took no pleasure in it. She thought about Malcolm. She wondered when a day would go by when she didn't think of him. Even with all of the insanity she had been through lately, she still thought of him daily. She supposed that sooner or later he would become a more distant memory. The concept both relieved and terrified her.

Her moment of contemplation seemed to satisfy the young valet and he nodded politely. "We're delighted to have you aboard, my Lady," he said graciously. "It's a little late, but we would be honoured if you would join us for dinner. "

Somewhere, in a moment long since forgotten to memory, the phrase "hard tack" had entered into Alice's consciousness. She honestly hadn't been sure what it was. It might have been something that you used to cover the roof on her house for all she knew. As it turned out, it probably would have been better used for that purpose than it was for eating, although Alice was far too polite to complain. Even with her ravenous hunger after a day lost at sea, the hard tack biscuits were a tough sell. An indelicate mixture of eggs, whole-wheat flour, and wallpaper paste, Alice would have gladly fed her entire meal to Grendel, if she hadn't been concerned that a violently ill dinosaur might not be a welcome addition to the crew. The rock hard biscuits were served with a cup of wine that appeared to be a mix of Merlot and soft dirt, with perhaps just a dash of some sort of root thrown in. She did her best to be polite and smile as she ate, since she was sure that this was the only thing the men on board the ship had eaten in weeks. They ate in the ship's galley, a tiny little room lit by an oil lamp that would not have outshone a lone Christmas tree bulb on a dark night. Still, even in the dim light, Alice could make out bright eyes twinkling in the darkness.

She knew that she was still in terrible danger – she was a woman among lawless men, in a time when women were treated as second-class citizens at best. Yet somehow she couldn't help but feel like these were little boys who needed their faces washed and their teeth brushed. Perhaps she might have felt differently if she had not had Grendel with her, but the little dinosaur had been the focus of so much positive attention that it was difficult to worry about her own welfare. (Grendel, for his part, was mastering the art of begging for table scraps, and already would have rivalled a sad-eyed golden retriever for proficiency.) Perhaps the danger was mostly in her head. After all, she had survived the Blitz. After that, pirates seemed like an improvement. She found herself starting to relax.

In the age before television and radio, men entertained themselves by drinking and telling stories. As the wine flowed freely, Alice heard a number of incredible tales – many of which might have been the true stories of real pirates or might have been the exploits of little boys pretending to be pirates. It was difficult to tell one from the other. They regaled Alice with stories of beautiful beaches, golden treasures, battles won, maidens swooned, and Frenchmen who were killed, seemingly by the dozen. Alice didn't see any eyepatches or peg legs, though, and in general it seemed that a pirate's greatest enemy was hygiene. Indeed, the smell in the little galley was quite potent, although Alice pretended not to notice. She smiled as the men related their adventures, reserving her remarks to short and mild exclamations of surprise. However, her ears perked up when one of the pirates mentioned having seen the King in London a few years ago.

"The King?" she asked, as if suddenly awakened from a dream. "Tell me, what was he like?"

"Well, I'll tell you," a young pirate with a long ponytail who had identified himself as 'Charlie' said. "He didn't look mad."

"Well, he's the King," another pirate insisted. "If 'e were mad, 'e would just blend right in with the rest of them, wouldn't 'e?"

"They say 'e's mad as a hatter," Charlie replied, shaking his head.

Alice thought of something. "Did you see his son?" she asked eagerly.

"The Prince of Wales? Yeah, 'e was with him. Nose way up in the air, that one."

"Well, he's the Prince," Alice said, trying to be objective.

"Yeah, but that don't him any better than me, do it?" Charlie insisted.

"Actually, Charlie," the bushy-bearded pirate said, "that's precisely what that means," and he took a swig of his wine.

"Yeah, but he thinks 'e's better than the King, an' everything. Thinks he's running the whole country an' all. He don't know nuthin', that one, 'cept maybe the best way to fluff his wig." Charlie grinned with derision.

It wasn't much, but Alice took the young pirate's mention of the King being "mad" and the Prince thinking he was better than anyone to mean that they were in the Regency, probably early on, judging by the sound of it. Alice had never been a history buff. Names and dates from her A levels tended to escape her, but she was pretty sure that Prince William had been regent in 1810. This would put them in the middle of the Napoleonic Wars, which made sense, given the profession of the crew and their insistence that they were privateers, not pirates. Although she didn't really want to think about it, this also fit with what Keith had told her back in San Tiempo: "As near as anyone can tell, time travel was invented by Alice Anderson in 1815." Alice would put all of this together in her head later on. In a little over a week, a dog-eared copy of The Times would confirm that it was April of 1814, and also that the American President had issued an attack against the city of New Orleans. However, all of these conclusions and discoveries would be in the future. In the present, one thought kept going through Alice's mind: *Two centuries,'* she thought. *'I'm two centuries from home. Two centuries from home, with no way to return.'*

Chapter 4
The Penultimate Problem

ondon, England, 1888

Doctor John Watson kicked off his slippers and pulled back the bedclothes. It had been a long day and he was looking forward to a good night's sleep. Watching people die all day was long and tedious work. He slid into bed, placed his pince nez on the bridge of his nose, and started to read. This, he felt, was life as it should be, and he was pleased to look up and find that his wife had entered the room. She was a proud woman, tall, and handsome, and Watson was pleased to note that she was already wearing a large green dressing gown. Watson reflected that a lesser man would have despaired at the thought of his wifecoming to bed wearing enough linen to cover a horse and he prided himself on *not* being that man.

(How Victorians reproduced is one of those mysteries lost to time. For his part, Doctor Watson had learned a great deal about human sexuality during his time at medical school and had pretty much left the knowledge there along with his cap and gown.)

"Missus Cruncher says that she needs more polish for the silver," Mrs. Watson said, sitting down at her dressing table and picking up her hairbrush.

Watson turned a page in his book and continued to read. "Very well," he replied. "Is there anything else?"

"Margaret said that her Uncle died yesterday, and she will be taking the day off tomorrow to go to the funeral, but I expect that you know that already."

"Yes," Watson admitted. "He was a patient, the poor man. Fatal bowel blockage, bad way to–"

Mrs. Watson looked up suddenly. "Did you hear something?" she interrupted.

Watson hadn't heard anything, but he put his book down out of deference to his wife. "What is it?"

Mrs. Watson's ear stretched toward the bedroom door. "I thought I heard–" she began, only she didn't need to finish the sentence, because then it happened a second time. A sharp knocking came from the foyer downstairs. Someone was at the front door. Watson rose from the bed. "I'll get it," he said.

Mrs. Watson put her hairbrush down. A look of frustration had crept into her eyes. "Please don't," she said.

Watson gave the long exasperated sigh of a husband who saw an argument approaching on the horizon. "It could be a patient," he pointed out, putting his slippers on. "Missus Burke is due in just two weeks."

Mrs. Watson stood up. She wasn't blocking the door, but she stood close enough to it that there was in implied sense of disapproval. "You bloody well know that it isn't Missus Burke," she said.

"I know," he agreed, "but it could be. You can always hope."

Mrs. Watson balled up her fists. "I'll take off my shimmy," she suggested, seriously.

Watson raised his eyebrows.

Mrs. Watson pleaded with her eyes. "I'm a modern woman. I've heard about those things that the French Ladies do. I'll try any of them that you want. Please, just don't go downstairs."

"Missus Watson!" the good doctor replied. "You're making a spectacle of yourself!" He stepped past his wife, giving her a conciliatory kiss on the cheek, turned the handle to the bedroom door, and went down stairs.

"He needs to let you move on!" Mrs. Watson cried as her husband walked past her.

"He can't," Watson said. He did not turn to face his wife as he said this; he knew it would be better if he let her have the last word. He was going to have to do this, no matter what the consequences were.

"Next time I hear something late at night, I won't tell you!" Mrs. Watson yelled. "It will probably be a burglar. Give us all a real laugh."

Watson walked down the stairs in the dark. He took pride in his role as a husband, but that he did not mean that he had forgotten his duty. His wife would always come second to the man that she usually referred to as his best patient. Watson crossed the hall to the front door, turned the handle and said, "Hello Holmes," before the shadowy figure even stepped in.

The man at the door dashed in without as much as a hello in return. Even in the dark, Watson could tell the man was agitated. "The game," Sherlock Holmes exclaimed, "is afoot!" He pointed his finger in the air dramatically.

Watson did his best not to betray any sign of exasperation. "Come into the parlour," he said simply.

The chronicles would always portray them as partners – the loyal sidekick and the genius crime fighter. Watson was responsible for this image – he had crafted it and shaped it – but in real life he knew that his wife's metaphor – the doctor and the patient – was equally apt. Watson stepped into the parlour and lit the lamp by the door. Holmes was obviously in the middle of a case, but in the dim light he looked sallow and unwell. Watson wondered whether he should grab his magnifying glass or his medical bag.

"What seems to be the trouble, old friend?" he asked, taking a seat by the fireplace.

Holmes paced excitedly around the room. He was dressed in his hunting cap and coat, a habit of his that boarded on the pathological. Everything about him, from his perfectly combed hair to his perfectly trimmed nails suggested a rigid adherence to the fastidious.

Only his manner and the red rims around his eyes gave even the tiniest hint of any lack of control.

"A case!" he shouted triumphantly. "Perhaps the most baffling of my career!"

The doctor wondered if it was too late to wake Mrs. Cruncher to make him a cup of tea. "A case, you say? Of what sort? Murder?"

"Worse!" Holmes shouted. "Murder is nothing compared to this!"

Watson nodded. "Worse than murder? What is it, then? Blackmail? Espionage? Regicide?"

Holmes games him a dirty look. "You mock me, Watson, but I am quite serious. I do believe that this may very well be the most important mystery I have ever encountered!"

"Very well," Watson said, giving his patient the benefit of the doubt. "What is it this time?"

"Someone has stolen my favourite pipe!" Holmes sneered.

Watson paled. "Tell me, Sherlock," he said, trying to sound calm. "Have you been at the cocaine bottle?"

"It was the large ivory one," Holmes said, ignoring the last question. "It has been missing for two weeks, possibly three."

"I don't suppose," Watson suggested in a very soft voice, "that you might have lost it?"

Holmes took a look around the room. "Your wife is upstairs right now. She's in her dressing gown, and she didn't want you to come downstairs. She thinks the housekeeper is stealing from you, but she knows that you're fond of the old girl, so she keeps dropping hints in the hopes that you'll catch on. She's right, by the way. The genuine Ming vase that was on the mantel last time I was here has been taken and replaced with a cheap imitation that someone bought in a shop. You ate shellfish for dinner tonight, mussels probably, it hasn't agreed with you. You've been working long hours for the past few nights, and you've been worried about your finances, and you think the problem is that *I've mislaid my pipe?*"

Watson swallowed. "Missus Cruncher has been with me for quite some time," he said, a little defensively.

"Yes, and I'm sure the missing pieces of silver and other small items that she's pilfered don't amount to much," Holmes snapped. "But you're missing the point. The point is that *I don't lose things.*"

"All right," Watson said, making a mental note to inventory the silver in the morning. "If you do not believe you've lost it, and presumably the maid didn't take it, then what on Earth do you suppose happened to it?"

"I've already told you," Holmes said. *"It was stolen."*

"Why on Earth," Watson sighed, "would somebody steal your pipe?"

"Why indeed?" Holmes asked. "It was an ordinary pipe, a little extravagant perhaps, but nothing you couldn't purchase for a reasonable price, so why steal mine?"

Watson searched for a reply. "Because it was convenient and the shops were closed?" he sputtered.

"I think not, my friend." Holmes answered. "Anyone clever enough to have pocketed it would have known my reputation, and would undoubtedly suspect that I would notice its absence and expect its return. No, Watson, I don't think that this was a simple case of pilfering. I believe that the person responsible for this had specific reasons for doing so, reasons that are not readily apparent at first glance. What do you suppose they could be?"

Watson thought that if he was ever going to get to bed, he might as well play along. "Because it's *yours*, Holmes, I suppose."

"Precisely!" Holmes shouted. He was so excited that his nose started whistling when he spoke. "I'm the greatest detective in the world. Stealing an object, even a fairly pedestrian one, from my personal residence has both professional and personal implications. It states a belief in one's intentions and abilities, I think. The thief wants me to know that he thinks he can beat me at my own game and that makes him an adversary worthy of my attention."

"All right," Watson said, doing his best to speak with a measured patience. "Who do you think took it?"

"A client," Holmes said, taking a seat in the chair opposite. "Or to be more precise, a man posing as a prospective client, who disappeared after our first meeting. He was an American and was oddly dressed. He looked like he was ready for an airship ride. Even his name was ridiculous. I was suspicious of him from the first. He had come to me on a fairly flimsy premise and disappeared the moment I quoted him my fee."

"And you think that this man stole your pipe?" Watson asked.

"I daresay, yes," Holmes said, "and I believe that he may be in league with someone else. A mysterious figure lurking in the shadows."

Watson didn't usually approve of speaking in extended vowels, but he did so now. "Sooooo…" he said, "you feel that this is some sort of pilfering conspiracy?"

"I do," Holmes said, standing up again. "In fact, I believe that this may be the beginning of an incredible quest. Come Watson, we need to find out who this mysterious Mister Quick is and who he is in league with!"

Chapter 5

A Ship on the Horizon

t was decided that as a guest, and the only female on board, Alice would be given the empty Captain's cabin, along with assurances that the Captain had not actually died in there. This was a chivalrous gesture on the part of the pirates, and Alice graciously accepted, although it occurred to her upon entering the room that her impression of what a Captain's cabin should look like had been largely informed by the animated version of Peter Pan. There was not, for example, a roll top desk and a harpsichord, which was a little disappointing. The real cabin was a fairly cramped closet, but it did have a bed, as well as a narrow but serviceable mattress, and a thin blanket.

After a long day of floating out in the great blue, Alice was understandably relieved to have a measure of safety, no matter how poor the accommodations were. She wanted nothing more than to lie down and fall into a blissful state of unconsciousness, preferably until the sun set on the British Empire. However, she knew she would sleep better if she took a moment to assess her situation. She took everything out of her handbag and coat and laid it on the bed. Everything, absolutely every item that she had on her person was anachronistic, and most of it worthless. In retrospect, there was probably very little need to carry American pennies around with her into another century, and even the useful items like the lighter and the ballpoint pens would require much more explanation than they were worth. Still, her personal effects were all that she had. Somehow she had to build a life out of the contents of her purse.

Even the money wasn't much good, unless for some reason she needed to prove definitively that she was from the future. The only item that struck Alice as being genuinely valuable was the Houdinometer that had inadvertently been left in her possession by Keith. Of course, it was so futuristic that she knew she couldn't trust to leave it where anybody else could find it. In another century, the cell phone would have been useful, but it couldn't be charged until the invention of electricity, and it wasn't like she could call anyone with it. The pocket watch might be valuable if she were to sell it, but she suspected that it wouldn't have a high market value. It felt light, which meant that anyone that might buy it would probably think that it was cheap. (To be fair, it was cheap, which made this an appropriate thing to think.) Alice supposed that she might tell a pawnbroker that it would never need winding. This was true, it never would, but it would also eventually stop working until the invention of the watch battery. (The watch also had the logo of a popular American superhero on it. Alice wondered if she could convince a pawnbroker that the stylized image of a flying rodent was some sort of emblem of her family's house. She suspected that she probably couldn't.)

All in all, it wasn't much to go on. Of course, the other thing she had was her knowledge and intelligence. She could say, without boasting, that she knew more about physics, astrophysics, chemistry, and mathematics than anyone else on Earth right now. *'I could discover the planet Neptune,'* she pondered, *'or the Andromeda Galaxy, or General Relativity,'* but even in the moment she knew it wouldn't ring true. She was a woman, for one thing. Even in her own era, male scientists were known for acting like trolls. She thought back to her last encounter with the Royal Astronomical Society; it was easy to picture the nineteenth century version as being populated with the same group of grey-haired men. It wasn't like they were going to be any better now, a century before Madame Curie and Maria Mayer. She was sure that if she tried to present as much as a new moon orbiting Saturn, they would laugh her out of the country. For another thing, she had a set of unverifiable and ridiculous sounding credentials. A twenty-first century graduate degree wasn't going to open a lot of doors during the reign of George the Third. She also had to admit that while discovering General Relativity a century early would be good for her, it certainly wouldn't be good for Einstein. Alice could picture him working as a patent clerk through the twenties and thirties, and trying to find a way out of Europe before the Nazis came to power. No, even if there was a timeline where Alice changed the future so that Einstein ended up marrying Marilyn Monroe, it wasn't fair to steal his work that way.

'I still have my wits,' she thought to herself. "And you too," she added, speaking to Grendel, to which the little dinosaur wagged his tail excitedly.

Somewhere in the back of Alice's mind was the idea that she was the Mother of Time, and that she would (or eventually might, at any rate) invent time travel, and get herself out of here, but she tried not think about that right now. It meant that there was hope that she might see the future again, but it was also a daunting prospect, as the whole idea flew straight in the face of absolutely everything she understood about the universe. It didn't seem like science, but magic, and she knew that the only way to do it was to tear through Einstein, quantum physics, and everything that she understood with a wrecking ball.

'Damned if you do and damned if you don't,' she thought.

Just as she was about get into bed (and she was truly exhausted by now, sleep wouldn't be a problem, no matter how thin the mattress was) there was a knock at the door. Alice opened it a crack. It was Jack Cassidy.

"I'm sorry to bother you, madam," he said, clicking his heels together and making a polite bow.

"It's all right," Alice said, although she was forced to stifle a yawn. "What is it?"

The young man pursed his lips and brushed his overlong locks out of his face. It seemed as though he was about to broach a difficult subject. "Are you aware of the difference between a pirate and a privateer?"

Alice sucked on her teeth. "No," she admitted.

Jack nodded. "The difference is that what a pirate does when he finds a woman on his ship is decidedly different than what privateers do."

There was a long pause.

"I understand," Alice said.

"Even so, I wouldn't want to put the men to the test," Jack added.

"I'm sure it will be fine," Alice said, after a long, heavy moment.

"The door, it locks," Jack said, and perhaps sensing the awkwardness of the moment, he turned around and walked away. Alice followed his advice and locked the door. She flopped down on the bed, and slept for what was literally the first time in centuries.

The ship never really slept. Alice heard the crew shouting on deck even in the dead of night, and from time to time footsteps went past her cabin. It hardly mattered. With the gentle rocking of the boat, Alice was asleep within minutes. Her dreams were fitful, and the culture shock of being stuck two centuries from home was an overwhelming theme of the evening. In one dream she was wearing an enormous ball gown and a powdered wig, and was being attended by Ludwig Van Beethoven. In another, Hiawatha and John Hudson asked for her help in finding the Northwest Passage. She tried to show them the way, but only ended up leading them into a primary school class room, where Keith, dressed in cap and gown, questioned them all on nineteenth century farming practices. When asked a question on plowing a field with oxen, the answer to which there was absolutely no way she could have known, he wrapped her on the knuckles with a ruler. "There are a thousand details," he shouted, "a million, and you have to know all of them," and suddenly Alice realized that she wasn't sleeping anymore.

Staring out the ship's porthole, she could see it was a beautiful day. It had been beautiful yesterday too, she reflected, only she had been too scared to really pay attention. Today the ocean was as lovely as it had been on San Tiempo. Alice dressed. The details of life on a ship are always difficult, even in the present, and the problems were compounded by the century that they were living in. This was an era of chamber pots, rotting teeth, and staph infections. The chances of a ship's concierge selling tooth powder and antiperspirant were decidedly small. Still, Alice was able to find a pitcher of fresh water, which she used to wash her face and rinse her hair, and a cracked mirror, which she used to check her reflection. With her appearance coming as close as was possible to something presentable, she found her way topside.

Alice hadn't been clear on what time in the morning the day really began on a pirate ship, but she suspected that the bulk of the crew awoke before dawn, because most of the young men seemed to be running about by the time she came up on deck. Alice's knowledge of pirates was largely confined to what could be gleaned from old movies, and as such she was secretly hoping that someone would touch on any one of a seemingly innumerable number of piratical clichés, even though she knew in her heart of hearts that this was a ridiculous idea. Still, she was a little disappointed to see that the ship was flying a Union Jack, and not the Skull and Crossbones. *'Of course, flying a pirate flag would just be asking for trouble,'* she mused. *'Maybe someone will shout 'Aye Aye Captain!' or something.'*

About half of pirates were up in the air, adjusting the sails to take advantage of the prevailing west wind. Jack was standing on the poop deck, steering the ship with a hand that was laying lazily on the wheel. He wore a black waistcoat, and there was an impressive-looking brass spyglass hanging from his belt. Alice looked at him and stifled a laugh. He looked as though he was as close to the living embodiment of Peter Pan as Alice would even see. "M'lady," he said with an oddly sincere nod. He swept his long black bangs out of his face and smiled at her.

With some difficulty, Alice managed to climb up the ladder onto the poop deck. The view from up there was beautiful. She took a deep breath and held it. It hadn't occurred to her before how fresh and clear the air was. Granted, sea air was always fresh and clear, but this was sea air that was unencumbered by pollution and greenhouse gases. Alice raised a hand to her forehead, shielding her eyes from the sun. "I'm sorry," she said, turning around and looking at Jack. "With everything that has happened, I'm honestly not sure where we are. I can tell from the sun that we're headed north, but beyond that I'm not entirely clear."

"We're headed home," Jack said, not precisely answering her question, but not completely ignoring it either. "We should sail around Brittany and reach port in Southampton in two days, if we're lucky." He turned around, not to look at Alice, but to mark the position of the sun. Alice noticed that he had pulled a pocket watch out of his waistcoat pocket. By the light of day, he looked even younger than he had the previous night. Alice wondered if he was even eighteen.

"The speed of these new ships is incredible," he said. "It's nothing to make it to the Virgins in a week, now. These ships, they are the future."

Alice smiled. *'He's trying very hard to act like a Captain. Probably because he's the only gentleman on board.'* The thought of a deeply ingrained class system made her a little queasy.

"You were saying last night that the Captain had been killed," she said, prodding him a little, in the hopes of finding out a little more of his story.

Jack nodded. His expression did its best to convey the gravity of the situation, but there was a bit of the pirate that hung around his eyes. "Aye," he said. "The First Mate, too. We lost them both in a battle with the French five days ago."

"I'm sorry," Alice mumbled.

Jack shrugged. "I cannot say he was the best of men," he admitted. "Still, he took me on, when very few others would."

Alice could only assume by his tone that she had been dead wrong about his status in the gentry. Perhaps with so many men who looked like grubby little dwarfs with dental hygiene issues, it was easy to imagine that this strapping young man was at least the son of some country squire. "I take it things were hard at home?" she asked.

"I would have to have had a home to judge how hard it was," Jack admitted. "I was in an orphanage till I was ten, then in a workhouse after that. By the time I was three and ten, I'd been on the streets of Edinburgh for a year. 'Twas the Captain who convinced me to go to sea, after he found me begging for spare change in front of a pub."

"I'm sorry," Alice said again, sounding more sincere than she had the first time.

"It's all right," replied Jack, except that it wasn't all right. The memory of begging on the street had turned his face sour. He turned back around to face the wheel of the ship.

"Without the Captain," Alice said, not wanting to prod, but not wanting to leave the conversation on such an odd note, either, "what will happen to the ship?"

Jack didn't want to face her, but stood straight. "Our pardon for acts of privateering was in the Captain's name. Without him, we must sail straight for home and turn the ship over to the Royal Navy. We must disband. This is our final voyage."

Jack looked as though the idea of starting a new life bothered him. If there was one thing that Alice had learned about in the last few weeks, it was the difficulty of making transitions. Between being accused of murder and then travelling to both the future and the past, she had certainly had an awful lot of new things to get used to. She would have liked to share her own experiences with Jack, but this was out of the question.

"What will you do?" she asked gently.

Jack still didn't want to look at her, but he shook his head. "I don't know." he admitted.

"Well, you're an experienced sailor now," she suggested. "I'm sure that you won't need to go back to begging."

"I am an experienced sailor," the young man acknowledged, "but the Royal Navy tends to frown upon associating itself with people of my chosen profession. Many of the crew believe that the golden age of piracy is over."

It occurred to Alice that she didn't have the foggiest idea what she was going to do when they got to the mainland either, but she let that slide. "There are always things you could do," she prodded.

Jack turned to look at her and smiled wickedly. "I could be a Member of Parliament," he said. "It would be just as cutthroat, but with better hours."

"You could be a doctor," Alice said. "You'd still get to be around blood a lot."

"I could be a barrister," Jack considered. "Good Lord, are all gentleman's professions this bloodthirsty? I suppose it will have to be the docks for me."

Alice would like very much to have responded to this, but at that moment the sailor up in the crow's nest shouted, "A ship! A ship! Starboard, ho!"

When you are at sea, a ship on the horizon is a little like a tiny drop of paint on a white canvas – easy to overlook until someone points it out and then impossible to ignore. Alice shielded her eyes again and looked out at the horizon. Even at this distance, she could tell that the ship was an impressive one. Its sails looked fluffier and larger than the ones on the Black Spot. It was south-southeast from where they were and it appeared to be headed towards them.

Jack pulled the spyglass out from his belt again and turned to face the ship. For a minute he stared through the glass, adjusting the lens. "Clipper," he mumbled, his voice betraying neither elevation nor concern. "Mister Tibbs, can you see her colours?"

"Red and white stripes with a blue square, sir!"

Jack spit. "Yanks," he grumbled.

The thought of an American ship momentarily hung around with no significance attached to it. It didn't occur to Alice that this might be dangerous, until she realized that this was a different era, filled with different alliances and strange, violent men. *I suppose if we're at war with the Americans, that narrows down the year, anyway,'* she thought.

"Mister Tibbs," Jack shouted, "can you see their arms?"

"I spot five cannons on the port side," Tibbs shouted.

Cassidy nodded and then he yelled, "All hands on deck!"

If the crew had seemed unprofessional or unseemly up until that point, this changed in an instant. The remaining sailors came running out from below deck, each man going to a different spot and attending to his position with a rigid alertness that suggested he would continue to man the sails, even if a cannonball had just blown a hole in the side of the ship. If anyone in the crew was afraid, their faces did not betray it. The men looked more disappointed than scared, like office workers who'd just been told that they had to work late.

'They must be brave,' Alice thought. She was fairly certain that first and foremost it would be her job to get out of the way of whatever was going to happen next. "Excuse me," she said, not being sure of how to broach the subject, "are we about to be attacked?"

Jack nodded. "We cannot be sure," he said, "but the enemy is on our doorstep. It seems likely that he will knock. I'm sorry, perhaps we should have left you adrift."

"What makes you say that?" Alice asked.

"I'm afraid this ship is rich in treasure, but poor in gunpowder," Jack admitted. "The Americans have fast ships. If they catch us, we may catch ourselves an early grave."

Alice thought about this. "You must have other weapons? Other than cannons, I mean?"

Jack laughed. "If we can get close enough to board their ship, there's a chance we can fight them hand to hand, but in a contest between a cannon and a cutlass, I think that you'll find that the cannon always wins."

"So we're in danger?" Alice asked.

Jack shook his head, his face taking on a grimace. "My lady, we are always in danger," he admitted. "It's in our nature. Today we are in more danger than usual."

"Surely there must be something we can do?"

"We have enough powder for three cannon blasts. That's all. The weapons have been loaded already, with no hope of reloading until we reach dry land."

A thought occurred to Alice, one that she was not particularly proud of. She realized that probably no one in this era would have heard of shrapnel. It was a simple rule of physics that a cannon packed with ball bearings could tear men apart in a way that a simple cannonball never could. She didn't like this idea. She was too far removed from this war and didn't feel its hatred. She couldn't see the Americans as villains, and she couldn't see the good in killing them, even to save herself. What she needed to do was come up with a plan to keep these little boys from playing at war, and she needed to come up with it quickly.

'If only there was some way I could use their own stupidity against them,' she thought bitterly – and then she thought of something. If she was lucky, it just might work. She put a hand on

the young man's shoulder. "If I can convince the Americans to leave you alone, would that be worth something?"

Jack shrugged in a manner that suggested that he did not really believe that Alice could convince a donkey that sugar cubes were tasty, much less talk a group of Americans out of firing their guns. "How exactly do you plan to do that?"

"With geography," Alice insisted. "And linguistics."

Jack raised his eyebrows. "I beg your pardon?"

Alice did her very best to look confident, even though inside she felt like hiding below deck would be a much better option. "Two underappreciated qualities of modern warfare, wouldn't you say?" she asked with a smile.

The conversation they were having seemed to be catching the attention of the crew. A few had climbed up onto the poop deck and were listening in. "And it's your belief that this will convince the Americans to leave us alone?" a dark-skinned pirate asked.

"If it works, I can get the Americans to sail away, without ever firing a shot," she insisted.

Jack nodded. "And if doesn't work?"

"Even if it doesn't work, I'll get you close enough to them to fight hand to hand," Alice reassured him. "Tell me, do you have any other flags besides the Union Jack up there?"

Jack stood so perfectly still that he might have passed for the figurehead on the front of the ship. "As a matter of fact, we do," he said softly. "Which one would my Lady have us fly?"

"A plain white one," Alice suggested. "Now tell me, how long before the Americans catch us up?"

The young man looked at the other pirates, but didn't answer. "If we sail away from them, 'twill be three hours before the Americans are within firing distance," a scruffy-looking pirate suggested.

Alice nodded. "And if we sail towards them?"

"One hour," Jack admitted. "Maybe less."

"It should be long enough," Alice said. "Set a course for the other ship. Raise the white flag right away. Assemble the entire crew. We have no time to waste."

Thirty minutes later, Alice stood in the middle of the bridge, with most of the crew of the Black Spot lined up in front of her, standing at attention.

"Everybody say it once more," she prompted.

"SHUUUURRE," the crew parroted back at her.

"Very good," she replied. "Remember, you can never use too much 'r.' Americans love their r's."

"Cheeky," someone shouted, and there was a laugh.

"This is serious," Alice insisted. "Your life may depend on it."

Alice's fee for saving the lives of pirates had been the loan of a three-cornered hat and a rapier. This was, she insisted, non-negotiable. If she could have haggled a fresh change of clothing out of the bargain she would have, but it didn't seem like laundry was a high priority on the ship. Still, it had made her feel important. The hat was comfortable and the sword was heavy. She hoped the hat would prove to be the more useful of the two, since she would probably end up slicing her finger off if she tried to draw the sword from its scabbard too quickly.

"All right," she said, one last time. "Say it again."

"SHUUURRRRE," everyone repeated.

"And the other one?" she asked.

"YEP," the pirates said, a little less evenly.

Their American accents only had to span two words, but even this was taking a great deal of practice. Alice could only hope that their enemies didn't ask too many questions. "Perfect!" she said, even though it wasn't. "That should get us through. We're ready. Does everybody remember what to do?"

There was a general murmur of agreement. It seemed that the stage was set.

"Mister Cassidy," Alice shouted, turning in the direction of the poop deck, "how long until the Americans get here?"

Jack was peering through his spyglass at the approaching ship. "They're lowering a boat for a boarding party even now," he said. "Ten minutes at most."

"Is their Captain among the party?" Alice asked.

"It appears so," Jack replied, tucking his spyglass away.

"All right," Alice said. "Man your stations, everyone. Remember, we're only going to get one shot at this."

The Captain of the American ship was a thin, grey-haired man with striking blue eyes that were about as warm as a windy night in February, and a long, thin nose that looked like it would have been the advanced slope at a ski resort in Vermont. He was tall, square-shouldered, and wore a double-breasted blue coat that looked like it had been dry cleaned only that morning. He was accompanied by a younger officer, tall and thin, who looked like he might have just left West Point, along with two grubby-looking oarsmen, who seemed like they might have been happy to join the pirates if they'd been offered a sufficient benefits package. Alice noted that although the Captain had an impressive-looking sword and gun, and the First Mate wore pistols, the oarsmen didn't have anything more dangerous than large daggers tucked in their belts.

"Good afternoon," the Captain said, having climbed aboard the Black Spot.

He had directed his comments to Alice, who was standing right in front of him, but it was obvious that he was uncomfortable addressing a woman. Alice found herself standing up straight, trying to compensate for her generally disheveled appearance. "Good afternoon, Captain," she said brightly. "Welcome to the SS Hamilton."

When you're faking an accent, it's absolutely physically impossible to know if you're doing it well. Alice *hoped* she *sounded* like an American. Certainly she had heard enough American dialects in the past year to give it a go, but these men were *actual* Americans, and they were going to be the judge. Fooling them would be tough.

"My name is Captain Michael Jameson," the Captain said. If he knew that Alice was faking anything, his face did not betray it. "You have surrendered to the SS Independence. What are you doing here?"

"My name is *Alice Adams,*" Alice lied. "I'm on a mission for *my father.*"

Alice had decided it would be a good idea to name-drop a former president, and she had judged Adams to be the most impressively inconspicuous. After all, there were two presidents who answered to that name, and neither one had the stature of Washington or Jefferson, whose relatives might be well known. (If Alice had been hard pressed, she might have been able to name one other classic American President, but Lincoln hadn't been born yet, so his would have been a bad name to mention.) If Captain Jameson had an idea that Alice was anything other than a young woman in need of a bath, though, he did not show it. "Before you flew the white flag, you had the Union Jack at the top of your mast. If this is an American ship, then why does it fly the colours of our enemy?"

If there was anything funny or even conversational about this subject, Captain Jameson's face did not own it. He looked like someone had carved a bust of a man in the middle of having a profound bowel movement. Alice did nothing to betray her nerves, breathing through her nose in slow, measured breaths.

"I thought that the flag might need explaining," Alice admitted. "As I was saying, I'm on a mission for my father, *President Adams.* A mission that, while unofficial, we believe to be of the highest importance to the war effort."

The American First Mate cleared his throat. "This ship's markings match those of a well-known pirate vessel," he said in a squeaky voice. "Why would a man as powerful as the President send a ship like this on a matter of state?"

"Our mission is classified *Top Secret,*" Alice said. "We will be landing on the English Coast to deliver a package. If we flew an American flag we'd get blown out of the water before we ever made it into the English Channel. As for the ship, it was a salvage, acquired by the US Navy roughly three months back. We picked this crew up in Newark a few days ago. Isn't that right, boys?"

"Yep," a voice from behind her shouted, to which another slightly shakier American accent replied, "Shuurre."

"We're to masquerade as a British Crew until we meet our contact. Young Jack Cassidy has even been working on a British accent. Haven't you, Jack?"

"Yep," Jack said, with something approaching a southern drawl.

"Don't be so modest," Alice beamed. "Show them."

"All right," Jack said in his normal voice. "I would like a cup of tea and a scone."

The American First Mate rolled his eyes. "No one," he said, "is going to believe *that*."

And at that point Alice knew that she had them. "May I offer you a drink, Captain?" she asked.

They brought the Captain and his First Mate down to the little mess hall, where they had eaten the night before. The Americans went willingly, but seemed to have their guard up. Alice sat on down at the table and encouraged them to do the same. It occurred to her that in the twenty-first century there was no way that this plan would ever have worked. It borrowed too much from bits and pieces of old spy movies. At the moment that didn't matter, since nobody was going to make a spy movie for a hundred and fifty years. Like the best lies, Alice had done her best to weave in as much of the truth into her story as she could.

"You'll forgive me for looking like rubbish," Alice said as she led the Captain below deck. "We were attacked by a French ship five days ago. They caught us unawares in the dead of night. We were able to get away, but we paid a heavy price. Please, have some wine."

The Captain eyed the tiny mess hall of the ship suspiciously. His First Mate stared at Alice wide-eyed, like a frightened child. Alice popped the cork on the bottle that was sitting on the table. In spite of any trepidation, though, the Americans both sat down at the table opposite her and accepted the wine when offered to them. *'Good,'* Alice thought.

"I believe I heard your name when I was in Ithaca," Alice said. "My brother was at Cornell, and he had a number of friends from West Point."

"I know Cornell," the Captain said, taking a sip. "It's nice there."

"Lake Cayuga is beautiful, and Taughannock Falls are amazing," Alice agreed, silently thinking that this was the one time in the past few weeks that she'd had the chance to use anything that she had learned at college. "I'll mention our meeting to my father, I'm sure that he will be most pleased."

"Espionage doesn't seem like a fitting position for a woman," Captain Jameson said, without any irony at all.

'Typical,' Alice thought. "Captain, if you were looking for a spy, then who would you suspect, the man in the black tie, or the woman standing behind him?"

"A fair point," he conceded. "You say that you're delivering a package?"

"Shuuure," Jack Cassidy said, sitting down next to Alice.

"What is it?" the Captain asked.

"An item that the British will find extremely valuable," Alice said, a little too carelessly.

When she said this, something strange happened that she hadn't anticipated – Jack got a look in his eyes that Alice could only describe as sheer panic. Alice had no idea what had scared him or why. Had they tipped their hand somehow?

"Can you show it to me? This thing that you're carrying?" the Captain of the enemy ship asked.

"Of course," Alice said, and at that moment she couldn't help it, she swallowed hard. "Would you like to finish your drink first?"

"Absolutely," the Captain said and he took a big sip. "I would actually love to have some more, if you don't mind," he added. Alice reached for the bottle of wine, and when she picked it up he grabbed her wrist. His grip was gentle but firm, and Alice knew that she'd been caught.

In a flash, pistols were blazing everywhere. The First Mate had drawn both his guns, and Jack had drawn his, and was doing his best to stare down the Captain, in spite of the fact that Captain Jameson looked like he could snap Jack's neck like a twig. Alice, whose sword was tucked underneath the table, decided to stay put.

"What gave it away?" Alice asked in her normal voice.

"The wine," the Captain said, leisurely pulling his own pistol out of its holster and pointing it at her. "I'm afraid I know English grapes when I taste them. You should really try a vintage from Virginia. I think you'll find that it's much drier and has more of a bite. Also, President Adams has been out of office for ten years, and to the best of my knowledge he never had a daughter." (It was Alice's bad luck that the second President Adams wouldn't be elected for another half a decade.)

The Captain took the liberty of pouring himself another cup of wine. "The accent wasn't bad," he commented smugly. "Americans don't usually use the word 'rubbish', though. Your crew don't seem to be as well practiced. Now let me explain to you just how much trouble you are in."

Alice wasn't sure if putting your hands in the air when a gun was pointed at you was a convention that anyone had invented yet, but in any case it seemed like a good idea, so she put her hands in the air. "You have the advantage of me, sir," she acknowledged.

"I do," Captain Jameson agreed. "More than you know. If I don't signal my ship within the hour they will blow this vessel out of the water – not that you will live that long," he added, holding up a hand.

Jack lowered his weapon. It was snatched up quickly by the Captain, who pointed it back at its owner. "My ship is faster and better gunned than yours," Captain Jameson continued. "You know this. Otherwise, you would never have sent up a white flag. Now tell me, in whatever accent you choose, why should I keep from sinking this vessel?"

It was funny, but Alice couldn't help but marvel that just a few weeks ago, the idea of having a gun pointed at her face would have been absolutely terrifying. Now, it seemed more like a moment of tense unpleasantness, like having a senior faculty member eye her chest while she was telling him about her research proposal. She supposed that if she could handle Nazis and a killer, then she could handle anything.

"The package," Alice said with gritted teeth. "Don't you want to know what it is?"

The First Mate snorted with contempt. "There probably is no package."

The Captain seemed less sure. "Maybe," he said. "Maybe not. We should search the cargo hold, just to make sure." He gestured with a gun towards the door, indicating that Alice and her companion should walk through it.

Alice stood up. She kept her hands raised in the air. "Right this way," she said. She walked quickly past Jack, who had taken a cue from Alice and put his hands into the air as well. He gave her just the smallest of sideways glances.

"This is madness," Jack whispered.

"Trust me," she said, in a voice so quiet that she barely heard herself speak.

The cargo hold was on the lowest level of the ship, and was small and cramped, with large barrels and wooden crates taking up most of the space. Undoubtedly, if he had been dealing with anyone whom he thought was even remotely competent, he would have been more careful, but Captain Jameson clearly saw no need. He followed the two of them down to the hold, where a large wooden crate sat in the middle of the floor.

A muffled voice from inside of the crate said the word "Nark" and Alice heard the unmistakable sound of dinosaur paws scraping against the inside of the box.

"What's that?" Captain Jameson asked.

"That," Alice said, maneuvering carefully out of the way, "is the package."

"Open it," Captain Jameson insisted.

Although he clearly had little respect for Alice, and even less for Jack, Captain Jameson wasn't overconfident to the point of recklessness. Whatever else might be said of him, he wasn't a stupid man. He might have come down to the cargo hold, but he hadn't been foolish enough to leave his back unguarded. The First Mate stood outside the door, looking out from the stairs for trouble from above. Alice and Jack walked to either side of the crate. They picked up the top and moved it aside.

Grendel's head popped up over the top of the crate. He sniffed the air hopefully. "Nark?" he asked, clearly hoping that it was all right to come out.

"What in God's name–" Captain Jameson said. It was just enough of a distraction to cause the Captain to forget himself. He stepped forward and stared at Grendel, lowering his pistols just slightly.

"What is it?" the First Mate asked, turning around and stepping into the room.

"Nark!" Grendel shouted by way of an explanation.

"It's some kind of rhinoceros, I think," the Captain said, but it was obvious that he had no idea. "I've heard tell of them, they come from Africa."

"It's not a rhinoceros," the First Mate countered. "It's got too many horns, and it's got skin like a lizard. Besides, it's too small."

"Must be a baby," the Captain insisted. "I think–"

But the American never got to the chance to finish that thought, because just then Alice shouted "Now!" and in a flash, three pirates appeared from inside the empty wine barrels on each side of the Captain, their gun barrels pointed right at the Americans' backs. Jack leapt forward, hit the First Mate, and tackled him to the floor. Alice, in a move that seemed to surprise even herself, yanked her sword from its scabbard and pointed it at Captain Jameson's throat.

"Drop your pistol, or you won't live another minute," she said.

The Captain obliged. If his expression had been unpleasantly businesslike before, now it was positively menacing. "My ship will still blow your vessel out of the water," he growled.

"It won't," Alice snapped. "You are going to signal your ship not to fire, and then you're going to go back to your crew and tell them to sail in the opposite direction. In return for this, I won't tell your oarsmen that you were bested by a woman. Only your First Mate has to know." Alice knew that she had him, and she could tell that he knew it. Even so, a caught fish doesn't always know when to give up the struggle, and she thought that she would do well to make it easier for him.

"Our crew was instructed not to speak to your oarsmen, unless they absolutely had to. As far as anyone else knows, you are on a friendly American ship, and as far as we're concerned, it can stay that way."

"Captain," the First Mate suggested in the gentlest voice, "maybe we should just let them go."

The Captain dismissed the first mate with a wave of his hand. "Our ship is faster, and better armed than yours," he countered, although the argument was less persuasive than it had been the first time. "Send me back to my ship and I can still rip a hole through your hull. By midday you'll be at the bottom of the ocean."

"You could," Alice acknowledged, "but I don't think that you will. Return the mercy of a woman with vengeance? It doesn't seem fitting, but if you need another incentive, I'll give you one."

"What's that?" the Captain asked.

"An opinion," Alice said, "but one I think you'll appreciate. I submit to you that this war is pointless, foul, and for the British, unwinnable. I believe that this isn't the reclamation of the Americas, but a last battle in war long lost. I believe that this is the last time there will ever be hostility between your country and mine, perhaps for centuries. I believe that any men who die today would do so needlessly and pointlessly."

The Captain didn't answer, but sighed heavily. Alice got the impression that dying pointlessly was probably a theme among men at war. She hoped that this was working in her favour.

"Captain," she said imploringly, "I swear to you, all we want to do is *go home.*"

There was a silence in the conversation that lasted for ten seconds, if not more. It was Captain Jameson who finally spoke.

"Just tell me one thing," he said with just the smallest hint of a smile creeping into his face. "*What the hell is this thing?*"

And Alice knew that they were going to be all right.

Chapter 6
Terra Firma

*B*ertha Wollaston *had been given* a fairly mean set of circumstances in life, as she was only too happy to tell you. Chief among her list of grievances was her hair, which was blonde and stringy. Her shoulders were oddly broad, too, and her head was roughly the size of a pumpkin, which gave her the look of a badly-made scarecrow. That her complaints about her own physical appearance came up much more often than the fact that her husband had been killed six years ago by a group of highwaymen did nothing to flatter her. This was unfortunate, because this was a woman who needed flattering. She greeted customers at the inn she ran with a thin-lipped, unpleasant smile. It was the kind of expression that implied that she had just done something absolutely awful and was very pleased with herself. She had fallen into the position of innkeeper as a matter of circumstance. Her late husband had been the original proprietor, and having died without issue, the tavern and the rooms above had been left to her. It was work that involved being friendly to people a lot more often then she wanted to, which was just this side of never.

She was behind the bar cleaning mugs when the bell by the door rang. A strange woman walked in. Bertha did not approve of strangeness; it made her feel like she was the butt of someone else's joke. The woman who had walked in was wearing a black dress that looked like it had been through a war, a black leather blazer, and a man's three-cornered hat. She was quite tall and had a round face with a head full of curls that seemed to go off in every direction. (Bertha did not approve of curly hair. She believed it was a sign that the owner of said hair was wild and carefree. The words 'wild' and 'carefree' implied that you were having fun, and Bertha would have no part of that.) Most offensive of all, the strange woman had a pair of blue spectacles perched on the end of her nose. Bertha had never seen blue spectacles before. She couldn't imagine why anyone would need spectacles that were blue, and she was reasonably certain that there could only be wickedness behind it.

"May I help you?" she asked, giving her prospective customer an unhealthy stare.

"Yes," the woman said in a quiet but confident voice. "I would like a room, please."

A thousand ugly thoughts ran through big Bertha's mind, each one slightly more unpleasant than the last. She wondered if she had any reason to refuse this woman. Certainly she was not respectable, no respectable woman would have dressed this way. Bertha was just about to say something awful when a young man walked in. He was little more than a boy, really – tall and good-looking, with the impossible thinness of his teens still on him. His long black bangs covered his face almost completely, but even so, Bertha could make out his sharp cheekbones and dark eyes peeking out from behind his long hair. The young man gave the odd-looking woman just the slightest glance, to indicate that they were together. Bertha had a weakness for handsome young men. They did not have a weakness for her, but this was beside the point. It would not do to be rude in front of him.

"Yes," Bertha said, mustering just the thinnest veneer of politeness. "I can help you with that. How long will you need a room?"

"I'm honestly not sure," the odd woman admitted. "Two weeks, at least."

"Two weeks," Bertha repeated, the slightest maniacal gleam of avarice flashing in her eyes. She explained the rates, meal times, and the rules of the house, adding, with a particular emphasis, that gentleman callers were not allowed upstairs. (The young man might have been handsome, but unless he was going upstairs with Bertha, he wasn't going upstairs at all. When sexual jealousy and modern convention fell in line together, Bertha's course of action was clear.) The odd woman paid with silver. Bertha bit it to make sure that it wasn't made of tin.

"I'll go and get your luggage," the young man said in a Scottish accent. He returned momentarily with a single item, a large wooden box with holes in it. "I'll just drop this upstairs, if that's okay," he added cheerfully.

"Just be sure you come right back down," Bertha said, shaking a finger at him. The thin veneer of pleasantness had got even thinner and there was a menacing gleam in her eyes.

"Of course," the young man said, flashing her a toothy grin before heading up the stairs. Bertha couldn't be sure, but just before the crate disappeared upstairs, she thought she heard something which sounded like "Nark!"

Alice had been back in Britain for two days, and this experience was fairly typical of her encounters with the locals. Any romanticism about the nineteenth century had been abandoned the moment she had reached dry land. The people she had met here had struck her as little more than peasants, and unpleasant peasants at that. They were unhappy, unhealthy, ignorant, bigoted, and had a tendency to smell. They looked at Alice with peering, suspicious eyes, a constant reminder that she was truly a stranger in a strange land. More than once, Alice found herself thinking of all the places that she had been before. In her old life she had travelled widely, attending conferences in such disparaging locations as Tokyo, Seoul, Los Angeles, and Bern. She would have traded for any one of those places and felt more at home than she did in this cramped house in London, less than an hour from her sister's house.

Except that it wasn't near her sister's house. The entire world seemed to have inflated, like a giant balloon. The trip from Southampton had taken most of two days by carriage, and they were two *exhausting* days. They had spent long hours cramped on seats that had clearly been made by some sadist who had been in a bad mood. The journey had been over long roads that had varied between dirt and brick, both of which were impressively uncomfortable. *'Shock absorbers,'* Alice found herself thinking as they went over a bump that felt like it had bruised her tailbone. *''*

Throughout these last two days young Jack Cassidy and Grendel had been her saviours. Jack had insisted that Alice, having saved the crew of the Black Spot from the Americans without firing a single shot, be given an equal share of the ship's plunder. He had then escorted her to London, an offer which she was eternally grateful for, as the process of finding transportation proved a little more informal than in the modern era. Jack had been able to make the necessary arrangements at a local pub within a few hours, where Grendel did his best to charm the pants off of absolutely everyone, wiggling his tail and sniffing hopefully at any one who cared to look his way. Nearly everyone found the little dinosaur interesting, and at roadside stops, Alice spent most of her time explaining what exactly a triceratops was, usually doing her best to be a little vague on the details. People were always happy to scratch his horn and let him put his front paws in their lap. There were one or two large men who mentioned that they thought Grendel would look handsome mounted on their wall and eyed their weapons hungrily, but for the most part people responded pleasantly to the little dinosaur in ways that they would have certainly not responded to Alice herself.

She told herself that once she brought a new dress she would blend in better, but she suspected that she would still look a little foreign – a little like an immigrant who had lived in the country and had learned the language, but still had just the slightest accent they couldn't quite shake. In her case, she had the language down, but she didn't quite look like the locals. She was too tall, for one thing. She towered over most of the era's men. There were other details, too – the way that she ate, her opinions of life and society, and her desire to speak her own mind didn't seem to fit in, and probably never would.

Still, it wasn't all bad. The fashions were truly impressive. They were probably seventy-five years before the invention of denim, and formality and splendor were pervasive to the point of absurdity. Nearly all the gentleman wore top hats, tails, and spats. The women wore bonnets and dresses. Dresses! Good Lord, you could have parked an automobile under some of them. Even the lower classes got into the act. Valets, footmen, and coachmen seemed to revel in their liveries. Even washer women and cooks never seemed to go anywhere without covering their heads. Everyone down to the lowliest farmer seemed to have at least a fancy jacket or hat for when they went into town. Alice had hated the idea of a class society, but it was easy to see where it came from. The gentry were cleaner, taller, more elegant, and more refined than the others. Money had bought them a lifetime of good meals and leisurely days, and they weren't afraid to show it. They were looking down their noses at people in large part because of a growth spurt that their underfed counterparts had never been allowed to experience.

'It's a new world, 'Alice thought to herself as she waited for Jack to come back down the stairs. *'At least the stars here are beautiful.'*

This was true. Alice had gone all the way to upstate New York to find a dark sky area. Here you didn't have to go any further than the outskirts of London. There was no electricity, so at night the sky went dark. So dark that on a clear night you could make out the Milky Way overhead, like it had been photographed by the Hubble Telescope.

'If I wanted to, I could discover Phobos and Deimos. I could find them with a spyglass with about twenty minutes of hard looking.' But this still struck her as the astronomical equivalent of solving The Times' crossword puzzle by looking up the answers and then filling in the empty spaces afterward. *'Whatever I do here, I will break new ground,'* she decided, somewhat defiantly.

All of which left Alice with an awful lot on her mind when Jack came back from delivering her luggage upstairs. "How is he?" she whispered to him.

"Curled right up on the bed," Jack said. "I should hope he doesn't roll over on his back like an old dog. He'll put holes in the mattress," he added.

Alice smiled. "Would you like a drink? I'm sure I could get the landlady to give us some ale."

She felt slightly guilty for procuring alcohol for someone so young, but it was clear that the conventions in the era were very different, and young Mister Cassidy was to no stranger to a drink. They sat at a table in a quiet corner, sipping their ale from large mugs and ignoring unpleasant glares from the innkeeper.

"So," Alice asked taking a sip, "what are you going to do now?"

Jack gave the landlady a sideways look. "There is something I have not told you," he said.

Alice raised her eyebrows.

"When we were on the ship, you told that American Captain that we had a package on board that the British would find extremely valuable. You were more right than you know."

276

He pulled a very dirty piece of linen out of the pocket of his vest. Alice could tell that there was something folded inside of it. Something that looked heavy.

"I have wanted to show you this for a long time," Jack admitted. He slid the package across the table. "It wasn't safe to tell you about it back on the ship. Privateers really are just pirates after all."

Alice unfolded the piece of linen. She looked at it:

"Oh my goodness," Alice said, clearly surprised. The Cross of King Arthur was a little smaller than she had expected it would be, but otherwise looked exactly like it had in the picture Professor Hopper had shown her back in the present. It was surprisingly heavy and appeared to be made of lead. The artist had obviously been drawing from real life, and had done an excellent job at recreating the object that Alice was now holding in her hand. She was shocked, not so much by the age and rarity of the artifact, as by the sheer coincidence that it had shown up in her life so quickly after she had discovered its existence. "I – my goodness!" she stammered.

"It's the cross from King Arthur's grave," Jack said, his eyes sparkling wildly. "The Captain took it off of a French marauder three months ago. When he died, I inherited it from him."

"I've – I've heard of it, actually," Alice said.

"I've been hiding it ever since the Captain died," Jack admitted. "But now, I expect to sell it to the Crown. Just think, the cross came from the grave of Britain's greatest King. What do you think the Prince of Wales would pay for *that*?"

Alice sighed. How was she going to tell him this? "Jack," she said, putting down the cross and reaching out to grab his hand. "It's a *fake.*"

Jack starred at her blankly. Alice wondered if perhaps the word hadn't been invented yet. "A counterfeit, a conceit, *it isn't real,*" she added, trying to get the message across without hurting his feelings.

"How do you know?" His tone was already defensive. This was not a good sign.

"You can tell from the *lettering,*" Alice said, and unfortunately she sounded just the tiniest bit glib. Jack had the expression of a wounded lion. Alice softened her tone and started again. "King Arthur died over a thousand years ago," she implored. "Anything from his grave would have had Celtic runes on it. These are *Roman* letters, in a medieval script. They were made later on."

There was a silence.

"I'm afraid that anybody you tried to sell that to would know that," Alice said. "I'm sorry."

There was another silence.

"I thought it would be the making of me," Jack admitted.

Alice wasn't sure what to say. Before she knew what was happening, Jack had stood up and started to leave. "Wait!" she said, standing. She didn't want him to leave, not like this. "I'm sure you won't have to go back to the docks. You've got enough left from privateering. You can make a new life."

"Yes," Jack said with the thinnest of smiles. "Yes, I suppose I can – but the question is, what should I do?

For one brief, shining moment, the educator inside Alice kicked in. "You could attend University! Get an education! Knowledge can make a gentleman out of anyone!"

Jack gave a little bow. "As you say, my Lady," he said, and without any other word he turned and left.

Chapter 7
Freaks

It has been remarked that the phrase "what do you want to do when you grow up?" was invented by adults who were looking for ideas. There is a certain truth to this. Alice had asked Jack about what he was going to do next in part because she had no idea what she was going to do herself. Having watched him storm out, she didn't have any better of an idea about what to do with her future, but at least she had a little time to herself to do a few things that she desperately needed to attend to.

The first order of business was a trip to the Gristle and Thorn. Alice set off that same afternoon. She found her way easily, although the city was very different from the one that she knew. It was a city of wood and plaster – smaller and brighter than the one she knew. It was also cramped and dirty. Still, the Thames was there, although the banks were very different, and the sight of the Tower without Tower Bridge standing next to it was strange. The smell was different, too. It took Alice about twenty minutes to discover that it was more than worth it to pay a street urchin (of which there was no short supply) a half-penny in order to sweep a busy intersection before crossing the street. Summer hadn't arrived yet, but the air was warm in a manner that suggested that it would be following quickly, and Alice enjoyed the walk over to the bar, relaxing for the first time in what felt like days.

When she got to the street, the Gristle and Thorn wasn't there. In its place was a shop selling fish.

Alice double-checked, and then triple-checked. The hotel she had been staying in the night before the conference hadn't been built yet, but she could tell that she was in the right place. The Gristle and Thorn was gone. She was the only Time Traveller here, with no way of getting home. This was, of course, precisely the outcome that Alice had expected, but it was heartbreaking just the same. She knew that there had to be *some* reason that she had been the inventor of time travel, and it didn't make much sense to invent it if there was a time orb nearby. Still, she would have gladly traded in the title of Mother of Time for the ability to check into a hotel with a Jacuzzi and Wi-Fi.

'There's nothing for it,' Alice thought to herself. *'I'll have to make my own way.'*

This was about as close as she could come to feeling ambitious. The truth was that the idea of inventing time travel was incredibly daunting. About the only thing useful that quantum physics had to say about time travel was that it technically wasn't impossible. The first theoretical solution to the problem was presented at MIT in the nineties, and it was so complicated that most of the graduate students working on it didn't realize what they were looking at until it was explained to them. Alice was familiar with the work. Putting the solution into practice would have involved finding a ball of antimatter roughly the size of the planet Jupiter. This was the best solution that the twenty-first century could come up with. Somehow, Alice had to do better than this, working by herself, two centuries before the Large Hadron Collider.

And yet…it was possible. They had proved that. She was here, after all. Once more, however the time orbs worked, they didn't seem to involve tremendous amounts of energy, so there must be a practical solution. The question was, how did work?

'I'm getting ahead of myself,' Alice thought. *'I'm thinking about how to do science. For the moment I need to focus on how to get through the day first.'*

The pirates had left Alice enough money so that she didn't have to worry about her future, at least in the short term. That didn't mean she was financially secure, though, and she certainly didn't have enough to support herself while she conducted some sort of time travel related experiments. *'I'm going to have to find a proper way to make a living,'* Alice thought, and she wondered which would be harder, figuring out how to travel through time, or figuring out how to survive as a nineteenth century woman.

Regardless of what she was going to do, the next order of business was getting a new dress, and having been summarily disappointed looking for the Gristle and Thorn, Alice turned her attention to the business of finding an entirely new wardrobe. This was trickier than it sounds. Marks and Spencer wasn't going to open for another seventy-five years or so. For that matter, directory listings and large signposts hadn't been invented either, so Alice could have walked past a clothing merchant and been blissfully unaware. She eventually stopped at a tavern, and after babbling the entire story of her shipwreck, asked a crowded room if anyone knew a seamstress. She was kindly directed by the barmen to a woman three streets over, who was all too happy to make her presentable to polite society. Alice bought dresses, shoes, and roughly enough underclothes to cover ten women in the modern era, paying more for the privilege than she really felt comfortable.

Money was high among the things that Alice found perplexing. In principle, she understood it, and didn't have a problem with it, but in practice, it was strange living in a society where a shilling was obviously worth more than she was used to a pound being worth. Goods that she tended to think of as fairly ordinary had taken on this rare, exotic quality. In the street she saw a man selling packets of cayenne pepper for more than she paid that morning for a new pair of shoes. "It's all the way from the Caribbean," the merchant said with a broad smile. "It makes everything taste incredible." Alice would have given anything for a curry, but politely declined. (The food so far had been delightfully bland and unappetizing, but she had also managed to avoid food poisoning. Sometimes you had to pick your battles.)

All in all, her arrival in the past had made for an enormous adjustment, one with a huge amount of culture shock involved, but Alice rose to this challenge, and by the time ten days had rolled around, she prided herself that she was managing quite well, thank you. Adjusting her new bonnet in the mirror, she looked every inch the proper lady, even if she didn't *feel* the part. It was around this time that she had one of what had become one of her daily conversations with her landlady about the continued presence of Grendel in her house.

"I'm just saying that if I'd have known that you had him, I'd have said no straight away," Bertha complained.

"Yes," Alice said. "You've just said that, but seeing as I've already paid—"

"At the very least, I would have charged you extra."

"You *did* charge me extra," Alice sighed. "I talked to Mister Gibb, he said that he only pays—"

"Mister Gibb, he's one of my regulars, isn't he? Never would have let you in if I'd seen that monster of yours."

Alice realized that this was a fruitless but inevitable conversation. The truth was, Bertha was right. She *had* snuck Grendel into the house, and she had done so knowing that he would be unwanted. Grendel had been extremely well behaved, it was true, but she knew that the landlady wasn't going to let her stay beyond the time that she had already paid for.

Grendel responded to this controversy by wiggling his tail and sniffing at Bertha hopefully.

"Don't know what he is," Bertha said, giving Grendel an unpleasant look, "but he don't look respectable, that's for sure. He looks like something they would have in that circus they've got over in Cheapside."

"Circus?" Alice said. She turned her attention from the mirror and spun around to face Bertha. "You say that there's a circus in town?"

The gap between Bertha's front teeth made a whistling noise. "That's what they call it, anyway," she said, making it clear that she didn't approve of a circus any more than she did of Grendel. "Nothing but a bunch of freaks, if you ask me. They put up posters all over town. It says they got a trapeze artist, and a bearded lady, and a dancing horse. God only knows what else. It just goes to show what this world is coming to."

"That's interesting," Alice said. "I didn't know anyone had invented the circus yet."

Bertha clearly didn't know what to make of this, which was just as well. It didn't matter. Somewhere in the centre of Alice's cerebellum, a pair of neurons had sparked. "That's an excellent idea," she said, patting her landlady on the shoulder. "Really top notch."

Bertha looked at her quizzically. Alice, having learned enough about this woman over the past week to know that explanations were completely pointless, simply turned to Grendel, and said excitedly, "How would you like to go to the circus?"

Alice had been to the circus when she was very young. She remembered her father taking both her and her sister Wendy. She had liked the little dogs best. Her sister had preferred the high wire.

(They both liked the ice cream and went home with stomachaches.) The memory struck Alice as pleasant, and after a week in the doldrums of the nineteenth century, she would have done almost anything to get out of the house. This was truly an era when boredom ruled Britain with an iron fist, and the idea of entertainment sounded wonderful. (Alice was already contemplating needlepoint as a way to pass the time, it was *that* bad.) However, a good time was not her only reason for heading out that day. Alice had a plan.

She first saw the circus from a distance, but even then, it was unmistakable. The comically striped red and white tent seemed like something out of a drama. It had been set up in a field, and was surrounded by a ring of wagons that looked like full-sized versions of the boxes they used to sell animal crackers in. A crowd was gathering around a carnival barker, who was shouting into a megaphone.

"Come one! Come all! It's the greatest spectacle you have ever seen! You will be simply amazed by Maximus! The strongest man to ever walk the Earth! Watch him lift two thousand pounds over his head with the greatest of ease! See Titania! The incredible seven-foot-tall woman from the icy fjords of Norway, along with her husband Oberon, the famous Dwarf of Gibraltar! Behold, the spectacle of Miranda, our contortionist extraordinaire!"

As Alice was listening, a man with a top hat and a bristly mustache but no shirt came through the crowd, walking a lion as casually as if it were a dog on a leash. "Make way!" he shouted. "Ferocious, man-eating lion coming this way!"

People parted like the Red Sea. The lion gave Grendel a sideways glance. "What do you say we follow him, boy?" Alice asked, and she and Grendel stepped into the lion's wake.

Alice followed the lion up to the front of the tent and stopped in front of the Carnival Barker. Like most of the men of the era he was spectacularly dressed, although his clothes were more flamboyantly coloured than most of the men in the street. His waistcoat was bright

purple and his top hat was bright red. Alice stopped right in front of him.

"And that's not all! You will witness the Flying Grace Brothers! And most spectacular of all, from the Orient, Eleanor Dragon and her incredible—"

As he was talking, Alice bent over to scratch Grendel on the horn. The Barker caught a glimpse of the little dinosaur and started to choke. Alice looked up at him and smiled. The Carnival Barker's eyes bulged until they looked like ping pong balls.

"I – agh! I'm sorry, Ladies and Gentlemen, I'm simply delirious from the excitement. Come one, come all, to the greatest spectacle you will ever see! Geoffrey Mac's Circus Spectacular!"

Alice and Grendel sat near the back. The circus was both smaller than any circus she had seen in the present and more entertaining at the same time. In the time since touching down in the nineteenth century, Alice had spent her free time staring at the stars, relaxing in the warm spring air, and reading the few novels that landlady Bertha had left around. In short, she had been bored to tears, and it was clear that she wasn't the only one. The circus was a nineteenth century phenomenon, and these people were right on the cusp of it. There was an energy here, an excitement, and Alice found herself getting caught up in the fun. The Carnival Barker doubled as the Ringmaster, and stirred the crowd into an appropriate frenzy. There were clowns, naturally, and a magician, that was new, and a talented high wire act. The giant and the dwarf were a comedy act who told bawdy jokes, at which the crowd laughed appreciatively. Alice bought a package of roasted peanuts, which Grendel ate greedily. The lion was obviously old and fairly toothless, but the crowd applauded when the lion tamer stuck his head into its mouth just the same. A woman with trained horses was quite impressive, and a bearded lady gave the crowd quite a laugh. They were reaching the end of the second act when a voice at Alice's left shoulder spoke, "You have my attention."

Alice turned sideways to find the Ringmaster sitting beside her. Up close, he was a kind-looking man, with tired eyes and a grey beard. He had removed his hat when he sat down, revealing a large mop of salt and pepper hair that looked like it had last been combed down in the eighteenth century.

"My name is Geoff," he said, with a small but polite bow, "and I would be happy if even one of my acts gave as good a performance as you did today."

"Thank you," Alice said with a smile. "My name is Alice. Alice Anderson. This is Grendel."

"What is he, some sort of lizard?" the Ringmaster asked.

"A reptile," Alice answered. (She was purposefully avoided the term 'dinosaur' for fear that it might attract suspicion somehow.) "He's a three-horned creature from the forests of Tasmania. Closer to a crocodile than a lizard, really, but still very friendly."

"He's an amiable fellow," Geoff remarked, scratching him on the horn. "A pity. Scary would be better. Scary always brings people in."

"He's one of a kind," Alice replied. "If I could find a fiercer one, I would."

"Can he be trained?" the Ringmaster asked.

Alice considered this. "I believe so, yes. He's demonstrated an understanding of basic commands."

The Ringmaster fidgeted with his hat in his hands nervously. "How much do you want for him?" he asked.

"He isn't for sale," Alice replied, with a small smile on her lips.

The Ringmaster sighed heavily. "I should have known," he said.

"He's not for sale," Alice elaborated, "but I need a job."

Geoff the Ringmaster's face showed the frustrated relief of a man who had just discovered that he was going to spend an awful lot of money on something that was going to make him very happy. "I need to close out the show," he said, placing a hand on her shoulder. "Afterward, we'll talk."

The show ended with a spectacular trapeze act done by a man and wife team who would have been a hit in any century. At the end of the show Geoff returned to the centre of the ring.

"Ladies and Gentlemen, thank you so much for your attention! We hope you had a wonderful time! Now, for your consideration, we have one final act for you to see! If you just head to the rear exit, you can witness our own exotic mistress of the Orient, Eleanor Dragon, the queen of the skies! Watch as she takes off in her incredible ship of the air! Ladies and Gentlemen, right this way!"

What happened next would haunt Alice for weeks to come. It was simply too surreal to believe. Alice and Grendel stood up and followed the crowd to the rear exit. That was where she saw it. It had been hidden by the tent when she had first come in, but it was clearly visible now. There was no mistaking the large blue dirigible with a pattern of golden stars on it. It looked exactly the same as it had when Alice had first seen it, before it had been ripped apart by the time vortex that had left her here. All of this was surprising enough, but even more shocking was the dirigible's passenger. Geoff the Ringmaster had refer to the pilot as Eleanor Dragon, exotic mistress of the Orient, but even so, Alice was frankly amazed to see the owner of the balloon was the severe-looking Asian woman who had attended her lecture at the Royal Astronomy Conference. She was wearing a pair of flying goggles and a different outfit, but there was no mistaking her. Alice watched as she dropped sandbags from the dirigible's platform, and floated gently up into the skies.

Chapter 8
Red and Black

There are times when you simply have to take the good with the bad. The appearance of the woman that Alice now knew as Eleanor Dragon was disturbing to say the least, but it came with the prospect of a situation, and with any luck a place in life where her day-to-day existence wouldn't be quite such a frenzy. Once more, Alice had arranged everything in a manner that might keep the rest of the world from noticing what struck her as glaringly obvious — that dinosaurs did not belong in the Regency, regardless of size. In a circus, Grendel would just seem like an oddity, a freak in a tent full of freaks. He would attract attention from everyone *except* for the scientific community, who were precisely the sort of people who would realize what an anomaly he was. This was all good.

The appearance of Eleanor, however, was another matter. What the woman's constant reappearance in her life meant, Alice couldn't say, but she wasn't keen to sit down with her and find out the cause of such a coincidence. So, instead of investigating, Alice sat down with the Ringmaster after the show and worked out an arrangement. She had been a little wary about this. Somewhere in the back of her mind she had this bad stereotype about ringmasters being glorified slave drivers, but Geoff Mac proved to be a nice man. He was very impressed with Grendel and thought he would make a spectacular addition to the show. He apologized that the salary he had to offer was so little, but he said that room and board would be included, and insisted that if Grendel proved to be a big draw, they could revisit the issue later on. (Geoff wouldn't know this, but the salary he had quoted Alice was actually less per month than she used to pay for a cup of coffee, so from her point of view the figure was really astoundingly low.) This wasn't about the money, naturally. What Alice needed was a place in the world.

"It's good that you came by today," Geoff said. "The circus is leaving for York tomorrow."

"I'm glad I caught you, then," Alice replied.

"Come back tomorrow, after lunch," Geoff suggested. "We'll give you the tour and then get you settled."

Alice thanked him and then left. She had a lot of things to do if she was going to leave the next day. First, she went out and bought a large carpet bag. It felt frighteningly good to have luggage again. After that, she purchased a bottle of ink, a quill, and a large leather-bound journal from a shop that sold stationary supplies, along with a blotter at the suggestion of the shopkeeper. (Alice was nervous about writing with a quill; she suspected that it would take some practice.) Then she went back to Bertha's Inn and packed up her things, informing her landlady that she would be leaving tomorrow. Bertha wished her well and told her that if she was ever in London again, she should feel free to stay absolutely anywhere else. Alice went to bed early that night, then after a good bath and a hearty breakfast, she went off to join the circus.

When Alice got to the field where the circus had been the previous day, everything had been transformed. The enormous striped tent had been taken down. Large men were pulling up the last of the stakes and organizing the remaining odds and ends. The wagons were lined up in a caravan, and the people milling about had a less showy, more businesslike quality than they had the day before. It was clear that everyone was in a hurry to move on to their next performance. Alice was surprised to find not just men and also women, but a fair number of children as well. Young boys and girls were running around, enjoying the last few minutes of freedom before a long ride north.

"Alice!" a voice called out. "Over here!"

Alice spun around. Geoff the Ringmaster was running up behind her. He was stripped of his ringmaster finery, and was wearing a fairly dirty white t-shirt. (Geoff the Ringmaster probably would have referred to it as a 'tunic' but Alice the Time Traveller was discovering that t-shirts seemed to be worn by men in almost every era.) He was obviously very hot and sweaty, but was happy to see her just the same. "Glad you could make it! Right this way!"

"Nark!" Grendel shouted, standing up on his hind paws.

"There's a bright little fellow!" Geoff said cheerfully. He put an arm around Alice. "It's quite a production, moving everything. We've been up since five, tearing everything down. It's a big day for us, so I'm just going to get you settled and then we'll be on our way in half a moment." Geoff began walking down the caravan. Alice followed. As they walked past the colourful wagons, Alice got a number of sideways glances. It was interesting to see that for the first time since they'd left San Tiempo, people's stares seemed to be directed at her and not Grendel, even though the little dinosaur was very happy to greet absolutely everyone who crossed their path.

'They're suspicious.' Alice thought. *'Or upset. Or something.'*

Indeed, Geoff had gotten oddly quiet. They walked back through the caravan, passing roughly six or seven wagons, and then stopped. They were standing in front of a beautiful wagon that looked like a little house on wheels, except that instead of more traditional colours, the shingles were painted in striking red and black swirls. It was harnessed to a chestnut mare. A woman with ebony skin and bright eyes was holding the reigns.

"Hello!" the woman said with a bright smile.

"This is Spring," Geoff said, with an unequivocally enthusiastic grin.

"You resemble one," Alice said. She spoke the words without really thinking about them, but truthfully she had never met anyone who was so aptly named. Everything about the woman seemed to radiate cheerfulness, even her hair, a yellow wig as bright as a daffodil, had springy coils.

"Thank you!" Spring said. "My mother thought so!"

"Spring is the head of the clowns," Geoff explained. "She'll be helping you get your feet wet, so to speak."

"And this is Harriet," Spring said, patting the mare on the hindquarters. "She's going to take us north. We're almost ready to go, so we'll need to get you settled."

Spring hopped down from the wagon. "Nark!" Grendel shouted, looking up at her happily.

"Well, you're a big boy!" Spring said, patting Grendel gingerly on the nose. "What is he, some sort of dog?"

"He's a tricera – a reptile," Alice answered, quickly correcting herself. (She knew that the phrase 'Triceratops' might attract the wrong sort of attention if it ended up on a poster, so she was determined not to use it.) "He's from Tasmania," she added. "Very rare."

"We're going to have to talk about what we're going to call him," Geoff suggested. "What do you think about 'The Tasmanian Three-Horned Puppy Lizard'?" he made a dramatic hand gesture, as if he were waving to a crowd.

"If you like," Alice agreed. "His name is Grendel," she reminded him.

"Perfect! I'll get to work on the posters," Geoff suggested. "Well, I'll leave you two ladies to it." Geoff turned and walked away. Spring walked around to the back of the wagon. Alice followed.

"Geoff likes to collect misfits," Spring said. "That's me, you see. Might be you, too," she added, sneaking a glance at Grendel. "If you don't fit in anywhere else, chances are that you might do well here." She climbed up into the back of the wagon. The inside was a perfect little room – it looked like everything had been lifted out of a Lord's mansion and placed inside the wagon's cab. There was canopy bed, a tall wardrobe, a small desk with an oil lamp, a pair of nightstands, and a washbasin. Several other wigs of different colours and styles hung on glass heads around the room. The windows had curtains, and the floor was covered in a thick Arabian rug. The air inside the cabin smelled of mint and almonds.

"This is home!" Spring said, cheerily. "Geoff's been wanting to get me a roommate for a while. Nobody wants to bunk with me, you see, and Geoff thought that you might, seeing as how you've ruffled a few feathers already."

"I – um, all right," Alice mumbled. "I'd love to."

"You can have the left side of the bed, then, if you don't mind. Just put your bag down and then we'll be off in just a few moments."

Alice put her carpet bag down on the left side of the bed, and they found their way to the front of the wagon. They sat down behind Harriet the horse and Grendel put his head in Alice's lap. "It's a beautiful wagon," Alice said admiringly. (Small talk had never been her strong suit, and she was eager to start somewhere.)

"Thank you," Spring said. "As I said, it's home. It can get a little cold at night, but it should be comfortable with the two of us."

As she spoke, the caravan began to move slowly forward. Spring picked up the reins and urged Harriet on. "Are you ready to go?" she asked the mare. Harriet the horse lumbered forward slowly.

This did not seem like one of the most important introductions in Alice's life, but it was. For the moment, it just seemed conversational. The weather was nice, and Spring was certainly a lively companion. The caravan rolled north through the city first, and then the suburbs, and then finally through the fields to the north, where the sun beat down on the grass, giving just the slightest hint that summer was on its way.

"It's a beautiful day," Alice said.

"Lovely," Spring agreed. "I love this time of year. The roses will be blooming soon."

"You must have been with the circus for a long time," Alice remarked, "to have become head clown."

"Oh, about three years now," Spring admitted. "Geoff picked me up working at a dairy farm in Cornwall. I didn't know much about clowning, but I like people, and I could juggle." Spring laughed. "I guess that's all it took. It's like I said, Geoff likes to find misfits. Even at the dairy farm, I never fit in. I never would have thought that I'd be sharing a room with a proper lady like you."

"Oh, I'm not a proper lady," Alice dismissed.

Spring laughed again. "Oh, of course you are!" she said, but Alice was adamant that this was wrong.

"No, really," Alice said, shaking her head. "I'm not a lady. I've been abroad for months, and my family is gone, and I have no idea what to do. I've studied science, but no one wants a woman scientist. Without my little friend here, I'd be lost."

"See, you are a misfit!" Spring exclaimed. "Just like the rest of us! Well, don't worry, it will be okay. You caused quite a little stir the other day, you know."

"Did we?" Alice asked. "I suppose that we did." She scratched Grendel's ridge plate. "We didn't mean to. Well, I guess we did, really, but we couldn't *help* it. We just wanted to join in, that was all."

"You did more than join in," Spring said. "You and this big boy managed to upstage the entire finale just sitting there on a bench! I'm telling you, if things go well, it won't be long till Geoff makes you a headliner! At least, he will if that's all right with your little friend here."

"Is that why people were giving me dirty looks a few minutes ago?" Alice asked.

Spring nodded appreciatively. "Just like I said. You ruffled a few feathers. Performers love a crowd, you know. They don't ever get enough of it, though, and they don't like sharing it. Now they're going to have to give up a few more minutes to you and they don't like it. We just had another big act join last week, you know."

"Who was that?" Alice asked.

"Oh, that would be Eleanor," Spring said dismissively.

Alice tried to not to look too startled. "Eleanor Dragon? The woman with the balloon?"

"That's her," Spring said. "Oriental woman. Strange lady. Seems to keep to herself so far. I tried talking to her. She was about as friendly as a grave."

"Is that right?" Alice asked.

"So far the crowd seems to love her," Spring added. "Or they love the balloon, at any rate. It is beautiful, watching her go up. Can't imagine what the world looks like from up there."

"There's nothing as beautiful as being up in the sky and looking down at the clouds," Alice agreed.

"Is that right?" Spring asked. "How do you know?"

The answer to this was that Alice had been in an airplane more times than could count, but as the Wright brothers weren't going to take off for another ninety years, it seemed that she was going to have to make something up. "Oh, I've been to the Alps," Alice lied. "From the mountaintops you can look down on everything. The clouds were the most beautiful."

"Really," Spring asked, wide-eyed.

"Oh, it's incredible," Alice said. "On a clear day you can see forever. You can touch the sky and watch the world from God's point of view."

Spring laughed. "I'd like to see that," she said.

"Then you will, someday," Alice said hopefully.

"Maybe," Spring said. "Maybe someday. Not yet, though. Right now we're just two proper ladies travelling north to find fame and fortune."

Harriet the horse chose this moment to defecate in the middle of the road.

"Make that three ladies," Alice said, and they both had a laugh.

Alice would think of that afternoon as the day that she learned to enjoy the joys of travelling slowly. The caravan moved at a sluggish pace, even by horse and buggy standards, but this meant that if you wanted to, you could get off and walk, or even stop for a minute or two, and get caught up afterward. This made Grendel very happy, as he could hop down whenever he wanted to, and drink from a stream or graze in a field, and still get caught up before the red and black wagon had gone over the next hill. Spring turned out to be one of those people who you could speak with for five minutes, and then feel like you had known your entire life. She had asked Alice about all the places that she'd been and Alice asked Spring for all her circus stories. In truth, most of the things that Spring had to share were the sort of idle gossip that you could hear almost anywhere, but Alice enjoyed the details that bled in around the edges and the cracks. She found the particulars of how the tightrope walker was having an affair with the fire-twirler less interesting than the fact that the fire-twirler made her own candles. She was fascinated at the idea that the performers made their own costumes and that Geoff the Ringmaster played the violin. The whole world seemed very new and very interesting, and for Alice, a woman who once considered applying to NASA and usually could not live without being connected to social media, the act of simply sitting and talking with one person as they lumbered down a dirt road was surprisingly invigorating.

About Eleanor, Spring didn't have much to report, although it was generally believed that Eleanor was making more money than most of the other cast, a fact which hadn't made her any friends. At any rate, Spring didn't care for her. This didn't seem to be personal; Spring didn't seem to have had any kind of altercation with her, Eleanor just seemed to have come off to most people as unfriendly, imposing, and severe. Alice made a mental note that she would have to find out more about her, although she had to admit that the thought intimidated her.

They pulled over that evening as the sun had just begun to set. Where they were, exactly, Alice couldn't say. Probably somewhere slightly north of where the more remote tube stations would be one day, but at this time, the city seemed like a distant memory. They had found their way to an inn, where a friendly innkeeper and his wife had their hands busy pouring wine for every clown, acrobat, juggler, and animal trainer with a pocketful of silver and a thirst to quench, and nearly all of them had silver. Circus people had performing coming out of their ears, and by the time Alice sat down at a table, there was a group of fiddlers and drummers playing along as a juggler tossed torches and a magician did card tricks. Alice was impressed.

"You're all so talented," Alice remarked, as Spring sat down beside her.

"Some are, some aren't," Spring said with a shrug, but then this turned out to be a bit of false modesty. Spring turned out to be the most talented member of the cast. She could juggle and sing; she did back flips and could walk on her hands. She had changed into shoulder-length black hair for the evening, which made her look elegant and sophisticated. Even the other circus people were impressed, all except one. Eleanor Dragon sat at a bar, wallowing in her own sorrows. She remained in the corner, doing her best to look inconspicuous and nursing a cup of wine like it was an old friend. She looked like the entire idea of a celebration was something completely anathema. In spite of herself, Alice found her gaze drawn to Eleanor, and more than once she caught Eleanor's sharp eyes gazing back at her.

"How are you making out?" Geoff the Ringmaster asked, having just sat down next to her at the table with a large cup of wine and looking a little glassy-eyed.

"Good," Alice said, trying to sound enthusiastic. Apart from the gala on San Tiempo, it seemed like it had been years since she'd been to a good party. It was nice that this time she was not the centre of attention.

"Tell me," Geoff said, slurring his words just slightly, "where's that little budding star of yours?"

Grendel had spent most of the afternoon running alongside the caravan and was thoroughly worn out. "He's lying down in the wagon."

"He'll need to be *trained*," Geoff insisted. "First thing in the morning, I'm going to have you sit down with my animal trainer, Fitzwilliam. Fitz has worked with everything from crocodiles to camels. If anyone can figure out what talents your little man has, he can."

"All right," Alice said. "I'm sure we can work out something."

"Of course," Geoff agreed. He took a little swig of his wine and then gave her a sideways glance. "Is he really one of a kind?"

"Yes," Alice said. "One of a kind. Does that surprise you?"

"Not really," Geoff admitted. "Most things are one of a kind. That's what makes life so interesting, and lonely."

The musicians in the corner of the room were starting up a waltz of some kind. Spring was sitting with them and looked like she was getting ready to sing. Geoff took another swig of his wine. "Shall we dance, my Lady?"

Alice didn't have the foggiest idea how to dance to the music that was playing, but she felt that it might be rude to refuse, so she stood up. "I don't know how to dance," she admitted.

"Neither do I," Geoff confessed. "But not knowing how to do something and then doing it anyway is basically my forte, so come on."

It must be said that Alice clearly wasn't Geoff's type. (She had caught him eyeing the strongman earlier in the evening.) Still, he was quite a gentleman, and led Alice around the dance floor at a merry pace. Neither of them seemed to know what they were doing, but it involved a lot of spinning. So much so that Alice almost didn't notice when Spring began to sing—

> *Magpies hunt for silver and gold*
> *In fields and summer skies.*
> *They chase beauty they can't behold*
> *Searching with unworthy eyes.*
> *Fly little bird, fly, fly away*
> *Take a trip to the Moon.*
> *If you need friends the stars will play*
> *Chasing fireflies to the Moon.*
> *Winds of change are on the morrow*
> *So spread your wings and soar.*
> *Do not dwell on your own sorrow,*
> *Just try and hope for more.*
> *Your heart's desire is up ahead.*
> *It's too soon to despair.*
> *Don't fill yourself up with too much dread*
> *When hope is in the air.*

What happened next was a blur. Alice was spinning around when Geoff let go of her. She lost her balance and found herself out of control. The world went off-kilter, and before Alice knew it, she was flying through the air. She came down hard, but not as hard as she would have expected. Alice was vaguely aware that the music had stopped. She was lying on top of someone. She just had to turn over to find out who. Alice rolled over and found Eleanor lying underneath her. How she had gotten there, Alice wasn't quite clear, but somehow she had ended on top of the strange-looking woman, who was staring back at her with dark, angry eyes.

"I'm sorry," Alice stammered, looking down at the other woman. Then, almost reflexively, a second set of words came tumbling out of her mouth. "Have we met?" Alice asked. If she hadn't said the words herself, she almost wouldn't have believed it.

Eleanor glared at her. "Yes," she seethed. "Yes, I believe that we have."

There was probably a bigger social faux pas than knocking someone over in the middle of a crowded room, but Alice couldn't think of one. Possibly trying to shoot someone with a gun. No, this was the nineteenth century. They had rules these days under which men could shoot at each other, if they wanted to. Knocking somebody over, on the other hand, appeared to go against all the rules of polite society. The solution for dealing with this breach of etiquette appeared to be removing both Alice and Eleanor from the area, and then sending them off in opposite directions. This was done with all the elegance of a swarm of bees and in seconds, a myriad of people had surrounded Alice and were moving her in the direction of the exit. This was understandable. It was also the exact opposite of what Alice would have wanted.

"Are you all right, honey?" Spring asked. She was holding Alice's arm. How they had ended up next to each other, exactly, Alice wasn't sure. Geoff had helped Eleanor up and headed off in the other direction, and somehow Spring had ended up at her side.

"My foot must have slipped," Alice mumbled distractedly.

"Of course it did," Spring agreed.

"I hope I didn't hurt her."

"She'll be fine," Spring said dismissively. "She's as tough as nails, that one. Come on, it's late, and it's been a long day."

It was *not* late by any modern definition of the word, but it *had* been a long day, and Alice thought that they might as well get some rest. They found their way back to the red and black wagon, where Grendel greeted them with big sweeps of his tail. "Nark!" he shouted happily when they came in the back door.

"At least *someone's* happy to see me," Alice said wistfully, scratching the little dinosaur underneath his ridge plate.

Spring and Alice both worked on putting on their nightgowns. Nineteenth century clothing was constricting in the extreme, and at the end of the day it was always a tremendous relief to undress, no matter what the circumstances were. Unencumbered, Alice took a deep breath.

"That song you sang," she said, sitting down on the bed, "it was beautiful."

"Thank you," Spring said, studying her face in the mirror. Her tone was warm, and she received the compliment courteously, but it was clear that she had heard the sentiment a number of times before.

"You have a beautiful voice," Alice added.

"My mother didn't leave me much," Spring admitted. "Just a beautiful voice and a cheery name. I've done my best to use both."

There was a quiet moment, as both women lay down on the bed. Grendel walked around in several concentric circles before lying down at Alice's feet.

"You didn't tell me that you knew Eleanor," Spring said, removing her wig.

A small stab of panic ran up and down Alice's spine.

"I don't," she blurted out, but she knew the words sounded false. "I met her once," she added. "It was years ago, at a scientific meeting."

"A scientific meeting? Really?" Spring asked.

"It was a long time ago," Alice said.

"*Women* at a scientific meeting, that is something," Spring said. "You said you were educated as a scientist, though, so I guess I shouldn't be surprised."

There was a pause, and Alice thought the subject had dropped, but then Spring spoke again, "Must have been quite a meeting to have gotten the two of you so upset like that."

Alice swallowed. "I don't know what you mean. She attended a talk I gave, that's all," but this was a lie, and a bad one at that.

Before she knew what she was doing, the words were coming out of her mouth, "She doesn't like me because she thinks I killed a man."

This time it was Spring's turn to swallow. "Did you?"

"No!" Alice insisted, her eyes wide. "Of course not! But I never got the chance to explain his death."

Alice would have expected there to be more shock at her admission, but much to her surprise, Spring seemed to take this in stride.

"What was his name?" Spring asked. "The man who was killed?"

"Malcolm Oliver," Alice said. He was my–" she paused. She realized that 'boyfriend' wasn't a word that anybody would recognize in this time. "I fancied him once," she corrected, and then added, "a long time ago."

"Some men deserve killing," Spring observed. "Some men need it. The man you killed, was he one of those?"

"I *didn't* kill him! And anyway, he wasn't like that. He was nice man."

"All right," Spring said. "If you didn't kill him, who did?"

"A man named Keith Quick. He was in love with me and saw Malcolm as a rival." Alice was pleased that although this was the short version of what happened between her and Keith, everything that she had said was true.

"Men," Spring said, and it seemed clear she felt this was explanation enough. "And Eleanor? She knew this man? The man who was killed?"

"I don't know," Alice admitted. "I only know she was there that day, the day I was accused. She sat there staring at me like I was the devil. I've been on the run ever since."

"I don't suppose there's any way that you could just explain all of this to Eleanor?" Spring suggested.

"I don't suppose there is," Alice said. "I don't really want to talk to her."

"I don't either," Spring said with a laugh. "She's a little scary."

"Can I ask you something?" Alice asked timidly. There had been something bothering her, and as long as she had spilled her deepest darkest secrets, she thought perhaps Spring might do the same.

"What is it, sweetie?" Spring asked.

"This morning you told me that no one wanted to stay with you," Alice recalled.

"That's right," Spring said.

"Is that because you're a woman and you're the head clown, or is it because–"

"Because of the colour of my skin?" Spring finished for her, and all trace of her cheerful demeanor was gone in an instant. "Truth be told, it's both," she said. "No one wants to treat someone like me as an equal. No one except Geoff. That's what makes me a misfit, even at the circus."

Alice had absolutely no idea what to say. "I'm – I'm sorry," she stammered after a very long pause. "It's a cruel world."

Spring laughed. Unlike her usual buoyant laugh, this one had more than a little pain mixed in with it. "It is a cruel world," Spring agreed. "I decided a long time ago that if I wanted to, I could choose to be upset about the ways things are, or I could choose to be cheerful. So every day I make that choice and every day I choose to put my best face forward. It doesn't always make things better, but it makes them a little easier."

How much sleep either woman got that night was tough to say. Alice felt immediately guilty for burdening her new friend with so much unpleasantness, and Spring may have not felt great about sleeping next to someone who was mixed up in a murder. Certainly, the evening had given Alice more than a little to think about. Maybe Spring was right, maybe she should try talking to Eleanor and do her best to be friendly. Perhaps Eleanor might even be able to help her get home. That was another problem for another day, though. In the meantime, she needed to focus on the here and now, and the here and now required rest. At some point in the middle of the night Alice realized that she was sleeping, if somewhat fitfully. It had been a long day, and Alice had a reasonable certainty that breakfast would not involve of a cup of tea, as the import of tea leaves was still being tightly controlled by the Dutch East India Company, an organization that made Starbucks look like a friendly group of people with very reasonable prices. Alice rolled over and did her best to get some sleep. In the morning, her new life would begin.

Chapter 9
A Sense of Foreboding

Fitzwilliam Trask had never been particularly good with people, it must be said. Talking came to him about as easily as ballet came to a rhinoceros. He was a quiet man, tall, grey-haired and lanky, with a way about him that made it difficult to talk to people. Fitz had grown up in the far reaches of Kentucky, a land where skill with a horse was more valuable than one's ability to talk to people, and Fitz had taken that idea and run with it, training horses first, then hawks, then almost anything that had feet. His own feet had gotten restless, though, so he found his way to the continent, where Geoff Mac had found him training monkeys on the island of La Grande Jatte and given him the job of training all the animals in the circus, or 'critters', as Fitz like to call them. He'd worked with lions, tigers, apes, elephants, and even an eagle once. So when Geoff came to him and asked Fitz to train a dinosaur, Fitz took one look at Grendel from across a crowded room and quietly said, "No problem," and it wasn't.

From Alice's point of view, Fitz was nothing less than a cowboy. The fact that his three-cornered hat was old and had a brim that was turned down, making it look more like a Stetson, only added to this effect. Fitz himself would have rejected this label; the golden age of cowboys was still a good sixty years off. In truth, Fitz wasn't so much a cowboy as what a cowboy aspired to be. In fact, several of his relatives in the ensuing decades would find their way to the old west, where they would often complain that their lives would never live up to his, but this is the way of the world, where each generation never quite feels like it lives up to the last.

Fitz sat down with Alice and the little dinosaur on their first day in York. The warm weather of early summer had spread, even to the north. When Geoff Mac found him that morning, Fitz was covered in sweat and shoeing a horse. He had caught a glimpse of the trike already, by that point everybody in the circus had, but he had shied away, preferring instead to wait for the animal to come to him. This was partly due to a natural awkwardness with members of the opposite sex, and also partly because Fitz knew that waiting would serve him well. The animal would need to know that Fitz was in control, and that he needed to be respected and understood. This would be a challenge, if only because deep down inside Fitz was the most excited he'd ever been in his entire life.

"Alice," Geoff said, smiling warmly, "this is Fitzwilliam Trask. Fitz is our resident trainer. He's going to work with you and Grendel to see what you can do to entertain the crowd, although I daresay that you shouldn't have too much trouble with that."

"Ma'am," Fitz said. Alice held out her hand and Fitz shook it. He felt awkward about this afterward. He was sure in retrospect that that she had wanted him to kiss her hand, but Alice had found the handshake refreshing.

"Alice is our newest addition," Geoff said proudly, "and I'm sure you'll have heard about our little man here already," he added, giving Grendel a nod.

"Nark!" the little dinosaur said once everyone had been properly introduced. He greeted Fisk with great sweeps of his tail, indicative of the idea that this was one the truly most exciting meetings of at least the last three or four minutes. Fitz knelt down and looked at his mouth.

"His teeth," Fitz remarked. "Never seen teeth like his. What does he eat?"

This was a line of questioning that surprised Alice slightly. She was much more accustomed to people asking what Grendel *was* first and then staring at him excitedly. (Fitz was excited, of course, but he expressed that excitement by sitting silently and frowning in a manner that suggested a state of deep constipation, so this was difficult to judge.)

"His name is Grendel," Alice said. Then, realizing that this didn't really answer his question, added, "He eats grass, and hay mostly, although sometimes he'll try some other vegetables."

Fitz gave her just the tiniest hint of a smile. "Let's see how you feel 'bout this," he said, and he took an apple out of his pocket. He handed it over to Grendel, who ate it greedily. Fitz scratched him behind the horn. Grendel indicated with a series of complicated butt wiggles that his true love could be purchased for the price of a second apple and horn scratch, but Fitz shook his head. "The first one is free," he said with a nod. "You've got to earn the rest."

Fitz worked with Grendel for almost two hours that morning, although in truth the one who was really being trained was Alice. In no time at all Fitz discovered mental abilities that Alice never knew that Grendel had. In a short amount of time he'd master sit, roll over, and walking on his hind legs. By the time midafternoon rolled by, Fitz was out two more apples, and they were ready for their first show.

They gave their first performance later that afternoon. While they had been training, the crew had put up the big tent, and before long a

crowd had begun to gather. Alice and Grendel weren't the headliners that night, as they would be on numerous occasions later on, and they didn't do much more than walk out and wave to the crowd, but even this was met with a fair amount of applause. Their appearance was punctuated by Geoff, who shouted in his best ringmaster voice. "You may not believe your eyes when you gaze upon this creature," he shouted into his bullhorn, over-enunciating every syllable. "Behold Grendel! The Tasmanian Rhino-Lizard! Unique among all God's creations! Part rhinoceros and part reptile, but don't worry, Ladies and Gentlemen, this is a monster that just wants to be loved!" Grendel seemed to enjoy the attention, although Alice enjoyed watching the show more, especially seeing Spring in all her clown regalia. Spring juggled, told jokes, and worked the crowd into a festive mood.

"How'd we do?" Alice asked Fitz when they got off stage.

"You did fine," Fitz said with a nod. "Next time we'll do better. This is only your first time, after all."

'It's not the career I imagined,' Alice thought. *'Still, it could be worse. I could be in jail right now, insisting that I* hadn't *killed Malcolm.'* She wondered if she would ever get the chance to prove herself innocent. Of course, before she got the chance to prove herself innocent, she had to get back to the present, which struck her as one of those monumentally difficult achievements along the lines of driving a car to the Moon. No matter how exciting the thought of being credited as the inventor of time travel was, Alice would have been much, much happier getting a lift back to the present with another time traveller and letting some alternate universe version of herself take the credit. Only there didn't seem to be any other time travellers anywhere to be found to get a lift from. Any, that is, except for Eleanor.

Eleanor had said that she had met Alice before, and it was clear from the look in her eyes that they had a past. It didn't quite ring true, though. For one thing, they *hadn't* actually met, at least not before Alice had knocked her down the other night at the inn. Alice had seen her at the Royal Astronomy Conference – that was true.

That event had been filled with intense drama, but they hadn't actually spoken on that occasion. It might be that Alice had simply made enough of an impression that Eleanor had felt as though she *had* met her, but Alice wasn't sure.

Of course, they had *also* met during the middle of the Blitz – only that clearly hadn't happened yet, at least not to Eleanor. The balloon was proof of that. Eleanor's was in perfect shape, and the one that Alice had stolen was at the bottom of the Atlantic. Once more, the large black engine that had dominated one end of the platform the last time that Alice had seen it in one piece wasn't there yet, which seemed to indicate that the events that she had seen in the future were still a ways off. *'I can't imagine she won't like me any better once she knows I've crashed her balloon,'* Alice thought miserably.

If Alice had no great love for Eleanor, the crowd certainly didn't feel the same way. The show that night ended as it did each night with the everyone heading out to watch the balloon taking off again, and the York crowd loved it as much as the Londoners had. Eleanor smiled and waved at the crowd with all the warmth and movement of a wax statue, but as the whole point was to watch her float away, this hardly seemed to matter. They would be in York for a week, and would play to almost everyone in the city during that time, most of them twice. Crowds grew with each performance that they gave and Grendel was a big part of this attraction. By the end of the week, Geoff was so pleased that he walked around with his chest sticking out about a foot in front of him. Alice felt good about the experience overall, but had the wind taken out of her sails just slightly by an incident that happened three or four nights after her first performance.

It was late in the evening, after the show. The sun had long since set, and Alice was getting ready for bed. The caravan was parked in a big field, much as it had been outside of London. Alice now knew that on these nights the cast usually built a bonfire, where wine and song were the highlights of the hour. Spring lived for these nights, but Alice usually avoided them, preferring instead to stay in their little wagon and write.

"It's a beautiful night," Spring said, entering the back of the wagon. "Why don't you ever come down and join us?" She looked like she'd had a good time. The bright blue wig she was wearing was askew.

Alice glanced down at the little desk where she'd been working. "Oh, I had other things I wanted to do," she said, a trifle dismissively.

Spring glanced down at the leather-bound journal that was open on the desk. The writing was in a small script that showed clearly that the author had found writing with a quill to be difficult. "What's this?" Spring asked.

What it was were some variations on Einstein's Theory of General Relativity, but this description would have been pointless. "That? That's science – mathematics, really. Something from my studies that I was working on."

Spring laughed. "It looks like Chinese," she said.

"It makes me happy to take part in my old studies again, at least, when I can."

"Well, I'm glad it makes you happy," Spring said. "The rest of us were singing 'Robin Hood and Guy of Gisborne' down by the campfire, and we were having a good time! Even Eleanor came down."

Alice raised her eyebrows. "Is that right?"

"Absolutely," Spring said. "She was smoking a hookah. I tell you, everything that woman does is odd, even by misfit standards."

"I'm not sure that can be helped," Alice replied.

"That's funny," Spring said. "She said something similar about you."

Alice felt a chill run up and down her spine. "What?" She stood up from the bed where she was sitting. "What did she say?"

Spring shrugged. "Something like what you said. She said that she thought that you couldn't be helped. No, wait. That wasn't it."

"What?" Alice asked. "What was it?"

"Half a moment," Spring said, biting her lip. "She said, no! I've got it – she said that *she* wasn't going to help. She said that she was just here to – to watch."

"Watch?" Alice repeated.

"Yes!" Spring said. "I thought that was odd, but then again, I guess you've got a whole lot of people watching you these days."

"I suppose," Alice sighed. The truth was that Alice didn't find this odd at all, but as with her notebook on General Relativity, she didn't think that the matter was within the realm of explanation. "Do me a favour, let me know if you hear anything else about me around the campfire," she said.

"Well, I'm not one to listen to gossip," Spring said, "unless it's about people."

They went to bed soon after that. In the middle of the night the caravan was dark and eerily quiet, but right before she went to sleep, Alice thought she heard the sound of someone laughing.

For the first time in months, Alice seemed to find a routine, where one day passed into the next, where her life was predictable, and the changes that she turned to face were subtle and less reactionary. Her days began at dawn. She would get dressed and go for a walk with Grendel. This was followed by a meagre breakfast with Spring, and sometimes Geoff Mac who made up for the frugality of the meal with hearty conversation. If it was a regular day, the rest of the morning would be spent training Grendel, sometimes with Fitz and sometimes not. In the afternoons they would perform, and as summer rolled on, the crowds began to grow, until only Eleanor's balloon act rivalled Grendel in terms of popularity. After the show, she would have a light supper with the other members of the cast, and in the early evening hours Alice would go back to the little wagon and work on inventing time travel.

She started out by writing down all the Laws of Physics, starting with Newton and working her way up past Heisenberg's Uncertainty

Principle. She was terrified that without the constant bombardment of University she would forget things fast, so she copied everything down before her memory started to slip. To all of this she added all the Calculus she knew, and a fair amount of Chemistry, running a few basic calculations just to keep her hand in. (She had been working on Einstein when Spring walked in the other day and he would feature in her work fairly prominently.) The work was rough, it must be admitted. Without hard data, or a calculator, it could be excruciating. After a few weeks of mental workouts, though, she felt like she was ready, and she started to work on the problem of time travel.

The astrophysicist inside of Alice frequently wanted to scream that this was patently ridiculous. The entire staff of CERN had never gotten as far as sending an electron back through time, and they had the Large Hadron Collider at their disposal. Certainly all of the initial ideas that she had about how to travel through time involved things that didn't make even the slightest bit of sense: speeds above and beyond the speed of light, energy levels that could only be achieved by smashing two galactic centres into each other, changing the acceleration due to gravity, and other ideas that bordered on the lunatic fringe of theoretical physics. The only thing about this endeavor that was helpful in any way was the undeniable truth that time travel was actually possible. Alice had been there. She had seen it happen.

The only real hope for the problem, as far as she could tell, lay in the unseen dimensions of string theory. It was an area of science so far removed from practical applications that you could practically replace the words "string" and "theory" with words like "fairy" and "dust" and it didn't change the science much. Theoretically, if you could access those extra dimensions, you might have something. Alice was sure that that was how the hole was created, that horrible hole in existence that they had travelled through every time they had gone backwards or forward in time, but how the devil did you get to it?

"The fifth dimension is choice," Alice mumbled to herself one evening as she stared bleary-eyed at several pages of detailed calculations, "and the sixth dimension is imagination."

"I beg your pardon?" Spring asked from her position on the bed. She'd been reading a small blue book, and had not really been paying attention to what Alice was doing. They were playing a two-week stint in Bath, and they were camping right out on the ocean. You could smell the sea air and hear the ocean in the distance. Alice was surprised that Spring was sitting in the wagon at all, instead of walking on the beach.

"I was remembering something an old friend told me once, a long time ago. He was trying to explain how there was more to life than we understand."

Spring nodded. "Like Mister Shakespeare said."

"Something like that," Alice said, smiling just a little. "Is that what you were reading, William Shakespeare?"

"Yes, except this is a different one," Spring said, flipping the book over and looking at the cover. "The line about more in Heaven and Earth, that was from 'Hamlet'. This is the sonnets. They're very beautiful."

'There's something about that,' Alice thought to herself. *'Something important. For the life of me, I can't think of what it is, though.'*

"I was reading the one about 'my love is nothing like the sun'," Spring continued. "It's lovely."

Alice remembered something from her A-Levels. "That was written about a man, you know."

Spring laughed. "It's just as well, it was making me *think* about a man. Have you ever been in love?"

Alice's smile faded just slightly. "Once," she admitted. "Or twice."

Spring raised her eyebrows. "I thought proper ladies aren't supposed to admit to being in love," she said.

"Proper ladies aren't supposed to do science, either," Alice pointed out. "I don't think I'm made to do the things that proper ladies do."

If Alice had been asked which was a likelier scenario, travelling back to the future or becoming a proper lady, she would have bet on a trip to the future, hands down. She might someday figure out how to ride their little red and black wagon to the Moon for that matter, but she would *never* feel like a proper lady, no matter what Spring thought. She could dress like a nineteenth century woman, but so did the large clown with the hairy chest every time he went out to perform. Alice didn't have a hairy chest like he did, but she didn't quite fit into this life, no matter how she tried. Too much of the twenty-first century hung about her. She wasn't appropriately afraid of her own body, for one thing. She had no qualms about hiking up her skirt on a hot day and showing off her petticoat, or wearing her corset on the outside of her dress if it suited her. She was too clever by half, too. Women in this era were accustomed to feigning ignorance in the presence of men. Alice wasn't having it and wasn't afraid to say so. In this respect she had something in common with the circus's other most recent addition – Eleanor.

Alice had steered clear of Eleanor like she was the plague, which seemed to suit Eleanor just fine. (Spring, who clearly understood people just a little too well, remarked that the real problem was that they were far too much alike to get along well, a suggestion that didn't help matters any.) Things came to a head one afternoon shortly before the show, as Alice was getting ready to go on.

Grendel was working on a new trick – Fitz had made some little loops out of rope, and was teaching Grendel to catch them on his middle horn. He did this standing on his hind legs, which was hard for him since his ridge plate made him extremely top-heavy. It was an impressive trick, and they would be performing it for the audience that night. Alice was nervous that the crowd wouldn't like it if they didn't do it properly. Grendel kept losing his balance, especially toward the end of the trick.

While they were working, Eleanor was heating up her balloon. It didn't seem to be going well. She was pacing around the partially inflated balloon, staring at it like she was going to heat it up with x-ray vision. She seemed to be missing something – at least, that was how Alice would remember it later on. She stormed off in the direction of her wagon, muttering to herself. This inconveniently led her into the path of Alice and Grendel.

What happened next would be a matter of great controversy. Just as they finished the trick, Eleanor walked into their path. She tried to walk around them, but of course at that moment Grendel lost his balance and went skidding into Eleanor's path, where he collided with her high-heeled black boot. If she had been paying closer attention, Eleanor probably would have avoided him, but her mind was elsewhere and she kicked him.

"Nark!" Grendel yelled. Judging by the tone in his voice, he was obviously more frightened than hurt, but even so, Alice reacted instinctively. "Watch where you're going!" she shouted.

Eleanor spun around. "He should watch where he's going!" she snapped.

Alice was incredulous. "I beg your pardon?"

"I *said* you should be more careful," Eleanor said in a tone that this suggested that this statement was both obvious and beyond reproach.

Alice paled. "You really are an insufferable woman, aren't you?" she asked, surprising even herself.

Eleanor narrowed her eyes. "Stay," she seethed, "out of my way." And having gotten in the last word, she spun around and stormed off.

"That woman seems to hate me with every fibre of her being," Alice whispered to Grendel. She gave him an inspection to make sure that he was all right. The little dinosaur was as tough as nails, but Alice still didn't like the idea of someone trying to hurt him.

"Nark!" Grendel said, indicating with his tone that a high quality butt rub would cure what was ailing him.

The show that night was big and energetic, but Alice felt just a little bit off somehow, even though the crowd thought the ring-catching trick was spectacular. The incident with Eleanor had thrown her for a loop, she had to admit. After they performed, she took Grendel out back, and then watched the other performers from the wings. There was no question that the circus was fun, but she couldn't help but feel a certain sense of wanton apathy. *'There's no denying it,'* Alice thought. *'What I really want to do is go home.'*

"You look tired," a voice said.

Alice spun around. Jack Cassidy was standing behind her.

"Jack! What are you doing here?"

It had been only a few months since she had last seen him, but Jack appeared to have grown about three inches and aged five years during that time. He was wearing a top hat and tails, and he had a walking stick in his right hand. He looked every bit the perfect gentleman. Perhaps he was.

"I came to meet the famous Alice Anderson," he said with a smile and a bow.

"I think that it's Grendel who's famous, not me," Alice said.

"Well, I suppose that's true," Jack agreed. "Who would have thought that our ship's little mascot would become world famous? From what I hear, the King has been wanting to take in your act."

"I – I hadn't heard that," Alice said, blushing. "I doubt that it's true."

"Well, the King doesn't have good taste, then," Jack acknowledged. "I first heard tales of the three-horned lizard while I was studying at Cambridge."

"Cambridge?" Alice repeated, surprised. "That's my–" she started to say *'Alma Mater,'* but caught herself. "That's impressive," she corrected.

"A wise woman once told me that University could make a gentleman out of anyone," he grinned. "We shall have to see if she was right. To be fair, I did gain acceptance to that particular institute of higher learning by crossing a number of learned palms with pirate gold, so its status as the accepted route to the gentry may have dimmed just slightly.”

“Actually, I think its status as an accepted route to the gentry is exactly what it once was,” she said, giggling. “What are you studying?”

“English, Latin, and Mathematics,” Jack said. “I’m a long way from taking my degree, so I haven’t focused yet. All in all, it has been an enormous challenge. I’m not sure that piracy wasn’t a more practical route to success, honestly. Where’s Grendel?”

“He’s in the pen out back, with the other animals,” Alice said. “Come with me, he’ll be glad to see you.”

They walked out of the tent toward the back, where Grendel was feeding on a bale of hay with a bunch of horses. “Nark!” he shouted excitedly.

“There’s a good fellow!” Jack Cassidy shouted back. Grendel ran up and Jack scratched him under the chin. “He seems glad to see me,” he added.

“Well, he’s usually glad to see *anyone,*” Alice said with a laugh.

“You won’t refuse me the honour of enjoying it just the same,” Jack said. “Without you, my little friend, my little ship would have been lost.”

“I’m sure that’s not true,” Alice mumbled. In truth, she wasn’t paying much attention to what Jack was saying, as she had just noticed that Eleanor was walking towards them.

It was towards the end of the show. Eleanor was usually in her balloon at this point, making the final preparations for her flight. Alice could only assume that something still wasn’t going right, as Eleanor was heading back to her wagon to get something again. This time she didn’t get anywhere close enough to them to force them into any kind of encounter. She simply stopped, and then stared, giving Alice and Jack a mean look. Then she promptly turned and walked back in the other direction.

‘*That was close,*’ Alice thought, relieved to have avoided another confrontation.

Jack, meanwhile, was still focused on Grendel, and hadn't appeared to notice the angry-looking Asian woman staring at them. "He's as cheerful as he ever was," Jack said, standing up to his full height. "It's good to see him again."

"Will you be in Bath long?" Alice asked.

"I'm afraid I just came up for the day. I've been staying with a friend in Somerset during the holidays. I'm heading back to University in the morning, but I didn't want to miss your show."

Alice related the details of her life in the circus, and Jack told her about life at Cambridge. For the most part it didn't sound like things at Cambridge had changed very much; undergraduates seemed to be as obnoxious as ever. They didn't take women, of course, and they wouldn't have accepted Alice as a teacher, or even a student, anyway, but at this point she had made her peace with this and moved on. Still, it was nice to hear slices of life from the world she'd left behind. Jack stayed for almost two hours, at which point he made his excuses and left politely. Alice said that she wished that she would see him soon, and he replied that should the circus come to Cambridge, he would make sure to call upon her again.

Afterwards, Alice found her way to the wagon, where Spring had once again decided to forego the usual evening of music and wine in favour of waiting for Alice and squeezing her for every last juicy piece of gossip she could get ahold of.

"You told me that you had been in love before," Spring said. "You didn't tell me he was so handsome."

"Is Jack handsome?" Alice asked. "I never really noticed."

Spring was wearing pigtails, one of which she pulled at excitedly. "With hair like that? Of course he's handsome, and a proper gentleman, too. I hope the day will be coming soon when I will be wishing you joy."

It took Alice a moment to realize that Spring was suggesting that she should *marry* Jack Cassidy, and then another moment to appreciate that the suggestion wasn't unreasonable, given the circumstances. It was easy to forget that dating hadn't been invented yet, and that marriages often had more to do with dowries and connections, neither of which Alice possessed. If Jack represented an eligible prospect, then Alice should consider herself lucky.

"Oh, I'm not in love with him. Jack isn't looking for a wife. He's at University," Alice replied.

"Well, he's looking for *something*, anyway," Spring said. She looked out of the window, as if she expected him to return.

"He's far too young, anyway," Alice added, hoping that would clear matters up a little.

"Uh huh," Spring said, a look of smug disbelief spreading across her face. "So, too young and unavailable. That makes two things that make no difference in matters of the heart. Do you want to try and suggest a third?"

Alice was about to respond to this, when at that moment Grendel walked in and climbed up onto the bed. Alice sighed, thinking that it was a shame that in spite of all of the training she had done, staying off the bed was one trick Grendel couldn't seem to master. "Off of the bed, sir," Alice suggested. "There isn't enough room for all three of us."

But Grendel didn't move. Alice patted him firmly on the shoulder. "I need you to get down," she said, but Grendel still didn't move.

"Spring," Alice said, "does Grendel look a little pale?"

Spring turned to look at the little dinosaur. Her expression was surprisingly serious. "Less like the ocean," she said, referring to the dinosaur's blue scales, "and more like the sky."

The little dinosaur stood up. He seemed to be trying to follow Alice's instruction to get off the bed, but his legs wobbled just slightly. He leaned over the edge of the bed and vomited all over the floor.

Alice looked at Spring, panic-stricken. "Quick," she insisted. "Get Mister Trask."

It took only five minutes or so for Fitz to come running, but it felt like an hour. Grendel looked miserable. His eyes were wide and he was panting heavily. He seemed aware that Alice was there, but didn't look at her or attempt to attract her attention, and his tongue hung out of his mouth in a way that seemed unnatural. Alice didn't know what to do. She sat there, stroking his centre horn, waiting for Trask to come.

When Fitz arrived, he was out of breath. He knew enough about animals to recognize the description of a troubled creature when he heard it, and had come running as fast he could. He stared deeply into the little dinosaur's eyes and smelled his breath, but seemed to learn the most from looking at the vomit on the floor.

"Bella donna," Fitz said, his voice not quivering even as his eyes betrayed an obvious concern. He pointed to some little berries that Grendel had vomited up. "We call it deadly nightshade back home. Most critters know to stay away from it. They must not have it in Tasmania."

'*Or in 100 million BC,*' Alice thought. Fitz scooped up Grendel and put him down on the floor. "We need to get him some water," he said.

Spring seemed to have anticipated this. She had already grabbed a pitcher of water from her side of the bed, and was pouring some into Grendel's water dish. "Here you go, my little friend," she said, encouragingly.

Grendel drank greedily, and then passed out on the floor. "Will he be all right?" Alice asked, her eyebrows turned up into all kinds of knots. After all that she and Grendel had been through, the idea of losing the little dinosaur was terrifying. In many ways, he was all she had.

"Can't say for certain," Fitz said. "He seems like he's a fighter, though. Throwing up was probably the best thing for him. Let him get some rest, and I'll see him in the mornin'." Fitz assured them that if there was any trouble in the middle of the night, that they should feel free to wake him. Alice thanked him profusely and assured him that she would. Spring suggested hopefully that Grendel's colour was returning, and that he looked a deeper shade of blue than he had a moment ago, but this didn't make Alice feel better.

"Spring," she asked when they were alone, "do you think Grendel could have gotten ahold of those berries on his own?"

Spring rubbed the little dinosaur's back. In his sleep, he gave a little kick. He looked so helpless. "I don't think so, honey," she admitted. "I think that you've got an enemy, and whomever it is, they're not afraid to hurt you to get what they want."

Chapter 10
Autumn in the Country

Although **Grendel had three days** of the worst sickness ever encountered by man or beast, he eventually recovered. Still, the incident with the bella donna was scary, and for weeks afterward Alice was frightened to let the little dinosaur out of her sight. She was undoubtedly overreacting, but after Malcolm's death, who could blame her? *'When the world is out to get you, being paranoid is just sound planning,'* Alice rationalized one night when Spring tried to get her to walk into town without the triceratops.

Alice and Spring agreed that Grendel had been deliberately poisoned, but they disagreed completely as to who the culprit might be. Spring believed that almost anyone in the circus could have tried to kill Grendel, and made a fair case for the idea. Alice had taken the circus by storm, and had taken the show's best performance slot, which had obviously upset people, more, perhaps, than Alice realized. Many of them probably wouldn't have looked at murdering the little dinosaur as anything particularly homicidal. Grendel wasn't a person, after all, so it wouldn't take a great deal of malevolence to attack him.

Alice, on the other hand, believed that Grendel had been poisoned by Eleanor, and by no one else.

"I don't think so," Spring said thoughtfully. It was the first day of autumn. They were in Warwickshire and the leaves were just starting to fall from the trees. They were in that shock of colour – red and orange and yellow were mixed in with green in a manner that seemed worthy of Van Gogh, or would be worthy of him whenever he got around to picking up a brush. It was one of their rare free days, when they were neither travelling nor performing, and Alice had reluctantly agreed to go for a walk on the condition that she be allowed to take Grendel with her. Nineteenth century people were much, much better at relaxing than their twenty-first century counterparts, and Alice had been trying to learn from Spring in this respect. Unfortunately, she had tried to bring up the subject of the attack on Grendel yet again, which by this point had become something of a broken record. (Which is, admittedly, an even more future-dated reference than Van Gogh had been.) Alice insisted for perhaps the tenth time that Eleanor had been behind the attack, but Spring wasn't having it.

"Eleanor is the one performer in the circus who the crowds like just as much as you," Spring insisted. She was wearing a black curly wig, which was up in a ponytail and gave her a certain air of respectability that made her difficult to ignore. "She wouldn't want your spotlight, anyway, even if she could have it. Her balloon always comes at the end. It *has* to. It gets the crowd out of the tent. That's the whole point."

"It isn't the spotlight she's after," Alice insisted. "I told you. She thinks I *killed* a man."

"About that," Spring said, chewing her lip, "I'm not really sure that I follow."

"What do you mean?" Alice asked.

Spring's eyes had the apologetic look of a nice woman who was on the verge of delivering bad news. "Well, I understand that you were accused of murder," she acknowledged, "but how does it work out that Eleanor would attack Grendel because of that? Grendel, and not you?"

"Nark!" Grendel said, taking this moment to chime in in a manner that Alice found irritating.

"I told you," Alice said, ignoring Grendel. "She wants to hurt me." Except that Spring was right, it didn't quite make sense. Eleanor's grudge was with her, not Grendel. Why attack the little dinosaur and not her? Did Eleanor think that forcing her out of the circus was an appropriate punishment for killing Malcolm? Alice didn't think so. The answer, of course, must have something to do with time travel, but what exactly Alice couldn't figure out yet, and she didn't feel that she could discuss it with Spring. That left with her with the one fact that Spring couldn't ignore – that Eleanor had kicked Grendel earlier and walked away in a huff. Spring had to acknowledge that this made Eleanor *look* guilty, but didn't seem to view it as anything more than an unfortunate coincidence.

"Another thing," Spring said, bending down to scratch Grendel on his ridge plate. "Poisoning seems like such a queer way to try and kill him. Why not just shoot him? After all, she's got that enormous musket stowed away in her wagon, it certainly seems like it would have a better chance of success."

That stopped Alice like an as-of-yet non-existent freight train. "Wait a minute," Alice said. "Are you telling me that Eleanor has a *rifle* in her wagon?"

"Yeah," Spring nodded. "It's a funny-looking long thing. Where she got it, I've got no idea, I'm sure. Most women have some kind of weapon for protection, of course, even I've got a little dagger in my bottom drawer. Still, it seems a little dramatic, if you ask me."

Regardless of how Spring felt, Alice was sure that Eleanor having a gun was definitely not a good sign. However, since she was alone in this belief, Alice decided to focus instead on inventing time travel.

It was October before she made a breakthrough. She'd been working with string theory, just fooling around really, when a thought occurred to her. It was a ludicrous, obscenely complicated, realistically impractical idea that might just get her killed. Still, it might work. The idea was to treat *time* as if it had the same properties as *matter* did. Then you could liquefy it and use its properties as a liquid to slice through the time space continuum like a knife through butter. You would need a few things that Alice didn't have – electricity, notably – but as ideas go, it was as close as you might get to being *possible*.

'Liquid time,' Alice thought to herself, one night after a long day's work. *'It does have a nice ring to it.'*

"My, it's cold out there!" Spring said, coming into the little wagon. This statement was really nothing more than a bit of passing conversation, but there was more truth in it than one might normally realize – the nineteenth century was *cold*. Alice, Spring, and Grendel were spending the entire month of October in little more than an unheated wooden box.

"Spring," Alice asked, "what does the circus do when winter comes?"

It was a fair question. Living in the little wagon was comfortable enough during the summer months, but in the winter the cold would be unbearable, and the circus tent equally so. What would they do once it was too cold to carry on?

"Geoff has a farm near Bristol where he and Fisk take the animals during the winter," Spring explained. "Most of the performers take to performing on the streets of London, although a few go up to Scotland. As for you and I, we could go anywhere, I suppose. What do you think? Where do you want to go?"

Alice looked down at the journal. She had been so wrapped up in the idea that she might be able to go back to the future that she had completely forgotten about the present. '*The present,*' Alice thought. '*When did the twenty-first century become the future?*' Then she said something she hadn't expected to say, "What if I told you that there was a way we could go anywhere? Anywhere at all, almost instantly? We could go to Paris, or Rome, or Ancient Greece, or Sherwood Forest for that matter. If we could go anywhere, anywhere at all, where would you go?"

Alice wasn't sure if Spring saw what she was saying as something serious, or if it was just some kind of game, but Spring seemed to consider her answer seriously enough. "It seems to me that even if you could go *anywhere* you always have to come back to the things that make you who you are. It doesn't matter, though. You can't just go anywhere. There's no such thing as magic."

"There's no such thing as magic," Alice agreed, "but there is a way to go anywhere. Anywhere you like, anywhere at all. We could go to America, Asia, Africa, the future, or the past. We could go anywhere you like, if only I could make it work."

Spring raised her eyebrows. "You sound pretty convinced. What makes you so sure?"

Now it was Alice's turn to raise her eyebrows. "You don't really think that Grendel comes from *Tasmania*, do you?"

Spring looked over at Grendel. The little dinosaur was curled up on the rug, snoring faintly. "What is he?" Spring asked. "He's not a dragon, is he? Because if he is, that would be disappointing."

Alice shook her head. "There's no such thing as dragons," she insisted.

Spring laughed. "That's too bad," she said, "because *that* I would like to see."

Alice sighed. "Barring the nearest dragon colony, if you could go absolutely anywhere, where would you like to go?"

Spring shrugged. "Someplace where people are judged not by what you see on the outside, but by what's in their hearts. But that seems about as likely as fighting a dragon."

Alice considered this. "There is such a place, a place where misfits fit in, and nothing is ordinary."

"Better than the circus?" Spring asked.

Alice nodded. "It might be. If we could get there."

Spring stepped over to the desk where Alice had been working, and studied the leather bound journal. "This *Chinese* you've been writing all this time…this has something to do with *that?"*

"This *Chinese* is a recipe that will bake a cake, but I am missing several ingredients. I guess wherever we go, we'll have to get there one step at a time, just like everybody else."

"There isn't anybody alive who at some point or another didn't wish they couldn't visit somewhere on a wish and a whim," Spring pointed out. "That doesn't mean that there isn't a real world out there that we have to deal with. The real question is, where do you want to go this winter?"

'Somewhere where I could find some liquid time,' Alice thought, but instead she said, "Personally, I think I would prefer the country to the town, but I have a feeling that you would enjoy something more exciting."

Spring laughed. "I'm not one for excitement, except in the evenings," she said. "Even then, I usually prefer to make it myself."

There might have been a person happier to have company than Geoff Mac was, but Alice had never met them. He was positively beaming when Alice asked if they could stay for the winter. "Absolutely!" he shouted, in his best Ringmaster voice. "We would love to have you! The more the merrier!" Fitz also seemed to be pleased with the idea. (In his case this was difficult to tell. He did raise his eyebrows at least twice.) Alice suspected that Fitz had different motives than Geoff did in welcoming them, but she let that pass.

It was strange to pack up her things again, even if it was only to take them out of the wagon when they had arrived. She, still had everything that she had brought with her from the twentieth century, but most of it seemed like part of a bygone era now. Her cell phone, identification, and other twenty-first century knick-knacks had been buried in the bottom of her drawer for months now. She still had the dress she had been wearing that night as well, although these days she only used it as a nightgown on cold nights. The leather blazer had been recently drafted into service against the cold. (Spring objected to this, complaining it was unladylike, but Alice felt that practicality outweighed the dictations of polite society.) She still had the Houdinometer, and its silver metallic surface glittered unnaturally when she threw it into her carpet bag. She knew that she should toss all of those things into the river and have done with it, but she couldn't bring herself to do it, somehow. It was difficult to let go of absolutely everything and pretend that she had always been this new person that she had somehow turned into.

Geoff called it Tennant Place, and it had apparently belonged to his grandfather, and while Geoff claimed that it wasn't much, after half a year of sharing a wagon with Spring it looked like Buckingham Palace. It was a stately country home made of stone – a little plain, and a tad disheveled, but with a majestic quality that implied a certain history. None of the floors were level, and all of the stairs creaked, which Alice supposed was part of its charm.

It probably would have been five minutes outside of Bristol by car, but that put it on the far side of the world, as far as they were concerned. There were only two other farms within walking distance and little else. The farm had only two servants (which Alice was privately grateful for) but it was a working farm with chickens, fields, and stables. Alice was most excited about the prospect of a sitting room with a proper fireplace. Geoff also informed Alice that during their stay she and Spring would be treated to that rarest of nineteenth century luxuries – separate bedrooms.

"You might be chilly at night," Geoff warned, "but there are five bedrooms, not including the servant's quarters, so I thought you might as well take the spare."

"The spare?" Alice repeated. There was something about that. Something that didn't quite add up.

"Yes. It's a little small, but I'm sure that you'll manage," Geoff spoke with the sort of warm smile you'd expect from an innkeeper. "Your room is right next to Eleanor's, so you'll both be sharing a bath."

'Ah,' Alice thought. There it was. There were five bedrooms. One for Geoff, Spring, and Fisk, as well as one for herself, and one for Eleanor. Alice nodded her head politely, and did her best to avoid looking like she was having a heart attack at this very moment. "Of course," she said calmly. "The spare bedroom. Where is it, exactly?"

"Just up the stairs," Geoff gave a grand wave. "Right this way."

Alice tried hard to focus on the positive. The room at Tennant Place was first and foremost a *room,* with four walls and a complete lack of wheels. It would stay in the same place, had a fireplace, and a bed that she didn't have to share. Even if she did have to bump into Eleanor on her way to the loo, it was definitely an improvement. Still, she worried about such close proximity. Eleanor would probably have more than ample opportunity to harm Grendel. She would have to be careful.

"It's not much," Geoff admitted, as they walked into Alice's new room. A little of the bluster seemed to be taken out of him, and he smiled apologetically.

"It's perfect," Alice said, and it very nearly was.

"It was mine, when I was a boy," Geoff said, giving the room a sad smile. "Or it was during the holidays. I'm afraid that I was never Granddad's favourite. I spent a good deal of time banished here, for one reason or another."

"It's lovely, really," Alice insisted, and then, trying to make what she said next sound as casual as possible, she asked, "When is Eleanor arriving?" Eleanor hadn't travelled with them to Bristol. They had seen the last of her when the circus split apart.

"She had to go to London first. I forget what it was, but she had some urgent business that she'd been wanting to take care of for quite some time. She'll be joining us in a week or two."

'Thank Heaven for small favours,' Alice thought, but rather than harping on the unpleasant realities, she asked, "What's for dinner?"

Geoff proved to be a gracious host. He had the cook prepare a roast chicken and mashed turnips, along with a loaf of fresh bread and butter. (After nine months of living in the nineteen century, Alice had become accustomed to treating what might have once seemed like an ordinary meal as if it was a holiday feast.) They ate in the dining hall, a small but elegant room with an elegant dining table, complete with ornate high-backed chairs that looked like they had been made by a group of fairies who had been suffering from obsessive-compulsive disorder. It was a pleasant meal, with all the trappings of home.

"We suffer from an excess of idleness while we're here," Geoff said as they sat down to dinner. "I try to make up for that fact with large quantities of gossip and food."

"I suppose we'll have to make do," Spring said, smiling. She was wearing her very best wig, a tiger-striped number with long straight hair, along with a new dress, and seemed to be very glad to be off the road for a while.

"What was your Grandfather?" Alice asked. "Some sort of country squire?"

"He aspired to be one," Geoff admitted. "Every generation of my family proves to be a misfit, and then hopes that the next generation will make up for it somehow. My grandfather was a foreigner. He made a living overseas and then retired here. I think he aspired to being a proper gentleman, but the locals always saw him as an outsider."

"I think feeling like an outsider is the normal state of existence everywhere," Alice replied.

"That's true enough!" Spring said with a laugh. "Although some of us tend to be a little further outside than the others."

"Eleanor isn't here yet," Alice chided, and everyone laughed. This was a pointed remark, and it achieved its purpose – it brought the subject of Eleanor up in a manner that seemed natural.

"Where is Eleanor?" Spring asked. "She didn't come here with us."

"Must have been some sort of balloon-related emergency," Alice commented.

"No—" Fitz said. "She went—"

"Mgmhm-mghm!" Geoff cleared his throat with all the subtlety of a clown walking through Saint John's Cathedral. The two men exchanged glances.

"It was a personal matter," Fitz said, but something about his deeply furrowed brow suggested that it wasn't. This time it was Alice and Spring's turn to exchange glances.

"I thought you said we would pass the time with gossip," Spring teased, but much to Alice's disappointment the subject was actually dropped.

Alice took a page from Spring's book and tried to focus on the positive again. She was positive that she didn't want to share a bath with Eleanor, she was positive that whatever had taken Eleanor to London was bad news, and she was positive that Eleanor would try and slit her throat if she didn't lock her door. Strangely, though, as the days stretched out, Eleanor never arrived. First a week passed, then two, then three. Where she had gone to was difficult to discern. Geoff claimed that he'd had a letter from her saying that she wouldn't arrive until after Christmas, but no one else ever read this letter, and when pressed, Geoff was more than a little vague on the details. Alice somehow had a feeling that she had not seen the last of Eleanor Dragon, but something about the oddly distracted look on Geoff's face troubled her.

If there was one good thing about all of this, it was that all the free time and the threat to Grendel's life encouraged Alice to put her nose to the grindstone and finish inventing time travel. Luckily for Alice, another big breakthrough was right up on the horizon.

It happened in December, just after the first snowfall. Christmas was a fortnight hence. (Alice was a proper nineteenth century woman now. She could use words like *hence* and *fortnight.*) The snow was a beautiful, gentle blanket of white, giving the fields a peaceful serenity. Alice was on a sofa in the sitting room with Grendel in her lap and listening to Spring read Shakespeare's sonnets out loud.

"That time of year thou mayst in me behold–" Spring began, but she was interrupted by Geoff entering the front door.

"Good Lord!" Geoff exclaimed, kicking the snow off his boots. He was wearing his Ringmaster's top hat and a warm muffler, both of which were covered in snow. This, Alice reflected, made him look a little like Bob Cratchit, a joke which made her smile, even if she couldn't share it with anyone.

"If it gets any colder out there, I'm going to bring the horses inside. You don't mind bunking with Harriet, do you Spring?"

"I love Harriet dearly, but I prefer a bedroom that smells of fresh flowers, not manure," Spring said. "Does Fitz need help feeding the animals?"

"He will not admit it, but he could use your aid," Geoff said. "Before you go, let me tell you about the news from town."

When you won't have access to a television set for another century, the news from town is a pretty big deal, so Spring immediately put the book away and sat up attentively. In practice, Alice had discovered that a local housewife preparing a new batch of strawberry jam tended to qualify as a big news day, but it was nice to hear about the outside world just the same. "Did Mrs. Field's dog have puppies yet?" Alice asked.

"Yes," Geoff said, "but there's bigger news than that. One of the new steamboats was heading down the river, and it got caught in the ice. I have it from a good source that the Captain tried to break her free and then ran aground against the rocks."

"A steamboat?" This was more significant news that Alice could have hoped for. A moment ago she was expecting *puppies* to be the lead story.

"Was anyone hurt?" Spring asked.

"Can it be salvaged?" Alice queried. She realized that asking this question before the first one had been answered was probably the single most callous thing she could have said. It was a little like asking if a Volkswagen Beetle had suffered any body damage in an accident that had crippled the driver. Still, she couldn't help herself.

"The crew and passengers are fine," Geoff said. "The ship will have to be scrapped, of course."

Alice pushed Grendel out of her lap and stood up. "Please," she said, "I need to go and see it."

Harriet was saddled within the hour. Geoff, Spring, and Fitz all gave Alice queer looks as she headed out into the snow. She was sure that all three imagined that she simply wanted to see the steamboat. Spring might have guessed that Alice would have a certain scientific curiosity, but clearly none had understood why she would need to see a sinking boat right this very second. To them, a steam engine was the absolute pinnacle of modern transportation, but in this case it was a pinnacle that not going anywhere, meaning that the ship had become an impressive paperweight, one which wouldn't warrant a trip out in cold weather to see. To Alice, it was power – potentially a source of electricity. With a little retrofitting, it could act as a generator, and Alice would be one step closer to completing her time machine. (For that matter, Alice would be one step closer to charging her cell phone!) She grabbed a hammer and the largest length of rope that she could find, mounted Harriet, and then galloped to the river with the urgency of a Jane Austen character who had just found out that her sister was carrying the wrong man's baby.

It took Alice two hours before she reached the steamship. It wasn't hard to find. There was a stream of people heading in that direction. Most were on foot, although a few here and there were on wagons. Alice was pretty sure that she knew what they were doing.

Historic people are usually revered not for the innocence of their souls, but for the lack of incriminating evidence. There were sure to be scavengers. Alice could only hope that no one had taken what she wanted.

By the time she got to the steamship the sky had gone black. The ship came out of the darkness like a mountain in the fog. A steamboat is an image that was ubiquitous in both the era that Alice grew up in and the one she lived in now, and yet she didn't think she had ever actually seen one, not in real life, anyway. It was enormous; less like a yacht and more like a mansion on water. Indeed, it was so large that it had a second floor with a porch, and inside Alice could make out a ballroom with a chandelier. Perhaps none of this was surprising, but it was so massive that in spite of the urgency of her business, Alice took a moment to pull Harriet up and stare. People were stealing everything in sight. They were grabbing chairs, tables, silverware, and plates – almost anything that might have had some value. It looked like the Titanic had looters.

Even if the ship hadn't been crawling with scavengers, it was obvious that it was done for. The front had smashed against a rock, and the boat was tilted out of the water in a manner that looked dangerous. Although it was winter, the river here was surprisingly wide and deep – deeper in fact than it would run in another era. *'It's an impressive-looking ship,'* Alice thought as she rode up, *'but it doesn't look like it could steer very well.'*

Alice scanned the shoreline until she saw a man wearing a captain's cap and uniform. He was sitting on the tree stump and looked stunned. *'Plain as day,'* Alice thought. *'This won't be easy.'*

As she approached, the Captain stood up. This seemed to be a reflexive gesture, as he didn't take his eyes off of the ship. "Excuse me," she said cautiously as she dismounted Harriet and approached the man on foot, "are you all right?"

The man nodded, although this confirmation wasn't born out in any way by the look in his eyes, which was equal parts fear and astonishment. "We lodged in the ice. I increased the engine power, but we thrust forward too quickly and ran aground on the rocks. I split the hull."

"I'm sorry," Alice said apologetically. "Was anyone hurt?"

"None of the passengers, nor crew," the man said. "They're all in the sitting room of a local farm, cursing my name. As far as these—" he pointed at the looters. "Two of them were washed away a few minutes ago, trying to carry off a chaise lounge."

"I'm sorry about that, too," Alice said, although privately she wondered if the Captain might think that the thieves got what they deserved. "My name is Alice. Alice Anderson. I understand that this ship is powered by steam?"

"Captain Josiah Smith," the man said. "And yes, it was, although I expect now that it's nothing more than a dam in the river."

Alice realized that there was probably very little that could be done to salvage the ship as a whole, but she wasn't positive that the Captain would be resigned to this fact. "Yes," she said, hesitantly. "Yes. I want to talk to you about buying the steam engine."

The Captain turned and looked at her. His eyes widened. It actually looked like he was about to laugh. "The engine?" he said, incredulous. "The engine is going to be at the bottom of the river by morning."

"In which case it won't be of any use to anyone, so you shouldn't mind parting with it," Alice pointed out.

The Captain stared at her. "Miss, I'm only trying to do you a favour," he said. "That engine weighs a quarter of a ton. "You won't be able to lift it, and even if you could, you'd drown."

"Leave that to me," Alice said. "I'm sorry, I'm afraid I don't have much money."

"If it's enough to get me a meal, a warm bed, and passage home, I'll be happy to say I never saw you," the Captain said. "It's not mine to sell, and I seem to have lost my living."

With permission to take the engine secured, Alice tied the rope to Harriet's saddle and then tied the other end around her waist. She climbed in the saddle and then rode out into the water. Harriet resisted this at first, and with good reason. Alice knew that even with fur, the icy waters must feel like daggers against the horse's legs. (In truth, she had ridden out into the water instead of wading out herself for precisely that same reason.) Harriet was loyal, though, and with a very small amount of coaching, they were out in the middle of the river. As they got closer, Alice's boots started to get wet, and she could feel the cold water against her skin. "Hang on, girl," Alice said, as much to herself as to Harriet. "This will only take a moment."

They reached the side of the boat, and with great difficulty, Alice hoisted herself over the railing and onto the ship's deck. Right away, a man and a woman carrying a large wardrobe walked right past her. "Careful, miss," the man said, pushing her to one side so that they could make their way past. "She's taking on water pretty quickly." The two walked to the far end of the bow, and much to Alice's amazement, threw the wardrobe over the side and started to float away down the river, using the top of it as a raft.

Alice was sure that the man was right. The boat must be sinking. As she walked up the ship's deck, she seemed to be climbing at a steep angle, with the stern hanging almost completely out of the water. *'That's good, though,'* Alice told herself. *'The stern is where the engine ought to be, which means it might be still dry.'*

Another man brushed past her, carrying tea cups. 'Madame,' he said, with a French accent and a polite little bow. Just as he passed, there was an enormous crash from the upstairs, as if something large and expensive appeared to have come down upon the floor. "What was that?" Alice asked, obviously surprised. The Frenchman stopped momentarily and looked up to where the noise had come from. "I expect zat iz ze chandelier," he said. "Best you get off zis boat, before eet goes ablaze."

The general crowd of looters seemed to agree with this assessment. They were all heading in a mass exodus toward the shore. Apparently everything good had been taken, and what was left didn't seem to be worth dying for. Only Alice seemed willing to head in the opposite direction. She walked to the far end of the deck and entered a small, functional-looking door, the kind that might have been used by the ship's crew.

The engine was surprisingly small for a ship this size. Alice imagined that it must have been a fairly slow ride. Bigger than a car engine, but smaller than the diesel motor of a large truck, it was roughly the size of two potbellied stoves stuck together. It was made of cast iron and looked relatively new. It was attached to the boat's paddle with a long leather belt, and was bolted to the floor next to a large coal bin, which appeared to have been emptied by the looters. Although Alice had very little idea of how a steam engine actually worked, she recognized its various levers and dials, because she had seen it before – it was the same black metal engine that had been in Eleanor's dirigible the first time that Alice had ridden in it.

'I suppose that's a good sign,' Alice thought to herself. Even so, she wasn't going to have too much time to get it ashore. The water was already seeping into the engine room and, the boat seemed to groan uncomfortably with every step she took.

First thing's first, she untied the rope from around her waist, and then secured it to the engine block. This was easy enough, although it was followed by another loud crunch, which Alice figured was probably part of the boat breaking off and floating down the river. Whatever it was, it caused the water to rush up to her feet. It was just as cold as it had been a moment before, but now it seemed to bother her less, in large part because the room was so warm. *'Why is it so hot in here?'* Alice thought, but as soon as she said it, she knew the answer. *'The boat is on fire.'* Looking up, she could see that smoke was coming through the ceiling quite clearly.

In retrospect, climbing onboard a steamship to drown with its engine and probably killing a horse in the process wasn't her best plan. Alice realized that the bolts holding the engine to the floor were much too big for her to simply rip out with the claw of a hammer, even if the ship weren't shaking as badly as it was. All she could do now was grab onto the engine and hope that she wasn't going to die. *'It doesn't seem fair,'* she thought, *'dying before I'm born, after surviving Nazis, pirates, Americans, and being wrongfully accused. It seems like my luck should have turned around at some point or another.'*

What happened next did not immediately make a whole lot of sense. The ceiling of the engine room collapsed just as the boat shifted, causing the entire ship to splinter apart. Alice found herself spinning in several different directions at once. A wall of water splashed against her like a tide, hitting her right in the face, but she still clung to the engine block, even as she heard the ship's paddlewheel smash behind her. When the dust and the smoke finally settled, Alice somehow found herself floating on something resembling a small raft. She and the engine were now floating downstream with the remaining pieces of the steamship. Alice was alive, and best of all, Harriet was just a short distance away, with the far end of the rope was still tied to her saddle.

"Harriet!" Alice shouted. "Get us out of here!"

Harriet didn't have to be told twice. The mare dug in and hauled toward the shore. In a few minutes, Alice and the steam engine were on dry ground. Alice was exhausted, aching, and freezing, but still alive, and in possession of the best Christmas present that she ever could have hoped for. "I'm really going to do this," Alice said, hugging the mare around the neck. "I'm going to make it home."

Chapter 11
The Library

Susan Moore was five weeks, four days, and three hours from retirement from her position as Chief Librarian in the rare books section of the British Library, and the thought of stepping down filled her with both fascination and dread. The rare books section was the library's most famous department, containing the most important and rare books in the entire world, and of course Susan loved working there. On the other hand, she was getting older, and she'd grown to dislike the hustle and bustle, the effort, and especially the weariness at the end of the day. Also, and she hated to admit this, but there were times when as much as she loved Chaucer, Milton, Dickens, and Marlowe (and the library had first editions of all of these), there were days when she wanted to sit down with a good old-fashioned bodice-ripper with a cover featuring a picture of a man with perfect abs making love to a woman with heaving bosoms. If the book was a dog-eared paperback, that would be a bonus, too. Susan had not been able to read a trashy romance for almost forty years now, as it would have been unseemly for the head librarian to be seen reading a book that would have made William Shakespeare seasick. Susan had never married and had devoted her life to her career, making sure the greatest books were preserved for all time. Now that her time as a librarian was ending, she wanted bosoms to heave, even if they were no longer her own.

Retirement is always bittersweet, at best. There were a number of sad things about leaving the library. It was nice to come in and adjust the case with the original copy of Beowulf. She had taken it out just once, ten years ago, when it had been photographed with a special camera. She had worn white gloves when she held it. The pages felt like dried oak leaves. There were the hand-written Beatle lyrics in the corner. Those were amazing to look at – so simple and careless, scrawled on loose leaf paper with less effort than it would have taken to take notes on a poetry lecture. There were the students, too. Susan had given tours to everybody from toddlers to graduate students, and loved giving lectures on the library's collection. Much to her surprise, she tended to like high school students the best. They were not as pretentious as they would be in their college years, but not as easily distracted as younger students, either. She liked the tourists, too – it was very flattering to meet someone from America, or Russia, or Japan, all of whom had come to see the collection. Some were strange, but most were friendly, eager, and excited. Truth be told, she liked the strange ones the best. It was hard not to be curious about them. So, in some ways it was fitting that five weeks, four days, and three hours from her retirement, the strangest of strangers walked in.

Susan had seen Eleanor Dragon on perhaps a dozen separate occasions – enough times that she had made a point of learning her name. Sometimes Eleanor seemed to know who Susan was and sometimes she didn't. It wasn't hard to forget Eleanor, though, since she always looked the same. Since the first time Susan had seen her, almost thirty years before, Eleanor didn't appear to have gotten even a day older. She didn't even seem to change her clothes – the black outfit she wore on her first visit seemed as unchanged as her austere expression. For more than thirty years, Susan had acted as if this were perfectly normal, never saying anything as time seemed to pass as Eleanor by. *'Well, not this time,'* Susan thought.

"May I help you?" she asked stiffly. She stood up to receive Eleanor as though she were the Queen. Susan looked far too much like the typical librarian to be intimidating to anybody. To the untrained eye she was all grey hair and horn-rimmed spectacles, but she was determined to try and be impressive just the same.

Even with Susan standing up straight, Eleanor towered over her. "Yes," Eleanor said gruffly. "I'm looking for a periodical, a first edition." She handed Susan a formal written request for the material, signed by the librarian downstairs. "Do you have it?"

Susan read over the request. "*The Final Problem* was first published in Strand Magazine in 1893, and yes, we do have a copy," Susan replied, professionally, "but before I get it for you, I want something."

This seemed to surprise Eleanor. She stared at the librarian impassively.

Susan swallowed hard. "The first time that you came in, I was new here. You requested a copy of the journal of a medieval monk. You looked about the same age I was, give or take a few."

Eleanor took no pains to deny this fact. "I remember," she said.

"You came back a few years later looking for an Early Edition of Thomas Malory."

"I recall," Eleanor said.

"You were back about ten years after that. You looked more like my niece by then. You come back decade after decade, and now you're here, looking like my granddaughter, and I'm an old woman less than six weeks from retirement. You haven't aged a day."

Eleanor clearly didn't know how to respond to this. "I'm sorry," she mumbled.

Susan found the answer frustrating. "I don't want an apology," she fumed. "I want to know how you do it. I want to know how to turn back the clock. I want to have *bosoms* that *heave,*" she insisted, and at that moment a lock of Susan's curly grey hair came undone.

Eleanor sighed, suddenly her face seemed a little less severe, and Susan wondered if perhaps she hadn't heard this question before. "I'm afraid the one thing I can't do is roll back the wheels of time," Eleanor said. "I'm sorry."

Susan frowned. "Then why don't the wheels ever seem to affect you? Or do you have some sort of amazing skin treatment that the rest of us don't know about?"

"I will admit that I am proof that there is more in Heaven and Earth than is dreamt of in your philosophy, but I'm afraid that I can't go into specifics," Eleanor said. "What I can tell you is that unlike any other petitioner to this department, when I request a copy of an ancient book, it may be a matter of life or death."

"Life or death?" Susan repeated.

"Life or death," Eleanor insisted.

Susan decided that perhaps it would be better to do her duty. "I'll get the periodical," she said.

It took her a few minutes to find it. It was tucked away in a dusty corner, where the nineteenth century periodicals were kept. It was a portion of the library usually reserved for elderly college professors who thought that the twentieth and twenty-first centuries were really just a passing fad, and didn't need to be trifled with. Susan made a mental note to dust and clean this area before she left. She took down a large volume of bounded periodicals and brought it out to the viewing table, where Eleanor met her.

"We use white gloves when handling anything over a century old," Susan told Eleanor, unnecessarily. She handed Eleanor a pair of cotton gloves. Eleanor slid them on and proceeded to inspect the aging journal. Susan hadn't been quite sure what to expect as Eleanor looked at the periodical. She knew from experience that most scholars who came to look at these documents were more interested in form, rather than content. The texts were available anywhere. Still, there was something about the way that this strange woman stared at the story's engraving that gave Susan pause. A thought occurred to her, one that was both exhilarating and scary.

"My god," Eleanor said, her voice barely above a whisper.

Susan usually refrained from asking people questions when she was showing rare books, but this time she couldn't help herself. "What? What is it?"

"I've been a fool," Eleanor answered, not taking her eyes off the page.

"I beg your pardon?" Susan asked.

Eleanor didn't answer, but responded with a question of her own. "Can I take a picture?"

"No flashes," Susan replied.

Eleanor took out her mobile and snapped off two pictures – one of the whole engraving and a close up of the details. "Thank you," she said.

Putting the mobile back in her pocket, Eleanor stood up and got ready to leave. As she headed to the door, Susan called out, "Wait!" She wasn't even sure what she was going to say. She was sure that she would never see Eleanor again, and she was also sure that this woman was somehow a part of something – some greater world, that was somehow bigger than the one she knew. "Please, just tell me – how is it that you've never aged, not even a day?"

The corners of Eleanor's mouth turned upward just slightly. "By learning to live with my regrets," she said. "Now if you'll excuse me, I really must be off." Eleanor turned with a sweeping gesture and headed toward the exit. She would need to act quickly, before everything was undone. She knew that even time travellers had some moments that they could never come back from. She strolled out of the building, turned the corner, and felt a knife jabbing into her back.

Witnesses who dialed 999 would later describe the kidnapper as a homeless man, remembering in particular his bald head and pointy beard. They didn't have the appropriate archeological background to recognize the man's bizarre covering of skin and furs as belonging to the Paleolithic culture. No one, not even the snootiest member of the Royal Geographic Society, would have been brave enough to call the kidnapper a caveman. It just wasn't done. If you do a quick search of the local adverts for career opportunities in your area, caveman isn't one that's going to come up. Eleanor, however, recognized the feel of the handmade dagger pressed into her back as belonging to someone ancient and dangerous.

"Whatever you do, don't move," Locrinus said, "unless you wish to die."

Eleanor didn't squirm, even an inch. "If you do this," she said calmly, "our world will die. The lives of everyone on Earth will shift."

Locrinus's voice was nothing more than a menacing hiss. "That is precisely what my master is counting on," he insisted. "But if you move, you'll never live to see it."

Chapter 12
Inventing Time

It has been noted that after the discovery of the Rosetta Stone it took twenty-two years to translate hieroglyphics, even with the ancient Greek laid side by side. Alice took comfort in this, as even with a working knowledge of physics and engineering it took her months to get the steam engine running. Everything about it was difficult and occasionally seemed to border on the impossible. Simply getting the engine back to Geoff's farm took the better part of three days. First, she had to return Harriet from her harrowing ride. Fitz was positively livid that Alice had rode the mare out into the freezing water, and had insisted that she be given a rub down and a full day's rest. Meanwhile, Alice cleared out the red and black wagon, and prepared it to haul the steam engine back to the barn. The engine itself was difficult to manage. Alice was forced to draft every single person she knew into helping her load it, including a group of local boys she found playing on a frozen pond that morning. No one had ever intended it to leave the steamboat, so it had no wheels. Alice was able to find a pulley, which assisted in getting the engine up to the wagon, but it was a long, exasperating effort. At the end of the third day, though, the engine was sitting in Geoff's barn.

Starting the engine took the better part of a week. This was less labour-intensive, although it did involve the purchase and shovelling of coal. The engine hadn't come with a manual, and wasn't entirely intuitive in many ways. Steam could be a harsh mistress. The combination of fire and water was awkward, even at the best of times. Fortunately, Alice was patient, and eventually the gears turned and the engine's pistons whirred and clicked, slowly and steadily.

"It is impressive," Spring said one morning as the machine was slowly pumping. Her mouth said the word "impressive" but her eyes were fixed on Alice, who was much less impressively covered from head to toe in soot. "What is it supposed to do, exactly?"

"Nothing yet," Alice said, "but it when it does, it will change the world."

While Alice had been working, life on the farm continued at its usual pace. The highlight of the winter was naturally Christmas, which was a little subdued compared with a modern Christmas, but was enjoyable just the same. Geoff's excitement at having guests on Christmas Day was both palpable and contagious, and as he ran around the house decorating, preparing food, and generally celebrating. Alice found herself almost as excited as he was. Although presents were somewhat lacking, the Christmas feast was one of the merriest that Alice could ever remember, even with just the four of them.

Spring was spending more and more time with Fitz. Increasingly the two of them could be found working in the barn together, enjoying the simple pleasures of life in the country. Fitz was quiet where Spring was talkative, and that suited both of them. Spring had found someone who would listen to her for hours, even when she had nothing to say, and Fitz had found someone who never cared if he was too embarrassed to talk. Fitz's idea of courtship was both painful and awkward to watch, but Spring was patient and seemed to understand him in a way that no one else did. Alice, for her part, was made both happy and sad by this news. She contented herself to spend her nights on the sofa, reading a book as Grendel sat curled up at her feet, and her days in the barn, transforming the steam engine into a time machine.

With the engine up and running, Alice began the work on changing mechanical energy to electrical power. This was less labour-intensive than the first two portions of the task. The biggest challenge here was supplies. She needed copper wire, magnets, gauges, and cylinders, a number of which hadn't been invented yet and whose construction would be difficult. Alice was able to find a compass maker in Bristol who was able to help her with many of the necessary parts, along with a blacksmith who could be employed in the construction of others. Even after the acquisition of everything that Alice needed, assembly and construction would take weeks, and it would be weeks more until everything was integrated into the engine and the output was consistent. The electrical output had to be spliced into a form Alice could use and the voltage had to be monitored constantly. Eventually, though, on a cold night in February, Alice did the unthinkable – she plugged in her cellphone and let it charge.

Alice was so happy when she saw the 'charging' logo appear on the front of the screen that she almost fell over laughing. Surely this was how Mission Control must have felt when Neil Armstrong landed on the Moon. Alice raised her voice to the skies and cheered. This drew the attention of Spring, who had been out riding with Fitz.

"What is that?" Spring asked. (Spring had never seen the mobile before; Alice had always been very careful to keep it out of sight.)

"It's a computer," Alice said. (She had decided that the words 'mobile' and 'telephone' would be inexplicable and inaccurate. For the moment, Alice would not be telephoning anyone. She was only interested in the mobile's computing abilities.)

"It's beautiful," Spring said, staring at it. "What does it do?"

"It's for storing and compiling information," Alice answered.

"You're speaking Chinese again," Spring said, with a sad shake of her head.

Alice smiled. "It's easier to show you." She beamed and pulled up her photo gallery.

Spring's eyes grew as wide as dinner plates. "My God," she said.

"Impressive, isn't it?" Alice remarked.

"How is this done?" Spring asked.

Alice considered what the simple answer to that question would be. "With light, and mathematics, and just a touch of electricity," she answered, hoping that this recipe wasn't too difficult to follow.

"Electricity?"

"Like lightning, only smaller," she explained.

Spring picked up the mobile delicately, touching the photo as if it were something fragile. "The likeness is flawless," she said, admiringly. "Who is it?"

Alice looked down at the photo. "My sister, Wendy," she said. The photograph was a picture of her sister from the Christmas before last. Wendy was wearing a little black dress and holding a glass of champagne. Alice remembered taking it. It seemed like a thousand years ago. Before she realized it, a tear was running down her cheek.

Spring stared at the photograph with a mixture of fascination and bewilderment. "Her dress is strange," Spring said, obviously taken aback by Wendy's modern style.

"That's just how she dresses," Alice said.

"She resembles you."

"Do you think so?" Alice asked, brushing the tear away. It seemed like so long since she'd thought about her sister.

"Absolutely," Spring said.

"I haven't thought about her in a long time," Alice admitted. "I miss her terribly."

"That's why you're doing all this," Spring concluded. "You want to go back to where there are things like this," and she held up the mobile.

"I would," Alice said, although as soon as the words were out of her mouth she realized that they sounded hurtful. "At least for a while," she added. The funny thing was, as soon as she had said this, she realized how true it actually was. She *would* like to go home, see her sister, and prove her innocence, but she would also love to see the future, the Roman Empire, and the nineteen sixties. She could see her parents when they were young, and her grandparents. Truth be told, though, she knew that sooner or later she would want to come back here. There was no traffic here, no pollution, and pound a month was enough to live on in downtown London. Best of all, at night you could see the stars – the Milky Way was so bright that you could reach out and touch it. It didn't make sense anymore to simply go back to the present and just stay there.

"When you go," Spring suggested, "maybe you could take one of those pictures of me with you."

Alice laughed. "Of course," she said. "Here, we'll take one right now."

"It doesn't hurt, does it?" Spring asked.

"Not a bit," Alice said, and a minute later Spring had her picture taken for the very first time.

"I don't know how necessary it is, but it is something," Spring said, looking at the photo.

It took until the end of March to get the time machine in proper working order. The steam engine attached to the generator would generate electricity. Alice's time travel formula was programmed into the mobile, which in turn would control their direction as they moved through time. This was wired into a special receptacle, which ideally should work in the same manner that the orb had. All Alice needed now was some liquid time and she would be on her way. This was a tall order, though, and having no feasible way of procuring liquid time, she was forced to set aside the time machine in favour of going through life one day at a time, just like everyone else. This was harder than you might think, especially since while Alice had been busy inventing time travel, the world had been passing her by.

Winter started to break, slowly but steadily, and while the farm was a giant mud pit once the snow melted, it did mean that the air was fresh and pleasant, and Alice and Grendel could go for a walk without having to bundle up like they were headed into deep space. They were on just such a walk one morning, enjoying the view from a hill nearby, when Alice spotted a figure on a horse galloping towards them. She had become used to the idea that any stranger coming within 100 metres of the house was a special occasion and she sheltered her eyes from the sun to see who was coming towards them. "Looks like we have company," she said to Grendel.

"Nark!" the little dinosaur said, bounding over towards the man.

Alice watch the man dismount from his horse. It seemed to her that Grendel was running over toward him with a little too much enthusiasm. It was only when the man that got off his horse, and scratched him under his ridge plate that Alice realized that it must be someone she knew. Jack Cassidy came walking towards them. Alice hadn't recognized him at first. His long black bangs were tucked underneath a large top hat, and he was dressed in a green riding jacket that Jane Austen would have found spectacular. Alice smiled, and waved, and began walking towards him. *'They must be feeding him well at University,'* Alice thought, thinking that if anything he looked taller and broader-shouldered than the last time. As she got closer, she noticed a thin scar on the left side of his cheek was healing slowly.

"I see you got my letter," Alice said. She had written him once, briefly, towards the end of the tour, just to let him know where she would be. She wasn't really sure why she had, except that she hadn't had anyone else to tell. She was surprised to see him; she hadn't invited him, and he hadn't written back.

"I did," Jack admitted. "You'll forgive me. I am a poor correspondent."

"Nark!" Grendel said, wiggling his tail.

"It seems he remembers me," Jack said, giving Grendel another scratch underneath the ridge plate. "I'm glad. I certainly would never forget him."

'His voice is different. He sounds like a gentleman now. That's the education, I suppose.' Alice thought. "Grendel's a smart fellow," she said, smiling. "He doesn't forget a face."

"I'm glad," Jack replied. He made an oddly formal bow. "Fancy a walk, my Lady?"

There was a little path that followed a creek towards the edge of Geoff's property, and they went for a walk, admiring the buds on the trees and watching Grendel munch on the sprouting daffodils. Alice, never sure of the best way to start a conversation, began by asking what struck her as the single most obvious question.

"Where did you get the scar?"

"Fencing with my betters," Jack said. His tone was surprisingly careless. "Someone thought it would be funny to spar with the pirate using a real rapier."

"I'm sorry," Alice said.

"You're not the only one," Jack said, rubbing his cheek and laughing.

"What are you studying in school?" she asked.

"Manners mostly. It seems to be the chief specialty in all fields. I may not know any more Latin or Greek then I did a year ago, but I've learned the proper way to introduce myself to a lady."

"Have you met very many ladies to introduce yourself to?" she asked him teasingly.

"No," Jack admitted. "There were more women on the ship than at Cambridge. I'm afraid if I want to fall in love, I shall have to return to piracy."

"Then you shall know the best of both worlds," Alice said brightly. "How to meet a woman and how to show one a good time."

"You have a point there," Jack conceded.

"Are you on holiday?" Alice asked.

"Only for the week," Jack acknowledged. "Having no real place to go, I thought I might as well come and see you."

They walked for a while down by the stream. Jack relayed some stories about University and Alice told him quite a bit about the circus, which Jack enjoyed because he said it sounded a bit like a pirate ship. Alice asked him if he would like to stay for lunch, but he declined, saying he had matters to attend to in town. Alice asked if he would like to return tomorrow, and he promised that he would.

It was that afternoon that Eleanor finally came to Tennant Place, landing her dirigible in the east fields. *'I suppose it was inevitable,'* Alice thought, watching from a distance as the balloon came down. Fitz aided Eleanor, guiding the dirigible to a safe spot in the field, not too far from the tree line. Eleanor looked a little windswept, but no worse for the winter. Lowering the balloon was a tedious process, clearly requiring a good deal of Eleanor's attention, but in the middle of securing the dirigible to the ground, Eleanor caught sight of Alice and stared at her open-mouthed, as if she had just seen a unicorn prancing through the field.

'Oh dear,' Alice thought. She had visions of another time flare up, and thought it would perhaps be best to give Eleanor a fairly wide berth, at least for the day. She went and found Spring and asked if she would like to go into town for a bit of shopping. Spring, who had been looking forward to her namesake season, was clearly delighted at the idea, and put on a lovely black-bobbed wig for the occasion. The two of them walked into town, where they engaged in the simple pleasures of a new dress shop that had opened during the winter.

"You should buy that bonnet," Spring suggested to Alice as they were wandering though the shop. It was true that Alice had been admiring it; it was very well made, with some lovely detailed flowers embroidered on the side.

"I don't know," Alice said. "I don't really feel I'm the sort for bonnets."

"*Gentlemen* prefer a lady in a bonnet," Spring insisted.

"I suppose that it will keep the sun off of my face," Alice said, and she found herself parting with a few shillings.

With the bonnet on outside, Alice stepped out of the dress shop, blending in better than she ever had before. Catching her reflection in a window, the woman gazing back at her didn't look any different than any other woman walking down the street. In fact, if anything she seemed to blend in better than Spring did.

"My goodness," Spring said. She pointed a finger at a stranger on the far side of the street. "*What is wrong with that man?*"

Alice looked across the road to where Spring was pointing. What was wrong with the man on the other side of the street was difficult to say. He wasn't sick or injured, he was just *odd-looking*. His head was entirely bald and he had a pointed beard, and he was dressed in a series of furs that seemed more appropriate for a hunting trip with an Inuit tribe than walking down the street in springtime. He was talking with a well-dressed man in black, who seemed to be trying very hard to act like he was somewhere else. They were definitely drawing some odd looks from passersby, but perhaps strangest of all was from Alice. She couldn't help but think that the well-dressed man in black in particular seemed vaguely familiar, as though she had met him at a party somewhere, but she hadn't really gotten to know him. It wasn't until the man in black turned to face her that she began to put things together. Alice had met Milton Chesterfield only once, on that night in the London Blitz that she had run away from Keith, but she hadn't forgotten him. Then, as now, he seemed a little nervous, although perhaps talking to the caveman was more than enough reason to feel that way. To anyone other than Alice he probably looked like a mourner, but Alice recognized the fashions of the Victorian era. Alice couldn't explain why, but she suddenly had a desperate desire to go unnoticed.

'*The last time he saw me, I was a twentieth-century woman,*' Alice thought, hoping that the bonnet covered her face. '*Of course, he may not have met me at all yet.*' She grabbed Spring's arm firmly but gently. "What do you say we head back?" she asked.

"Are you sure?" Spring said. "There's another shop, just around the corner."

"I'm sure," Alice insisted. "Geoff will be expecting us home for tea."

Spring sighed. "All right, all right. Let's go."

They returned to Tennant Place quickly and quietly, where they were greeted at the front door by Eleanor.

"Alice," she said, staring at her open-mouthed.

"Hello," Alice said, a little unsure why Eleanor had chosen to meet them at the door. There was an awkward pause that Alice couldn't have held her breath through if she had wanted to.

"I'm glad to see that you are well," Eleanor said.

Alice smiled. "Thank you. I'm glad to see that you are also well. We expected you months ago."

Suddenly Eleanor seemed to want to look anywhere but at Alice's face. "Thank you," she said politely. "I was delayed. I would have been here sooner, if I could."

There was a certain inflection in Eleanor's voice that made Alice wonder what she was on about, but just as she was about to say something, Geoff called from the other room. "Alice! Eleanor! Spring? Everyone, come and eat!"

The conversation over dinner was stilted, as if everybody had something they were trying very hard not to say. After dinner, Alice spent the remainder of the evening listening to Spring read Shakespeare's sonnets, and then headed off to bed early.

Jack returned the next day around midday, bringing the sun with him. It was a beautiful day. Everything had gone green. This time Jack knocked on the front door, and was greeted by Geoff and Spring, who were curious to meet him. Spring wore her best powdered white wig and Geoff wore his Ringmaster coat. Jack suggested that he and Alice should go for a walk, and Alice was only too happy to oblige.

"Wear your new bonnet," Spring said in an exaggerated stage whisper as Alice headed out the door.

Alice rolled her eyes.

"Gentlemen prefer a woman with a bonnet," Spring insisted.

Alice sighed. She felt like a teenager being scolded by her mother, but nonetheless she left the house with the bonnet on her head.

The day was warm and pleasant. They sat down in a field, where they sat staring at the horizon, as Grendel enjoyed grazing on clover. Just for entertainment, Jack pulled a small leather-bound book out of his jacket, and opened it up.

"What's that?" Alice asked.

"A small book of verse," Jack said, noncommittally.

"Well, go on, let's have a go," Alice said.

Jack casually flipped through the volume. "The time of year thou mayst in me behold," he said.

And there it was. After all this time, Alice was back in the dream that she'd had on the night that Malcolm was killed. All the improbable things that she'd seen that night – the bonnet, the dinosaur, the sonnet (which of course she now knew), and the faceless man in fancy dress trying to romance her, it was all there, all of it. Only this time, it wasn't a dream, it was real, and the faceless man wasn't faceless – he was Jack Cassidy.

The funny thing about déjà vu is that when you get it, there's almost no way for the recurring moment to play out in the exactly same way that it did the first time, if for no other reason than you are simply aware of the pretense, so when Alice mumbled "Shakespeare," a moment later, it seemed to have a very different connotation than it did the first time.

"You know it, then?" Jack asked, flipping the book over and looking at its cover.

"Of course," Alice said, "and now I know why. I'm about to make a joke about how you're trying to woo me. Then you're going to kiss me. I'm going to find it surprising."

In spite of the romantic implications, this statement was just strange enough to make Jack raise his eyebrows. "What are you on about?" he asked.

"Nothing. Nothing. It was a dream. A dream I had about you a while ago. It was rubbish, probably."

Jack nodded. "I had a dream about you last night. It was the strangest dream I ever had."

"Is that right?" Alice asked.

"We were in London," Jack said, "only it wasn't London. It was monstrous, huge and complex. There were all these carriages moving about, even though they didn't have horses. Everything was loud, and fast."

"Horseless carriages?" Alice repeated.

"I suppose so," Jack said. "I don't really know what else to call them, at any rate. They were smoothed and curved, mostly, like wine bottles."

"You're drifting," Alice said. Suddenly a thought came to her. "What day is today?"

"The twenty-ninth of March," Jack said. "Why?"

And suddenly Alice realized that she was headed home. She sat up, grabbed Jack by the face, and kissed him firmly. "You were drifting!" she said excitedly.

Jack found the moment a little too perplexing to make any sense of what was going on. "I – I beg your pardon?"

"The dream you had is from the future. You are a time traveller. You just don't know it yet, because you haven't been on your first trip. The dream is a sign that you're going to be travelling to the future soon." Alice stood up, raised up her dress, and started walking toward the house at a pace approaching a run. "The only reason you would be about to travel through time is if I brought you with me," she concluded.

Jack had stood up and was following after her. He had Grendel nipping at his heels and appeared to be struggling to keep up. "Brought me with you?" he repeated in a tone that suggested that he very much *didn't* want to be the person who pointed out that Alice had gone mad. "I'm sorry, but what are you talking about?"

"If you are having dreams about automobiles, it's because you're about to travel into the future. I know, because I've been there. I've been trying to get back to the twenty-first century for months now, and if you're about to go there, it's because I'm going to take you. And if I'm about to take you, *it means that my time machine is nearly complete.*"

As explanations go, this one was probably only really successful in giving Jack information about the nature and depths of Alice's lunacy. She didn't care. "I'm sorry," Jack said politely. "Are you feeling ill?"

"I haven't felt this good for a year," she said. "A year almost exactly," she added, quietly to herself.

The past few months, it hadn't paid much to look at a calendar. One day was so much like the next that it didn't really matter. It wasn't like she had any appointments to keep. When she had woken up that morning, it hadn't occurred to her that it was the anniversary of the day she had left America – the day that Malcolm had been murdered, the day that she desperately wanted to get back to.

All of which led Alice to the conclusion that there had to be some liquid time around somewhere close by. That was the only explanation for Jack having a dream about cars on the *one day* that Alice wanted to return to the present more than any other. And if Eleanor wasn't going to provide her with it (after all, she said she was only here to watch) then it must be that Alice was going to use her own time machine to get back to the present. It seemed that this only left one inevitable conclusion – Alice must already have some liquid time with her, or near her somewhere.

She burst into the house and ran up the stairs. Jack followed her inside.

"Where are you going?" he asked.

Alice spun her head around. "My room," she shouted. "And before you start to go on about waiting downstairs, I'll ask you to spare me the pre-Victorian sensibilities. We have a man's life to save and there isn't a moment to spare."

She had stored all of her twentieth century paraphernalia in the carpet bag under the bed. She pulled it out now and then dumped everything onto the bed itself. There had to be some liquid time here somewhere: the question was where. The Mobile? No, she didn't think so. If it was inside she would need to break it apart, and she would need that to program the time machine, anyway. Nothing else really made sense, though, except—

"The Houdinometer," Alice exclaimed to herself. It was the only logical conclusion. Everything else she'd brought from the future was something she knew and understood, but the Houdinometer was an *unknown* entity. She had no idea how it worked, or why. Something had to be powering it, though, something powerful. Alice picked up the shiny beetle-shaped metal object and stared at it, her eyes wide.

Jack had entered the room in the manner of a doctor visiting a patient who was in hospice. He stared at the Houdinometer, bug-eyed in disbelief. "What," he asked, "is that?"

"Something from the future," Alice said. "Something I need to break."

She pushed past him and headed downstairs. Jack followed. Spring was standing at the bottom of the stairs, looking up at the two of them, obviously concerned. "Are you all right?" she asked.

"Never better," Alice answered, "only I need something to crack this open with," and she held up the Houdinometer.

It was to Spring's credit that she simply accepted this statement on faith, rather than trying to back up and have Alice explain what was going on. "Fitz has a hammer in the barn," she said, after just the briefest glance at what Alice was holding. "Let me fetch it."

Spring came back with a rusty old hammer. Alice took it, got down on her knees, and placed the Houdinometer on the floor. "You might want to stand back," she said to Spring and Jack.

Alice raised the hammer and brought it down onto the Houdinometer with a thunderous clap. The device cracked open with the sound of a stained glass window being dropped from a skyscraper. The casing shattered, spilling a cornucopia of what looked like the pieces of a pocket watch. There were gears, coils, and springs, and – there! Right in the centre was a tiny glass vial filled with the strangest liquid that Alice had ever seen. It looked a little like magma, and a little like moon rocks, with perhaps just a dash of cinnamon thrown in, and when Alice picked it up, it glowed a brilliant bright blue.

Confronted with the first evidence that Alice was not absolutely bonkers, Jack took a second to let the moment soak in. "I feel like I'm repeating myself," he said, "but what is that, exactly?"

"It's called liquid time," Alice said. "It's going to take us anywhere we want to go – the past, the present, the future. We can go to distant lands that you've scarcely dreamed of. This little vial puts the world at our fingertips."

Spring seemed to understand the significance of what Alice was saying more than Jack did. "So you really were born in the future, then?"

Alice smiled and then nodded. "My grandparents won't be born for another century. Why, didn't you believe me?"

Spring sighed. "It's hard to believe you when you aren't making any sense," she said. "Which is often."

Alice laughed. "This time, I intend to back up what I say. This was the missing piece to my time machine. It will work now. All I need is Eleanor's balloon."

Spring's shocked expression became, if anything, more incredulous. *"Eleanor,"* she said, doing her best to speak in italics, *"is never going to give you her balloon."*

Alice's eyes flashed wickedly. "I have no intension of asking her for it," she said. Turning to look at Jack, she asked, "You were a pirate once – what do you say we steal a balloon?"

Chapter 13
Stealing Time

"**I**'d like to repeat that I think this is a bad idea,**"** Spring said for the third time.

"Stealing an object the size of a house in broad daylight does take a certain amount of courage," Jack pointed out.

"You were a pirate," Alice said defensively. "You should have plenty of courage."

"Ah, you see, that's a myth," Jack explained. "Most people think that pirates are very brave, but in fact we are surprisingly cowardly. I would have thought you'd have figured that out by now. Are you sure you wouldn't rather do this at night? Or not at all? I'm thinking 'not at all' is an idea that could use a little more discussion."

"When you travel through time, you can only travel to the same day of the year as the day that you're leaving," Alice explained. "I need to go back *today*. Otherwise it will be too late."

"Too late for what?" Spring asked.

"To stop a murder," Alice said. "Now let's get to it."

They had just loaded the time machine into the back of the wagon. Since bringing it back to the barn, Alice had put casters on it, making it easier to move, but it was still a tough job. Alice had hooked her mobile and the vial with the liquid time up to the machine, and loaded up the wagon with coal. She was nearly ready to travel through time.

"Are you sure this plan will work?" Spring asked.

It wasn't much of a plan, really. Jack would ride up ahead of them, and then check to see if the coast was clear. If Eleanor wasn't near the balloon, they would load the time machine onto the dirigible's platform. If Eleanor was there, they would ride on past and hope that she didn't ask any questions. Alice knew that nothing was certain, but the fact that she had already seen the time machine on the dirigible's platform made her fairly confident that this was going to work. They hitched Harriet up to the red and black wagon, and then started to roll out towards the dirigible, which was anchored out in one of the farm's far fields, near the tree line.

Jack rode out towards the balloon, doing his best to act as if he was simply interested in looking at it, as it was certainly an impressive sight. "I don't see anyone over there," he said, after riding back towards Alice, "although I suppose that she could be hiding."

"Hiding? That's ridiculous," Alice said.

"It does beg the question, where is she?" Spring asked. "She wasn't in the house either."

"I'm sure she must have gone into town or something," Alice said, dismissing their concerns.

It was a nervous few minutes as they hauled the time machine towards the dirigible. The fields were on uneven ground and the work was slow. By the time they made it out to the balloon thirty minutes had gone by and Spring was so nervous that her teeth were chattering. "Don't worry," Alice said, patting her on the shoulder. "In another minute, we'll be off."

Jack, who was riding alongside the wagon, shielded his eyes from the sun, and stared at the dirigible's platform. "How do you want to do this?" he asked, as they closed in on the balloon.

"There's a door on one side of the platform," Alice said, knowingly. "Here, I'll show you."

Jack dismounted, and Alice got down off the wagon. They walked around to the other side of the dirigible's platform. Suddenly Eleanor sprung up and drew her gun in a single fluid motion, pointing it with the cool menace of a woman skilled in its use. Alice, unsure of what to do at this point, raised her hands in the air and she started to back away slowly.

"Stop," Eleanor commanded.

Alice stopped. What Eleanor said next would change the course of her entire life.

"That man is Professor Moriarty."

Alice realized something. It was difficult to tell from where she was standing, but she realized now that the gun wasn't actually pointed at *her*. It was pointed at Jack, standing behind her. Alice stared at Eleanor. "Professor Moriarty?" she asked, not believing what she was told.

"The same," Eleanor repeated.

"Sherlock's Moriarty?" Alice said.

Eleanor's gun didn't move an inch. "The very same," she said, her eyes narrowing.

Alice didn't know how to respond to this. Fortunately, Spring did.

"You're wrong," Spring insisted. "His name is—"

"What?" Eleanor asked. "John Smith? Michael Casey? Something else, maybe?"

"You're suggesting that Moriarty is a pseudonym," Alice surmised.

"If you were Sherlock Holmes's nemesis, would you tell him your real name?" Eleanor asked.

Alice gave just the slightest stammer before answering. "Th – that doesn't mean he's Professor Moriarty." Alice pointed out.

"I'm sorry," Jack said, taking just the slightest step forward. "I have absolutely no idea what you are talking about."

"She's saying that you're one of the most notorious criminals the world has ever known," Alice said. "Or at any rate, that you are going to be."

"I'm saying more than that, I'm saying that he's a murderer."

There was a silence.

"I don't believe you," Alice said.

Eleanor's body seemed to collapse in on itself, like a balloon that had lost some of its air. "I'm sorry," she said. "I know that you have no reason to trust me. I have acted in a manner that was both suspicious and unpleasant. I'm sorry. I thought that you killed the man I loved." A tear ran down Eleanor's cheek. She brushed it away. Alice didn't know what to say. Stunned silence seemed the best approach.

"I met Malcolm Oliver after you left him," Eleanor said. "He was a broken man after you went to America, did you know that?"

Alice tried to speak, but no words seemed to come out. Silence seemed to be the only communication she was capable of.

"He was a wreck," Eleanor said. "Broken, pushed to the limits – but also wonderful. That was how he was when I met him. I helped him to move on with his life. It was the happiest I've ever been."

"Did he know that you were a time traveller?" Alice asked.

"I never talked to him about it," Eleanor admitted. "I think he started to suspect, though. Probably after I left a few things that aren't supposed to exist around the house. Once he started to suspect what was really possible, he started to explore Fictional Realism, which of course only made him look crazy."

Alice smiled. "It did, at that," she said.

"I was so happy, happy like I'd never been before. We had so many plans. I had thought about quitting my job at the museum and living in just one time and one place, but I'd gotten a lead on an object the museum would want. It was one of the most important objects in history, the broken sword of an ancient king, one whose existence stretches the bonds of credibility, even in our world. It's an item that any time traveller would find extremely valuable, because it's a symbol of all the unknown realms we have yet to conquer."

"Excalibur," Alice said. "Professor Hopper, he was at my last lecture. He said that Malcolm had been asking about Excalibur, and whether or not it was real."

"The stories of King Arthur are shrouded in magic and mysticism," Eleanor said. "They violate the laws of physics. They shouldn't exist. That's what makes them so valuable. But I was given information that a gang of renegade time travellers were starting to get close. I was sent in to infiltrate them, and that's when I met the Professor."

"Moriarty," Alice repeated. It was interesting to note that it was not a question.

"He never told me his name," Eleanor admitted. "We only called him 'the Professor.' More often than not he ruled in absentia, but I did meet him once or twice. He was an older man, easy to recognize, and distinguished by a long thin scar on his cheek."

Alice considered her next words very carefully. Jack did not.

"I'm sorry," he said. "I don't believe in prophecies."

He looked as though a glass curtain had come down over his face. Alice couldn't blame him. She wasn't sure how much Jack understood about what Eleanor was talking about, but it was clear that nothing she was saying was flattering. Alice gave him a sympathetic look. "No," Alice agreed. "Neither do I."

"If you don't believe me, perhaps you'll believe your own eyes," Eleanor said. She reached into her pocket and pulled out a piece of paper, handing into Alice without ever dropping the rifle.

Alice stared at the piece of paper. It looked more than a little dog-eared. "What is this?" she asked.

"An original illustration from '*The Final Problem,*' by Arthur Conan Doyle."

It was a pen and ink drawing, very well done, in a style that looked like it might have been fashionable in another fifty years. The drawing wasn't Jack, not yet, anyway. The man depicted was much, much older, so much so that you might not have recognized him, except that there was something familiar about the eyes. The eyes and the pencil-thin scar that ran down the subject's cheek.

"That's the original. Over the centuries images of him have evolved and changed, but if you look close, you'll see it."

Alice's denial kicked into overdrive. "No," she insisted.

"Alice, it's him. He's Professor Moriarty. He's going to steal the Mona Lisa one day. He's going to push Sherlock Holmes over Reichenbach Falls, and *he's going to kill Malcolm Oliver.*"

"No!" Alice shouted. "No, it was Keith. Keith lied to me. He was in love with me. He had gotten in touch with Malcolm the night before he was killed, and he killed him because Malcolm wanted to get back together with me."

Eleanor's tone was surprisingly calm, at least compared with Alice's. "No," she said. "Malcolm never intended to do anything with you other than give that lecture. It was Malcolm who had contacted Keith because I had finally found Excalibur, and stashed it in Malcolm's apartment."

Alice shook her head. "No," she insisted.

"I didn't want to believe it either," Eleanor admitted. "Mostly because I couldn't get myself to admit that I'd done something so stupid. After months of undercover work, I had finally gotten a tip. The sword had been discovered at an abbey and was being moved to Scotland. All I had to do was get there first."

"Did you?" Alice asked.

Eleanor nodded. "I did. I took it off a pair of monks. I brought a rifle and fired a shot in the air. It scared them so badly that one of them took a vow of silence afterward."

"Sounds serious," Alice commented dryly.

"The sword is one of the most valuable and dangerous objects the world has ever known. It was important that it not fall into the wrong hands," Eleanor dismissed. "I did what was necessary, but I made a mistake."

"Is that right?" Alice asked.

"I assumed that Moriarty would never be able to find me in the vast oceans of time," Eleanor explained. "Even walking though London, I was never concerned. It never occurred to me that one of us would go to Moriarty and let him know where Excalibur was."

Alice shook her head. "What do you mean?" she asked.

Eleanor sighed. "I never thought another time traveller would tell him where he could find it."

"Who?" Alice asked. "Who told him?"

Eleanor shook her head. "It was Keith Quick. He didn't mean to, of course. Keith went looking for–"

Alice suddenly started to catch up. "Keith went looking for Sherlock Holmes' pipe," she said.

"He did," Eleanor agreed, "and when Keith went after the pipe, he needed information. So he talked to the one man who would know Holmes's secrets, and would have a desire to divulge them."

"Moriarty," Alice said.

"Moriarty had found his way to the Gristle and Thorn by then," Eleanor said. "He was happy to help Keith get the pipe. In exchange for helping Keith, Moriarty had gotten the one thing that he wanted, information about you."

Alice rolled her eyes. "What did Keith tell him? That he was married to the *Mother of Time?*"

"I don't think so," Eleanor said. "Keith only played the fool. He wouldn't have been stupid enough to mention you by name, but he might have told Moriarty that his wife was a twenty-first century astrophysicist. It's possible he simply told a few stories about you, or mentioned your podcast, or the colour of your hair. Whatever he said, it was enough. Once he knew about you, it would have led him to Malcolm, and later, to me. Once Moriarty knew who you were and where he could find you, he could find out about your public appearances, in particular your appearance at the Royal Astronomy Conference.

"It must have seemed like the perfect opportunity. He knew that I had the sword, and he knew that I was with Malcolm. He knew from the podcast that you had been living in New York, and he would have known that you hadn't learned of time travel yet, and that you hadn't met Keith Quick. He knew you were going to do the conference with Malcolm. It was a chance to net one of the one most important objects in the world and to influence the direction of all of time and space. He had to move quickly and carefully. There was a very precise moment when he had to act, and that would have been the night that you flew in from New York.

'This is embarrassing to admit, but I had left the sword hilt in a small handbag, under the bed. I had gone out that evening to the Gristle and Thorn, where I got a message from the Fergus on staff. My father, who lives in medieval China, was sick. I left immediately, barely taking a moment to leave Malcolm a message that I would be out of town. The message about my father was a lie, of course. Moriarty knew that you were coming to the conference, and he knew that with me out of century, the sword would be with Malcolm. What he did next was tricky. First, he contacted Malcolm, and told him that the sword was in his flat. Because of Malcolm's work with fictional realism, he would have believed Moriarty when he told him what it was."

Alice stared at Eleanor. Even as the tears ran down her face, Eleanor never dropped her rifle. It was strange. Alice had always thought of Eleanor's features as striking. It had never occurred to her before that someone else might also consider them strikingly beautiful.

"Moriarty had no fear of the local police, of course, but he would have wanted to make his acquisition of the sword look legitimate. He told Malcom he could verify the sword's authenticity by making a phone call, then he gave him Keith Quick's number. The call would ensure that Keith would be wanted for questioning by the police, which at the very least would make him look guilty, especially to you."

Eleanor sighed deeply. "I don't like to think about the moment, the moment when Malcolm was killed. He would have been such an easy target. He was so trusting. It probably wouldn't have taken anything more than an old man knocking on the door to his flat, and asking if this was the third floor, or the fourth. All he would have had to do is open the door for a moment. A moment that would change my life forever."

At long last, Alice knew everything – why she was here, why Malcolm had been killed, why she was the Mother of Time. The final pieces of the chaotic puzzle of her life were finally falling into place.

"I thought it was Keith," Alice explained. "He lied to me about our relationship. Then he told me that Malcolm had called him on the night that he died."

"I know it sounds cruel, but Keith would have had good reason to lie to you. He knows about your future, and he wouldn't want to affect it adversely."

"I suppose that's true," Alice admitted.

"So that's what all this was about?" Spring asked. "A robbery?"

"Indeed," Eleanor agreed. "One that was almost perfectly executed. Once Moriarty had the sword, he replaced it with another object – a cross. The cross was inscribed with Arthur's name and was manufactured in the Middle Ages to fool King Edward. The cross had been switched with the sword before, doing so again would simply make any claim I made against him look like a case of misidentification, or sour grapes. Where he found the cross, I don't know, but–"

"He found it," Alice interrupted, "last year. On a pirate ship."

"I wondered," Eleanor said, and for the first time she lowered the barrel of her gun, just slightly.

During her time as an astrophysicist, Alice would have gladly told the greater podcasting community that when a scientist is confronted with data that clearly disproves a hypothesis, then the hypothesis must be abandoned, no matter what the cost. This was true, but it didn't take the sting out of Eleanor proving her wrong. For a moment, Alice was so wrapped up in her own bitterness that it took her by surprise when a very young-sounding voice behind her said, "Alice?"

Alice spun around. Jack looked pale. Any maturity he had acquired over the last year seemed to have been drained out of him over the last few minutes. Even so, he had a brave look on his face. *'He's just a boy,'* Alice reminded herself. *'He isn't responsible for all this. At least, not yet.'*

"I can't pretend that I understand what the two of you are talking about," Jack said quietly.

"No," Alice said. The word seemed to be ringing in her head like a church bell. "We were talking about things that might be. Shadows of the future, cast by a very bright sun."

Jack pushed his bangs out of his eyes. "I don't know anything of the future. I only came to ask you a – a question," he stuttered slightly as the words came out. There was a hidden meaning there, an implication that the rest of this conversation was a fait accompli.

Alice looked at her shoes. "I know," she admitted.

"I thought you might."

There was no easy way to put this. "The answer will be no," she said.

The silence was deafening.

Jack gave Eleanor a very slight but definitely menacing glance. "I take it that my reputation precedes me," he said.

Alice wasn't sure how to respond to this. The truth was that even if she hadn't run into Eleanor, the answer would still have been no. She had fallen under the spell of the nineteenth century, and in many ways it had seemed like a dream, but it wasn't who she was. Even if Eleanor's news hadn't woken her up in the way that it had, there was no way she was going to sleep forever. Still, it didn't mean she had to hurt his feelings any more than was necessary. "It's not your reputation," she insisted, a tad disingenuously. "It's me. I am not the person that you think I am."

"It sounds like I am not the person you think I am either," Jack observed.

Whatever happened, Alice didn't want to encourage him down a dark road. "You are no different than you were this morning," she insisted, but it seemed that Jack was finished. He held up a hand in protest.

"Madam, this is the second time that I have come to you with news that I thought would be the making of me," he replied. "I have been disappointed both times." He gave a curt bow and turned to leave. Alice grabbed his arm.

"Wait!" she said. "Don't leave, not like this. You still have your education. That's what's really important."

Jack sneered at her. "You said that education could make a gentleman out of anyone, but I think all it has made me is a gentleman pirate. The worst of both worlds, after all." He smiled bitterly, and then walked away at a pace approaching a run. Alice would have run after him, but Eleanor grabbed her by the arm. She watched him walk away, cutting a handsome figure as he strode across the fields.

She would see him again two centuries later.

Chapter 14
The Return

Eleanor's willingness to help meant that Alice didn't have to sneak away with the balloon, but there was very little time to spare. Alice could only travel back to the same day she had left, which meant that since today was March twenty-ninth, she only had a couple of hours to get back to the present. Still, there wasn't any need to steal away, and she took a few minutes to say goodbye.

"I'm still not clear," Geoff said. "Where are you going again?"

"For the purpose of conversation, let's say London," Alice replied. "After that, I'm not sure."

Geoff hadn't been able to confirm all of Eleanor's story, but he had affirmed what Eleanor had told him before she parted company

– that she was travelling a long distance to prove Alice was innocent of a murder. The confirmation made Alice feel better about what had happened, although it didn't change matters any.

"I could send for a coach," Geoff suggested. He knew the dirigible was not the most reliable means of transportation, and didn't understand why Alice would want to use it, but since there were a myriad of other things that Geoff didn't understand, Alice decided not to worry him.

"This is one trip where we need to travel by airship," Alice insisted, doing her best to sound reassuring.

"I hate to lose three performers who are so talented right before the start of the new season," Geoff said with a sigh, "but it will make the trapeze artists happy. No one has paid attention to them for ages."

Alice smiled. In spite of the unpleasant incident with Jack Cassidy, the mood was considerably lighter than it had been. Spring seemed relieved that Alice had avoided becoming a burglar. She had packed a bag, and changed into a black and blonde wig with lovely curls. Fitz had changed too, from somewhere he had dug out a moth-eaten black jacket and a bow tie. As usual, he said very little, but there was a haunted look in his eyes.

"Are you sure you want to come along?" Alice asked.

Spring grinned. "Oh, you know me, I'm always up for an adventure. Besides, we can always come back, can't we?"

"We *can* always come back," Alice agreed, "but things may seem different afterwards."

"Good," Spring said. "It's been a long time since I've been homesick. It does a body good to miss the ones we love. Besides, I've never left the country. We are going to leave the country, aren't we?"

"We're going to leave the country, the century, and the continent, although not necessarily in that order," Alice assured her. "Probably the millennium before the weekend."

"I'll settle for leaving the country," Spring said. Before she left she kissed Fitz on the cheek and promised she would be back soon.

Eleanor was most anxious to get moving. She adjusted the dirigible's sandbags, and watched the skies nervously. "We should get up in the air," she said. "I don't like the look of those clouds moving in."

In keeping with the season, the weather had gone from sunny to cloudy in manner of moments, and already the sun was beginning to get low in the sky. *'If the sun is setting for me, it's also setting for Malcolm,'* Alice thought. In attempt to project an air of confidence, she stepped onto the dirigible's platform. "We're ready," she insisted.

Fitz, who was standing near Grendel, gave the little dinosaur a final scratch on the horn. "Watch yourself," he said.

"Nark!" Grendel said cheerfully, and after a final butt wiggle, both he and Spring climbed aboard.

Alice turned to look at Eleanor. "I suppose that I didn't need to go through all of this," she mused. "You probably have a time orb, don't you?"

"I do," Eleanor admitted. "And you're right, I could get us back home. Afterward, we could stop by Kitty Hawk in a 747 and offer to fly them back to Dayton. We are time travellers. Sometimes we have to get out of the way and let history work its magic. Today that history is being made by you."

Eleanor untied the balloon from where it was staked to the ground. She dropped one sandbag, then another. Slowly, carefully, the balloon started to rise into the air.

The effect was as impressive, as always, but had the biggest impression on Spring, who admittedly had never been in a building over three stories tall. "I always wanted to ride in this," she said, her eyes getting wider as the ground retreated from them.

"You might want to hang on," Eleanor suggested.

Spring, still a little nervous, took this suggestion a little too literally, and latched onto the side of the platform with both hands. "Just wait until we get above the clouds," Alice said.

Spring nodded and made no other reply. Her death grip on the railing didn't budge. Alice turned her attention to the time machine.

The flame was already lit, and the coal was heating the boiler, although it would take a few minutes for the engine to work itself up to full pressure.

"Is this this really going to work?" Eleanor whispered to Alice while Spring had her back turned.

"No idea," Alice admitted. "It should work."

"*Should?*" Eleanor asked.

"Well, it's an untested experimental piece of equipment, designed to rip a hole in the space time continuum," Alice pointed out. "I think that *should* is a fairly confident-sounding word."

"Fair enough," Eleanor conceded.

"My biggest concern is precision," Alice admitted. "I'm just hoping we end up in the right place."

"Wherever we end up, it will be historic," Eleanor said. "But if we can get me back to Malcolm, I will be the happiest woman alive."

If you've never seen the setting sun from above the clouds, rest assured that the view is truly spectacular. No less so if you are viewing it from a dirigible, where everything is still and you can enjoy the fresh air. The clouds had covered the ground completely, making it seem like a new world, one which was beautiful in its stillness, which is why Alice was so surprised when she heard Spring shout out, "What is that?"

Alice spun around and shaded her eyes. Spring was facing almost due west, which made it difficult to see with the setting sun, but if you squinted, you could just make out something coming towards them in the distance. As it approached its shape became clearer. Alice swallowed hard.

It was an American B52 bomber.

"Good Lord," Alice said. "Are they here to shoot me down again?"

Eleanor spun around. She looked at the plane and smiled. "No. Don't you see? They're here to see you off." She turned in another direction and shouted, "Look!"

A group of F16 fighter jets flying in V formation were cruising just behind them. They were flanked by what appeared to be the airplane built by the Wright brothers and a pair of men in Victorian garb wearing enormous mechanical wings, which they flapped like birds.

"Yeeehah!" someone yelled. This didn't come from Alice, Spring, or Eleanor, but from a group of cowboys descending from above. They were riding robotic winged horses and firing their six-shooters into the air. There was a space shuttle, too – it was cruising at a high altitude in the north, above a group of Apache helicopters that were rising up from the clouds.

"Great Scott!" Spring shouted. "What *are* those?"

"Whirlybirds!" Alice shouted back, laughing.

"I am never going to complain about dragonflies again!" Spring said.

The helicopters hung motionless in the air, as did two men wearing jetpacks, and a futuristic chrome contraption that Alice could only describe as a flying saucer. Other flying machines seemed to run and skip about on the air like small children, a pair of stealth bombers twisted through the air, and – there! Way off in the distance, an old biplane with the π symbol painted on its tail was doing barrel rolls behind a pair of flying robots. "It's beautiful!" Alice said "All of it! I can't believe it!"

"You wouldn't want to disappoint them!" Eleanor said. "You'd better punch it, quick!"

Alice turned her attention back to the time machine. She pulled up her time traveller formula and began running the program. It took a minute for the program to boot. Alice held her breath. At first, she thought it hadn't worked. There was a silence that lasted almost three seconds. Then the little vial of liquid glowed bright blue.

A hole opened up in the universe. It was slightly smaller than the ones they had opened up before, but it was no less impressive for the effort. The wind began to howl and the other flying machines backed away.

Keith had needed to fly the biplane into the hole, but Eleanor wouldn't need to direct the balloon. The dirigible travelled on air currents and immediately got sucked into the empty void. Alice grabbed Grendel and Spring and crouched down. The last thing she saw before they plunged into blackness was Eleanor staring straight into the empty void, her arms raised like a woman who had just been released from bondage.

The world was spinning, and Spring was screaming at the top of her lungs. The platform had tilted backward at an uncomfortable angle and the wind pressed against them. Alice wasn't particularly surprised by either these events, but she worried about Spring. The night and day flickering past had been traumatizing enough for her the first time that she had travelled through time, and she had the benefit of an education in science. She could only imagine how surreal this all must seem. She grasped Spring tightly, who was hugging the floor of the platform for dear life.

"What," Spring asked, still screaming, "did you do to the sky?"

"Nothing!" Alice shouted. "We're just moving very, very fast."

"What do we do to slow down, then?" Spring asked.

Alice swallowed. The truth was that she had no idea how to slow down the dirigible. (It *would* slow down eventually, of course, but Alice would prefer to avoid crashing into the Atlantic a second time.) "Eleanor!" she shouted. "How do we stop this thing?"

"Leave it to me," she shouted. She grabbed something that looked like a little round ball connected to a long silver chain. Slowly, she made her way to the rear of the platform, and then threw the ball off the stern of the ship. What it did next was amazing. It exploded outward, over and over again, except that instead of breaking apart, with each explosion it got bigger, twisting and transforming until it looked like something that resembled the spoiler on the back end of a race car. How it worked was difficult to say, but the balloon seemed to be slowing down quite quickly. In a matter of moments, the balloon was drifting gently above a large landmass that Alice could only hope was Great Britain.

"Anti-Grav anchor," Eleanor said, answering Alice's question before she had a chance to ask it. "It's a twenty-third century invention. It slows us down, making sure we go where we want to go." This seemed to be true enough, and in a few minutes the balloon was coming down over the outskirts of London. The sight of the skyline as she knew it, complete with skyscrapers, brownstones, automobiles, electric lights, and Tower Bridge, was amazing.

"Good Lord!" Spring exclaimed. "What on Earth is that?"

Alice looked at where Spring was pointing. She was staring at a large, round, bright object not far from the river. Alice was so happy that she could burst out laughing. "That," she explained, joy positively bubbling out of her, "is the London Eye. We're in the twenty-first century now. We did it!"

Spring stared at the Ferris Wheel. "It's enormous," she said. "What does it do, exactly? Does it watch everyone, or something?"

"It's a ride," Alice said, and then realizing that this didn't really provide Spring with any point of reference, she added, "it has carriages on it. I'll explain it later."

With the help of a Fergus, they drifted into H.G. Wells airport. Alice was so happy that she could have kissed the ground. She hardly noticed that the Fergus was staring at her open-mouthed. "Miss, Miss Anderson," he said through an Irish brogue. "Are you—"

"In a terrible hurry," Alice said stepping off the platform. "Can you see that the dirigible is stored away safely?"

"Yes, mum," the Fergus said politely. He took something out of his pocket and handed it to her. "I was told to give you these," he said.

Alice looked at what Fergus had put in her palm. It was a set of keys.

"He left them," the Fergus said simply.

Alice nodded. "I understand," she said. She walked with big strides towards the airport. She strode past the other aircraft, and out into the airport parking lot, where a black Triumph motorcycle was waiting for them.

"Do you know how to drive this thing?" Eleanor asked.

"What *is* that thing?" Spring asked, yet again.

"It's called a motorcycle, and yes, I know how to ride it," Alice insisted, not telling anyone how much trouble she'd had the first time.

Spring stared at it. "It's funny," she said. "I think that I've seen it before. It was in–"

"A dream that you had?" Alice asked.

Spring nodded. "Now that you mention it, I think it was."

Alice smiled. "I'll explain that later as well," she said. "Eleanor, can you sit with Grendel on your lap?"

A quick glance over at the two of them confirmed Alice's suspicion that neither one of them thought that this was a good idea.

Eleanor scooped up Grendel and stared at him "I suppose so," she said through gritted teeth.

"Good, the two of you can share the sidecar," Alice said. She removed her bonnet and climbed up onto the motorcycle. "Hold on tight!" she shouted, giving it a quick start as everyone climbed on board. She grasped the throttle and in a matter of seconds, the motorcycle sped away into the city.

It's difficult to imagine what it's like seeing traffic lights, automobiles, and skyscrapers after not seeing them for a year. Alice had been convinced that those were gone from her life forever and she could have kissed everything she saw. She was back, back in the age of information and technology. She couldn't wait to celebrate by checking her email, watching television, and having a latte, only there wasn't time just now. The sun was setting, and as the lights came on in the city, Alice didn't know how much more time she had left. She tried to remember – had the detective who had questioned her told her the time of death? She didn't know, she only remembered that he was killed in his flat. She steered the motorcycle off towards Piccadilly Circus and Malcolm.

By the time they arrived, it was dark. Alice parked the motorcycle on the street and then looked up at the window that she knew from days gone by had belonged to Malcolm's flat.

The light was on.

She pulled the motorcycle into an alley. As she stopped the engine, Eleanor reached up from the sidecar and grabbed her arm. "You realize that we're walking into a trap, don't you?"

Alice stared at Eleanor. Eleanor still had the rifle strapped in a special holster on her back. "Are you concerned?" Alice asked.

"About Moriarty?" Eleanor said. "I think we should be."

Alice nodded. She got off the bike and turned to look at Spring. Spring didn't look frightened, not exactly, but her eyes were wide. She had ridden on the bike behind Alice, clutching her with tight grip most of the way, and didn't seem to feel any better for having come to a halt. "Eleanor and I just need to pop in for a moment. Would it be all right if you stayed here and watched Grendel?"

Spring nodded. "All right," she mumbled.

"Thanks," Alice said, doing her best to sound as if she were heading into a shop for a loaf of bread. "Be right back."

She wondered if she would be.

Malcolm's flat was on the third floor of a skinny brownstone with a rickety staircase. As soon as they walked in, Eleanor drew her rifle. "The hall light is off," she remarked. She found the switch and turned it on.

"Could be a coincidence," Alice said.

Eleanor nodded. "It could be," she agreed. "I'd better go first."

Eleanor kicked open the door to the stairs and walked up slowly. The stairwell was dark as well, but this time Eleanor seemed to prefer to leave the light off. When they reached the third floor, Eleanor pushed the door open a crack and then peered through. For the first time since Alice had met her, Eleanor smiled. "It's for you," she said, somewhat cryptically. Alice pushed the door open and walked through it. Keith was standing at the end of the hallway.

He looked exactly as he had on the day that she had first met him, because of course it *was* the first day that she'd met him. His

World War One aviator's cap and goggles were slightly askew, and his white scarf was tied instead of undone, but he remained perfectly in sync with Alice's memory of him. Not even a shoelace was out of place. He smiled, and then he grinned, and then he smiled again.

"Have we met?" Alice asked.

Keith didn't answer. Instead, he ran forward and kissed her.

It should be noted for the record that Alice kissed him back. It should also be noted that this kiss was Keith's expression not so much of passion, but more of relief – the exhausted exasperation of a man who mistakenly thought that he was at the end of a long day. For Alice, the moment was overwhelmed by a new thought, one which she could barely admit to herself.

"You will not believe the day I've had," he said. He seemed tremendously relieved to see her. "I just met you at the Gristle and Thorn. You looked like you had just turned *eleven*. Why didn't you tell me you were double-tracking?"

'*I'll just pretend I know what that means,"* Alice thought. "I'm having a bit of a day myself," she said, furrowing her brow.

"I'm sorry," Keith said. "What did you do?"

"I invented time travel."

There was a pause, and silence, and a pause again.

"You invented time travel? Today?"

"Yes."

"And when did you do this exactly?"

"About an hour ago."

"So that kiss you gave me was–"

"Technically not the first time but still a bit of a surprise."

"Ah. My wife gets annoyed when I kiss other women, even when they're her."

"I could see how that would be a problem."

"Okay, I'm caught up now. Now, as a follow up question – what am I doing at your ex-boyfriend's place, and who is the woman with the gun pointed at me?"

"The woman is Eleanor. She's with me. The gun isn't pointed at you, but at Malcolm's door. You're about to walk into a trap.

Moriarty figured out who you are and is going to steal Excalibur and frame you for murder."

Keith smiled, and he smirked, and he smiled again. "I got in trouble, and you broke the time barrier to save me?"

Alice opened her mouth, and for just a moment, the only thing that came out was air. "I – I suppose that's true," she stammered.

"All right," Keith said. "I'm sorry, Miss–"

"Dragon," Eleanor said with a nod.

"Well, I won't forget that one. I'm going to have you poke that thing through the door first, if that's okay with you."

Eleanor nodded. Keith nodded back. He grabbed the handle of the door. There was a click, a turn, and a creaking.

Alice, Eleanor, and Keith walked into the room.

It *was* a trap, but it *wasn't* a very subtle one. The man whom Alice had known as Jack Cassidy was standing on the other side of the door, pointing a gun at Malcolm Oliver. Except that it wasn't Jack. The man in front of her was gnarled and twisted. His long black locks and young face were long gone. Moriarty was little more than a shell of what Jack had once been. Only the eyes seemed to be the same. Although watery and pale now, the eyes were those of the young man she'd met on a pirate ship, two centuries before. The eyes, and the thin scar that now ran down the edge of a crumbling jawline.

Malcolm, on the other hand, was Malcolm, although he had been beaten pretty badly. He was bound to a chair and had a rag tied over his mouth. Saying he looked scared was one of those fairly obvious points along the lines of stating that the sun sets in the west, but the fear was nonetheless palpable and spoke to everyone else in the room. However, the sight of him was, if anything, more impressive than seeing Jack's transformation. Alice was still relatively new to time travel, and she had no idea the waves of sorrow, exasperation, and sheer relief that come from staring at a face that you'd thought you'd never see again. It was enough to make Alice's lip quiver, but this was nothing compared to Eleanor. Although her hands on her rifle never shook, she gave out a cry, her face exploding in a river of tears. This did nothing to discourage Moriarty and he stepped forward, leering at them with a menacing scowl. All of this was so visually assaulting that Alice barely noticed the rusty bit of metal that lay on the coffee table in front of Malcolm.

It was funny; it didn't look like much. It might have been a bit of waste from a construction site – a pair of bolts that would normally hold a pair of beams together, maybe, not the sword of a mythical king. At one end, though, there was definitely something that resembled a handle, and on the other end a hard jagged break, as if someone had shattered it, flinging it against steel plate in the last battle of a heartbreaking war.

"How long has it been, child?" asked Moriarty.

Alice saw no reason to lie. "A few hours," she admitted.

Moriarty scowled. "A lifetime for me," he said, gasping. "No matter. After half a century, all is going according to my plan."

Alice gave Malcolm just the briefest sympathetic glance. She tried to convey with her eyes that everything would be all right, but the trouble was that she wasn't sure that it would be.

"I came here as soon as I could," Alice insisted. "I wanted to keep you from becoming a murderer, Jack."

Moriarty gave a sickly, weak, cough. He stepped forward, and in the faintest, most delicate whisper, uttered two words: "Too late."

Alice swallowed.

"It took me a lifetime to get here," Moriarty admitted. "Decades of searching, experimentation, and frustration have finally led me here, to the perfect moment, when the fate of the world balances on the point of a knife."

"It's not the world that concerns me."

"It should."

Alice stared at the pistol in Moriarty's hand. The hand that held the gun was arthritic and withered. Chances were that Moriarty would have difficulty pulling the trigger. She wondered if she could get the gun from him if she got close enough.

"I knew you would come here," Moriarty sputtered. "I knew you would want the sword. I knew you would want to save your friend, to protect your life and your reputation in this former world."

"I don't want the sword!" Alice insisted. "I only want to make sure that everyone is all right. If you want the sword, you should take it. Just leave Malcolm alone!"

"Foolish child," Moriarty sneered. "I don't want the sword! Do you think that this is some kind of get rich quick scheme? I want something much, much more important. I want your time machine!"

"Take it!" Alice screamed. "If that's what you want, take it! Take it and the sword, just go!"

But Keith put a hand on her shoulder. "You can't," Keith said. His tone and his grip on Alice's shoulder were surprisingly firm.

She could tell that he thought she was making a mistake, but she didn't care. "Take the dirigible! And the engine! All of it!" she shouted "Just don't hurt anyone!"

But Keith's hand stayed firm on her shoulder. "You can't," he repeated. "Even if he shoots."

"But–" Alice began.

"But nothing," Keith said. "It doesn't matter. You can't give him the time machine."

"Your husband is quite correct," Moriarty said. "You would be better served letting me kill this man and keeping the machine for yourself. Fortunately, it does not matter. My associates are currently acquiring the time machine from H.G. Wells airport."

Alice didn't say anything, but glanced down at her handbag. She knew that her cell phone was in her bag. The cell phone was an integral part of the machine. It wouldn't run without it. Did Moriarty know that? She didn't think so.

Moriarty clearly saw this as his moment of triumph, and decided to expound. "All of the choices we make affect our path through the emptiness of time," he said. "Each choice directing us, each point creating new opportunities, some seen and some unseen. For each trip we make through time, you have the opportunity to revisit those choices, creating new moments, and opening up a universe of time like a rose in the summer sun. Every time, that is, except this time. This time, the rose isn't open yet."

"If you give him the time machine it will give him dominion over all of time," Keith clarified. "It will rewrite the lives of everyone who ever set foot on San Tiempo. You'll drop the future at his feet, like it was a rug."

"Precisely," Moriarty said, glaring at Alice. "You were about to make one of the most noble and foolish mistakes. You were going to take time travel, one of the most valuable and powerful pieces of technology, and you were going to share it with the world for free. I assure you, I won't make such a costly error. I intend to mold the new future with a firm grip."

Eleanor stifled a sob. "The time machine will let you go back and forth in time," she pointed out. "It won't make you any younger."

This seemed like a bit of a non-sequitur to Alice, but it was apparently closer to the mark then she would have thought, because Moriarty exploded with rage. "I SAY IT WILL!" he screamed, his face turning red. "I AM GOING TO START MY LIFE OVER AT THE BEGINNING, STARTING WITH THE MOMENT THAT YOU LEFT ME, STANDING IN A FIELD, WISHING THAT I HAD NEVER MET YOU. THIS TIME, IT WILL BE MY TURN!"

Moriarty paused for breath. He stepped forward and picked up Excalibur. "This is all academic," he said, more quietly. "I have the time machine, and I have the sword. All I need now is that item that you happen to have in your handbag."

'Damn,' Alice thought. She supposed it was too much to hope for that Moriarty wouldn't know about the mobile. Alice reached into her handbag and grabbed it. It was true that he knew her mobile was there, but how much did Moriarty really know about how it worked? She pushed one button, then another.

"Alice," Keith said. "If you do this," his voice cracked, "you and I will never meet."

Alice shook her head. "If given the choice between life and love, I have to choose what is over what might have been," she said. She stepped forward, pulled her phone out of her pocket, and handed it to Moriarty. Moriarty took it, and with a nod, headed for the door.

Eleanor lowered her weapon and dropped it to the floor. She ran over to Malcolm and threw her arms around him, her face exploding in sheer unadulterated joy. "I thought you were dead," she blubbered.

Keith was the only one who saw the danger. "Watch it!" he shouted, but he was too late. Moriarty had turned and cocked his gun. "No!" Alice shouted, and of course, this was it, the moment when it happened, the moment that Malcolm died. This was the moment that changed Alice's life forever, which changed all of their lives forever. Moriarty raised the gun. Malcolm was going to die – except that this time it didn't happen. Just then, the horn of a miniature triceratops tore through Malcolm's front door like it was paper. Grendel broke down the door and plowed into Moriarty. The old man went down with the little dinosaur, the door coming down on top of him.

Spring leaned casually against the doorframe. "We thought you might need a hand," she said. "I didn't know that it would be this bad."

Alice reached over and grabbed the pistol out of Moriarty's hand. "It's over," she said. She walked over to the nearest window, opened it, and then threw the gun out onto the street below. "You might not be from this century, but if I were you I'd get used to it. You're staying here now."

Keith picked up Eleanor's rifle and pointed it at the old man. "Move and you're dead," he said.

Moriarty pushed the door and the dinosaur off him. "Foolish children," he said, "how little you understand." Then he clapped his hands together and vanished.

Chapter 15
Reichenbach Falls

Alice stared at the empty space where Moriarty had been. It must be some kind of trick. It had to be. Still, she couldn't see how it was done. "How did he do that?" she asked.

Keith stared at the empty space where Moriarty wasn't. He and Eleanor exchanged glances of dead wonder. "No idea."

Eleanor nodded in agreement. "That's impossible," she said. "It violates the laws of physics."

"It must be some kind of trick," Alice said. She bent over and pushed the door that had been on top of Moriarty out of the way, running her hand on the floor where Moriarty had been. "There must be a trap door, or something." She felt around for an edge or a hinge that might reveal a secret way out of the room. Of course, there wasn't one. It was a ridiculous idea, one borne out by a refusal to believe what she had seen. Moriarty had vanished into thin air, like it was–

From behind the gag in his mouth, Malcolm made a choking noise. Eleanor was untying him, taking breaks as she undid the knots to kiss his face. Tears kept flowing down Eleanor's face, but she didn't bother brushing them away. Alice stood up and turned toward the window, to give the two of them a moment's privacy.

"Are you all right?" Keith asked in a quiet voice. He wasn't looking at Malcolm, but at Alice, who was staring out the window and trying not to look forlorn.

Alice nodded. It was funny, the street seemed so embarrassingly pedestrian, but it had been so long since she'd been able to look out the window and see a street lamp. Before any of this happened, she would have travelled to the end of Western Civilization to find a dark sky area. Now, it seemed like the most wonderful thing in the world, being able to look outside at night and see the street lit up. It occurred to her that she must be nearly within sight of the inn that she stayed in when she first arrived in the nineteenth century. It was hard to tell exactly where it would have been, the streets had changed so much. Bertha must have been dead for over a hundred years.

"You tried to tell me something once, a long time ago," Alice said. "I had asked if you had a time machine why I couldn't go back and save Malcolm. She turned her head just slightly, so that she could catch Malcolm and Eleanor out of the corner of her eye. They looked blissfully happy together, like the hero and heroine of fairy tale. "You tried to tell me that saving him wouldn't make me happy."

"I did?" Keith asked.

"You did. I wouldn't listen," Alice said. She turned back around and looked at Keith. (He really was quite handsome, wasn't he?) "Anyhow, it turns out that you were wrong."

Keith smiled. "I'm glad," he said.

Alice sighed. "I have loved three men in my life, one from the past, one from the present, and one from the future. I have misjudged them all."

Keith nodded. "As one tends to do with moments in time."

From behind her, Alice heard Malcolm say, "Could someone please tell me what's going on?"

Keith stepped forward "Alice invented a time machine, the odd iron-looking thing on your coffee table a moment ago was Excalibur, the man who took it was apparently a wizard of some kind, and the little animal sniffing at your feet is a miniature triceratops. Oh, and I'm Keith," he finished, holding out a hand.

There was a pause. Malcolm looked exhausted, and pale. "I'm just going to ask the obvious question. Have I gone mad?"

Eleanor squeezed his hand. "No, darling, it's the world that's gone mad. You are in the unfortunate position of having been right all along, about everything. I was afraid to tell you, and I'm sorry."

Malcolm nodded, his eyebrows raised. "So when that man said he was Professor Moriarty, that wasn't a metaphor of some kind?"

"No," Alice said. "No, that was really him. Your theory about fictional realism, as it turns out, you were correct."

"I was?" Malcolm asked.

Alice nodded. "Right as rain."

"Right," Malcolm said. He clearly wasn't sure how to take this last bit of news. "Quick question – that whole mad thing, we're sure that that isn't the problem here?"

"No," Keith said. "You're just as sane as I am. However, Alice just gave one of the most valuable pieces of technology in the universe over to the world's most notorious nineteenth century criminal, probably causing the entire time space continuum to tilt dangerously off course, like a gasoline tanker driven by an orangutan, so going mad now might not be bad thinking."

Alice rolled her eyes.

"I didn't give him the most valuable piece of technology in the universe. I gave him a balloon, a steam engine, and a mobile phone," she said, a smug look of self-satisfaction on spreading over her face. "It wasn't the Rosetta Stone or anything."

Keith frowned. "You gave him the time machine," he insisted, "the only one ever created, so far. Moriarty isn't going to share his toys with the other children."

Eleanor nodded. "Mister Quick is correct. Without the influence of San Tiempo, an unscrupulous time traveller could use that power to control the entire world. Moriarty's influence will spread over the continuum like an oil spill on the ocean of time."

Alice was so pleased with herself that she could barely contain her laughter. "Moriarty stole the time machine, but he doesn't understand how it works. What makes time travel possible is the formula."

"The formula was on your mobile, wasn't it?" Eleanor asked.

"It was," Alice agreed, "except I emailed it to Malcolm twenty minutes ago. As long as he shares it with someone else, everything should be fine."

From somewhere inside Malcolm's pocket, there was the sound of a mobile vibrating.

"Moriarty was a genius," Alice said, "but he was a nineteenth century genius. I had a feeling he might not understand email."

There was a pause, and then a silence, and then a pause again. "Is it just me," Keith said, "or is everything all right?"

"I realize that this isn't the usual run of things, but yes, for the moment we're all fine," Alice conceded. "I'm sure that it won't last."

Eleanor was clutching Malcolm's hand tightly. "It is a shame that I lost Excalibur, but if it was a choice between losing the sword and losing Malcolm, then my choice is clear." Eleanor grinned at Malcolm, who grinned back. Alice felt queasy. She remembered something else that Keith had tried to tell her once. He had started to say that "Malcolm wasn't" something when she had run off. She had never heard what it was. She supposed it must have been *'Malcolm wasn't in love with you.'*

"It is a shame, though," Keith said, sound a trifle remorseful. "The sword would have made a great addition to the museum."

"It's too bad we don't know where Moriarty went to," Alice said, "but I suppose that it can't be helped."

Malcolm frowned. "Who? Moriarty? I know where he's going."

Alice blinked. "You know where Moriarty is?" she asked, her eyebrows raised. "Why, did he tell you?"

Malcolm shook his head. "He didn't *tell* me, but I know where he went."

No one in the room seemed to follow Malcolm's logic. "How could you *know* where he's headed?" Keith asked. "Did you see him trying to book a hotel room or something?"

"Well, Moriarty looked pretty old," Malcolm pointed out. "Seems like a man his age might be facing the Final Problem."

Alice and Keith exchanged open-mouthed glances.

"It can't be that simple," Keith said. "Surely, he wouldn't be that stupid."

"Or that egotistical?" Alice asked. "I don't know. It's worth a try."

Alice saw a wild spark in Keith's eyes. "All right then. Let's go get my biplane. With any luck, we can be back in the nineteenth century before the sun rises."

She almost said yes. It would have been the easiest thing in the world to run off together to the past or the future, or to wherever the wind might take them. In her mind, she could see a million adventures crumbling into dust. She could see that he was a nice man – fun-loving and kind, which made what she had to say next that much more difficult.

"Stop," she said, holding up a hand. "This isn't right. You can't go with us."

Keith looked like he had just swallowed his own testicles. "I can't?" he said.

Alice nodded. "If Malcolm isn't dead, that would mean that another Alice is lying in bed, asleep, and that no one is going to wake her up and accuse her of murder, the way I was."

Keith nodded. "Yes, that's true."

Alice bit her lip. "And that means that you're not really my Keith, doesn't it? You're hers."

Keith nodded thoughtfully. "No. This isn't your timeline. Yours is still out there, but this world is different. An alternate universe, if you will. Your world is the one where Moriarty killed Malcolm, I take it."

(Malcolm mouthed the word 'murdered,' but Eleanor told him to shush.)

"If that's true, then you need to stay here and find your Alice, because right now her life is simple, and rational, and makes perfect sense."

Keith shook his head and grinned a little in spite of himself. "That's a shame," he said.

"I know. I agree. What your Alice needs now is a heavy dose of chaos in her life, because it will drive her to greatness. Besides, Eleanor is right – love is more important than anything. The sword, that's just a knick-knack."

There was sorrow and laughter in Keith's eyes. "When I first met Alice Anderson she was the saddest woman I'd ever met. I think I understand why now."

There was a kiss, and there was an embrace, and then there was kissing again.

"If you're going to do this," Keith said, "I want you to take someone with you, someone who I know and trust, who has been there for me in my darkest hour."

Alice nodded. "All right," she said. "I understand. Who did you have in mind?"

"Spring?" Keith asked. "Do you mind going on a trip?"

"Sure!" Spring said. "Where are we going?"

"A place called Reichenbach Falls," Keith said. "Haven't you always wanted to go to the Alps?"

Sherlock Holmes found the fact that the fall hadn't killed him to be an interesting curiosity. He had spent the last five minutes coughing up water onto a rocky shore. Pushing himself up from the dirt, he preferred to focus on the improbability that he was still alive and ignore the pain that was coursing through every inch of his body. Surely it *should* have killed him. The height was easily high enough, and the water at the bottom of the falls didn't appear to be that deep. Once he got back to his residence at Baker Street, he would have to work out exactly how it was done. *'I will have to relay the particulars to Watson,'* he reflected. *'Provided I survive, of course.'*

Holmes felt something that was roughly the size of a dog sniffing at his foot. Using his brilliant powers of deduction, he concluded that it was a hunting dog, most likely a retriever of some kind. With any luck, there might be a shooting party nearby. With great effort, he rolled over to have a look at the animal sniffing him.

The creature at his foot *wasn't* a dog. What it *was*, exactly, was difficult to say. It was blue and had a wide, flat face with three horns on it. It had skin like an alligator, eyes like Chihuahua, and teeth like a cow. If someone had told the great detective that sixty-three million years of evolution separated the two of them, it might have explained a few things, but no one ever did.

"Nark!" the little animal said.

Holmes stared at it. He didn't know what to say. The animal was so strange-looking that for a moment he didn't notice the three women standing right behind it.

The first was an Asian woman, dressed from head to toe in black. She was wearing a large black hat, had a severe look on her face, and a had Winchester rifle slung over her shoulder. The second was a woman with bright red curly hair. She was wearing a brown dress with a black corset. (For reasons lost on Holmes, the corset was on the outside of the dress.) She had hiked her skirts up to reveal a pair of shapely legs covered in silk stockings. The third was the most modestly dressed of the three – an ebony-skinned woman with a bright smile and cheerful eyes. She might have been the most normal-looking of the bunch, if she weren't wearing a tall powdered wig. Even further behind them was a large blue dirigible with a pattern of stars on it. (*'Had that been there before?'* Holmes wasn't sure.)

The redhead stepped forward and scratched the lizard-dog-thing behind its ear. "Give him some space, Grendel," she chided.

Holmes pushed himself up from the dirt. He surveyed the scene. "A question, if I may–"

"You're not going mad," the redhead said sympathetically, "but you will require medical attention. Come on, give us a hand."

Holmes held out his left hand and she pulled him to his feet. His right hand was gripping something tightly, a strange bit of iron he had grabbed from Moriarty as they quarreled. The cheerful ebony-skinned woman in the powdered wig grabbed him by the hand, putting her arm around her shoulder to support him. "Come on, sweetie," she said. "Let's find you a doctor."

"I don't think you'll be needing this," the Asian woman said, taking the iron cross out of his hand.

"It belonged to my foe," Holmes said wearily. "My opponent, he attacked me with it."

"Probably just something that was handy," the redhead suggested.

"My enemy," Holmes gasped. "He went over the falls with me. Is he alive?"

The three women exchanged knowing glances with one another. "He didn't come out of the falls," the redhead said. "His body may have been lost."

Holmes nodded. "The balloon, is it yours?"

"Yes," the Asian woman said. She slipped the iron cross into a large pocket in her overcoat. "Or at any rate, it is now. Come, sir, let's get you to the nearest town."

They eventually left Holmes under the medical care of a questionable Zurich physician, who told them in broken English that he thought the great detective's pelvis might be fractured.

"I suppose that explains why he disappeared for so long in the books," Alice mused.

"There are books?" Spring asked. "About *that* man?"

"Oh yes," Alice said "Stories of all kinds."

"I suppose I've got two centuries worth of literature to catch up on," Spring mused.

Alice looked at Eleanor. She knew that they were both thinking the same thing; the only question was which one of them would say it.

"If Moriarty could disappear from Malcolm's apartment, then he could have survived going over the falls," Alice said.

"It would seem so," Eleanor agreed.

"I didn't want to tell Mister Holmes," Alice said.

"Neither did I," Eleanor agreed. "Sherlock Holmes is a man of truth and consequences. Wherever Moriarty has gone, it is somewhere he can't follow. We can, though, and we will, but maybe not today."

They found their way back to where Moriarty had left the balloon. It appeared he had come straight here, or nearly so. "It's a pity Malcolm couldn't be here," Alice said.

Malcolm had been in pretty rough shape after spending most of a day tied to a chair, and hadn't been up to the trip. "The doctor recommended a few days of rest," Eleanor said. "When he feels better, I'll take him on his first trip. Somewhere relaxing."

Spring laughed. "Where's the fun in that?" she asked.

"With any luck, it will be less fun than we've been used to," Eleanor said, glancing at Alice. "We have a few things to take care of, and then I think I'll take him somewhere nice. The Italian Renaissance perhaps. Travelling in time is always a little chaotic, no matter where you go."

"What about that iron thing you've got in your pocket?" Spring asked. "Where does that go?"

Eleanor couldn't resist the excuse to take out the sword and look at it. "This goes to the Time Traveller's Resort and Museum," she said. "It will be safe there."

Alice shook her head. "I don't understand why Moriarty thinks that I would want this thing," she said. "I know it's valuable, but–"

"I've thought about that," Eleanor said. "The sword represents a link between this world and something different. A dimension filled with magic and mysticism, where the laws of physics don't apply. At first I thought you would want it for the same reasons that I would – as proof of a world out there that's unexplored and untouched, with powers greater than anyone could imagine. In light of the events of the last few days, I've been thinking there may be a more pedestrian reason."

"What do you mean?" Alice asked.

Eleanor handed the cross over to her. "Here. Have a look."

Excalibur was heavier than Alice would have expected, but other than that, it was very similar to the cross she had held in London two centuries earlier – the inscription was about the same, at any rate. Its edges though, were sharp, and the end of the blade had been shattered. Alice wondered how that had happened. Had Arthur broken it? She supposed that he must have.

"I've seen a copy of this," Alice admitted. "It had been fashioned into a cross, but it was very similar. I don't see what it has to do with me, though."

"It isn't the inscription that's important," Eleanor clarified. "It's the other side that you'll want to have a look at. Flip it over."

The other side was plainer and in better shape than the side the bore the inscription. Alice notice that the pummel had an odd mark on it – a series of concentric arcs and circles, with a number of lines sticking out at odd angles:

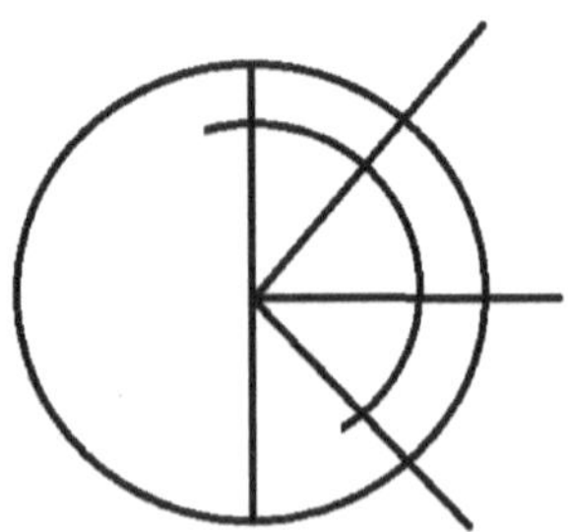

Alice stared at the mark. "What is that?" she asked.

"I wondered about that, at first," Eleanor said. "I think it's a manufacturer's symbol. One that was chosen for a specific reason. You'll notice if you look closely, you'll see that–"

"It's letters," Alice finished for her excitedly. She could see it now. It was as plain as day. The symbol was four letters written on top of each other. Alice traced each letter with her finger. A A K Q.

Alice Anderson. Keith Quick.

"Keith is still alive," Alice said. "The Keith Quick from my timeline. I dropped him from the balloon. I thought he was dead."

Eleanor smiled warmly. "As someone who knows what it feels like to lose someone and then get them back – congratulations. You're very lucky."

"I didn't even realize what I was losing," Alice admitted. "Now that I know, I'll have to get him back."

She didn't know what to do next, so she hugged Eleanor awkwardly. "At some point I'm going to steal your balloon and crash it into the ocean," she admitted.

Eleanor laughed. "I suppose that's why it never ended up in the museum. Come on, let's get back to the present. Then we'll see what we can do about getting you home."

Chapter 16
There's No Place Like Home

Detective Inspector Enid Williams had been working on the Malcolm Oliver case for most of a week and it had been driving her batty. The main suspect had been the victim's ex-girlfriend. She had flown into London the day that the victim was killed, had no alibi, and had definitely acted suspiciously in the aftermath of the victim's death. Unfortunately, Enid had lost her. Somehow this woman had managed to slip a dragnet at her hotel, and then had absolutely disappeared off of the map. No one had seen her, and there hadn't been a hit on her telephone, credit cards, passport, or bank accounts. Her sister hadn't been in touch, her father was estranged, and her mother had died a number of years ago under strange circumstances. She simply didn't have the kind of contacts that could have provided her with large sums of cash. She seemed to have blown away on the wind, like the smoke from a chimney. It was bizarre.

Assistant Detective Inspector Charles knocked on Enid's office door. His expression was wide-eyed.

"Yes?" Enid asked.

"Your suspect turned herself in," he said.

Enid stood up. "You're kidding," she said.

"I'm not," Charles insisted.

"Where is she?" Enid asked.

"Central booking. Patrolman Harry is processing her now," Charles said. His face was an open book of astonishment. "I don't understand. She just walked in the front door."

It was usually considered rude to run inside New Scotland Yard unless there was an emergency of some kind, but Enid found herself running now. She ran through the corridor, past the lift and down the stairs, then down another hallway to central booking, where she found the chief suspect in the Malcolm Oliver murder sitting in a hardback chair in front of Patrolman Harry's desk.

Wherever Alice Anderson had been was not immediately clear, but wherever it was she had been hiding, it was obvious that she hadn't been suffering. In truth, she appeared to have gone and raided the closet of PT Barnum. She was wearing a black top hat with goggles on it and a red jacket with tails that was made of crushed red velvet. She was sitting comfortably, with her legs crossed, presumably to show off the red flame pattern on her knee-high leather boots. She had apparently come in with an entourage. She was accompanied by an Asian woman dressed all in black, and another woman, who, judging by the way she was dressed, might have been an extra in an upcoming production of Moll Flanders if it weren't for the strange colour of her hair. There was also a man with them. Unlike the others, he was more conservatively dressed, and appeared to be looking in the other direction.

Enid directed her attention to Harry. "Has she been read her rights?" she asked.

Harry looked up at her and nodded. There was something strange about his face, as if he had just seen something very surprising, like a ghost. Enid supposed that it was probably Miss Anderson's strange appearance.

"Alice Anderson," Enid said. She cleared her throat and stood up straight. "At this time, I will be formally charging you with the murder of Malcolm Oliver."

For a woman who had been charged with murder, Miss Anderson took this news surprisingly calmly. Her expression seemed to convey understanding, even pity. "Before you do that, you're going to want to talk to him," she said, looking over at the conservatively-dressed man with just the slightest hint of a smile.

Enid turned to look at the man. *'Oddly informal for a solicitor,'* she thought. He was wearing a black jumper and a pair of beige trousers. Perhaps he'd been called in suddenly. She glanced up at his face, and her jaw dropped.

"My name is Malcolm Oliver," Malcolm Oliver said. He stretched out a hand and smiled feebly. "It's nice to meet you."

For once, Wendy sat alone in a pub, stone cold sober and waiting patiently. Normally, at this time of day she would have at least have a glass of wine, but the past week had shaken her badly, so badly that she was starting to rethink some of her bad habits. This was something that required a fair amount of self-reflection. Wendy didn't approve of self-reflection. It usually made her look bad.

Her sister had reappeared last night, and had appeared to have gone a good way round the bend, as their mother used to say. She showed up looking like the driver in a nineteenth century auto race (if such a thing was possible) and immediately blurted out, "Okay, I invented time travel," and then marched in a miniature triceratops and the man she was accused of murdering as proof. It was a little too much to take in. (The triceratops in particular had been an unpleasant surprise. Wendy's living room had thick white carpets.)

Alice had seemed to be a different person, one who was evolving right before her eyes and moving at the speed of light. Wendy had been worried enough about her living in America; the idea of her living in the nineteenth century scared the willies out of her. (If Wendy had been in a period of even deeper self-reflection, she would have wondered if perhaps expressing her concern in a manner other than sarcastic comments might have been an interesting choice, but frankly there just wasn't enough water in the pool.)

When at last Alice walked in, Wendy breathed a sigh of relief. She was alone this time, which struck Wendy as a step toward normalcy, although her outfit this afternoon was just as strange as the one she had been wearing last night. Something of the nineteenth century still seemed to hang about her, and she couldn't get rid of it, no matter how hard she tried. Much to Wendy's surprise the bartender had brought her sister a drink almost the moment she sat down. Alice nodded to the waiter and said, "Thank you, Fergus," before taking a long sip. When they had met in this same bar a week ago, that time it had been Wendy's idea. This time, it was her sister's suggestion. Even though it had only been a few days since they had been here, Alice seemed to fit in now. In addition to the drink, her newfound fashion sense seemed to fit in with regulars' taste in clothing, and several patrons either smiled at her or waved in her direction.

Alice had sat her sister down last night and told her everything, and there had been an awful lot of everything to tell. Even with the supporting evidence of the undead Malcolm and the triceratops it was a difficult story to believe, but then again maybe it was easier than thinking that Alice had gone mad. Wendy stared at her sister. *'I always admired your beautiful mind, and I never told you,'* Wendy thought, again not telling her.

"Grendel is sorry about the carpet," Alice said.

Wendy took a sip of her tea. "It's all right," she said. "I've been meaning to have them cleaned."

"Sorry I'm late. I had to drop my friend Spring off at the hotel. She's from the Regency and I just wanted to make sure that she got settled okay."

Wendy didn't really know how to respond to this. "How does she like it here?" she asked.

"Spring has declared the ice cream sundae to be the best invention of the modern era and the motorcycle to be the worst. A fair assessment, I would say."

"What about Malcolm?" Wendy asked.

Alice's face seemed to do something completely inexplicable. "He's gone back to his own timeline. I think he felt a little uncomfortable here, in a world where he's supposed to be dead. Anyway, I think he and his girlfriend have a little catching up to do."

Wendy nodded. "And did you take care of everything?" she asked.

"Ultimately, they decided that they couldn't prosecute me for a murder if the victim was sitting there with me saying that I didn't do it. They were a little frustrated by this fact."

"I'm sure," Wendy agreed.

"I feel bad that Moriarty got away, but there wasn't much I could do about that, at least not at the moment."

Wendy swallowed. "This man who killed Malcolm, are you going to go after him?"

Alice took a sip of her drink. "I don't know," she admitted. "Not right away certainly. First thing's first, I need to go and find Keith. My Keith. What happened to him was my fault. I need to find him and rescue him. After that, we'll see."

"Now, I don't understand that part. Where is he, exactly?" Wendy asked.

"I don't know," Alice said a second time. "Somewhere beyond anything I've seen so far. I have a feeling that Moriarty would know, but I'm a little hesitant to ask him."

Wendy shook her head. "All this time I've been hoping you would meet a man and settle down. Be careful what you wish for, I suppose."

Alice sighed. "I knew you weren't happy. Listen, I know this has been a lot to take in. A lot. I sat in this same bar a year ago, and I shook my head back and forth and said, 'No, no, no.' I was practically stomping my feet I was so mad. Keith sat across the table from me and basically just tried to tell me in the nicest possible way what was happening. Then it happened, and I was stuck back in the nineteenth century with no way home, and do you know the one thing that kept me sane? It was *you*. The thought that if I did this insane thing, if I built a time machine, I would get to sit down in a restaurant and relax and have a drink and talk with my sister. Every person who will ever travel through time is going to get to do so because more than anything else, I wanted to see you. Now I'm back, and I'm here, and I know I seem like I've changed completely, but at least I'm here, and *we're together*. Isn't that worth something?"

Wendy shook her head. "No," she insisted. "I'm sorry, but no. Yes, I'm happy that you're all right. I'm absolutely over the Moon that you're not going to prison, but what you are doing, what you are going to do, strikes me as dangerous. I think you're messing about with powers you can't really control."

Alice sighed. "You're probably right. I wish I could reassure you that everything is all right, but the truth is I don't know. You never know. I could give this all up and head back to the wilds of upstate New York and still end up getting hit by lightning tomorrow. There's a lot of lightning in New York. The University is up on a tall hill. I want you to do something, though. If you ever worried, just call, and when you call, let's try and begin by saying nice things to each other, like I'm glad to hear from you, and I love you, because you never know. Anything could happen."

Wendy took a sip of her tea. "It's a little sad to think that sending you back off into the middle of nowhere again suddenly sounds like a good deal."

Alice did her best to smile. "This is just something I have to do," she said. "But for right now, for today, I'm here with you, and I'm happy. If it helps, though, you might want to remember that I've actually been gone for over a year now."

Wendy frowned. "So?"

Alice smirked. "So, that means that you're only six months older than me, doesn't it?"

Wendy groaned. "Little sister, see if you can get that waiter that you seem to know so well to bring me one of those fancy drinks of yours. If I'm going to have to suffer with your catching up with me, I will need to start catching up with you."

The sisters laughed, and talked, and enjoyed a few moments of peace in an otherwise chaotic world.

Epilogue

Keith Quick lay on his back, his eyes closed, trying to ignore the fact that he needed to come to terms with the unpleasant reality that he was still alive. Really, in all honesty, almost any other alternative would have been better, as basically every fibre of his being was in pain. Somewhere in the deep part of his subconscious, he began to make a list of things that hurt. His back was sore and stiff, his left shoulder throbbed, and his ankle stung. His right wrist smarted and his left burned. His fingers tingled and his toes twitched. His lips, oddly enough, felt fine, but they were caked in sand. His heart – well, his heart was weary, and not for the first time.

'*You married the Mother of Time,*' his subconscious pointed out. '*A certain degree of trouble was probably inevitable.*'

The desert stretched out endlessly in every direction. Keith wasn't aware of this. As far as he knew, the desert stretched out as far as the end of his lips. He was aware that it was blisteringly, miserably, uncomfortably hot, and he was wearing a leather aviator hat, which, to the uninitiated, is not a piece of clothing that breathes well. With a herculean effort, he lifted his right hand to the top of his head and took the hat off. His thick brown hair was covered in what he hoped was sweat. His head pounded. That was a new one; he would have to add that to the list.

"Are you all right?" a voice asked.

"No!" Keith shouted, his eyes closed. Privately he hoped that would be the end of it. *'That's it,'* his subconscious said, encouragingly. *'You told him. That's the end of that. Now, you can go back to taking a nap on this large pile of sand that somebody provided.'*

"Are you awake?" the voice inquired.

"I told you, NO!" Keith repeated. He tried to roll over, but his back announced that this wasn't a good idea. It seemed like it wasn't going to help, anyway. Keith had a sense that the voice was coming from at least fifteen feet above him, and it wasn't going to be put off easily.

"Why not?" the voice asked.

"Because I have a feeling that if I open my eyes I won't like what I see," Keith said. "Nothing personal."

"What makes you so sure you won't be happy with your surroundings?"

"I've been dumped by my wife, you see, and in this case that statement is depressingly literal. I'm afraid that I've used up my quota of depressing news for the day, so if it's all the same to you, my friend, I'm just going to continue sleeping on this sand dune here."

"What makes you think that I'm your friend?" the voice asked.

"Well, I was just being conversational," Keith said. "You seem like a nice enough man."

"What makes you think I'm a man?" the voice asked.

Keith opened his eyes.

Keith was a sophisticated enough traveller to recognize the Sahara Desert when he saw it. Its distinctive rolling sand was different that of the Mojave, or the Gobi, but this observation was pushed to the back of his mind as he stared at the creature in front of him. Standing at the top of the sand dune was a large scaly green dragon.

"Hello, lunch," the dragon said, beating its wings.

Keith Quick sat up and began to scramble backward.

The dragon blew smoke through its nostrils.

ABOUT THE CREATORS

David McLain is the author of the two novels: *Dragonbait*, and *The Life of a Thief.* His stories have been published in the anthologies *Metastasis*, *Penny Dread II*, and the Doctor Who Anthology *Time Shadows*, as well as over two dozen magazines. He has been featured on NPR's Off the Page and the History of England podcast. He lives in New York.

Felix Eddy graduated Magnum Cum Laude from Alfred University. She is the author and illustrator of *A Bestiary Alphabet,* and has illustrated several book covers and children's books. You can find out more about her at www.felixeddy.com

Love this book?
We appreciate every like, tweet, facebook post and review and
we love to hear from you. Please consider leaving us a review
online or sending your thoughts and comments to
info@mirrorworldpublishing.com
Thank you.

Also, if you liked this book, chances are you'll like the rest of
what we have to offer.
To find more great titles and information about our
membership program, visit: www.mirrorworldpublishing.com

Or keep reading for a sneak peek of...

UNCHARTED

by Justine Alley Dowsett
and Murandy Damodred

Chapter 1

"Sam!" Reginald exclaimed, making a point to sound jovial while addressing the sour-face postmaster. "How're the kids? How's Frank?"

"Har, har," Sam replied in a flat monotone, barely looking up enough to glance over the edge of his half-moon glasses. "Like you care. I don't even know why you bother to stop in here, you're just going to throw out the letter from your mother without even reading it."

"You're reading my mail now?" Reginald raised a quizzical brow in Sam's direction.

The postmaster shrugged lazily instead of answering, reaching below his desk to pull out a familiar looking manilla envelope to hold it out to Reginald. He did all of this without taking his eyes from the newspaper article he was reading. Leaning forward,

Reginald took note of the headline: *Kevlan warship spotted off the Eastern coast; coincidence or portent?*

Reginald shook his head. *Kevlans, our modern day boogeyman. Sure, relations with Kevla aren't great, but one ship in our waters is hardly a declaration of war.*

Regarding the man suspiciously now, Reginald took the proffered letter and ignored the wastebasket this time in favour of stuffing it into the breast pocket of his sailor's jacket. Sam, with his gaze still on the newspaper before him, didn't seem to notice the change in Reginald's routine, or if he did, he simply did not care.

"So if anyone comes this way looking for passage, you'll direct them along then, right Sam?" Reginald fought to get Sam's attention one last time even as he backed away intent on the door.

"Especially if it's a Priestess," Sam repeated dutifully, still without looking up, "yes, yes, I know."

"Thanks, buddy. I knew I could count on you," Reginald forced a smile in the off chance that Sam should look his way.

"You mean you knew you could count on your coin buying my discretion," Sam commented drily directing his words to the paper in his hands more so than Reginald.

"That too," Reginald mumbled half to himself as he let himself out of the trading post and into the early morning sunlight. "Rat bastard."

The street was bustling, at least bustling for the Temple District in early spring. It wasn't cold out, and perhaps that was the reason; this being the first real nice day since winter broke. Kids laughed as they ran in the street chasing one another and Reginald nearly tripped over one of them as they got near enough to be underfoot.

"Hey! Watch where you're going!" He called out, but the little girl with twin ponytails and a smudge of dirt on her freckled cheeks just laughed at him and kept on with her friends.

"You're the one walking the wrong way on the street, mister!" One of her friends, a boy, yelled at him as he too, ran past.

Reginald looked up and realized belatedly that the boy was right. Everyone else on this side of the street was headed away from the docks and he, like an ignorant fool, was trying to head in the opposite direction.

And this *is why I hate the Temple District,* Reginald reminded himself. *All their stupid rules and superstitions… why can't they just walk on both sides of the road like regular people?*

Without trying to be too obvious about it, he ducked his head and scurried to the far side of the street where he swiftly merged with foot traffic. He soon blended inconspicuously with the crowd, and before long he was back where he'd docked The Clover.

Just seeing his majestic ship made him feel better. *Alright,* he admitted, *it's not 'majestic' by any stretch of the imagination, but it's mine as so few things are in this world are.*

Of a smaller than average size and with an even smaller than average crew, The Clover was still a proper naval ship registered with the Saegardian navy. Painted navy blue and grey, Saegard's colours, it sported a strip of white paint across the middle with a brightly painted green four-leaf clover. Before Reginald had inherited the ship, the Clover had belonged to his father and the only reason his father had become a Captain in the navy in the first place was because he had won this ship in a poker tournament and had the misfortune of needing a job at the time. The Clover was supposed to have been named after the winning card in that poker game, *Le Roi du Trefle,* but a misunderstanding with the English-speaking painter at the shipyard had resulted in the current design. And as Reginald's father had been a man who believed strongly in luck and fate, he had simply laughed at the mixup and called it his 'lucky ship.'

Reginald didn't care what the ship was called. It was his and he was the Captain now, and that's what mattered.

A loud booming sound spit the air. Reginald jumped, caught off guard, but his panic deepened as he realized that the thunderous sound reminiscent of an explosion or a cannon, only not quite as deafening, was coming from his ship. Before he knew it, Reginald was running full speed up the gangplank.

His boots thudded against the wooden gangplank, but the sound they made was nothing compared to the second round of cannon-fire, or whatever it was he was hearing. *Why in the world would anyone be using their cannons* here *of all places? I can't imagine there are any Saegardian Priestesses that need to be fired upon!*

No sooner had he reached the deck than he identified the source of the noise. His private charter turned business partner, Grey Rhodes, stood near the center mast, his left arm extended with what looked like a mini hand held cannon. As Reginald watched, Grey lit the end of a short fuse and did his best to hold his arm steady as the booming sound filled the air once more.

Reginald watched open-mouthed in horror as the ball bearing thudded into the wall of the captain's quarters, splintering wood already weakened by his first few shots.

"Etes-vous fou?!" Reginald's French roots escaped him despite his best efforts.

"Ah, there you are," Grey responded, smiling as if taking notice of him for the first time at his exclamation. "How did your trip to town go?"

Reginald spluttered, his face going red with the effort needed to contain himself. He forced his next words out painstakingly one by one, being extra careful to make sure each one was in English. "Why. In. The. World. Are. You. *Firing shots at my boat!?"*

"Well, you don't need to get all up in arms about it," Grey answered, calmly cleaning out the barrel of his contraption with a scrap of cloth. He waited until he'd gently placed the mini-cannon on a nearby barrel next to what looked like the rest of his shooting supplies. "I've taken precautions."

Reginald looked from the splintered wood of his boat to the calm expression on Grey's face and then back again before crossing the deck to the scene of the crime. He pointed at the evidence. "You call *this* taking precautions?! What precautions? You may technically be sleeping in the Captain's Quarters because you pay more to keep this boat afloat than I do at the moment, but they're still the *Captain's* Quarters and the last time I checked I'm still the *Captain!"*

"Of course you are," Grey agreed in that same infuriatingly calm tone. "And I told you that I'm more than happy to take the First Mate's cabin or any other cabin you choose to give me. I didn't choose this wall because it was the Captain's Quarters, I chose it because I could get a clear shot from a decent distance. I can't very well be firing off shots into the city and the boats are so close together here on the docks that if I shot out that way, I'd risk hitting someone else's boat."

"Oh, I get it," Reginald stated, flatly. "You didn't want to damage *anyone else's* boat…"

"Right," Grey agreed. "Well, now that that is sorted. How'd you make out in town? Do we have any jobs lined up? Any passengers that need a lift?"

Unable to contain himself any longer, Reginald opened his mouth ready to give Grey a piece of his mind when a familiar voice broke in, stopping his tirade before it could begin.

"Did you want me to take it down now, milord Grey?" Pierre, the deckhand addressed himself to Grey, as usual not taking notice of the fact that he was butting into a conversation that was already in full swing. "Are you finished with it?"

"Best leave it up, I think," Grey told Pierre with a smile and a sidelong glance at Reginald. "It seems to me that your *Capitaine* may want to blow off some steam later and we wouldn't want to risk him damaging his *own* boat."

The particular emphasis in Grey's words made Reginald stop and consider the situation for a moment. He turned and really took in Pierre for the first time and realized that the lanky red-haired boy had his hand on what appeared to be a large plank of wood mounted to the exterior wall of the Captain's Quarters. At Reginald's glance, Pierre dropped the plank and it made a slight clanging sound like a cooking sheet might make if dropped onto a wooden floor.

"It's really quite ingenious actually," Grey noted, crossing to take Pierre's place next to the makeshift target. "Pierre's idea. He's got a rare mind."

"He does?" Reginald looked over the awkward teen with the oversized nose and dull looking brown eyes.

"Oh yes," Grey insisted. "I told him I needed a place to practice with my new pistol and he came up with this all on his own. And look," he lifted the panel far enough off the wall that Reginald could see what lay beneath it, "it works. The wood here is just as smooth as the day it was installed… well, at least as good as it was yesterday."

Reginald instantly felt foolish. He'd made a big stink about nothing. He could see, however, by the twinkle in Grey's eye, that his reaction had been perfectly anticipated.

"Yes, well," Reginald cleared his throat trying to regain some amount of his authority. "Next time you want to install something on *my ship,* Pierre, you talk to me."

"But Lord Grey, sir -"

"*Lord* Grey," Reginald said, for what he felt was the millionth time, "is not the Captain of The Clover!"

"*Oui, Monsieur.*" Pierre hung his head. "I mean, yes, sir. Sorry, sir."

"All right," Reginald felt a little better, "go on with you then. Keep lookout from the crow's nest and give a whistle if you see any likely passengers looking to board. Got it?"

Pierre sighed as if Reginald had just asked him to swab the deck. "Fine…"

"I'm sorry, I didn't hear that properly," Reginald commented.

"Fine… *Sir?*"

"That'll do."

Pierre scurried off, leaving Reginald alone with Grey. "I swear I wonder if that kid's worth the trouble most days."

"He's not so bad," Grey allowed. "He still has some growing up to do, but he looks up to you."

Reginald raised a brow. "You think so?"

"Yeah, sure."

Another person may not have picked up on the lie, but Reginald had spent nearly two years in this man's company and he was beginning to detect when Grey was putting him on. Reginald shook his head. *It's not that Grey thinks that Pierre has the talent needed to do this job, it's that he doesn't like to see anyone down on their luck. He knows just as well as I do that if I sent Pierre home to his mother, she'd kick him out on his ear. She's got too many mouths to feed as it is.*

Reginald sighed. "Yeah, maybe you're right."

Grey smiled. "Of course I am!" He put his arm around Reginald's shoulder. "And speaking of me being right, there's something else I wanted you to see…"

Folded between two barrels and wrapped in damp silks, Meredith woke slowly from an uncomfortable sleep. She didn't even have the time to stretch the kinks out of her neck before she became aware of the sound that had woken her; two sets of heavy footfalls on the wooden stairs that led to her hiding place in the cargo hold of a ship.

Struck with immediate panic, she reached out for the nightgown she'd draped along the barrel next to her to dry. It was still damp, but she pulled it to her chest anyways and carefully arranged it so she could slip it over her head quickly and easily. It wouldn't do to have someone find her in the the state she was in.

The men's voices drew nearer and their conversation became clear.

"So while you were gone I took it upon myself to do some shopping."

"You bought all this without ever leaving the ship?"

"I know some people."

"I'll bet."

"So, like I was saying..."

Meredith's heart stopped in her chest as one of the barrels hiding her from view suddenly slid aside. She was halfway to lifting the shift over her head. Her body was by and large covered by a thin layer of silk, but that was all.

Her eyes met those of two men who couldn't look more dissimilar. The one on the left wore sailor's clothes; worn, but of decent quality. His hair was dark brown and cut short, though it had the slightest hint of a reddish tint and an unruly curl. His eyes were blue and warm like his skin which was sun-darkened probably from being on deck most of the time.

The other, the one holding the barrel, looked as if here in the cargo hold of a ship was the very last place he belonged. He was tall and well-dressed in a navy suit jacket over a pressed white shirt with a ruffled collar. His ash-blonde hair fell straight over steel grey eyes and his features were smooth and not those of a sailor or labourer, though he was tanned as if he too spent considerable time outside.

The noble-looking man's eyes were wide, but his surprised expression was nothing compared to the shock evident on the sailor's face.

A moment passed where nothing was said at all and then Meredith started screaming.

Uncharted is coming soon.
For more information, please visit our website:
http://www.mirrorworldpublishing.com/new-releases